He was created, molded, formed from life, love, and misery…

Lethally daring and ruthlessly passionate. He invites death to his door, welcomes it with each breath he draws, each step he takes. And thus, he *is* danger—a volatile storm that will sweep across the calm realms of humanity and shake it to the depths of its core.

And that storm is… Sterling.

THE *Storm* THAT IS
STERLING

LISA RENEE JONES

sourcebooks
casablanca

Copyright © 2011 by Lisa Renee Jones
Cover and internal design © 2011 by Sourcebooks, Inc.
Cover illustration by Aleta Rafton

Sourcebooks and the colophon are registered trademarks of Sourcebooks, Inc.

Published by Sourcebooks Casablanca, an imprint of Sourcebooks, Inc.
P.O. Box 4410, Naperville, Illinois 60567-4410
(630) 961-3900
FAX: (630) 961-2168
www.sourcebooks.com

Printed and bound in Canada
WC 10 9 8 7 6 5 4 3 2 1

To Diego—for everything and more.

Glossary

Area 51—Another name used for Groom Lake.

Blood Exchange—A part of the Lifebond process done by choice, after the Lifebond mark appears on the female's neck. This completes the female's transformation to GTECH and links the two Lifebonds in life and death. (See Lifebond Process.)

Dreamland—Though Groom Lake/Area 51 is often called Dreamland, in the Renegades series, Dreamland is the fictional military facility opened eighty miles from Area 51 by General Powell to take a stand against the Zodius who overran Area 51.

Green Hornet—Special bullet that is so powerful it not only shreds human muscle and bone, it permeates the thin bodysuit armor that the GTECHs—both Zodius and Renegades—wear when no other bullet can do so.

Groom Lake—Also known as Area 51, this is the military base where the Project Zodius experiments with alien DNA took place. It was later taken over by the Zodius rebels.

GTECH—The Super Soldiers who were created under Project Zodius and who divided into two groups—

Zodius and Renegades. GTECHs are stronger, faster, and more agile than humans; they heal rapidly and have low fatality rates. They can wind-walk. Over time, many are developing special gifts unique to them, such as telepathy and the ability to communicate with animals.

GTECH Body Armor—A thin bodysuit that fits like a second skin. Extremely light and flexible. The material is made from alien technology recovered from a 1950s crash site. Until the Green Hornets were created, no standard issue ammunition could penetrate the suits.

GTECH Serum—The serum created from alien DNA that was gathered at a crash site in the 1950s and then used to create the GTECHs. The original sample was destroyed. Since the alien DNA will not allow itself to be duplicated, there can be no new serum created without new scientific discoveries. The remaining serum disappeared the day Area 51/Groom Lake was taken over by the GTECH Rebels known as Zodius Soldiers. The GTECH serum cannot be created from GTECH DNA. This has been tried and failed.

Lifebond Mark—A double circle resembling a tattoo that appears on the back of a female's neck after her first sexual encounter with her GTECH Lifebond. After the mark appears, it will tingle whenever her Lifebond approaches. Only sexual encounters with one's Lifebond will result in a Lifebond Mark appearing. After the mark appears, the female feels a tingling sensation whenever the male Lifebond first approaches.

Lifebond Process—A Lifebond is a male and female who are bonded physically for life and death. If one dies, so does the other. This bond allows the GTECH male to reproduce, and it offers the females the same physical skills as their male Lifebond. The Lifebond mark, a double circle resembling a tattoo, appears on the back of the female's neck after the first sexual encounter. A blood exchange is required to complete the physical transformation of the female to GTECH, if the couple makes that decision. There is physical pain and illness for the female during conversion.

Neonopolis—The Las Vegas satellite location for the Renegades, covertly located in the basement of the Neonopolis entertainment complex off Las Vegas Avenue.

PMI or **Private Military Intelligence**—A company run by General Powell, the officer who created Project Zodius. PMI is used as a cover for top-secret military projects that the government doesn't want to officially show on the books.

Project Zodius—Code name for the government's top-secret operation—two hundred Special Operations soldiers who were assigned to Groom Lake (Area 51) and injected with what they believed to be immunizations, but which was, in fact, alien DNA.

Red Dart—A red crystal found at the same UFO 1950s crash site where the GTECH DNA was discovered. The crystal enables a red laser beam that enters the bloodstream and creates a permanent tracking beacon that is sensitive to sound waves. These sound waves can also be used for torture and control of the GTECHs. Thus far, U.S. military attempts to use Red Dart have been fatal.

Renegade Soldier—A GTECH who protects humanity and stands against the rebels known as "Zodius." The Renegades are led by Adam Rain's twin brother, Caleb Rain.

Shield—A mental barrier that a GTECH uses to block their psychic residue from being traceable by Trackers.

Stardust—An alien substance that is undetectable in human testing and causes brain aneurisms.

Sunrise City—The main Renegades facility, an advanced, underground city located in Nevada's Sunrise Mountain Range.

Trackers—These are GTECHs with the special ability to track the psychic residue of another GTECH or a human female who's been intimate with another GTECH. If a female possesses this residue, then only that female's Lifebond can shield her from a Tracker.

Wind-walking—The ability to fade into the wind, like mist into the air, and invisibly travel far distances at rapid speed.

X2 Gene—A gene that appears in some, but not all, of the GTECHs by the fifteenth month after injection of the GTECH serum.

Zodius City—Still known as the top-secret U.S. military facility. Located in Nevada and often called Area 51 or Groom Lake, it was taken over by the rebel GTECHs led by Adam Rain. This facility is both above and beneath ground level.

Zodius Soldier—A rebel GTECH soldier who follows Adam Rain, the leader of the rebel movement. Adam intends to take over the world.

Prologue

REBECCA BURNS WAS SITTING BEHIND A SCUFFED wooden table in the Killeen, Texas, library when he sauntered by, and every nerve ending in her body went on alert. "He" being Sterling Jeter, the hot blond hunk of a guy who'd graduated a year ahead of her. And try as she might to keep her attention on Bobby Johnson, the second-year high school quarterback who she was tutoring for his SAT test, she failed pitifully. As if drawn by a magnet, her gaze lifted and followed Sterling's sexy, loose-legged swagger as he crossed to the computer terminals he'd been frequenting the past three weeks.

Sterling yanked a chair out from behind a desk, and she quickly cut her gaze back to Bobby, who was still struggling through the worksheet she'd given him. Unable to resist, she slid her attention back to Sterling only to find him looking right at her. He grinned and winked, holding up a Snickers bar. She blushed at the realization that he'd brought it for her, after she'd confessed an undying love for their peanuty goodness just the afternoon before.

"I just don't get why I need to know algebra on the football field," Bobby grumbled. Reluctantly, Becca tore her gaze from Sterling's and refocused on Bobby who, at six foot two with brown hair and eyes and stud status at the school, was no grand dictionary of knowledge.

"Either you meet the required SAT score for the University of Texas," she reminded him, "or you'll be passing your ball to whoever is open somewhere else."

He shoved the paper away and scrubbed his hand through his hair. "This is bull. I don't want some fancy NASA-sponsored scholarship like you got, so I don't see why I have to be some geeky bookworm like you either."

She stiffened at the familiar jab, wondering why she let it bother her, why every once in a while she wished she was the cheerleader or prom queen. It wasn't like she wanted to be some brainless blonde beauty. Her mother was a teacher, both pretty and smart. Darn it, Becca liked having her mother's dark brown hair and brains, and she was proud of the NASA scholarship. Her parents were proud of her, and that's what counted.

Resolved to ignore his remark, she pushed the paper back toward him. "Let's try again."

"I'm done," he said. "I'm going to talk to Coach. He has to get me out of the SAT."

"Get you out of the SAT?" she asked. "You can't be serious."

He pushed to his feet. "As a touchdown." And with that smart remark, he headed toward the door.

Becca tossed down her pencil and sighed. Please let the summer end. She couldn't get to Houston and her new school soon enough.

The chair in front of her moved, and a Snickers bar slid in front of her. "You look like you need this urgently." Sterling sat down across from her, his teal green eyes a bright contrast to his spiky blond hair. She decided right then that her summer goal was to run her fingers through that hair just one time before she left for Houston. And kiss him. She really wanted to kiss him.

"It's a wiser and safer man who brings a Burns woman chocolate when she's upset. Or so says the Burns men. They swear it's a better survival technique than anything they learned in basic training." Both her father and brother were career military, same as her grandfather had been. She reached for the candy bar. "Thank you, Sterling."

He grabbed the worksheet Bobby had abandoned and started working an algebra problem with such ease that she assumed he was just doodling. They chatted while she waited for her next tutoring session, and she decided he was the best part of her summer wait for college. He took care of his grandmother by doing computer programming work. She thought that made him amazingly sweet.

When it was nearly time for her next student, he abandoned the worksheet and studied her. "I should go."

"Okay." Dang it, she really didn't want him to go.

He didn't go. He sat there, staring at her, the air thick with something—she didn't know what—but it made her stomach flutter.

"You want to catch a movie or something Friday night?"

She smiled instantly, knowing she should play coy—after all, Sterling was older and more experienced—but not sure she would know how if she tried. Dating wasn't exactly something she'd excelled at.

"Yeah," she said. "I'd like to go to a movie."

His lips lifted. "With me, right?"

She laughed. "Yeah, with you."

Once they'd arranged to meet at the library at seven the next evening, Sterling headed back to the computers. She glanced down at the math he'd done and smiled all over again. He'd gotten all the questions right. Good looking *and* smart. She might just fall in love with her hot cowboy.

———

With a smile on his lips, Sterling whipped his battered, black Ford F-150 into the driveway of the equally damaged trailer he called home and killed the engine.

He leaned back in the seat and pulled the wad of cash from his pocket. Ten thousand dollars and a date with Becca tomorrow night. He was going to kiss her, see what honey and sunshine tasted like, because that's what she reminded him of. Ah yeah. Life was good.

"Yeehaw," he whispered, staring at the cash again. How many nineteen-year-olds had that kind of dough? He was liking this new job. Hack a computer, get cash. He snorted. "And they say that government databases can't be hacked. This low-life trailer trash proved them wrong." That's what the kids at school had called him after his grandmom had gotten arrested for public intoxication. Trailer trash. Misfit. "Screw you," he mumbled to the voices of the past. "Screw you all."

Once Sterling had counted the money, down to the ten thousandth dollar, he grabbed a hundred for his date with Becca and stuffed the wad of cash back in his pocket. Then he snatched the bundle of flowers on the seat. He left the Snickers bar for himself and then decided better. Candy had worked with Becca, after all. And he'd need all the sweetness he could muster to convince Grandmom to head to that fancy alcohol-rehab center he'd arranged for her to enter up in Temple, Texas. It was even close by, only twenty miles away, which he hoped would help convince her to go. She'd curse and probably hit him. She was good at that, but it didn't hurt anymore. Hadn't for years.

He knew she couldn't help herself. He'd read enough about alcoholism to know she was sick. Yet she'd raised him despite that. Heck, he was to blame, he supposed. He was why his mother had died—the trigger that had set Grandmom off.

He climbed out of the truck and whistled down the path to the front door. The whistle faded the instant he entered the trailer. Grandmom sat on the couch, wrapped in the same crinkly blue dress that she'd gone to bed wearing, a big bottle of vodka in her hand. Two men dressed in suits sat next to her.

"Look what these men brought me," she said, grinning, holding up her prize.

"We know how you like to take care of your grandmother," one of the men said, his buzz cut flat against his skull.

"Kind of like your father took care of his family," the other man stated, a clone of the first one. They had to be army or government. *Fuck me!*

"The resemblance between the two of you is amazing," the first man said, picking up a picture of Sterling's father. He was standing in front of a helicopter, his blond hair longer than it should have been because he wasn't normal army. He'd been Special Forces, working undercover all over the map. And it had gotten him killed when Sterling was barely out of diapers. The man set the picture back down on the coffee table.

Grandmom grabbed the picture, mumbling to herself. "They're the spitting image of each other." Her gaze lifted, her voice with it. "But Sterling ain't got no clue who his daddy was. Man was never here. Neither was his mama." She took a drink. "They died. Didn't they, Ster… ling?"

The captain focused on Sterling. "We think you're a lot like him. For instance, you both showed an interest in official government business."

Sterling's gut twisted in a knot. He was busted. Big-time freaking busted and going to jail. "I don't know what you're talking about." He wasn't admitting shit. He wouldn't go down without a fight. He had Grandmom to take care of.

"You know," the second man said, "there's a lot that can be forgiven if you serve your country. Enlistment is favorable in certain circumstances."

The first man took the picture from Grandmom. "I'm Captain Sherman, son." He gave a sideways nod to the second man. "This is Captain Jenson. We served with your father."

Thank the Lord above. They weren't Feds. "What do you want from me?"

The captain answered, "Your father was part of a Special Forces unit where certain 'skills,' say— computer expertise, can be useful." He wrapped his arm around Grandmom's shoulders. "In exchange for service in this unit, your family will be well taken care of. It's time you enlisted, son. Be all you can be, like your father."

Grandmom gulped from the bottle, and suddenly Sterling realized he was still holding the flowers—those damn flowers that weren't going to erase his problems any more than the wad of cash sitting in his pocket.

"And if I say no?" he asked.

"I don't remember asking," the first man said.

"I'm not a soldier," Sterling said. He was just a kid in a trailer park who knew how to hack a computer.

"You are your father's son," the man said. "Mark my words, boy. You will be a soldier when I'm through with you."

Sterling looked at his grandmother, watched as she gulped from the bottle, her teal green eyes that matched his own the only familiar thing left in her. He saw the hint of contempt that lurked in their depths—the blame for his mother's death. The booze could never quite kill that. Sterling realized right then and there that the best thing he could do for her was to leave and give her a chance to heal. To get as far away from her as he could and stay there.

His gaze shifted to the man to his grandmother's right, and Sterling fixed him in an accessing stare. "She'll be taken care of?"

"You have my word."

"Mister," he said. "I don't know you from anywhere. I'll expect that in writing."

A hint of respect flickered in the man's expression. "As well you should."

"Don't suppose you'd wait until after tomorrow night to sign me up and ship me off?" They gave him deadpan looks in reply. "No. I didn't think so." His date with Becca was officially canceled.

Chapter 1

STERLING SLIPPED INTO THE SHADOWY RECESSES OF A dark Las Vegas alley, hot on the trail of what was one of the ever elusive, nearly impossible to locate ICE dealers pedaling the newest variety of "sin" in the city. But then, Sterling supposed that when you were selling top-secret, Area 51 military technology laced with alien DNA, you tended to be more careful than the average scumbag drug dealer. ICE was a dirty little number created by the leader of the Zodius movement, rebels formed from a group of GTECH Super Soldiers created under the government's Zodius Project. Their sorry SOB of a leader, Adam Rain, planned to force the city into dependency and grow his "perfect race," the evolution of humanity.

"Not on my watch," Sterling murmured. He, like all the Renegade GTECHs led by Adam's brother Caleb, lived to blow the Zodius movement to hell, starting with the ICE warehouse.

The dealer stopped in front of his buyer—an Ice Junkie, or "Clanner," as they were being called on the streets. Two burly dudes flanked the dealer like bodyguards.

This was the break Sterling had been waiting for.

"Where's the money, Charles?" the dealer demanded.

"I won't have it until tomorrow," Charles replied, hugging himself, his teeth chattering. "But I'll get you the money. I just need a hit. I'm begging you, David. Please. Give me a hit." He wheezed, a loud wet noise that sounded like death barely warmed over. Considering withdrawal from ICE had already produced six dead Clanners in only a month, all with their organs shriveled up like prunes, Sterling was pretty darn sure the dude really did need that hit.

The dealer didn't seem to care. "No money. No ICE."

"Tomorrow," Charles promised, his voice quavering. "Tomorrow I get paid. I'll pay you double. Please, man. Please. I need… that hit."

"Is this what you want?" the dealer taunted, producing a small vial of ICE from his pocket. The clear liquid contents slid down the user's throat with a sub-zero effect and delivered a temporary boost of superhuman power and speed. ICE, the Renegades' scientific team knew for certain, was a synthetic version of the original GTECH serum but with unidentifiable components. And identifying those components had proven critical to developing a method of safe withdrawal.

"Yes, please David!" Charles shouted desperately. "Please! I have to have a hit." David pocketed the ICE vial, and Charles grabbed for his arm. David flung him across the alley with the kind of ease that said he was feeling the super strength of his own ICE addiction.

Sterling cursed, hitting the mike by his ear and speaking to his team. "Hot ICE on the move and so am I."

"Wait on backup," Caleb ordered.

"No time."

"Sterl—"

Sterling clicked off the mike in the middle of the angry reply and did the one thing he knew the Clanners couldn't. He grabbed a strand of wind and faded into it. In a blink, he reappeared at the outside corner of the alley and then stepped in front of the dealer, blocking his exit.

"Howdy there, fellas." He ignored the bodyguards. "I'll be taking that vial of ICE you've got there in your pocket. Then you can mosey on along and take the rest of your lifetime on vacation. You know, do whatever retired drug dealers do. Play the casino tables. Watch *SpongeBob* for all I care. Just get the *hell* off my streets."

David cackled a laugh. "Your streets? These streets belong to Adam Rain, as you will soon find out." He gave Sterling's black fatigues a once-over and spoke to the man on his right. "Looks like we got us some army wannabe who's been ICE-ing too much. Thinks he's superhuman or some shit like that. Thinks he can push us around."

"See," Sterling drawled. "That's where you're mistaken. I already attended the army party and left. I'm what you call an independent contractor. We Renegades write our own rules. The good, bendable kind that let me kick your ass all over the curb and then do it again just for fun."

David made a less than successful attempt at a hand signal, and the three men instantly rushed at Sterling. Bring. It. On. Sterling could have wind-walked away, but what fun would that be? Standing his ground, he kicked one of his attackers in the chest and landed a fist on the other's jaw. The two bodyguards—or whatever the juiced-up bastards were—came back at Sterling before he could make a move toward Charles and David, neither of the guards fazed by his attacks when they should have been.

Sterling punched one of the men and sent him stumbling backwards. Then, taking the offensive, he reached for the other man and did the same to him, but not before the man ripped off Sterling's hat and took a chunk of short, spiky blond hair with it.

"Now you're fighting like a girl," Sterling mumbled irritably. Both men were already getting up as he turned his attention to David, who was running down the alley, leaving Charles lying flat on his face in the middle of the street.

Sterling wind-walked and appeared in front of David.

"How did you—"

Sterling grabbed David and jacked him up against the wall, David's feet dangling above the pavement.

"Give me the ICE."

"Where'd you come from man?"

"That's what drugs do to you," Sterling said, digging inside David's pockets and retrieving the vial. "They make you see things." Sterling held onto David and turned in preparation to face the two bodyguards, but they had disappeared.

That left only Sterling, Charles, and David in the alley, and Charles was lying on the ground, foaming at the mouth. David threw an ICEd-up super punch that landed hard on Sterling's jaw.

Sterling grinned. "Feels good," he said about the time the wind lifted, and Caleb appeared at his side.

Caleb took one look at Charles and hit his headset. "Get me an ambulance and a military escort." Every agency and hospital in town had been set up to notify a military hotline about all ICE-related activity, which went directly to Sterling, as he was the Renegade in charge of the inner city.

Caleb grabbed David from Sterling, his ability to sense human emotions, truths, and lies, about to come in real damn handy. But first he looked pointedly at Sterling. "You don't know the meaning of 'wait,' do you?"

Sterling grinned. "You wouldn't love me if I did."

Caleb grunted and jerked as the dealer placed a well-planted knee in his groin. "That was really uncalled for," Caleb choked out, pinning his captive's neck under with his arm. "Now. Play nice, and I might let you live. I want the location of the ICE warehouse."

"I don't know that," the dealer said. "You really think I know that?"

"Okay then," Caleb said, seeming to believe him. "Who's your source?"

Sterling turned his attention to Charles, bending down next to him and noting the blue tinge to his skin. He was dying. Damn it to hell. He would need the vial of ICE Sterling had planned to hand over to a scientific team desperate for samples.

The dealer's barked laugh echoed in the alley. "Adam Rain. Adam Rain is my source."

"Yeah?" Caleb demanded. "What does this Adam Rain look like?"

"Let me go, and I'll tell you."

Caleb growled in frustration and eyed Sterling over his shoulder. "He's a waste of time. Hand him over to the army, and be done with him."

The dealer squirmed worthlessly under Caleb's tight hold. "I can tell you what you need to know! Just let me go."

"Adam Rain's my twin, you idiot," Caleb muttered, lifting the man by his shirt so that his feet dangled off the ground and tossing him into the nearby Dumpster. Ignoring the man's protests, he slammed the lid shut and used army-issued plastic cuffs to secure it.

Sirens sounded in the distance as Caleb kneeled beside Charles and withdrew a syringe from his pocket, quickly taking a blood sample before their company arrived. Caleb and Sterling shared a silent look, both knowing they were in a bad spot. For all they knew at this point, all ICE wasn't created the same—maybe some of it killed, and some did not. All theories were good theories, not to be ignored when you had no answers. In other words, they didn't know if they were killing this man or saving his life.

With a heavy sigh, Caleb said, "One day soon I'm going to make Adam pay for all of this." He scrubbed his jaw. "Give him the ICE, but hold back a few drops for the lab."

It was a good call, the right call. Sterling tossed the ICE down the dying man's throat and pocketed the remaining contents of the vial just as the army arrived. Caleb excused himself to take a call, and Sterling waded through the erupting chaos created by the various official personnel.

Caleb returned, motioning Sterling to a location out of hearing range, and looked grim. "That slim list of six scientists our team thought might be able to develop a withdrawal antidote has turned into one. The other five were MIA when our teams arrived. We have to assume Adam got to them before we could."

"What about the sixth?"

"We thought Adam had her," he said. "But turns out she was in Germany the past few months. She showed up on our radar when she booked a flight back to the states. I want you to be there when she arrives."

Sterling scrubbed his jaw. "Caleb, man, you know I'll do whatever, whenever you need me to do it, but we need me here. I know these streets better than anyone, which makes me the best shot we have of finding that warehouse."

"She's from Killeen," he said. "So are you."

"At least ten of our men served at the Killeen Ft. Hood army base, and they're all damn good soldiers. Surely one of them can handle this."

"None of the others went to her high school three of her four years there. It's a connection you can use to earn trust. We need this woman's help, Sterling."

Sterling went utterly still, warning bells ringing in his head. The same high school, the same years? That was a monster-sized coincidence, and Sterling didn't believe in coincidence. The look he shared with Caleb said, as usual, they were in agreement. He didn't either.

"What's the woman's name?" Sterling asked, though on some core level he couldn't explain, he already knew.

"Rebecca Burns."

―――⁓―――

Twenty-four hours later
Houston, Texas

Three months of hiding was long enough. Becca pulled her blue Volvo to a halt in front of her quaint, two-story stucco house surrounded by miles of grassy hills and droopy willow trees, ready to embrace whatever the future might bring. She came from a family of fighters—of military men and the tough women who knew how to hold their own. She could almost imagine her father and brother crawling out of their graves to shake sense into her if she didn't fight to the end.

Battling the strong wind gusts that threatened a midnight storm, Becca somehow managed to shove the car door shut, her black cotton dress flapping around her knees, her loose, long hair lifting around her shoulders. It was near ten o'clock after a tiring day of travel, so her baggage was going to have to wait until morning. Anxious for the comfort of home, Becca hurried down the sidewalk hugged by a stone border she'd laid with care a year before. The high moon peeked from the cloud cover, casting the path in dull light. A smile touched her lips as the house came fully into view, a sense of knowing this was where she belonged, where she was strongest. Her territory, her turf.

Her smile was short-lived. As she reached the stairs leading to her porch, the motion detectors flickered to a soft glow before they should have. Poised for flight, Becca's heart thundered in her chest as a man stepped from the corner, the rocking chair creaking with his exit. Dressed in jeans and a T-shirt, with thick blond hair, the stranger seemed to consume the porch, to consume the very air around her.

When she should have turned to dart away and reached for the cell phone in her purse to call for help, she found herself staring at him and not because he was absolutely gorgeous—tall, broad, and defined, the kind of drool-worthy body and good looks that fantasies were made for.

There was something familiar about this man, something that stirred a distant memory of a youthful crush that sent a magical shimmer of warmth through her limbs.

"Hello, Becca," the sexy stranger said in a deep, sandpaper-rough baritone.

Becca blinked at the remarkably familiar voice, a ripple of awareness becoming full recognition. It couldn't be—*he* couldn't be here—could he? "Sterling?"

"It's been a long time," he said softly.

"I... I can't believe you're here." But he was. Sterling Jeter was standing on her doorstep. This was an older, even hotter version of the boy she'd once known—a man now, his face more defined, his body more sculpted—but there was no question, it was him. "*How* are you here? How is this even possible?"

"I'd rather explain inside, if you'll invite me in."

The wind gusted, lifting her hair and then her skirt. Becca gasped and grabbed the hem, pushing it back into place before Sterling got a bird's-eye view of her unmentionables.

Recovering from her near-exposure, Becca expected to see amusement in Sterling's face, but frowned as she watched him scan the yard, as if he were looking for some unknown threat.

"We should really go inside now," he said, his gaze settling back on her face, and though he hadn't moved, there was a new edge to him, a sense of increasing discomfort.

Unease flinted through Becca, her own senses tingling with awareness, telling her that something was behind her, watching her, *stalking her*. It was all she could do not to run up the stairs toward Sterling. Instead, she hesitated, forcing herself to remain in place. No matter how sexy and familiar Sterling might be, she hadn't seen or heard from him since high school.

Caution prevailed, despite the continued tingling sensation of being watched from behind, telling her to run for cover. "You still haven't told me why you're here or even how you found me."

"Invite me inside, Becca," he said, his voice low, tense, bordering on a command.

She opened her mouth to speak and stopped when a droplet of rain smacked her forehead. That was all the encouragement she needed to go with her instincts. Becca ran up the stairs toward Sterling.

Chapter 2

WITH HIS GTECH SENSES SCREAMING IN WARNING, Sterling followed Becca inside her house, leaving his team covertly nestled around the exterior perimeter. He shut the door behind him, welcoming any added barrier between them and the Zodius, who he was certain were nearby.

Becca turned to face him, close, so close that the soft floral scent of her insinuated into his nostrils and warmed his blood. Close enough that he could see the infinitesimal specks of amber sunshine and honey in her gaze. She was a woman now, beautiful, confident, with curves in all the right places, and the most amazing mouth that made him want to claim the kiss he'd never managed to steal.

They stared at one another, the air crackling with a mixture of unmistakable, surprisingly clear and present shared attraction along with something edgier, darker, that said she'd probably smack him if he kissed her. And he'd deserve it for standing her up so long ago, even welcome it if it would get the past out of the way. But there was more to what was in the air between them— uncertainty, distrust. She was on edge, suspicious of him, which only made him more suspicious of her. The coincidence of her involvement in something so near to him—her months in Germany could have easily been spent in a lab with Adam Rain—encouraged caution.

Even so, his eyes traced those lush lips again, heating his blood.

His gaze lifted to her cautious one. "You should lock up," he told her, wanting to do it himself, but afraid he'd put her more on edge if he seemed like he was trying to hold her captive.

She set her purse on the slim mahogany table against the wall. "Locks will slow my escape if you turn out to be some sort of crazy stalker."

Good thing he didn't lock the door himself, he thought with amusement. His lips twitched at the playful accusation, though he knew she wasn't completely joking. "Since when does a crazy stalker wait for an invitation to come inside?"

She crossed her arms in front her. "I've heard stalkers are quite patient and calculating."

"I don't have fourteen years of patience, which is how long it's been since we last saw each other." Especially where she was concerned. In fact, he was pretty darn sure he was going to give in to temptation and kiss her if he stood in this tiny hallway a minute longer. "Is there someplace we can sit down and talk?"

She studied him another several seconds, her intelligent gaze sizing him up before she motioned down the hall. "This way."

Sterling flipped the locks into place and followed her into a shiny, all white, rectangular-shaped kitchen that sparkled with the kind of perfection you expected of a soldier's home. But then, she'd grown up a soldier's daughter, so that didn't surprise him.

She brushed the windblown brown silk of her hair from her face and motioned to the table, offering him a seat, but without any indication that she planned to sit down herself. He arched a brow. "You're not going to join me?"

"Not until I know how and why you're here," she said, leaning against a counter. "And frankly, I'd rather you sit while I stand. It makes me feel like I have a running chance if this reunion turns bad."

Sterling chuckled and grabbed a wooden chair from the table, straddled it, and rested his arms on the back. "Happy now?"

She studied him a moment and then said, "No. No, I am not happy. I feel like I am in the Twilight Zone. And I can't think of one reason why the boy who stood me up for a date fourteen years ago would show up at my doorstep out of the blue like this. How did you even know where to find me?"

Damn, there it was. The reason he deserved to be slapped. "That night—"

She held up a hand. "I don't need to know."

"I want—"

"Please don't," she said, shaking her head. "It's awkward. It's over. And actually, just thinking about how I sat in that library for hours waiting for you is making me ridiculously and irrationally mad." She crossed her arms in front of her chest. "Maybe you should just tell me why you're here."

Damn. He wanted to explain the past, and he'd push the issue, but that prickly instinct telling him something was wrong just wouldn't let go of him. "We need your help, Becca."

"We—being who?"

"We—being my special operations unit."

"You joined the army?"

He nodded. "Fourteen years ago."

She blinked and seemed to process the timeline to their missed date, but didn't comment. "Why in the world would a Special Operations unit need my help?"

"There's a highly addictive street drug being circulated around the general population. And when I say addictive, I mean once you use this drug, you can't stop without dying. If we don't come up with a method to safely wean people off the drug, we're looking at mass casualties. We're hoping you can help us make that happen."

"Oh God," she said, paling. "I want to help. I do. I will, but I'm an astrobiologist, Sterling. I don't know the slightest thing about street drugs."

Sterling. Damn he wanted to hear her say his name again, which he was pretty sure meant he was too personally involved to be objective, but he'd be damned if he was passing her off to someone else. "This isn't a typical street drug," he continued. "The drug is created from military technology, and by that I mean of an *otherworldly* nature."

The look of utter horror on her face defied his suspicions she had knowledge of ICE before this. She sat down next to him, the space barrier between them forgotten. "*Please* tell me I'm misunderstanding, and you don't mean an alien organism, because an alien organism in our environment could have devastating, unpredictable results. Maybe not immediately, but over time. It's what we fear at NASA, what we work sunup to sundown to prevent."

He scooted his chair a few inches to face her. "I

don't know if you would call this an organism. Then again, maybe you would. We don't know at this point exactly what we're dealing with. The lab reports have an unknown component. What we do know is that almost three years ago, the army created a serum made from a DNA sample obtained in a… shall we say, a unique aircraft, back in the 1950s. They proceeded to tell a group of two hundred soldiers they were being immunized against a chemical agent the enemy had obtained. Those men became what we now know as GTECH Super Soldiers. Not long after the injections were completed, the DNA that created the serum was destroyed, and with it the ability to replicate it. Our scientists believe this street drug is a synthetic recreation of the serum."

She squeezed her eyes shut. "He really went through with it."

Sterling stiffened. "He *who*? What does that mean, Becca?"

She drew a taut breath and expelled it. "I was approached by someone named General Powell several years back to help with what he was calling the 'Project Zodius' immunization program."

"Powell was responsible for recruiting soldiers under false pretenses to Area 51," Sterling confirmed, "then injecting them with the DNA." *And then trying to control his creations with torture devices that their immune systems destroyed, but he left that part out.* "So he approached you and then what?"

"I was eager to help save the lives of our soldiers," she said, a tightness to her tone that made him suspect she was thinking of her father and brother, both killed in combat only a few years before. His mind slid to Caleb, and Sterling wondered what was worse. Losing a family member you loved to war, or fighting a war against your only remaining family member, as Caleb now had to.

"I was intrigued too," she continued. "The scientist in me reveled at the chance to study the unknown."

"But you said no."

"I had to. Powell wanted this immunization ready for use in a few months. I knew he was treading on dangerous territory, pushing too quickly with an unknown pathogen, and I wanted no part of it. In fact, I went to my superiors and requested they get involved to ensure he was stopped."

"And what happened?"

"I was told to leave it alone in no uncertain terms. As in, told it would be dangerous to pursue any action against Powell, with a distinct underlying threat. I was shocked." She paused. "Are they dead? The men he injected?"

"You didn't let anything happen. Powell was too powerful. No one could have stopped him."

"Did they die?" she repeated. "Please, Sterling. I need to know."

"No," he said. "They didn't die."

"Thank God." Her shoulders relaxed marginally, but her eyes narrowed on him almost instantly. "What aren't you telling me?"

Sterling hesitated, though he knew she had to know the truth to effectively work on an ICE antidote. "Once I tell you this information, Becca, I can't untell it. That threat to leave Powell alone was nothing compared to what we're talking about now. This is the kind of secret people get killed over."

"You're Special Ops, which means you checked me

out before you came here." There was a slight rasp to her words, as if they were uncomfortable in her mouth. "You must know any liability I represent is short-lived."

He drew in a breath that ripped through his lungs like a blade, sharp and painful. There it was. The reasons she'd supposedly been in Germany that he'd rejected—an experimental noninvasive treatment for a rare, rapidly progressing lung cancer that hit nonsmokers. He saw the truth of it in her eyes—her death, her *fear*. Regret, anger, and an undeniable ball of protectiveness settled where his breath had been and then roared through him with the force of a nuclear bomb. She didn't look sick. She hadn't lost her hair. The cancer was a cover story— she was working for Adam. Her anguish was guilt, regret. That had to be it. He could pull her back from the dark side, but he couldn't pull her back from the grave. But her eyes, her beautiful amber eyes told the truth he wanted to be a lie.

Before he could stop himself he was on his feet, pulling her into his arms, lacing his fingers in her hair.

"You'll die over my dead body," he vowed, pulling her mouth to his and parting her lips, tasting her with a long slide of his tongue. That was when the patio door and the window above the kitchen sink shattered.

Chapter 3

DISTANT ECHOES OF SHATTERED WINDOWS CLAMORED through the air from around the house as Sterling dragged Becca to the ground, covering her body with his, the skintight Area 51 body armor he wore beneath his clothing offering them both protection from injury. Seconds ticked by in slow motion as foreboding silence settled around them, smoke rising in the air, flooding them in fumes and toxins meant to force Becca from the house. Well, Adam could kiss Sterling's Texan ass. The only person leaving with Becca tonight was him. As if mocking his vow, another smoke bomb exploded through the patio door and then another.

"I can use some help here anytime now, Damion," he murmured into the invisible mike he wore, already pushing to his feet. He pulled Becca up with him and silently cursed when his second-in-charge still hadn't replied.

"What's happening?" She sucked in air and wheezed, her balled fist on her chest, panic flaring in her eyes. "Oh God. I can't… breath. We have to get out of here." Her gaze flickered to the patio door a moment before she bolted.

Sterling lunged for her, shackled her wrist, and dragged her back to him. "Easy, sweetheart, you're running straight to the enemy."

"Let go," she hissed, shoving against him, even as

she tried to suck in more air and choked on the smoke. "You don't understand. My... I—"

"Can't breathe," he said, positioning her back to his chest and wrapping her in his arms, before she could make a run for it. "I know, and so do the people who threw those bombs in the house." He spoke low, against her ear. "The same people who will kill you before they'll let you help us with an antidote."

"Kill me?" she gasped, trying to look over her shoulder at him. "They're trying to kill me?"

"Yes. Kill you." It was vital she know the extent of the danger and listen to him, to trust him when he'd given her no reason to do so. He turned her to face him, his hands on her arms. "I'll get you out of here safely. I promise you. But you need to do exactly what I say, when I say it."

She nodded earnestly. "Yes. Okay. I'm normally not so... I shouldn't have panicked and run. Tell me what to do."

Brave and beautiful. Exactly his kind of woman. Sterling yanked a towel off the counter and ran water on it before handing it to her. "Keep your face covered."

With her hand in his, Sterling silently urged Becca behind him and headed toward the hallway, but not toward the front door where they'd be expected. He rounded the corner, and holy mother of Jesus, *he* couldn't see squat for the suffocating smoke that consumed every flipping inch of the house, transforming the hallway into one big cloud of white and gray.

Becca coughed and then wheezed, but even more important than this announcement of their location was her need for fresh air.

He pulled her down to a crouch by the wall in an effort to get beneath the smoke, only to discover there was no "below the smoke." There was only more smoke. "Are you okay?"

"Alive," she said. "That's what counts."

Indeed, and that was enough to set Sterling into action again, leading her to the stairwell where he paused and tapped the mike by his ear. "Damion, damn it. Where are you?" Nothing. Not one damn word. He started up the steps, but Becca stumbled and almost fell. Sterling quickly wrapped his arm around her, only to feel her go limp in his arms.

"Becca. Becca." His heart thundered in his chest, his blood frozen with fear. "Don't you dare die on me."

He sat down on the step, held her close, and pressed his lips to hers, praying for her warm breath and finding a trickle of air. Yes, thank you, God.

Damion's voice sounded in his ear bud, welcome as hell. "What's your position?"

"Stairwell, and about damn time. I need a fast exit. Becca's passed out and in trouble. I need oxygen, and I need it now."

"Top floor. Bedroom to your left. Meet me at the window."

Before Damion even finished the directive, Sterling had scooped Becca up and started running up the steps. Smoke pumped through his lungs like motor oil, but he didn't slow down. He'd survive; he'd heal. He had to get Becca out of here, or she wouldn't.

Visibility was near zero at the top of the stairs, and Sterling didn't hesitate to contemplate what might be in waiting for him. He cut to the left and kicked open the bedroom door to find a thankfully smokeless room... and Damion leaning in at the window.

"The Zodius are MIA," he said, motioning Sterling forward and offering his arms for Becca. "Retreating or regrouping."

Or waiting for Becca to come out of this house before attacking again, Sterling thought, hesitating to hand Becca over to him. Sterling's senses tingled with warning a second before Damion turned away as if he felt it too. The sound of battle followed—grunts, punches, thundering jolts against the wall. Then a yell that grew distant before the silence that followed. Damion and his attacker had gone over the edge of the roof.

Sterling took one look at Becca's pale, nearly lifeless face, and knew even before he bent close to her mouth that she wasn't breathing. Sterling shoved aside the emotions stabbing at his chest and forced the trained soldier to react. He rushed her to the side of the bed and settled her on the floor, out of sight of the window. The two guns beneath his pant leg went on top of the bed, within reach and ready for action.

And damn, he wasn't what one might call a religious man these days, but he was darn sure praying when he bent over her and pressed his lips to hers, alternating a breath with a pump of her chest. "Come on, baby. Come on." Still she wasn't breathing. "Fuck!"

In a distant part of his mind, he heard the sound of activity by the window, but he couldn't think about it being the enemy, couldn't let a second go by that might mean Becca would never breathe again. Breath, pump, breath, pump. She gasped then, her lashes fluttering and then shutting again, and he brushed dark hair from her

eyes. She raised up on her hands, looking around, dis-
oriented. "Sterling…?"

Relief washed over him at hearing his name on her
lips, the proof she was alive and present in mind. His
instincts kicked back in as he reached for his weapons.

"Don't even think about it," came the growl from
above.

Sterling rotated to a squat to find himself staring down
the barrel of a weapon held by Tad Bensen, the brawny
bulldog, second-in-charge to Adam Rain. He'd known
him well during their Area 51 service. Didn't like him
then and liked him less now. "It's not good to play with
guns," Sterling said dryly. "You might get yourself shot."

"Bravely spoken by the man without a gun," Tad said.
"Pick up the woman, and carry her to the window. Hand
her over to my man. Then, you will return to Zodius City
with me for debriefing."

Translation. Tortured until he gave up Renegade
secrets. *When donkeys fly.* Their eyes locked, held.
They both knew there was enough wind coming in the
bedroom window to allow Sterling to escape. They also
knew wind-walking was potentially lethal for humans,
which meant taking Becca with him was a risk, especially in her present condition. Tad jerked one of his
weapons toward Becca.

The man seemed to read Sterling's thoughts. "Just so
you know, my orders are to bring the woman back, dead
or alive. Adam would rather have her alive, but either
way works just fine by me."

"Nothing like a man who knows how to please his
man," Sterling taunted, trying to keep the attention on
himself, not Becca.

It worked better than expected. Tad growled and without warning, shot him in the arm. Sterling's armor was no protection against the Green Hornet Area 51 bullets that ripped through the material and then his flesh and bone.

"Sterling!" Becca gasped, and he felt her move behind him, press closer to his back.

"I'm fine," he said, feeling her hand closing over the wound to stop the blood that already oozed down his sleeve, sticky and warm. Pain radiated clear to Sterling's teeth, but he wasn't about to give Tad the satisfaction of showing it or a reason to refocus on Becca. "You should really work on self-control, Tad."

"She goes to the window now, or I unload a few more bullets in your chest and be done with you."

"I'll go," Becca said quickly and started around him.

Sterling shackled her arm. "I'll carry her. She's too weak to walk."

With his eyes locked on Tad, Sterling pushed to his feet, Becca rising automatically with him, behind him. Time seemed to stand still as his eyes locked with Becca's, silently telling her to prepare herself for what came next. Understanding seeped into her eyes, readiness that defied her physical limitations. And to his surprise, her gaze flicked slightly toward the bed, to his weapons. Surprise, surprise, surprise, indeed. His little Becca was a real fighter.

He bent to pick her up, positioning himself to block her from Tad's view. At the same moment she grabbed the gun. Sterling ignored the second weapon, unable to get to it and hold Becca. He started for the door, and Becca twisted in his arms and started firing on Tad, clearly trained to shoot.

Tad was firing too, and one Green Hornet and then another, pierced Sterling's left shoulder blade, ripping bone and muscle with their unique splintering action. But the weight of Becca in his arms, her sheer bravery as she fired his weapon over and over, kept him moving down the stairs through the smoke and furniture.

Another bullet penetrated his armor, ripped into his back. Sterling groaned with the intensity of the impact, with the grind of bullet against flesh, but somehow, he kept running.

He kicked open the front door and charged onto the porch to find Damion here, reaching for Becca. Sterling handed her over, while fighting the ache in his gut that told him it was a mistake. But he was in no physical position to protect her now, and he knew it. With every last bit of energy he had left, determined to give Damion a chance to escape, he turned to face Tad, armed for his exit, but taut seconds ticked by with no sign of Tad.

A bad feeling curled inside him, and Sterling jerked around to check on Becca, sticky blood clinging to his shirt front and back, dripping down his legs. Spots floated in front of his eyes, and he clung to the frame of the doorway to keep from falling, trying to process what he was seeing. Damion wasn't holding Becca any longer, Tad was, nor was Damion injured, fighting, or trying to save Becca. He was nowhere to be found. Damion had handed her over to Tad. It was the only explanation.

"No!" The shout exploded from Sterling's lungs in a rush of fury that had him reaching for the wind, but he was too weak to control it.

He charged across the porch toward Becca, but the instant his feet touched the stairs, a bullet ripped through his knee. More spots filled his vision, and he reached for the banister, but found air. He reached for his phone even as he began to fall... had... to tell Caleb... Damion was a *traitor*. That thought echoed in his mind... in the darkness. He slid down the stairs, his mind barely processing what had happened. Sterling had found Becca and once again let her go... let her down—failed her.

Chapter 4

"STERLING!" BECCA SHOUTED, FIGHTING THE GRIP OF the man carrying her away from the house, the one who'd shot Sterling in the bedroom, twisting and turning in a struggle to get free.

Her gaze reached beyond her captor's bulky shoulders to latch on to Sterling, the sight of him bringing a moment of hope. "Sterling!"

He saw her. She was sure of it, but then he stumbled. He was falling. Becca screamed, realizing he'd been shot again, and watched as a group of soldiers charged him, praying they were his men, that they would save him. He'd taken those bullets for her. She was supposed to die, not him—she was already dying.

The injustice, the terror for Sterling, tore through her, and adrenaline launched her into action all over again. She fought against the bulky man holding her—teeth, nails, fists. She was fighting for her life, fighting to get back to Sterling. God, he was going to die. She just knew it. She had to get him help.

"Fucking bitch," the man holding her muttered and then flung her across the bed of an eighteen-wheeler that had appeared at the back of her house. She flew across the hard steel floor and hit the wall, gasping, her bones rattling with the impact. Somehow she scrambled to a sitting position just in time to see Sterling's bleeding, broken body flung across the truck bed toward her, a trail of blood following his body. So much blood… too much blood.

She scrambled to his side, only to realize the big man was standing over her, as if he'd traveled superspeed, jerking her head back by a large chunk of her hair.

He produced a vial of clear liquid. "Swallow it."

"No!" She tried to shake her head, and he pulled her hair. "No!"

A gun appeared in his hand, and he pointed it at Sterling's head. "He won't survive a bullet in the brain. You decide. Does he live or die?"

He meant it. She saw it in his eyes. He hated Sterling. He wanted to kill him, if he hadn't already succeeded. There was too much of Sterling's blood on the steel floor pooling around his body for him to survive. Too many bullets were buried deep inside him, but she couldn't—wouldn't—give up on him.

"I'll take it." She held out her hand and received a gloating smile in return. He disposed of his gun and handed the vial to her, but the grip on her hair tightened mercilessly.

Becca sucked down the chilly liquid, coughing at a bitter cold sensation that felt more like fire than ICE in her throat, seconds before the burn in her lungs began.

The man squatted beside her, his big body pressed to her side, his lips to her ear. "My name is Tad, and I'm the man who just cured your cancer and became your drug dealer. That makes me your new sugar daddy." He held up another vial. "When you start shaking, and you need another hit, we'll talk about what payment we expect in return. And just so you know, in case you get any ideas about being disloyal to us, if you miss just one dose of your new cure, you die from withdrawal. In other words, we *own you*." He motioned to Sterling. "Not him. Not any of his kind."

His kind. Becca had no idea what that meant. He let go of her and stood up, glaring down at her with a lusty dark look that made the ICE in her veins downright arctic. When he finally turned away, he was a blur of movement before the steel doors slammed shut, sealing them inside with the same suffocating effect she imagined her own coffin would deliver. Only a small light flickered overhead.

Her fingers balled in Sterling's shirt, feeling his wet, thick blood on her skin. Fear and anger collided inside her, exploded from her in a fierce yell. "Who are you people?"

The only answer was the sound of her heavy breathing. It filled the trailer, bounced off the walls and back at her. Her body tingled, her lungs expanded, and she felt air filtering through them without one hint of pain or discomfort. But she felt no hope, no joy. The cure was a drug-induced facade, and this was a nightmare.

"Wake up," she whispered, pressing her hands to Sterling's body, to his face, the damn blood clinging to her hands. "Wake up! Damn it, Sterling, wake up!" She collapsed over the top of him, pressed her ear to his chest, searching desperately for a heartbeat, and sighing in relief when she found it. Slowly Becca relaxed against him, his soft rhythmic heart calming her even as the truck began to move, the last thing she remembered before blacking out.

Sterling came awake abruptly, but he didn't move, didn't so much as breathe. Training and instinct kept his lashes securely closed, allowed him to absorb the hard and unforgiving concrete beneath his body. Discreetly, he inhaled, reaching with his enhanced GTECH senses to find the familiar scent he'd hoped to never experience again—Area 51, now Adam's Zodius City.

Stickiness clung to his shirt, but remarkably, considering the number of Green Hornets Tad had unloaded in him, his GTECH immune system had kicked into gear, and his body felt nearly healed. He translated that to mean two things—his body would have needed at least twelve hours of sleep, maybe double that to heal. And in order for that to happen, someone had removed the Green Hornets from his wounds and given him an injection of vitamin C to offset the chronic depletion, common to GTECHs, that worsened in the healing process.

He inhaled deeper, and another softer, sweeter scent touched his lips. "Becca." He jerked to a sitting position, back against more glass, finding himself alone in some sort of glass cage overlooking a lab, where several white coats worked.

He dropped his head against the wall, squeezing his eyes shut, willing her to be alive—he'd find her and get the hell out of here.

A television screen hung from the corner wall flickered to life, and Sterling brought it into focus, only to bolt to his feet at the sight of Tad kneeling over Becca's limp body, pouring a clearly evident vial of ICE down her throat. Tad turned to the monitor and smiled, running his hands down Becca's hair, petting her.

"You sonofabitch!" Sterling roared, every nerve in

his body on fire, every pore seething with anger. "I'm going to kill you. I'm going to kill you and enjoy it."

Tad came closer to the camera. "I'm sure you can imagine all the things I'm planning to do to her." The screen went black, and the doors behind him slid open.

Sterling whirled around, ready to launch himself on the visitor, only to find two wolves snarling at him with the promise of attack. *Adam's wolves*. His command of the beasts was well known, his use of them for punishment and entertainment also well known. Defy Adam, even look at him wrong, and you'd end up in an old Roman-style coliseum beneath Area 51. With thousands of Zodius citizens watching, you'd battle the wolves until you were near death. And where there were wolves, there was... Adam.

Dressed in desert camouflage fatigues, Adam entered the room, leaving the glass wall open behind him. Well over six foot two with a muscular frame and light brown hair, he was his brother's evil doppelganger, as if the GTECH serum had somehow divided them between good and evil.

"You want to kill me," Adam said, assessing Sterling with a smile on his lips.

"Damn straight I do," Sterling ground out between gritted teeth.

"You want to kill me over the woman."

"The reasons to kill you are many," he replied cautiously, certain this conversation was going nowhere good fast. "Should I count them out, or would you rather hear the many ways I've fantasized about completing the task?"

Laughter roared from Adam. "You have balls to

stand here in my cage, in my world, and dare to threaten me. I like you, Sterling." He leaned against the wall, the wolves settling at his feet. "More importantly, my brother likes you, and he will not want to see you dead when we finally reconcile and rule as one."

"He'll die before he joins you."

"Sooner or later he will stop fighting what is truth. That I am in him as he is in me," Adam said, tilting his head to study Sterling. "Did you know your little Rebecca Burns took her first dose of ICE because Tad held a gun to your head? The irony is that the ICE is curing her cancer. A few more doses, and she should be good as new."

Sterling went colder than ICE, his emotions shredded by conflicting reactions. The cancer was being cured, but Becca was addicted to ICE. And just like the original serum, no one else could figure out how to replicate ICE, which made Adam her only source of survival until an antidote was found.

"Of course," Adam added. "There is the risk of death during withdrawal if she discontinues the use of ICE, not to mention the risk her cancer might return. I'm sure you would agree. She shouldn't take any chances."

"You're a bastard, Adam."

"But I'm her bastard hero."

Anger coiled inside him, and Sterling lunged forward. The wolves snarled and blocked his path.

"You want her," Adam said. "Good. I'll give her to you. I'll keep Tad and all the other men away from her. That's right. As much as my wife wants to use her for fertility testing, I won't let her." He paused, letting the implications fill the silence.

Sterling's fingers curled by his sides, his thoughts going exactly where directed. To the sex camps where the women were traded from soldier to soldier in hopes one of them would find the rare Lifebond connection that mated them and allowed the production of offspring.

"You can save her from such a fate," Adam offered slyly. "She'll be yours and yours alone, and you don't even have to give up my brother's secrets to get her."

Right. And Sterling was going to become the president of the United States. Adam was manipulating him, playing a game to get what he wanted. "Get to the point, Adam."

"Dead ICE addicts do me no good. Nor do junkies who cannot think while anticipating their next hit. I want them lucidly addicted and under my command. Becca will perform better to aid this effort if she is functioning of her own free will. You will see to it that she does. As long as you make sure she cooperates, no one touches her but you."

Chapter 5

TWO HOURS HAD PASSED SINCE STERLING'S MEETING with Adam, when he'd been locked in the luxury officers' quarters that he and Becca were to share. He spent the entire time pacing, and pacing some more, ready to climb out of his own skin. Over and over, his mind tortured him with images of Tad touching Becca, images of her begging for ICE, willing to do anything to get it.

But I'm her bastard hero, Adam had said. Becca's hero. Adam had saved Becca from cancer and given her a reason to be loyal to him at the same time. Sterling had done nothing but stand her up for a date and get her kidnapped. She wouldn't trust him any more than he could trust her. He scrubbed a hand over his nearly two-day-old beard and glanced at the clock on the security panel that said it was exactly noon, only five minutes later than the last time he'd checked.

"Damn it to hell," he mumbled, eyeing the leather sofa, full kitchen, and entry to a bedroom complete with a king-sized bed that made up his new prison cell. One might think he was a welcomed guest if not for the locks on the doors. He should be wolf bait inside the coliseum, where he'd be mangled until he healed, and mangled all over, until he told the Renegade secrets. So why wasn't he? Why… when Adam had Becca's ICE addiction, did he think he needed Becca's help? Unless… Adam was using Becca to get to him. He didn't have time to contemplate the many ways Becca might be used against him, before the door burst open and Becca was shoved inside.

Tad filled the doorway behind her. "Take care of her," he said. "Or I'll enjoy doing it for you." He barked out laughter and pulled the door shut. A glow of red lights appeared on the knob as he activated the electronic locks.

Any thought he'd had of her rushing to his side glad to see him faded when she leaned against the door, leaving several feet between them, and accused, "You're one of them."

She still wore the same black dress, one side of it ripped, one section matted with blood, *his blood*. The dark length of her silky hair rested in disorderly waves around her pale face, where not a drop of makeup remained. And she was beautiful, absolutely freaking beautiful. There was just something about Becca that called to the man in him, even before he'd fully been one.

"I'm not one of them, Becca," he promised.

She shook her head, rejecting his answer. "You were bleeding to death. They shot you at least a half dozen times." Her voice lifted, cracked with anger, and turned to a shout. "You should be dead right now."

Okay, he hadn't seen that one coming. She was pissed he was still alive? "Sorry to disappoint you, sweetheart, but I'm not dead, nor do I intend to be anytime soon."

"Don't say it like that," she said. "Don't say it like I did something wrong. I cried for you. I… took that damn drug for you."

Understanding washed over him, the reason Adam needed Sterling's help. Either Becca was a damn good actress, or she not only wasn't happy about being an ICE addict, but she now thought he'd been part of an elaborate scheme to make her take it.

"I'm one of the two hundred men injected by Powell at Area 51 before Adam Rain got power hungry and took it over. That makes me a GTECH, and yes, I heal quickly, among other abilities. But I am not, nor will I ever be, one of Adam's men."

She studied him a moment, her gaze sharp, but her body eased slightly, melting against the door. "So you work for the army?"

"The Renegades," he said. "A private Special Operations group composed of both GTECHs and civilian human members."

"Human," she repeated.

"Most GTECHs don't consider themselves human."

"Do you?"

"No."

She seemed to digest that a moment, accept it, before moving on. "They want me to help them with the drug," she said. "Just like you did."

He didn't miss the slight hint of accusation to the statement. "For different reasons with the same outcome," he said, starting to realize the opportunity they had before them. The DNA source was here, where he could destroy it if she could come up with an antidote. "So people don't die."

"They gave me the drug."

Cautiously, he moved a few inches closer to her, encouraged when she didn't object. "It cured your cancer."

"It made me an addict and a slave to whatever that man wants of me. That's not a cure."

"We'll find an antidote."

"More than an antidote," she replied vehemently. "I'll make an immunization that keeps ICE from working. I'll make sure he doesn't turn anyone else into a slave at his mercy, if it's the last thing I do on this earth, so help me God."

Sterling stiffened at the words, despite his approval. They were being taped, watched, and listened to, and her statement was the kind that would get them both killed or thrown into the sex camps.

She was fired up, angry. "I'm going to destroy—"

Sterling reacted before she could finish her statement, doing exactly what he knew Adam would expect him to do, but doing it for himself with his own intentions. He closed the distance between himself and Becca, pulled her into his arms, and kissed her to shut her up. No. He kissed her because he had to, because every fiber of his being needed to feel her next to him, to claim her in a way he didn't try to analyze. His tongue parted her lips, brushing past her teeth, to delve deeper. She moaned and melted into him, sliding her arms around his neck, rising to her toes to taste him.

"Sterling," she whispered.

Possessiveness flared inside him like nothing he'd ever felt before. If anyone tried to touch her—Adam, Tad, or anyone else in this damnable place, he'd kill them. She was his to protect, his to save… his.

She had cancer. She didn't have cancer. She was now Adam's slave, kept alive by ICE. It was all a roller-coaster ride of emotions, and while Becca knew she should resist Sterling, knew she should be cautious about trusting him, she couldn't make herself. He was alive when she'd been certain he was dead, and she needed to feel him, to convince herself he was real.

To escape the nightmare of the past day, the past months of her life. And kissing him was good, so good, the escape she had desperately craved for months now, even before he showed up on her doorstep. And she did trust him… on some core level *she trusted Sterling*.

It's why she'd let him in her house, why she was able to lose herself in the mindless bliss of his lips, his tongue, the blessed warmth of his powerful body pressed to hers. There was no cancer, no drug addiction, no monster with grand ideas of ruling the world, and no Tad. There was just this moment in time with Sterling, with his hand sliding over her waist, her hip. Becca moaned as his palm rounded her backside, and he lifted her. Still kissing him, she wrapped her legs around his waist, her arms around his neck.

She barely remembered him walking, carrying her, nor how she found herself sitting on the bathroom sink. Bathroom sink? On some level that was an odd choice of locations, but Sterling's lips were traveling her jaw, her neck, driving her wild.

"Cameras and recording devices," he whispered. She sucked in a breath, tensed at the implications, but his mouth was on hers again. His tongue stroked hers with one last long caress before his hand ran down her hair, and he stepped away, yanking back the shower curtain and turning on the water.

The absence of his touch left her suddenly cold, the memory of ICE sliding down her throat a vivid, immediate memory. Tension curled in her chest and spread through her body, her fingers closing around the edges of the vanity beneath her. She was addicted to ICE, a drug that might have who knew what side effects on those who used it, even if they were safely weaned off of it.

Sterling returned to stand in front of her, pressing his hands to the vanity at her side. The other went to her face, his fingers gliding over her cheek, gently drawing her eyes to his. "We're getting out of here," he said. "Both of us alive and well." He tilted his head, near her ear. "They need to believe we are doing something other than talking." He reached up and turned out the light.

"What are you doing?" Becca asked, stiffening both from the shock of complete darkness, and the idea that his kisses had been nothing more than a cover story.

"Letting their imaginations run wild," he explained. "And I can hear you thinking, Becca. No, I didn't kiss you just for a cover. I've wanted to kiss you since the day I met you in that library fourteen years ago. And now that I have…" His fingers trailed her lip. "I want more." He slid his hand up her back, sensual and strong, soothing her, exciting her, adding to the heat of his words. "I want that date we never had, and I want to convince you I deserve to make love to you. But not here, not in this hellhole of place where you don't belong." His lips brushed hers. "So what do you say? Let's destroy Adam, and get out of here?"

"Sterling," she whispered, conflicting emotions welling in her chest at the absolute impossibility of his words ever becoming reality. They were trapped, and she was enslaved to ICE.

His lips brushed hers. "You should know... it drives me so wild when you say my name."

Heat swam through her as the very core of her clenched with desire, and she pressed her hand to his chest, feeling the racing of his heartbeat. She wanted him so badly she could almost forget she needed ICE to survive.

"We'll stockpile ICE from the lab every day," he said, seeming to read her mind. "And the minute we have enough, and you either have an antidote, or you believe you have what you need to make one, you tell me, and I'll get us out of here."

A sliver of hope slid inside her that they could escape, that they could save the city, maybe the world, from ICE addiction. That she was really cured, that she would be free and have a chance to live life, and just maybe Sterling would be a part of that life.

But hope was something she'd been burned by; hope was something that had lifted her up and stomped on her too many times to count. Hope was the one thing that could still terrify her, destroy her. She didn't want hope. She didn't want Sterling to offer her a façade. She wanted to scream at him, to tell him hope didn't solve anything. But suddenly, his mouth closed over hers, stealing the thought, melting her into the moment. It was a claiming, passionate, hungry, devouring kiss that did exactly what she needed—it pulled her under a spell, made her forget hope, forget fear. There was just need, and a hard, hot male body pressing against hers.

Something ignited inside her, a wild, urgent burn for this man like nothing she had ever felt. Becca clung to him, touching him, pressing her hands under his T-shirt—taut skin and rippling muscle beneath her palms—and she couldn't get enough of him.

"Sterling," she whispered, arching into him until she felt the thick pulse of his arousal in the intimate V of her body.

He growled at his name, his hand curving her backside, molding her to him. "You're killing me woman. I said not here, not now."

"We don't even know if there will be a tomorrow." She covered his hand on her waist and urged it to her breast. "I don't want to wait."

His forehead rested on hers. "I only have so much willpower."

"I don't want you to have *any*."

His fingers laced into her hair, his lips brushing hers. "This isn't how I wanted this to happen."

She lifted her lips and pressed them to his, being bold when she would otherwise not be, sliding her tongue into his mouth. A low moan slid from his throat, before he slanted his lips more fully over hers, before he tasted her deeply, fervently.

"I won't take you like this," he whispered.

"I won't forgive you if you don't," she rebutted, feeling as if she had nothing to lose by being bold, nothing except the escape, the pleasure—the opportunity to be with this man she wanted so very much. Her hand slid down his pants, tracing the hard line of his erection.

He covered his hand over hers, held it there a moment, kissed her. "We'll compromise," he whispered by her ear, nibbling the lobe.

"What does that mean?" she asked breathlessly, a

sizzling chill racing over her skin as he pressed her shirt down her shoulder and kissed the delicate skin there.

"Actions speak louder than words. I'll show you what it means." He moved in the darkness, and oh God, he was on the floor, pushing her skirt along her thighs as he kissed a path up the length of one of them.

"Sterling," she whispered.

He kissed the silk of her panties. "Do you like the way I compromise?"

She swallowed hard, warmth sliding to her lower body. "Yes."

"Good," he said, and eased her panties down her legs. Her fingers curled around the edge of the sink. His big, powerful hand slid back up her legs, his lips following one of them... slowly—too slowly.

"Sterling," she said urgently, needing his mouth in her most sensitive, intimate place.

He laughed, low and sexy, filled with the mischief of a man enjoying his power. He licked her clit, and she arched her hips, her nipples aching as if they, too, had felt his tongue. The moments that followed were a haze of desire that stretched into blissful minutes. His fingers slid into the slick wet heat of her body, his tongue flicking her clit, delving where his fingers had been, where they were once again—mimicking lovemaking with skill that only made her burn more to feel him inside her.

By the time his fingers were caressing her inside, him suckling her nub, she was ready to explode, ready to tumble over the edge of pleasure into absolute pleasure. "Oh... I..." She inhaled a breath and then stiffened. A rainbow of sensation ripped through her, shaking her to the point that there was nothing else, nothing but the intense explosion of sensation. His fingers and tongue stroked, licked, caressed her into a slow ease downward, that left her gasping and blushing to the point she thought he might see it in the darkness.

When finally he stood, sliding his fingers back into her hair, he whispered, "Next time, the lights are on, so I can see every second of your pleasure."

New hunger rose in her, so fiercely it shocked her. "I need you, Sterling. Inside me. Now."

Suddenly, he stiffened, the mood in the room thick with tension, as if he didn't like her bold words. Insecurity rippled through her a moment, before he said, "Get in the shower now." He flipped on the light and started to undress.

"What? I don't—"

He leaned in and kissed her. "Someone just came in the front door. Get in the shower and stay there until I tell you to come out."

His shirt came off, the sprinkle of blond hair across his broad chest, making her gulp for air. He leaned against the wall and reached for his boots. She couldn't seem to get herself to move off the vanity and just rip her clothes off. Somehow it had been easier with the lights out and passion on.

He picked her up and set her on the ground. "Shower. Now."

Right. Shower. She bent down to unlace her flat sandals, and his pants fell to the floor. Good Lord, he was commando. And he had a backside to make grown women cry.

A knock sounded on the door. "Open up."

Horror ran down Becca's spine at the sound of

Tad's voice. Sterling wrapped a towel around his waist and looked over his shoulder with a silent command in his stare. Becca unzipped her dress and let it fall to the floor, then pulled back the shower curtain and got in, bra and panties still intact, but not before she saw the heat in Sterling's eyes. The door opened and shut, and Becca leaned against the wall, passion quickly turning to fear as she heard the male voices raise in a gruff exchange.

The bathroom door opened, and Becca held her breath. Tad was there. She felt the menace of him as readily as she had her trusted Sterling. Time stood still as she waited for what would come next. Finally, there was movement, and the door shut. Becca let out a relieved breath, but worried for Sterling. She jumped out of the shower and grabbed a towel, wrapping herself inside it, and pressed her ear to the door.

Sterling eyed the handgun on Tad's belt, prepared to kill him if he stepped one foot past the entrance of the bathroom. Tad's insistence on going inside didn't surprise Sterling. The lights had been out, the conversation muted, and Adam had demanded confirmation Sterling wasn't up to something.

Finally, Tad turned back to Sterling, but Sterling didn't relax. The time wasn't right to kill Tad, he knew this, but he wanted it to be on a downright primal level.

"No lights out," Tad said. "Ever."

"If you think I'm giving you a kinky freak show you can forget it."

"Then I guess you better keep it in your pants," he

said, and reached in his pocket, removing a vial of ICE. "Get her out here. I need to dose her."

"Adam and I have an agreement," Sterling said. "She's mine. I dose her."

Tad stared at him with hard, bulldog eyes. "You're pissing me off, Sterling Jeter. You don't want to piss me off."

"I'm under Adam's protection," Sterling said. "So you don't want to piss *me* off."

Tad turned away, and Sterling walked him to the door and made sure he exited. That man was going to be a problem, and he knew it. He quickly headed back to the bathroom and entered to find Becca wrapped in a towel and sitting on the edge of the tub, her hair dry.

"What did you mean you have a deal with Adam?"

Sterling set the ICE on the vanity and kneeled in front of her, reaching for her, but she leaned away. He lowered his voice. "I told Adam I would make sure you help him. It's what I had to tell him."

Her bottom lip trembled. "And you get what in return?"

"You," he said. "I get you, Becca. And an assurance Tad and none of the other men touch you." His gaze narrowed, noting her hand was trembling too. "You're cold. I'll get you another towel."

She grabbed his hand. "I'm not cold." She hesitated. "It just started. I… I think I'm in withdrawal."

———

"Under Adam's protection, my fucking ass," Tad murmured, sitting behind a security panel, watching Becca exiting the living quarters, his teeth grinding together like steel on steel. Sterling was a problem that needed to go away. Sterling was close to Caleb, and therefore, Adam wanted Sterling to convert to Zodius and help him bring Caleb over as well. If Sterling continued to grow close to this woman who was now permanently dependant on the Zodius to survive that might just happen. Which meant Tad fell down the power chain, and he wasn't going to let that occur. It was time to turn the woman against Sterling.

Chapter 6

THE TREMBLING HAD STOPPED FIVE MINUTES AFTER Becca had downed the dose of ICE Tad had left for her. Now, an hour later, she sat at the silver kitchen table, reading research material that had apparently been left there for her before her arrival. The room was even stocked with toiletries, makeup, and clothes that included the black jeans and T-shirt she had on. Apparently, the façade of comfort was meant to be a reward for willingly helping Adam discover his new serum—like those things made up for the locked front door that screamed prison.

"You need to eat," Sterling said, returning from the kitchen to sit down across from her and eyeing her half-eaten sandwich with disapproval.

Becca blinked at him, wondering how in the world they'd ended up back in each other's lives. He'd showered and shaven and changed into a tan army T-shirt with tan fatigues that somehow made his eyes pop a more brilliant green than usual. And for just a moment, she found herself transported back to that Texas library, sitting across from him in casual conversation, while wondering what it would be like to kiss him. Only the fantasy kiss had graduated to memories of his perfect naked body she'd glimpsed far too briefly.

He arched a brow at her, the twinkle in his eyes saying her expression showed more than she wanted it to, and she delicately cleared her throat. "I see stress doesn't affect your appetite," she commented, noting his second large stack of sandwiches. "And what's with all the orange juice?"

He finished off half the glass. "GTECHs have a chronic vitamin C deficiency and a rapid metabolism that requires fuel. Lots of it and often."

He'd told her about the GTECHs' superspeed and superstrength over his first stack of sandwiches, but not much more than she'd already known, except that ICE users supposedly had those skills on a limited basis.

"Interesting. ICE users don't experience rapid metabolism or a vitamin C deficiency from what I've read. So far, all I've felt is expanded lung capacity and that horrible trembling when I start to withdraw."

He studied her closely. "Nothing else? You're sure?"

"Not that I know of," she said, and surprised herself by actually smiling. She remembered that about Sterling. The way he said things, the way he did things. He made her loosen up. "If you tick me off, I might test my superstrength on you."

He wiggled an eyebrow. "Might be fun."

Yeah, it would, but minus the superstrength, the city of Zodius, and an ICE addiction. She shook off the thought with a darkening mood and shut the file. "The material left for me is generic at best. I'll never find what we need from this kind of data."

Abruptly, the door to the apartment opened.

"Stay where you are," Sterling ordered Becca, already on his feet to confront the two soldiers dressed in desert fatigues who had entered the quarters.

"We're to escort the woman to the lab."

"All right," Sterling said, his gaze unwavering. "We'll go to the lab."

"Not you," one soldier corrected and jerked his head at Becca. "Just her."

Becca didn't move, but her heart exploded in her chest. Without Sterling, she'd have to contend with Tad by herself, and no matter her earlier claim that she feared nothing but false hope—that man terrified her.

"Where she goes, I go," Sterling insisted. "That's non-negotiable."

Both soldiers moved their hands to the weapons on their hip holsters. "We have orders," one of them said. "She comes alone."

Becca took one look at Sterling's face, and she knew he was going to do something crazy and get himself killed. She stood up, and her hand must have hit her glass of orange juice, because it flew off the table and shattered. "I'll go." She glanced at Sterling. "I'll be fine. I need a lab to do my work."

"Forget it," he said.

Becca was in front of him now, pressing her hand on his chest. "I have to do this. I'll be okay."

The two soldiers walked up behind her and pointed guns at Sterling. "She'll be okay, but you might not," one said.

"I'm going," she said softly and turned toward the door.

Sterling pulled her back and kissed her, and then with a tormented look, let her go.

—◦◦◦—

Becca sat at a tall table in the concrete confines of the Zodius laboratory, staring at the slide under the viewer, studying what turned out to be Adam's six-month-old's DNA. Only six months for him translated to twelve years. He was aging at a rate of two years a month. And this boy's DNA was supplying the drug she was ingesting twice a day.

A folder landed on the table in front of her, and hot breath touched her neck. "Open it."

Tad. She knew his voice like one knew a bad dream, all too vividly. She flipped it open. There was a picture of Sterling with another man, two wolves at their feet. She flipped through several more, all similar, but obviously taken in different locations.

Tad turned her around, his hands going to the table on either side of her, his big body too close. "That's Adam he's with," he said. "He's one of us. He wants to be Adam's second, and he promised to fuck you into submission to get that title."

Becca's stomach knotted. "You're lying. Why would you tell me this if it's what Adam wants?"

"Because I'm Adam's second," he said. "And he means to replace me. I'm going to kill him before he has the chance. So I suggest you make it clear you're loyal to me or I'll see you thrown in one of the sex camps." He shoved away from the table and headed to the back office.

Becca had no idea what a "sex camp" was, but she was screaming in her head. Nononono! Sterling was not a Zodius. He wasn't one of them. He wasn't! Those pictures had to be of Sterling with Adam's brother Caleb. Her gaze slid around the lab, looking for an escape. She needed to escape. A water glass on her table shattered. Then a slide.

Milton Wright, the only other non-GTECH scientist

out of the six present, rushed to her table and began picking up glass. A thirty-something scientist who worked for the military, he too had been kidnapped and forced to help Adam.

"That was odd," he said, tossing shards in the trash. "The glass just shattered. I never saw you touch it."

She agreed, remembering the orange juice glass a few hours back shattering in much the same way, but too twisted in knots from Tad's visit to give it much thought. "What's a sex camp?"

He glanced up from what he was doing and then walked to her side and sat down at the table adjoining hers. "Adam's son, Dorian, is very powerful. Like freaky powerful. They want more like him, which means finding the rare woman who can bond with one of the males and convert to GTECH. It's like a physical marriage. They have sex. They bond. They have scary offspring like Dorian."

Becca felt sick. "How do they know they bond? They just get pregnant or what?"

"Some strange tattoo marking appears on the woman's neck right after sex. I hear it hurts, like someone is carving it in their flesh. Then they do a blood exchange, and the woman converts to GTECH."

"Blood exchange?" she asked, aghast at such an idea.

"They slice their palms and press them together. There is a plus side for the female. She becomes a GTECH complete with eternal youth and immunity to all human illness, among other things. Of course, she has a really nasty Zodius soldier hanging around all the time, and if he goes and gets himself killed, say by pissing off Adam—" He held up a hand. "I know that's hard to believe, but it happens—well, then she goes bye-bye right along with him. One dies, the other dies."

She still couldn't quite get her head around this. "Okay, back up because I feel like I'm living in bizarro world. Are you actually telling me they basically pass women from soldier to soldier until one of them bonds with her, and this mark shows up?"

"That's pretty much the sum of it."

"That's barbaric," she said. "It's just—" Becca paused as he wiped his forehead. He didn't look good. Sweat gathered on his upper lip and forehead; the lab jacket clung to his clothes. Becca rolled her stool to his table. "You okay, Milton?"

He sat back on the lab stool and ran his hands over his thighs. "They didn't dose me this morning."

"What?" Worried, she turned to study him more closely. "Are you sure they didn't think you'd dosed—"

"No, Becca," he said sharply. "They know what they're doing. And of course, they dosed you. I've failed to find the answers they seek. You're the new kid on the block. They don't need me anymore. Out with me. In with you."

She drew back, shocked at the harshness of his words.

He scrubbed his jaw. "I'm sorry. I'm not myself. It feels like I've swallowed acid, and it's eating me alive."

She softened instantly and touched his hand. It was clammy, yet he shivered as if cold. She cut the other scientists a quick look, contemplating complaining, but the men cast an evil smile, clearly amused at Milton's suffering.

A buzzer sounded, and the electronic steel doors, the only entrance or exit to the lab directly in front of their table, slid open. Dressed in green army fatigues, a tall man radiating power entered with two wolves by his side. Becca wanted to throw up. This was Adam Rain, and this man and these pet wolves of his had been in the pictures with Sterling.

Beside him was his son Dorian, dressed in matching fatigues, and looking every bit twelve at six months old. "So nice of you to join us, Ms. Burns," Adam said, motioning to Dorian. "Meet my son, who cured you of your cancer."

The boy's gaze settled on Becca, his black eyes boring into hers with such darkness and depth she felt as if she were being sucked into them.

"What good news do you have for me, Milton?"

Adam's question jolted her from whatever hold the boy's eyes had on her, and she glanced at Milton, who looked like he was about to choke on his tongue.

Becca quickly came to his rescue. "Since every ICE user who goes into withdrawal doesn't die, pre-existing conditions or some inconsistency in the ICE doses would be an obvious place to begin looking for cause of death."

"Read the files, Ms. Burns," Adam snapped. "There were no pre-existing conditions and no difference in one vial of ICE from the next."

"That we know of—"

"No pre-existing conditions and no difference in one vial of ICE to the next," Adam repeated. "Your failure to be more informed disappoints me."

He cut his gaze to Dorian. "Show the lady what happens to people who disappoint me."

The boy's lips curled upward, his dark eyes expressive, excited as if he'd been rewarded with a toy, and

Becca was that toy. He raised his hands, and the wolves charged at her. She screamed, unaware that the boy, too, could control the wolves. She scrambled to her feet and backed against the concrete beam behind her, trapped as they crowded her so close their breath fanned the bottom of her lab coat.

Dorian laughed. "I do believe she's frightened, Father."

Becca's gaze swept toward Milton in the misdirected hope of intervention. His head was on the table, his body shaking.

With bravado she didn't feel, Becca pushed herself upright. "I'll do what you want. But please, I need Milton's help. Don't make him suffer."

"I take it from your desire to cling to the aid of this human scientist that my scientific team has displeased you?"

"No," she said quickly, afraid an insult to his men would get both of them killed. "They're fine. They're great. Very helpful."

"Good then," he said. "You would be better served to focus on the big picture and not on a few humans without purpose."

"I'm human," she said softly.

"You are female," he said. "You will soon learn how purposeful that is around here."

He meant the sex camps. Her mind flashed to those pictures of Sterling with Adam and the wolves as proof she had no allies in this place. Adrenaline and emotions rushed through her, but somehow she stayed focused. Milton was dying. "Please," Becca said. "I need Milton's experience and knowledge."

Adam glanced at his son. "Give him the drug."

"As you wish, Father," Dorian said, approaching

Milton, that evil look of his ravishing her with dread. A sense of something not being right settled hard in her stomach. Dorian grabbed a handful of Milton's hair and jerked his head backward, shoving a pill in his mouth.

Oh God. Panic rushed through Becca. "That wasn't ICE! What did you give him?"

Dorian's attention settled on Becca, callousness beyond his age etching his finely carved features as he slammed Milton's face into the table.

Becca's stomach rolled at the hard crash of skull against wood.

"Lady," Dorian spoke, tilting his head to study her as if she were a specimen to be evaluated. "I've given him what you wished for. He will suffer no more. This should please you."

Milton convulsed and fell off the chair.

"What does that mean?" she screamed, taking a step forward, only to have the wolves growl, warning her to hold her position. "What does that mean, he will suffer no more?" She turned a pleading stare on Adam. "Adam, please! Please, help him. I'll do anything you want."

"You'll do what I want, regardless," he replied. "But it will be without him. He is dead. And you are not the only scientist here with your expertise. But you *are* female, and I do not wish you dead, just motivated. So here is your motivation. Every time I feel you are failing me, I will kill one of the humans. And you are failing me. Consider Milton's blood is on your hands, Becca."

Becca choked on her breath, and this time it had nothing to do with cancer. This wasn't happening. She squeezed her eyes shut and told herself she'd wake up soon. This was a bad nightmare, a side effect of her treatments in Germany. Minutes of slumber had passed, not hours of captivity.

Suddenly, Adam was in front of her, the wolves parting to allow him to stand almost on top of her. Becca gasped, shocked at his nearness. He didn't touch her, yet she could almost swear she felt his hands on her throat. She tried not to move, but he stared at her, the depths of evil in his black, spiraling eyes pouring through her like acid, eating her alive.

"I suggest you get to work," Adam said, his voice low, poisonous. "Before I decide to kill another human simply because… well, it's entertaining. Especially when I watch you worry for them." He paused as if for effect, then, "Am I clear?"

She nodded. "Yes," she whispered, but the word was barely audible, her voice lost in the bile forming with his nearness.

For several seconds, he studied her, his features stony, intense. "Then do it," he finally said. "And I'll leave Milton here to remind you of the consequences of displeasing me."

He gave her his back, his wolves following on his heels. Dorian fell into step beside his father, but not before casting Becca a mocking glance. The boy was evil. Born evil. Growing more so with each passing day.

And when Becca was certain this day could get no worse—a second before the doors closed—Tad's big, obnoxious self stepped inside.

"Good news, Becca. Sweetie. Darling. Honey bunch. We have some quality time together. I'm to look out for you." He smiled and winked. Then walked to Milton and shoved him onto the ground as if he were nothing but trash in the way. "You heard Adam," he shouted at the group. "Let's get to work."

Anger, pain, and yes, fear, collided inside Becca with a force so mighty, she thought she might collapse. Something happened with that force—energy crackled in the air—glass shattered in various locations of the lab. It was as if her emotions waved through the air with electricity. Her head spun, her chest tightened. Remotely, she heard Tad yelling. And then he was on the floor and so were the other scientists. They just dropped like rocks and hit the concrete with hard thuds.

Becca's eyes went wide. Her heart jackknifed and then raced. What just happened? She balled her fist over her heart and willed it to stop racing, but her hand was unsteady, shaky. She forced herself to inhale and exhale and count to ten slowly. The dizziness subsided; the room came back into focus.

Then, and only then, did she scold herself for standing still. She raced to Milton's side and rolled him over, cringing at his blank, open eyes even as she checked for a pulse she knew she wasn't going to find.

Her stomach twisted, and she reached up to close his eyes. More glass around the room shattered as she whispered, "I'm sorry I didn't save you." But she didn't cry—the fury over this cruelty still eating her alive.

She pushed to her feet and faced the scientists where they lay on the ground. Items in the room began to float. A chair jumped and turned over. Becca could feel the energy coming off her—the power that damn ICE created. And she knew she was the reason those men were on the ground.

Becca stared at them and then at the locked doors. Badge. They had badges to open the door. Tad would have the highest security clearance she assumed. Without allowing herself time to think, Becca charged forward and bent over Tad, repulsed as she touched his wrist and found a pulse. He wasn't dead; she didn't know if she should feel relieved or disappointed. She had no idea what was wrong with them, but she wasn't going to stay around until they woke up.

She unclipped the badge from Tad's shirt and rushed to the doorway. Then she stopped, went back, and yanked his gun from his holster.

It made her think of how her brother had forced her to handle a gun despite her objections. "Thank you, Kevin," she murmured. He'd insisted she needed to know so that when he was away at war, she was protected. And so she'd learned.

One last thought filled her mind. Money. Did she dare hope Tad had any on him? She cringed at the idea of touching him and then reached into his pocket. Nothing. She hopped over him and tried the other pocket. Bingo! A money clip that had a decent amount of cash.

In a flash, she was at the exit, swiping the security card over the key device. A light turned green, but the doors didn't open. She punched the keypad next to it in random combinations. Nothing. She tried again. Suddenly, water burst from the fire sprinklers, and the doors opened. Becca stood there under the spray of water, having no idea what to do next. She didn't know how to get out of this place, and she didn't know how to get to Sterling, or even if she could trust him if she did. Or anyone else for that matter. Muffled voices sounded down the hall. Time was up. She took off running in the opposite direction.

Chapter 7

No way was Sterling leaving Becca to deal with whatever was happening in Zodius City on her own. The minute the fire alarm went off and water started spewing all over him, Sterling did what he'd wanted to do for hours. He busted open the electronic panel by the door and unlocked it himself, immediately heading down the deserted hall for the lab, knowing exactly where he was going. Not only had this section of Zodius City existed when it had been Area 51 and his assigned post, but he'd studied the maps Michael had provided while undercover as Adam's second.

Down a flight of stairs, he paused at a door and eased it open only to discover something was blocking it. Holy crap. There was a Zodius soldier face down in front of the door. What was going on, and where was Becca while it was happening? Sterling reeled back and shoved his weight against the door, the water puddle at its base adding resistance. He managed to create a space large enough for him to examine the vacant corridor before he exited. Bending down next to the soldier, Sterling retrieved the man's weapons, slicking his wet hair back as the uncompromising water covered his face.

Sterling took off in a light jog and stepped over two more Zodius soldiers lying face down, before he rounded the corner to find the lab door open. His gut clenched as he entered, and he didn't breathe until he'd confirmed none of the six bodies in the lab were Becca. Fear for Becca seeped into him, twisting him into knots.

His gaze landed on the computer by the doorway, water pooled around it. Not optimistic, he headed toward it, setting his weapons down to punch some keys. Against all odds, the screen came to life, and he worked his magic. In a minute flat, he had the security feed live and had opened several windows at once, confirming that whatever had happened in this area of the city wasn't happening elsewhere. Soldiers gathered at a distant corridor, and Sterling had no doubt the only reason this place wasn't swarming with them was that whatever had set off the alarm and flattened everyone but he and Becca wasn't contained.

A few more screens and he wanted to shout from relief. Becca was alive and on the move. He punched in a code to shut down the security cameras and then snatched his weapons. A search of the lab for ICE followed and came up dry. Cursing, he headed after Becca and vowed to find a dealer and the ICE that Becca needed in the city.

Her path ended at an underground ventilation tunnel he knew would lead to deserted terrain near a highway. Obviously, she'd put her brains to work to figure that out or taken a calculated risk.

He pulled open the steel door to the tunnel and climbed inside, resealing it behind him. He didn't dare call out for fear of being heard, but the farther he traveled with no sign of Becca, the more worried he became. When he reached the end of the tunnel, he went topside to discover that Becca was nowhere in sight. He'd lost her again, and she was running on borrowed time. He

had no idea if she had a supply of ICE, and he didn't
have the serum.

———*———

Once the sprinklers were off and the security feed was
analyzed, Adam entered the lab with Dorian by his side.
He grimaced with disgust at the sight of his second-in-
charge knocked out on the floor—the worthless piece of
shit. Half the men who'd taken a nap, compliments of
Rebecca Burns, were already awake, but Tad lay there
sleeping in a puddle of water. He kicked Tad.

"Get up, you moron. Get up now!"

Tad jerked to a sitting position, a stunned look on his
face. "Holy crap. What the fuck happened?" He jumped
to his feet and glanced around to see the scientists on the
floor as he had been. "Where's—"

"You tell me!" Adam demanded furiously. "She
and Sterling are both gone. How is it that your prisoner
dropped all of you flat on your asses without lifting a
hand, and now she's missing and the cameras are out?
How does that happen with my second-in-charge here?
And you idiot, she used *your* badge to get out of the lab."
Adam motioned to Dorian and then the rest of the men.
"Wake them all up."

Dorian quickly began kicking the other men with the
force of an angry elephant. Despite his irritation, Adam
found himself amused at the display.

The doors to the lab opened, and the lead scientist
for the ICE program rushed into the room, his lab coat
neatly buttoned, his glasses sliding down his nose. Adam
had expected the world when he recruited the brilliant
Chinese scientist from under General Powell's nose, and

he'd been given ICE in all its failing glory. Chin was wearing on his nerves and outstaying his welcome, if he wasn't careful.

"I just finished watching the camera feed," Dr. Chin said. "The woman levitated items in the lab and caused the men to pass out. It's remarkable, like nothing we've seen before."

Adam ground his teeth, barely containing the urge to snap the man's neck. "Yet another side effect of ICE we should have known about."

Chin pressed his glasses up his nose. "Thousands of people have used ICE, and no one else has developed anything remotely similar to the skills this woman has demonstrated. Perhaps ICE reacted to her recent cancer treatments. I need the woman and her records from the Germany hospital to be certain." He held up a hand. "I make no promises, but if my theory proves correct, we could combine ICE with the treatments and recreate her skills in your men. But we must locate her quickly before ICE withdrawal kills her. The camera footage showed her taking a small supply, not more than a few days at most."

Adam wanted no part of giving anyone the kind of power this woman had, unless it was him and him alone. He eyed Tad. "Find her, and you kill her. Bring her body to Chin to study."

"I need her alive," Chin argued.

"I want her dead," Adam said. "*Now*, before she can be used as a weapon against us, which means before Sterling manages to get her to Sunrise City and under my brother's protection."

He cut the three dripping wet scientists a look. "You

have all failed me, and that comes with a price." His attention flicked to Tad. "Kill her, and you will be forgiven. Fail… and you will suffer worse than all three of them together."

Becca reached the highway and stripped her jacket off, hiding the gun in its folds. Waving her hands, she raced in front of an oncoming truck and prayed the driver stopped. Her heart racing as he got closer and closer, a huge sigh escaped her lips as the semi came to a screeching halt inches from hitting her.

Shaking, Becca ran toward the passenger's door, which popped open, only to have the ICE vials in her jacket crash to the ground. No! No! She bent down and tried to recover them, but they were gone. Her lifeline was gone.

"You comin', lady?" the trucker asked.

"Yes," she said. She had no other option. She couldn't go back; she could only go forward and pray she could find a stock of ICE on the streets. Either way, there was a good chance she would die, but she'd be damned if she was doing it before she stopped Adam from hurting anyone else.

Becca climbed inside the truck and started rambling about a made-up, crazy boyfriend who'd left her on the side of the road, when all she could think about was her supply of ICE being lost. *The ICE was gone*. Sterling was gone. He'd deceived her, she reminded herself. He wasn't what he'd seemed. He was never her friend, never her lover, and thank goodness for it. But as her gaze settled on the road, and she was traveling farther and farther away from him, she found herself replaying every moment with him, questioning his true agenda. No matter how she justified leaving him behind, no matter how she told herself she had taken her one chance to leave Zodius City alive and warn the world about Adam, leaving without Sterling hurt.

Chapter 8

AFTER A GOOD THREE HOURS OF SEARCHING THE AREA 51 desert terrain for Becca with no luck, Sterling wind-walked to the Nevada mountains and the underground headquarters for the Renegades. He entered Sunrise City with murder on his mind—Damion's to be precise. He charged through the facility, and with a few inquiries, went straight for his target in the "war room," the Renegades operation center.

Kicking the door open, he found Damion sitting at the conference table with Caleb and Michael on either side of him, along with four other high-ranking Renegades. One look in Sterling's direction and the room seemed to get the message. No one dared any "welcome homes," and Caleb motioned for them all to leave. Everyone stood and quickly complied, except Michael, who considered himself Caleb's personal bodyguard, which was fine with Sterling. He and Michael had their personal battles, but they were friends at the core. Michael and Caleb were about the only two people he would trust if his life depended on it right now. There was a time not so long ago, when Damion would have been included on that short list.

Sterling stepped out of the doorway to let the four other men pass, as he waited for Damion, adrenaline rushing through his limbs in anticipation of his approach. The instant Damion was within reach Sterling grabbed him and flung him onto the conference table.

Michael arched a dark brow as Damion slid to a halt between him and Caleb. "Bad mood, Sterling?"

"Bad mood doesn't even begin to describe it," Sterling said, already stalking toward the table.

"What the fuck, man?" Damion demanded, starting to get up.

Sterling jumped on the table and was on top of Damion in a flash, grabbing a handful of his shirt again. Pumped up on anger and fear for Becca, Sterling had Damion against the wall in another blink.

"You fake, Mr. All-American, do everything by the book, piece-of-shit traitor, with your GI Joe haircut and morals of steel," Sterling ground out. "You gave her up. You gave *me* up."

"What the fuck are you talking about?" Damion demanded.

"Don't pretend you don't know," Sterling warned. "Because that's only going to piss me off more, and you don't want to do that right now."

"Wow," Caleb said, pressing them apart with an assist from Michael. "What's this about?"

"Damion handed Rebecca Burns over to Tad Bensen. That's what the fuck this is about."

Damion glared at Sterling. "*You* handed that woman over, not me."

Sterling lunged at Damion. "You lying sack of shit."

Michael cursed and shoved Sterling to the table, blocking his view of Damion. "Take a breath, man. Let's figure this out."

"He's Zodius," Sterling seethed, enunciating every word tightly. "And you know me well enough to know I wouldn't make such an accusation if I wasn't *dead* certain."

Michael narrowed his gaze before he stepped aside to glance at Caleb, but not without maintaining a handful of Sterling's shirt for good measure. Sonofabitch. Sterling was going to kick Michael's ass, too, if he didn't let him go.

"This is insane," Damion mumbled furiously, talking to Caleb, who had his hand pressed to his shoulder, holding him immobile. "He's crazy. He was hurt and delirious, and I'm not taking the fall for his stupid, daredevil mistakes that got that woman killed." He glared at Sterling. "Stop trying to prove you're as GTECH as the rest of us before you get someone *else* killed."

Fury exploded in Sterling at the reference to Sterling's limited wind-walking ability and a few other shortfalls that only a handful of people knew existed. Sterling lunged forward, managing to land a blow on Damion's jaw, before Michael and Caleb could gain control again.

Michael held Sterling against the table and looked over his shoulder at Damion. "Why did you go there, man? Seriously why?" He returned his attention to Sterling. "That shit he just said doesn't matter," Michael said, shared understanding in his gaze, the feeling of being an outcast. While Sterling had a few limitations, Michael had a few extra assets that scared the shit out of people. "You're both pissed and saying things you don't mean."

"Oh yeah, I'm pissed," Sterling agreed. "I have *never* risked anyone's life but my own, and I've damn sure saved a hell of a lot more than him."

"Oh Jeezus, Sterling," Damion said. "Why don't we get out our dicks and measure them too?"

Sterling kept his gaze locked on Michael. "Maybe

you should remind him I'm as good at taking lives as I am at saving them."

"I *said* meet me at the upstairs window," Damion yelled behind them. "Why the hell did you go out the back door? And why the hell did you hand her over to the Zodius without a fight?"

"Oh, that's priceless," Sterling said in the midst of a bitter laugh as Michael moved from between the two of them. "You were at the window. You think I don't remember that? And we both know you were on the back porch, that I handed Becca *to you*."

"You came out the back door before I ever made it to the window."

Anger uncurled in Sterling, calmer now, more calculated. "Your lies are going to get you nice and dead, Damion."

"I am *not* working for Adam," Damion insisted vehemently, his chin lifting in Michael's direction. "You were undercover inside Zodius until only a few months ago. If I was working for Adam, wouldn't you know?"

"A lot can happen in a few months," Michael stated.

Damion made a frustrated sound. "I am not working for Adam!"

"Why didn't we hear about any of this until now, Damion?" Caleb demanded.

"Because it was done," Damion said. "For all I knew Sterling was dead, and I wasn't going to throw accusations at a dead man you considered a friend."

Caleb considered him a moment, then released Damion and indicated the door to Michael. "You and Damion leave Sterling and me alone."

Michael cast Sterling a warning look before releasing

him. Sterling stood rock steady, his eyes locked on Damion. "She's not dead. But I can promise you this. If anything happens to her, I will kill you."

Several tense seconds passed before Damion pushed off the wall and walked away without another word. Neither Sterling nor Caleb spoke until the door to the war room shut behind Michael.

"He's not lying," Caleb said softly.

"The hell he's not," Sterling said. "I saw him hand her over. I don't care what your damn Spidey senses tell you."

"I know you believe that," he said. "I know you're not lying, and I wouldn't need my 'Spidey' senses to know that, because I know you. But I can tell you without any question, you both believe what you're saying is the one hundred percent truth." He paused a moment. "I thought you were dead."

Sterling ran a hand through his hair and sat on the edge of the table. "Yeah well, I should be, and she will be, if I don't find her and find her fast." He recounted the past few days, including Becca's ICE addiction and ending with the details of their escape. "I have no idea what happened in that section of Zodius City, but Becca and I were the only ones who were conscious."

"Were they dead?" Caleb asked from the spot where he'd perched against the wall.

"No clue, and there wasn't time to spare to find out," he said. "And it can't be a toxin, or Becca and I would have been affected."

They talked a few more minutes, and while debriefing was necessary, Sterling was once again feeling that "ready to climb out of his own skin" sensation. He needed to be out of here. He needed to find Becca.

"She's personal to you?" Caleb asked, watching him closely.

"Yeah," he said. "She's personal." There was no reason to deny the truth he didn't quite understand. Not only would Caleb sense his feelings, Caleb was the brother he'd never had. And Becca mattered to him more than anything had in a very long time.

Caleb pushed off the wall. "We'll find her," Caleb promised.

But would they find her before it was too late to save her?

Sterling left Sunrise City near ten o'clock, early for Vegas, especially on Friday night, and he planned to use every second he had available to find Becca. With a few phone calls to both his street team and various outside contacts, he determined that ICE had gone underground, dealt through some sort of private club system.

When the words "private" and "money" were involved, Sterling, or rather his bounty hunter who did anything for the right price, knew where to go. By ten thirty, Sterling was exiting the elevator of the Magnolia Casino, one of the biggest moneymakers on the strip, and followed a cushioned, red-carpeted path. Expected, he entered the security booth, where a front windowpane overlooked the casino. Computer monitors lined walls and hung from the ceiling.

In the center of the room stood Marcus Lyons, the head of security for three of the largest casino resort operations on the strip. Tall and athletic with dark hair, he wore the same black suit as his staff, but with a blood-red tie that said, look at me, I'm George-freaking-Clooney. *Whatever got the guy off*, as far as Sterling was concerned. The man was connected like a lightbulb in this city. That's all that mattered. And the man would be king as far as Sterling was concerned if he led him to Becca. With a lift of his chin, Marcus motioned to the office in the back of the booth, and Sterling followed. Shutting the door behind him went without saying.

"What was so urgent?" Marcus asked, turning to face him.

"I have a client who wants a large stock of ICE," he said. "He's willing to pay premium plus. And don't tell me you don't know what it is. This is worth too much money to play games. He wants what he wants, and he wants it tonight."

Marcus studied him a long moment. "If I give you this information and you make a contact, I want a piece of the action."

"*If* I make a contact?"

"I've got a location, and that's it," he said. "But it took some serious bullying to get it." His lips lifted as he added, "I like to be prepared for occasions such as this one. But if you go to this place, opportunity may or may not present itself. But I'll have someone nearby. Someone watching. I'll know if you make contact. I'll expect to be paid."

"I've always paid, and paid well for information," Sterling said, legs in a V, arms crossed. The Renegades had deep-pocket funding, in part, from Renegades like Michael and Damion, who were born with silver spoons. "Why would that change now?"

"What's your 'take' on this deal?" Marcus inquired, a keen look in his blue eyes.

He hesitated intentionally, playing the negotiation game expected of him. Not an easy task when he wanted to shake Marcus until he told him what he wanted to know. "Fifty Gs."

Marcus arched a brow. "I'll take thirty."

Sterling snorted out a laugh and fixed Marcus in an "are you whacked" look. "And the real number is…?"

"We both know you didn't tell me your full price," Marcus countered. "You lowered the number. I want thirty, or you get nothing from me."

Sterling whistled, putting on a show. "That's steep, you greedy sonofabitch."

"Not when you're talking about stockpiling something as hot and impossible to find as ICE," he said. "So take it." He folded his arms in front of his chest. "Or leave it."

"I get the location now. Tonight."

"I get a retainer now, or no deal," Marcus countered.

Sterling sauntered over to the desk and hiked one hip up on the edge. He reached into his pocket and pulled out a wad of cash secured with a clip and tossed it on the desk. "That's ten. I figured that would be enough to get you one of those fancy manicures you like so much."

Marcus laughed, noticeably relaxing. "I don't know who's a bigger asshole. You or me."

"I like to think we have our own brand of assholeness," Sterling said dryly. "You're the suit-wearing, talk-down-to-you, and then bust-your-wallet-in-the-balls, kind of asshole. I'm the dirty-boxing, back-alley kind of asshole." He pushed off the desk. "Now where am I going?"

"When do I get the rest of my money?"

"When I get the ICE."

Marcus considered a moment. "Don't fuck me over, Sterling."

"Back at you, *asshole*," Sterling replied snidely. "You have my ten grand."

Marcus considered a moment then he said, "Nebula," naming the newest addition to the club scene, located inside a competing casino property. Marcus gave Sterling's attire of jeans and a T-shirt a once-over. "You might want to make sure to blend with the crowd. It's not your typical Vegas hot spot. This place is more leather and chains than denim."

Dryly, Sterling replied, "And here I thought you might come with me." He shrugged. "Too bad." The tension between them evaporated. Despite all their mocking exchanges, they almost liked each other. They'd done too many of these deals together not to respect each other's value. "Later, Marcus."

"Bring us both back some money, Sterling."

Sterling waved as he exited, ready for action.

———

To hell with changing clothes to fit into some goth-themed drug bar. By eleven thirty, Sterling was standing in the far corner of the smoke-filled, three-story portion of the Empire Tower Casino's Club Nebula, nursing a beer for show and thinking of that moment when he'd handed Becca over to Damion. It had been Damion, he was sure of it.

Nonchalantly, he tilted back his beer again, studying the far corner by the bar where two punkers—one with a Mohawk and the other with a spiked 'do—were talking with a woman. One of the punkers partially blocked his view. A glimpse of long black hair and he set the beer down with a thud, waiting for a better line of sight, hoping like hell it was Becca, which was insane. He was making himself crazy. The place was crawling with goth-black hairdos.

"Hey, sugar," came a purring female voice, as a raven-haired beauty shoved up close to his chair, nuzzling her ample breast on his arm. A dealer... that was the buzz in the bar. The ICE dealers were hot chicks that sized you up and decided who they offered the drug to. Apparently, the dealers sampled the goods, because this one had Clanner eyes. They weren't black, but they were darn near it; the pupils were dilated, the dark ridge around the eyeballs wider. He wondered if Becca's eyes would look like that after a few more doses... if they already did. *If she was even alive.*

He forced a smile, reminding himself that any amount of ICE he could get was important to Becca and for their scientific team. "That's sugar pie honey bunch to you, darlin'."

"So," she said, wrapping her arm around his. "Want some heat with your ICE?"

"Depends," he drawled, his gaze going toward the bar, trying to find his mystery woman again, but his view was still blocked. Reluctantly, he flicked his attention back to his ICE babe. "You gonna share a little ICE buzz with me first?"

"Whatcha gonna give me if I do?" she asked, stroking his arm.

He flicked another look toward the mystery woman just in time to see her profile. Becca. It was Becca. He stood up.

The woman clung to him, blocking his view. "Where you going?"

"Beer goes right through me, baby," he replied, untangling himself only to find Becca missing. Damn it.

He charged up to the bar and into the face of the bartender. "The prim little black-haired princess who was standing here... where did she go and with who?"

"I'm not a baby-sitter," the man said.

Sterling reached over the bar and yanked him across it. The man's eyes were wide, dilated, and filled with panic. "Headed out the back door with two of the regulars."

Fuck! Sterling dropped the man and shoved his way through the crowd before cutting down the side hall past the restrooms. He burst through the steel door exit and into a back delivery area for the hotel, a loading dock to his right. A muffled voice reached his ears, cutting through the sound of the churning industrial fan inside the warehouse.

Easing under the open entrance of the dock, Sterling surveyed the dimly lit warehouse, but saw nothing. A stealthy GTECH leap and he was on top of the ten-foot-high dock floor. To his left, stacked pallets stretched in long, neat rows, as far back as they were high, the concrete floor that separated them shiny and clean.

Sterling inched past several stacks of pallets to his left and found the last row, where he went still, colder than any hit of ICE could make him. Becca was backed into a corner with the two men who were crowding her.

"Quid pro quo, baby," one of the men said to Becca. "Pull that shirt up, and show me what you got. You give me some of you, and I'll give you ICE."

Sterling bolted into action. The only person touching Becca was him.

Chapter 9

Sterling was behind Becca's attackers in five seconds flat. He grabbed a handful of both men's shirts and flung them into a stack of pallets.

"Thank God, Becca," Sterling said, shackling her arms, ready to hug her just to prove to himself she was real.

"Don't touch me," she hissed with such unexpected vehement anger, he almost released her. "I know you're one of them. I saw proof. Damn you, *I know*."

"What are you talking about?"

"I saw pictures…" Her lips were trembling. "Of you and Adam. Tad showed me."

He really hoped Tad had died on that lab floor. "Not only are Caleb and Adam twins, but—"

"He had wolves with him! You had wolves with you. It was Adam. *You with Adam*."

The sound of a gun cocking echoed through the open, high ceilings. Becca inhaled sharply, and he didn't miss the difficulty that she had doing so.

"Get down on the ground, man, or I'll shoot," Mohawk guy ordered, pointing a Smith & Wesson.

Sterling had half a mind to ignore the kid, but he needed the ICE the kid had on him for Becca and for study.

"Be right back," he told Becca, and turned and held his hands out to his sides. "Whatever gets you off, man. Take your best shot."

Mohawk's thin face turned puffy with anger, and he

pulled the trigger. The bullet hit Sterling's chest and bounced off his body armor like a rubber ball.

"That was fun," Sterling said sardonically. "But sorry. No time to do it again." In a flash, he'd closed the distance between himself and the Clanners, snatched the weapon, and turned it on Mohawk man. "Then again, maybe I should take a shot of my own. Quid pro quo, and all that shit. Right asshole?"

"Look, man," Punker said. "He didn't mean it. Just let us go."

Mohawk held his hands up in defeat. "Yeah, man. It was a joke."

Sterling arched a brow. "Do I look amused?" He motioned with his fingers. "Hand over your ICE, and *that* ain't no joke."

"We don't have any—" Mohawk started to say.

Sterling fired at the ground, popped two shots damn close to their feet, and cast Becca a quick inspection while the men squirmed. She was leaning against the wall, watching with wide eyes. Safe. That's all that mattered.

Sterling's lips twisted with a wry taunt. "The next two bullets won't hit the ground. Think of all those little bones in your feet blasted away by the steel force of a bullet." He shook his head. "Ouch. That hurts just thinking about it. Even on an ICE high, that's gonna bite like a bitch. After that, we'll move upwards." He pointed the gun at Mohawk's knee. Then his thigh. Then shoved the gun toward his crotch. "About midway up is where all the fun starts. If I blow it off, will ICE grow it back? Wanna find out?"

"Okay!" Mohawk said. He was shaking worse than Becca now, digging in his pockets and producing four vials of ICE.

"Come now," Sterling said, still holding the gun at Mohawk's groin. "That can't be all you got. I really don't want to see you two buck naked, but if I have to make you undress to get the rest of the ICE—that's what we will do."

Punker dude handed over another vial, obviously deciding he didn't want Smith & Wesson giving him a visit down under, too.

"Good," Sterling said agreeably, pocketing the ICE. Doc Kelly, the Renegade's medical chief of staff, was going to piss her pants or maybe go orgasmic on him over five vials of ICE. He jerked the gun hard against the guy's crotch and received a guttural grunt in return. "Now hand over your IDs. That way, if you say a word about this, I can hunt you down and use you for target practice." He shook the gun in the air. It took all of sixty seconds for their compliance. Sterling motioned them away. "Get out of here."

The two Clanners shot into action, darting away while Sterling shoved the weapon under his belt. Sterling tucked the ICE in his pockets and turned to Becca, who was huddled in the corner. "Stay back!" she yelled, her hand pressed to her stomach.

She was scared of him, truly scared of him. And pale as a new winter's snow, her dark hair tangled around her face.

"Becca, honey. It's me. Sterling. You know me. You know you can trust me."

She hugged herself, her teeth chattering. "I saw the pictures, Sterling."

"All the GTECHs were stationed at Area 51 before Adam took it over. I was in the same unit as both Caleb and Adam." He removed a vial from his pocket, taking the risk of giving her ICE their team hadn't inspected first. The fear that it wasn't withdrawal killing people but tainted ICE was a long shot their team was giving limited credibility, but one he felt like a twist of a knife in his gut right now. "You need to dose."

"How do I know that doesn't have poison in it to kill me like you killed Milton. How do I know this isn't a setup?"

"I don't even know a Milton, Becca. Please. Sweethcart. You need to take the ICE, and then we'll go meet Caleb. He'll tell you I served with Adam."

"I'm not going anywhere with you," she shouted and tried to dart past him.

Sterling wrapped his arms around her and pulled her close with no intention of letting her go. He'd found her quickly, as if he were meant to find her, meant to protect her, to save her, and he was damn well going to do it.

"Let me go!" she demanded, shoving weakly against him, determined to use the energy she had left to escape him. He turned her in his arms as he had in her kitchen, her back to his chest. "Damn you, Sterling." Her voice dropped to a whisper. "Why can't you just let me go?"

"I would never hurt you," he said softly and repeated it as she continued to squirm. "I would never hurt you, Becca."

Seconds passed, and she stilled in his arms, but she whispered, "Let me go, Sterling."

Sterling opened his mouth to reply when a tingling awareness rushed over him, and wind gusted through the warehouse. He grabbed Becca's wrist and pressed the vial in her palm a second before he drew a gun into each hand and rotated to block her from danger.

At the same moment, a good half dozen Zodius soldiers materialized at quick count. Sterling took them in and knew he was screwed. "We'll be taking the woman," one of the soldiers said, confirming what he'd feared. They were here for Becca, tracking her, not him.

Before Sterling could decide his next move, the soldiers dropped to the floor like sawed-off trees. Just hit the ground with hard thumps.

"What the—?" He used his guns to scan from unmoving soldier to unmoving soldier, then above, checking the pallets for another attack. At the same time, he nudged the leg of the nearest Zodius. Nothing. Totally limp. He felt for a pulse and found one. They were asleep.

He turned to Becca, one eye still on the Zs, finding her standing against the wall, hands pressed to the concrete, accusation in her eyes.

"Why are you still standing, and they aren't?" Becca demanded from behind him.

"Why are *we* still standing, and they aren't?" he countered.

"You… oh God." She curled forward, holding her stomach.

Sterling rushed to her, bending down and taking her with him. He lifted her face so she would look at him, knowing he needed to get them out of here before more company arrived, but needing to get the ICE down her first. "I didn't deceive you."

She blinked at him. "I don't know what to believe."

His hand closed over hers, where it clutched the ICE. "Believe in me." He removed the vial from her palm and popped the seal before holding it near her mouth. "Drink."

She hesitated, but her hand came up to his, and she helped him tilt it back so she could swallow.

She gasped as the liquid slid down her throat before curling forward again. "Please God, let it work quickly."

Sterling scooped her up in his arms, and she snuggled into his chest and shut her eyes. She didn't fight... didn't ask where they were going... didn't have any fight left in her. Sterling went icy inside and not from the drug. From the sheer terror that he'd found her too late.

He started for the door, feeling her shake in his arms, and for the first time in a very long time, he was shaking too.

—ᴡᴡ—

More than a few people turned to look at Sterling as he carried Becca into the dimly lit, highly populated parking lot behind the club, directly adjacent to the main hotel. Responding to their silent, but forceful inquiries, he jokingly called out to the populace. "Told her it was more fun to have sex on the beach than to drink Sex on the Beach."

Laughter followed, and one male voice said, "Keep her on a leash, dude. That's what I do with my woman." The man's grunt filled the air before he grumbled, "Ouch. Don't hit me, *woman*." Apparently *the woman* in question wasn't on a leash after all. Either way, he'd created a diversion that allowed Sterling to travel onward without being approached.

Sterling stopped beside "Carrie," the black Ford Mustang he'd confiscated from the private garage of the Renegades' inner-city headquarters. The muscle car was Michael's pride and joy, right after his Lifebond Cassandra, of course. Which is exactly why Sterling had taken it upon himself to borrow Carrie—because it would piss off Michael.

Well, bring on the fight, Michael. You should have helped me convince Caleb to lock Damion up when I went to you. But no. Michael had said he'd trusted Caleb's ability to read Damion. Sorry son of a bitch, so did Sterling—except this once.

He glared at the car. "Pride and joy, my ass," Sterling mumbled, as soft, wayward strands of Becca's hair floated against his face. Holding her like this, seeing her helpless, ripened his anger. Michael should have dealt with Damion, rather than taking the wait and see attitude. Screw wait and see. Becca wouldn't be half-dead now if it weren't for Damion.

Carefully, Sterling settled Becca onto the warm leather seat. Her lashes fluttered and lifted as she blinked him into focus with a pleading look. "Cold," she murmured, wrapping her arms around herself.

It was a hundred degrees outside. From the backseat, he snatched the leather jacket Michael sometimes wore to hide his weapons and covered Becca. Instantly, she huddled beneath it, teeth chattering, eyes shut.

"Hang in there, princess," he whispered, brushing his knuckles over her cheek.

She rolled toward the driver's seat, curling her legs under the leather, and he shut her inside, his cell phone already in hand by the time he reached the driver's side and climbed in. He hit the speed dial for Kelly Peterson, the lead scientist and doctor on the ICE project.

"Fuck!" he yelled, hitting the steering wheel when her voice mail answered. He shifted the car into drive, peeling out of the parking lot.

Then he dialed Caleb who answered in one ring. "I've got Becca. I found her trying to buy ICE off a couple users. And before you ask… yes, I've got samples. Four more vials."

"I was going to ask how she is."

He glanced at her as a streetlight illuminated the car, noting with growing concern the blue tinge to Becca's lips. "Bad. I dosed her, but it doesn't seem to be working."

Caleb gave a low curse. "Hold on." Sterling could hear him say, "Get Kelly over here now. We've got Rebecca Burns, and she's in ICE withdrawal." Michael's voice sounded in the background and then Caleb was back on the line. "Where are you now? I'll send backup."

"Don't." He cut to the right on a back road and shifted gears to hit the three-minute highway stretch they'd follow to Freemont Street. "I just had an encounter with a six-pack of Zs. The next thing I knew Becca and I were the only ones not taking a nap on the pavement. It… well, it seems to have something to do with being near Becca."

Caleb was silent a moment. "But you're immune?"

"Yeah. I can't explain it."

Silence a moment. "You can't take her to Neonopolis until we know she isn't a risk to the other men there." Neonopolis was the hundred-thousand-square-foot entertainment complex off Freemont Street, where they retained an entire underground floor for their inner-city operation.

"I'm on the same page," Sterling said. "I'm headed to the rattrap two blocks over, until we can figure out what to do with her."

"Sterling," Caleb said grimly. "Should she be underground where the Trackers can't find her?"

Sterling ground his teeth at the question. Sex with a GTECH marked a woman with a certain psychic residue that allowed her to be located if she wasn't underground. "No, she did not have sex, willingly or unwillingly, with a GTECH. I was with her the entire time." Except when he'd passed out, and she'd been with Tad.

"Except the past twenty-four hours."

And then. Damn it to hell.

Clearly reading Sterling's silence, Caleb said, "I'll put a team on your location and tell them to keep a safe distance. One of them will be a Tracker. We need to be sure we know what we're dealing with."

"Copy that," Sterling said, ending the call, feeling like he'd been kicked in the gut. The Tracker would try to get a read on Becca, and if he could, she'd need to be underground and fast. Sterling felt like he'd been punched in the gut. If another GTECH had touched Becca, he would be to blame. He was the one who'd let her get captured in the first place.

Chapter 10

ICEMAN SCREECHED HIS PORSCHE 911 TO A HALT IN the back parking lot of the 66 Briar Street warehouse location. It was one of three ICE storage facilities he ran for the prick who played the role of "muscle" for Adam. Tad was pathetic. He actually thought being the bully for a man like Adam gave him power. It gave him nothing. What an idiot for not being able to see the writing on the wall!

Iceman had only met Adam once, but he could see the man was volatile. In a blink of an irritated eye, Adam could squash Tad like the inconsequential fly he was. Because he let himself be.

Iceman knew how to make himself indispensable. He'd learned that lesson years ago from his father. It didn't matter how hard he'd worked to prove to that man he could run his little fast-food empire, he'd never been good enough. *For chicken*. The old man sold chicken. He could keep his fucking chicken empire. He'd make his own. He was Iceman.

Stepping out of the Porsche, Iceman clicked the locks in place and sauntered toward the back door of the facility. The location, two miles off the "Strip Area"—as the Gaming Commission called a certain radius—was by design, to stay off their radar. Not that they were "gaming," but he didn't need those bulldogs snooping around.

It was enough to keep up appearances for Tad. But

that would change as soon as he figured out how to duplicate the baseline ICE formula himself. And with the money he was paying to have it analyzed that should be any day now. In the meantime, he had a plan moving forward, working to claim the control Adam wanted for himself. Well, screw Adam and his GTECH kingdom. Humans outnumbered GTECHs, and it would remain that way.

His gaze shifted to the remarkable sky—starless, moonless—yet not a rumble of thunder, near or far. It was as if there had been an eclipse—an ICE Eclipse. Yes. He liked that name.

Tonight he would celebrate taking his own special formula of ICE from small-time distribution to mass market by naming it and his clan of followers: ICE Eclipse and the Eclipsers. This pleased Iceman. It pleased him immensely.

Satisfaction rolled though him at the thought of the empire *he* was building, his black dress shoes scraping the gravel-riddled pavement. Hidden cameras tracked his progress and followed him up a steel stairwell.

The instant he reached the single heavy metal door, a buzzer sounded and the seal popped open. As it should. The security guard had the good sense not to keep him waiting as he had once before. Waiting did not please Iceman. He had long ago grown tired of waiting for people. Serving them. He would not serve. Not even Adam. Not for long, that was. Exactly why he didn't do ICE himself. That was as good as handing his puppet strings to Adam.

Promises of a GTECH serum that he didn't even know existed did nothing for him. He'd let them think it did, that he wanted it, that he was pining for conversion to GTECH. He wasn't.

Iceman entered a long rectangular office with a glass window overlooking the warehouse, where rows of neatly palleted vials of ICE were stored. Sabrina Walker, his version of Tad—a much easier on the eyes version to boot—leaned a fine leather-clad ass on the worn, white wooden desk.

She discarded the clipboard in her hand on the desk. "Hi sugar," she said, her long, red hair a fiery mass that traced delicate white shoulders, exposed by her barely there, leather halter top. No matter how delicate her skin, how sensual her body—she was far more leather than lace. She'd kick your ass in an ICE-induced high in three seconds flat. Or just shoot you with one of the guns she had strapped under her pant leg above those spike heels. He got hot just thinking about it.

She pursed her full, red lips. "Thought you'd never get here." He knew what she needed all right. Iceman advanced on her, tugged her hard against his body, grabbed her palm, and pressed the deep circle tattoo in the center to his mouth, his tongue sliding over the surface, over his *brand* that allowed fast absorption of the Eclipse portion of his ICE. She moaned softly. "I need a hit, baby," she whispered. "I've waited an hour too long."

His lips curled. "If you need it so badly," he challenged, "go down on your knees and ask nicely."

"There isn't time," she purred. "The girls will begin arriving any minute."

Unfortunately, she was right. "Pity," he said, reaching into his pocket and retrieving the tiny silver star that appeared harmless. It was, in fact, the method of dispensing Eclipse. "I would have liked you on your knees." He motioned to her desk where a rack of ICE vials sat. "Take your dose. You can thank me later."

She didn't hesitate, grabbing a glass tube. She held it out to him. "Join me?"

When hell froze over. "It's all yours, my little ICE bitch."

She smiled. Pleased. "I *am* a bitch, aren't I?"

"Indeed," he said. A dominant, controlling bitch, who kept the rest of the bitches in line. He took her hand again, finger sliding over the tattoo on her palm. "But a lovely bitch deserves her reward." He urged her to drink, knowing her addiction gave him the same control over her that Adam wished to have over humanity. The control he would soon have over his Eclipsers. "Do it."

She popped the top of the vial and brought it to her lips. At the same time, Iceman dissolved the silver star over the mark on her hand, the etched skin allowing the unique formulation of ecstasy mixed with a few secret ingredients, that he and he alone controlled, to be absorbed into the bloodstream almost instantly. The boost, when taken in conjunction with ICE, delivered enhanced senses—made everything taste better, smell better, feel better.

Her lashes fluttered, the vial all but falling from her hand. He kissed her wrist, and she shivered, pleasure rolling across her face. Most users would have orgasmed right then and there. But not Sabrina. She was fiery and hot, demanding more.

"ICE Eclipse," she murmured. "God, I love this stuff." He rewarded her agreement, his lips moving up her arm until she shivered and fixed him in a bright green stare. Desire and lust poured from her gaze. "I really love it."

He reached up and unzipped her vest, intending to enjoy her ICE-induced arousal. Time for her to get on her knees. He urged her downward, and she smiled, sensually sliding down his body until the buzzer went off on the door.

She pursed her lips again. "The girls are arriving," she said. "Bringing you all that money you're making. They'll wait until we're done. They like their 'Eclipse' as much as I do." She smiled. "Or we could make a party of it. Have them join the fun."

He yanked her up, kissed her hard, and then set her away from him. She was a toy, nothing more. "Business before pleasure. Need I remind you we've expanded our distribution tonight? Monitor the results as I pay you to do."

Only two weeks before, they'd had a dealer go MIA, and they'd been forced to regroup, rethink.

Sabrina stiffened, sliding into the comfortable shell of badass bitch. "The results…" she said, zipping those perky nipples back inside her leather vest and heading toward her left, "will be as expected. My girls will deliver."

"Go see to it they do," he ordered tightly, giving her his back, dismissing her to the duty he expected, staring out at the warehouse that he expected her to clear out twice a week, not twice a month.

She had a dozen new women on staff on his dime, all trained to approach prescreened targets, frequenters of certain bars, clubs, casinos, and restaurants to convert them to users.

Abruptly, an alarm sounded in the office, a warning the guards delivered the minute a wind-walker appeared on the property. Shit. Tad. But he wasn't due for his ICE payment for days.

Iceman reached for the remote to the security monitor to flip the channel, when Tad appeared in the office, Sabrina in front of him, held close to his body. She didn't look happy, but she didn't fight to get away. She'd learned the hard way when a previous confrontation had gotten her backhanded and flung across the room.

"We need to talk," Tad blistered out.

Such brilliance. Like that wasn't obvious. Clamping down on his immense irritation, Iceman crossed his arms in front of his chest. "So talk."

"Rebecca Burns," he said, offering nothing more. Ah yes. The woman whose picture he'd been shown for identification and told to capture.

And for reasons he'd yet to determine, the woman scared the crap out of Tad and his Zodius cronies. Interesting. What could one little woman do to a Zodius Nation? Whatever she had on them, he wanted it for himself.

He arched a brow. "What of her?"

Tad's hand stroked Sabrina's hair as if she were a pet. "You were to keep her away from ICE. You were to bring her to me. Tonight, she not only found her way to an ICE dealer, she found her way into the path of a Renegade."

"That's impossible," Iceman said. "None of my dealers gave that woman ICE. They don't randomly deal. Not anymore."

"Ah," Tad said. "But they did." He tossed a DVD at Iceman. It hit the floor with a thud. "That came from your club where your men lured her to a back warehouse."

"We don't have male dealers," Sabrina said. "That's ridiculous."

Tad yanked her hair back, and she bit her lip, whimpering. "Then a user," Tad said, staring down at her a moment before letting her hair go. He eyed Iceman. "One of your customers, which means you have no control, and that is unacceptable. If you can't do your job, I'll get someone who can."

"Any customer who sells a dose of ICE does not get a replacement," Iceman said. "That means withdrawal. I find it hard to believe that any man would be that foolish over a piece of ass." He wasn't convinced withdrawal was killing the Clanners, but he was making it work in his favor anyway. He was convincing users that buying the Eclipse boost made dosing safer.

Fucking beautiful. Worked like a charm. And Adam got none of his Eclipse profits.

"You watch the DVD," Tad said, running his hand over Sabrina's neck. "Or maybe you'd rather watch me bend your woman over the desk. She is your woman, isn't she? She reminds me of Adam's Lifebond, Ava—red hair, stubborn."

"I'm sure Adam would appreciate knowing you have a hard-on for his Ava," Iceman said, hoping to anger him enough to get him to let go of Sabrina. He didn't give a damn if Tad screwed her, but he knew what sex with Tad meant—she could be tracked. That was a problem. "You should have fucked this Rebecca chick and marked her for your Trackers, and then you wouldn't have me trying to find her while also running the ICE distribution process." He bent down and snatched up the DVD. He wanted to know who the hell was pawning off ICE—if Tad had managed to get the facts right.

By the time he straightened, the DVD in hand, it was clear there was no saving Sabrina. Tad had her bent over the desk, ripping away her vest. He'd have to replace her. Irritating. He didn't have time for such delays.

He turned his back to Tad and Sabrina, about to pop the DVD into the computer on the desk, when he was suddenly lifted off his feet and slammed against the floor, the air shoved from his lungs. Tad's foot landed in his ribs over and over again, and then slammed into his chest.

"You lie there and watch me enjoy your woman," he said. "Then we will discuss how you will repay me for your failure."

Blood dripped from the corner of Iceman's mouth, his physical vulnerability the price he paid for being unwilling to take ICE. But he had a team working on creating his own version of the drug, just as he was growing his Eclipsers. Tad could have Sabrina. He could relish his moment. It would only make the day Iceman killed him all the sweeter. This was his game, and everyone would know when he made his final move.

Chapter 11

STERLING HAD NO IDEA WHY THE WOMAN IN HIS ARMS felt so important to him, but as he carried Becca into the piece-of-crap motel room with powder blue walls and nary a piece of furniture, there was no denying what he felt. Protective. Almost possessive. Like she was his. Like she'd always been in some way. With a few awkward maneuvers, he managed to lock the door before carrying Becca to the lumpy, full-sized bed with an ugly floral bedspread. He was ready to figure out what was causing everyone around her to pass out so he could take her to Neonopolis where she could be truly safe.

Flinging back the blankets, Sterling laid Becca on the mattress, tossing aside her shoes, and then covering her. Black hair fluttered over her pale, heart-shaped face, and he reached down and stroked it gently away from her brow. He didn't even know he had "gentle" in him, not anymore, and not since, well, those days back in the library with her. And here she was now, bringing out the tenderness in him when he would have sworn it wasn't possible. He checked her pulse; it was steady, and so was her breathing. Even her skin tone had color now. The ICE seemed to be finally working.

A series of coded knocks sounded on the door. Sterling stalked across the room, rubbing his jaw, while mentally scrubbing the emotion from his face. Caleb,

Michael, and Damion, all dressed in street clothes, awaited him on the other side.

"You drove my fucking car," Michael growled. "If we didn't need you right now, I'd freaking kill you."

Sterling ignored him, too angry at Damion's presence. He eyed Caleb and motioned to Damion. "Why is he here?"

"In case you forgot," Damion said dryly. "I'm the best Tracker we have. Becca is clear. No psychic residue."

Sterling cut an urgent look in Michael's direction for confirmation. Michael might have limited tracking abilities, but he trusted him. He didn't trust Damion.

"No residue," Michael confirmed. "But before you get all excited about what that means—check her neck for the Lifebond mark. A male Lifebond can shield his female from Trackers."

Sterling's vision went momentarily red with Michael's words, his blood—cold. Becca—another man's Lifebond? Why did that make him want to punch the wall? Caleb held up a bag, jolting Sterling out of his red haze of anger. "Kelly wants her to take the ICE in the bag that she's already analyzed in case there's some variation in the formula causing the fatalities. She included supplies to draw blood and some tranquilizers."

"Tranquilizers?"

"If Becca's asleep, she can't put other people to sleep. At least, that's the theory. Kelly wants to analyze her blood and make sure there are no red flags that could be dangerous to others before we move her. In the meantime, I'm having the west end of Neonopolis cleared, so you can take her there once we clear her to travel."

Sterling wasn't tranquilizing her if he didn't have to, but he needed the ICE. He took the bag. "I'll control her."

"Kelly wants that blood ASAP," Caleb added.

Sterling nodded and dug the vials of ICE from his pocket, hesitating a millisecond as his eyes collided with Damion's. He didn't trust him as far as he could throw him, not with the ICE samples Becca needed to survive.

Caleb and Damion turned to depart, but Michael stepped forward, as if he intended to enter the room.

Sterling blocked him. "Where the hell do you think you're going?"

"She has twenty-four hours of unaccounted for time with an addiction to a drug only Adam can provide. We need to interrogate the woman and ensure she's not a spy, and you're too personally involved to do it."

"Says who?" Sterling demanded.

"Says me," Michael replied.

"Figures," Sterling said dryly. Michael was known for being as cold-hearted as they came, the Dark Knight behind Caleb's Superman persona. "Try using some of that decision-making and paranoia to get Damion the hell away from Caleb before it's too late. Becca isn't a spy."

Michael ignored the comment and focused on getting into the room. "I'm coming in."

He really wanted to punch the SOB. "When you pass out, I'll be sure and give you a blankie and teddy bear."

"I'm not like the other GTECHs any more than you are," Michael said, but he didn't advance, as if Sterling's words had given him pause.

Sterling snorted. "Yeah well, I'm thinking about that.

Becca was around a nightclub filled with humans, and they didn't pass out. And then there's me, who doesn't pack as much GTECH juice as the rest of you. I didn't pass out. And I hate to tell you this, Michael, but you aren't human. Not even close." Only recently he'd discovered he had gone off and grown an extra gene no one else possessed.

Michael glared a moment and then apparently dispelled any concern. "She's weakened by her withdrawal." He stepped forward. "I'll take my chances."

Sterling didn't give a damn how powerful Michael was. He stepped forward, toe-to-toe with him. "I swear to the good Lord above, if you set foot in this room, I will find a cliff and drive Carrie over the side."

"I'll buy another," Michael said, his stone-cold expression a permanent feature.

"That's the worst load of crap you've fed me since you said you would never get the healing illness and then you did," Sterling ground out between clenched teeth. "You can't buy another Carrie, and we both know it. She's got sentimental value." He lowered his voice and added before he could stop himself, "If this were Cassandra, would you let *you* in this room?"

"I'd kill to protect Cassandra," Michael said, narrowing his eyes on Sterling. "Are you saying this woman is your Lifebond? Because that changes everything in my eyes if she is."

What? He opened his mouth to speak and shut it. For a rare instant, he was speechless, the idea that Becca and he were Lifebonds resonating far deeper than he realized. "All I'm going to tell you at this point is to back off, Michael. I've got this situation under control."

Michael's gaze bore into Sterling's, and Sterling knew Michael had noticed his lack of confirmation or denial. Tense seconds ticked by before he stepped back. "I'll be nearby."

"Do us both a favor," Sterling said. "Be nearby Damion, not me."

Michael gave a reluctant nod, and Sterling didn't stay around for more discussion. He entered the room, slammed the door shut, and locked it. His cell phone buzzed. Reluctantly Sterling maneuvered Becca to the pillow and moved to the end of the bed where he'd left his phone. He punched the button to hear Kelly's voice.

"How is she?"

"She almost died in withdrawal," he said. "She turned blue like the other Clanner did and it took way too long for the ICE to kick in. At least half an hour. It took five minutes the last time I saw her dose."

"I'm not a Clanner," Becca murmured in a hoarse whisper that drew his attention. He shifted toward her, finding those amber eyes peeking beneath heavy fluttering lashes. "They forced this on me."

His eyes met Becca's amber ones, the briefest of contact, before her lashes fluttered, and her breathing slipped back into an even, steady rhythm. It was as if the very thought of being called a Clanner had ripped her from a healing slumber and elicited a rebuttal. He'd seen it in her eyes, heard it in her voice. Felt it in that momentary melding of eyes.

"Sterling?" Kelly asked. "Is something wrong? How is she?"

Tough, he thought. She is tough and brave and beautiful. "Considering she just woke up from what I thought was a near-death sleep to tell me she is *not* a Clanner," he said, "I'd say she's improving."

Kelly laughed. "Busting your chops and barely back from the dead. I think I might like this woman. And we both know you get off on having your chops busted."

Sterling crossed to the corner behind the table and yanked open the minifridge he kept loaded down with Dr. Pepper and cold M&Ms, his two favorites.

"Is that how you justify your abuse?" he asked, snatching a soda. "By pretending I like it?"

Kelly snorted. "I know you do. It's your deep psychological way of dealing with a misguided sense of no self-worth."

Sterling ground his teeth, the comment going down about as well as broken glass. "I'm not the patient, Doc," he said. "Can we focus on Becca?"

"Ouch," she said. "I guess I hit a nerve. Get me the blood. Damion hacked the German cancer center's records. I'm working on helping her and hoping she can help us."

Damion... if he had to hear that name one more time! Sterling claimed a chair and sat down at the wobbly mockery of a table. Ten minutes later, Sterling hung up, having taken a verbal lashing for not drawing Becca's blood before dosing her, and with instructions to allow Becca to sleep until she woke before moving her.

Sterling set the phone on the table and glanced at Becca where she rested a few feet away. His gut clenched at the sight she made. Innocent in slumber— soft and feminine.

He picked the phone back up and called his bud Eddie at the Las Vegas Metropolitan Police Department and had him check up on the two Clanners. The phone went back on the table, his eyes back to the bed—to Becca.

Tension charged his body, and he tried to dispel it, turning the empty soda can around and around, his mind spinning with it. His eyes followed the movement, focused on the can, not Becca. In bed. Making him think of, well, Becca in bed with him, when she might hate him when she woke up. Worse, she might be the Lifebond to another.

He stopped spinning the can. That made no sense. A Lifebond would be fully converted. ICE wouldn't send her into withdrawal. Then he cursed under his breath and leaned back in his chair. Or would it? Could GTECHs dose on ICE for an extra boost?

Abruptly Sterling got up. He stalked to the bed, a man on a mission. Becca lay on her side, and he approached her from behind. His knees went down on the mattress. His hand slid to her hair and pushed it aside.

She moved, turning onto her stomach. Like the Renegade that he was, a man who knew what he wanted, he pursued. Sterling climbed fully onto the bed, leaned over her, and brushed her hair away from her neck where the Lifebonds would have formed a tattoo—a circle within a circle if she belonged to another man, an unbreakable physical connection, bound in life and death. He stared at the creamy white perfection of the delicate skin and let out a silent breath of relief. No Lifebond mark. Unable to resist, Sterling ran his fingers over the bare spot at the base of her neck. He was one step closer to being able to trust her. And he wanted to… more than he should.

"Mmmmm," she murmured. "That feels good." The

words purred out of her. Soft. Seductive. Like a woman talking to her lover.

His hand froze there on her neck; the bittersweet rush of uncontrollable raging hormones and pure, hot lust shot through him, thickening his cock. He inhaled, telling himself to back away. She was asleep, drugged for all practical purposes. He started to move, but she reached for his hand and then turned over. She blinked him into focus.

"You came for me," she whispered. "I knew you would come." There was a hazy, blank expression on her face that said she was home but not taking calls. She was still dreaming, experiencing some effect from her near withdrawal perhaps. Maybe not even seeing him. Maybe seeing someone else. But as she stared up at him with hope and relief overflowing from her into him, he wasn't about to take away the peace he sensed in her. The woman had been through enough. She deserved some peace.

"I came," he assured her and pulled the blanket around her, the air in the room churning fast and hard. His knuckles slid over her cheek. "Rest… so you can heal."

She reached up and wrapped her hand around his, dragging it to her chest and lacing her fingers with his. His heart froze at the intimate act, and when she nuzzled her chin to his fingers, her lashes fluttering to a close, the message was clear. She had no intention of letting him go.

He wasn't sure how to react or why his chest felt like a steel thousand-pound ball had been placed on top of it. He was a wham-bam, see-you-some-other-time kind of guy, who didn't do the touchy-feely kind of stuff—a necessary evil of being Renegade. It wasn't fair to be anything but a wham-bam guy when you woke up every day facing death. Inviting death. Laughing at death. Especially when the female could be put in jeopardy, on Adam's radar, just knowing you. So Sterling did what was right, and he avoided intimacy—it wasn't like relationships had been lucky for him. His mother was gone. His father too. His grandmother—well, she had died, but she'd had ten years of sobriety and happiness after he'd left. All that said—right here and now with Becca, he wasn't sure he had it in him to pull away.

There was a connection between them, a silent, understood connection. Maybe because Becca, like himself, woke up every day facing death too. Only, unlike Sterling, who'd been doing so by choice, Becca had no choice. A cancer diagnosis had stolen it from her, and now Adam had too. She'd faced the cancer diagnosis alone. Her mother had moved to Europe, remarried, and lived in a happy bubble, which Sterling had a sneaking suspicion was why Becca had decided not to burst it with news of her cancer.

Slowly, Sterling eased onto the mattress, facing Becca, his legs parallel to hers. For several moments he studied the dark half moons of her long lashes resting on pale perfect skin, and with that image in his mind, he closed his eyes. His senses flared into overdrive, the warmth of her nearness invading him, consuming him, rolling through him like the wind, only more like a soft summer breeze. Silently, he vowed that Becca would not wake up her first day outside of captivity facing death alone. She would wake to face it with him. And it was then that he allowed himself the first peaceful sleep since Becca had been taken from him.

—⁓—

Only minutes after Tad had finally finished fucking Sabrina into a trackable liability, Iceman stood in the security booth of the warehouse, waiting as his personal bodyguard, JC Miller, inserted the DVD in a master panel that fed ten security monitors. Tall and athletic, JC was shrewd, calculating, a badass in all possible ways—a black belt in judo, a master with weapons, a lethal killer even before he became a Clanner.

He was also a necessary evil considering Iceman didn't "ICE" himself. And he was smart enough not to ask why Iceman didn't juice. He knew and didn't mention it because Iceman had him by the balls—he was his ICE distributor, and he had records of every kill the man had made sealed in a safe, ready to deliver to the authorities. Knowledge assuring JC's loyalty to Iceman in a way Iceman would never be loyal to Tad or Adam. Or anyone for that matter.

"Shall I dispose of Sabrina?" JC asked as nonchalantly as if he were talking about a bag of trash.

"Not yet," Iceman said, stroking his clean-shaven chin and considered. "Perhaps there is a way we can use her against Tad." The DVD footage started to roll, illuminating images of club Zeus that flickered to a woman he recognized from photos as Rebecca Burns. At the obvious urging of the Clanners, she headed to the back of the club. A second later, a man flashed across the screen in pursuit.

"Sterling," Iceman said, lips thinning in a mixture

of irritation and admiration for the bounty hunter who walked both sides of the law, a man he knew well and kept at a measurable distance. Of course, Sterling did not know he was Iceman.

"He shows up where there's trouble far too often," JC commented dryly, having long tried to convince Iceman to force an ICE addiction on Sterling. "We need to control him."

"His free agent status serves us well," Iceman stated flatly and pointedly added, "We have his resources at our disposal, and he's not a risk as long as he's properly monitored."

JC's jaw noticeably flexed, his gaze shifting to the monitors, and Iceman had a distinct impression he was soon to discover JC did not have Sterling as well monitored as he should. JC hit the remote, and another monitor flickered to life with new feed. "Tad didn't see this footage. The manager of Zeus managed to keep the cameras inside the warehouse a secret, despite being beaten to a pulp by Tad and his goons. He's been rewarded as you would expect."

That meant paid and paid well. Iceman believed in extremes—learned that one from Pops. Beat 'em until they can't see straight when they fuck up; lots of ice cream—translation, cold hard cash—when they did well.

The warehouse feed began to play—the two Clanners from the bar cornering Rebecca Burns, teasing her with the prospect of ICE. It was clear they planned to rape the woman, not give up their ICE. A code of conduct existed for Clanners, devised to stay off police radar, and this was not it. Their Clanner movement had been one of silence—a slow, sinuous takeover of the city.

As if reading Iceman's mind, JC said, "They will be dealt with."

Iceman didn't respond. JC doing his job was expected—the man didn't need to be patted on the head like a dog.

With interest, Iceman watched as Sterling pocketed the IDs of the Clanners, even greater interest when Tad's men appeared in the warehouse and then dropped to the floor, lights out in a flash. No indication as to why. Immediately afterwards, Sterling carried the woman away. JC killed the visual.

"Are they dead?"

JC shook his head. "They were knocked out about half an hour."

"What weapon did this, and why don't I have it?"

JC shook his head. "I've enhanced the footage every way possible, and there's no weapon, at least nothing visible to the eye. I'll get it, whatever it is."

"Judging from Tad's urgency to get the women, I'd say she holds the weapon. Find her, and bring her to me by whatever means you find necessary. Just make it happen."

Chapter 12

BECCA WOKE INSIDE A DREAM, TRYING TO BLINK THE darkness into light, but there was no light, only damnable, inescapable darkness. She inhaled a surprisingly easy breath, a warm scent rippling through her senses, familiar to her dreams—the one she knew instantly to be Sterling. She relaxed into the moment, no longer fighting the darkness. She needed this familiar place, this dream that had led her through darkness far worse than that of her slumber. Becca searched for his image in her mind, sought out those teal green eyes, frustrated when it wouldn't come to her. Greedily, she inhaled his smell again. God, she loved that masculine spicy scent.

Strong arms wrapped around her, and she smiled at the touch, the dream taking a shape in a way it never had before, solidifying. It was as if Sterling was there, touching her, holding her. Becca moaned at the feel of him next to her, long legs entwined with hers. His breath trickled along her lips, promising her seductive, hot kisses.

She ached for more, needed more. Her arms wrapped around his back, her hips curling against his, the thick bulge of his erection tucked against her stomach. Never before had her dreams felt this real... this erotic. She could feel him everywhere, feel the ripple of muscle beneath his cotton T-shirt. Her hands skimmed his back, his chest, the warmth of taut skin as she caressed hard muscle. His moan near her ear drove her wild. It was a

low, masculine sound that sent a delicious shiver down
her spine and tightened her nipples a moment before
his fingers laced through her hair. He kissed her then,
a deep hungry kiss that swept through her like a rain
shower that turned to raging downpour. It was wild,
unleashed. It was her dream, and it was going exactly
how she wanted it to. She couldn't get enough of him.
He couldn't get enough of her.

Somewhere in the midst of the sensual slide of his
tongue, a glimmer of awareness formed outside the
shadows of her dreams. She shoved it aside, not ready
to wake up, allowing Sterling's tongue to draw her back
into delicious escape. It was a deep kiss, a passionate
kiss, a kiss that made love to her the way she wanted to
make love to him.

She arched into his hips, her fingers curling on a strong
jaw, rough stubble pressing erotically against her delicate
skin. The other hand rested on a bare, muscular chest, with
springy hair that teased her palm. But still the light threatened, and somewhere in the distance, a horn honked, per-
meating the soft moans that she knew to be her own. The
sound of that horn bounced around in her mind and faded
into the pleasure of his tongue trailing hers. It sounded
again. Loud enough this time that Becca stilled instantly.

Her hands pressed to Sterling's chest—or her dream
version of Sterling... She gulped as light flooded her
vision then blinked as she stared at the location of her
hands, the solid wall of muscle sprinkled with light
blond hair. Her hips straddling his... and the distinct
bulge of his erection pressed to the wet heat of her core.

Her gaze lifted and collided with a familiar teal green
stare. Familiar eyes framed by a chiseled face and spiky

blond hair. And then there was the ultra sexy dimple in the middle of a chin she had a random memory of kissing. Oh God. It really was him. She was on top of Sterling.

"I'm not dreaming, am I?" she whispered.

"Feels pretty real to me," he confirmed.

Her throat went dry, her gaze scanning the light blue scuffed wall and equally scuffed nightstand that were definitely not what dreams were made of. She was in a cheap motel sprawled wantonly across the man, and she had no idea how it had happened. She tried to slide off of him—more like launch herself away from him—only to find herself on her back with his powerful body over the top of hers.

"Easy, sweetheart." His whiskey-rough voice rippled down her spine, making her limbs heat despite her resistance. "I have no idea what just happened, but I saw the sudden awareness and instant panic in your eyes. We were sleeping, when—"

"Why were we in bed together?" she demanded, as a brief flash of the two of them in a warehouse brushed her mind. *A warehouse*. Not a bed. "Why are we in some sleazy hotel together?" The phone slid across the nightstand and crashed to the floor. She jumped, adrenaline spiking through her at not only the crash, but the realization that she had caused it. Memories of the lab assailed her. Milton had died; they'd killed him. Emotion clawed at her. The tawdry flower picture beside the bed fell off the wall. She was shaking, invisible, prickling spears poking her forehead. The faded picture of Las Vegas to her right clamored to the ground.

Sterling arched a brow. "Aside from moving things around with your mind and being a walking, talking

GTECH sleeping pill, are there any other surprises I should know about?"

Another flash of memory washed over her. *The soldiers in the lab passing out*. Flash-forward to the warehouse and an image of Sterling standing in front of her with guns locked and loaded when a group of Zodius attacked. They'd passed out, but he hadn't. Sterling wasn't like the other GTECHs, but he wasn't human either. She didn't know what he was—besides on top of her, making her crazy.

"You didn't pass out." She started to struggle, shoving and wiggling left and right, while pounding his rockhard, too bare, too delicious chest that she had to get away from. "Let me up!"

"I have no idea why I don't pass out when you put everyone else to sleep." He shackled her wrist in front of her, holding her with ease. "Why is it that me not passing out like the other GTECHs is freaking you out, Becca? Because if I had, you'd either be dead or back in Adam's clutches instead of here with me."

"Instead I ended up in a cheap motel with no memory of how I got here!" He smelled good. He felt good. He was dangerous. She knew the devious ways of Adam, his boss—his friend.

"You're alive," he said.

"Because you need me," she said. "Because Adam needs me." The inference was that he was working for Adam. He was GTECH. Adam was GTECH. That was a dangerous parallel when Adam intended to destroy humanity. And Sterling had managed to show up every time Adam was hunting her, with his charm and seduction in full glamour.

"I am *not* Zodius," he clipped out shortly.

"Yet here I am," she said bitterly, "in bed with you, almost having sex, and barely remembering how it happened. Dreaming of you too, Sterling. I'm no fool. GTECHs have special skills. I know you're messing with my dreams. I know—" She lost her words to the heat deepening in his eyes.

"You dreamed of me?"

Heat flooded her cheeks. "I… yes, but—"

His eyes melted into hers a moment before he kissed her, a warm, wonderful impossible-to-resist kiss seeping through to her very bones. Too soon, and yet not soon enough, he tore his mouth from hers.

"That's why we woke up all over each other," he said softly. "Because we want each other and have since the moment we met fourteen years ago. If I'm brainwashing you, you're doing the same to me." He rolled off of her and left her shocked, panting, and wishing for that hard body back on top of hers. And angry. The man had just accused her of brainwashing him! *He'd betrayed her*, made her fear for him… made her trust him.

The picture lying on the floor flew across the room with a crash. The chairs at the table tumbled to their backs. She knew she was doing it. She didn't know how, but she was doing it, and she hoped it made him afraid, like she had been on the street, fighting withdrawal.

He didn't react to the objects in the room. Instead, he simply stood there at the side of the bed facing her, wearing a dark expression made more foreboding by the shadow carving his jaw. The lamp on the nightstand crashed to floor with the shatter of glass. A bag once lying on the stand landed on the bed between them, several vials of ICE bouncing onto the mattress.

Becca swallowed hard at the sight, her eyes lighting on Sterling's, colliding in a standoff. Silence folded around them, their eyes locking in a stormy, erotically charged confrontation. She didn't dare trust him, and he knew she felt that way. Those vials of ICE would give her a few days' freedom without consequence. He knew that too. It was in that deep, hot stare of his.

Adrenaline pumped through her, liquid bubbling energy, her mind justifying the risk. This man was far more dangerous to her than anyone inside Zodius City. Because she wanted to trust him. Because she simply wanted him to the point of aching to feel him next to her. The intensity of the attraction was too much. It defied reason and supported brainwashing.

She had to get out of here, and she intended to make as much noise and cause as much trouble as it took to do it. The police would come. The neighbors would complain. Becca lunged for the ICE.

—⁓—

By the time Tad finished with Iceman, his team of soldiers had used the GPS tracking device they'd covertly inserted into Becca's arm to locate her—a precautionary measure taken when Adam deemed it necessary to keep her out of the sex camps.

Tad appeared on the rooftop a mile from the motel where Sterling had holed up in hiding, a safe distance from the Renegades guarding the perimeter. A convoy of his men waited for him. Why he'd thought that Sterling would be dumb enough to take the woman to the Renegades' highly sought after inner-city headquarters, he didn't know.

His hand went into his pocket, feeling the vial of ICE there, hungering for a hit. It was his secret addiction and the source of some unique abilities that he had yet to disclose to anyone. No one even knew ICE had an impact on GTECHs. They foolishly thought it, like all drugs, had no effect on a GTECH. Even Adam and Tad planned to keep it that way. He didn't want other GTECHs, neither Zodius nor Renegade, to dose with ICE. He wanted the upper hand, to stay in Adam's sights, to become one of the leaders of the new world. ICE hits made him stronger than the average GTECH—faster too. But it was his other abilities, the unique ones that really made dosing the ultimate fix, the ride he needed to stay on top. His ability to—

"Sir," the officer in charge said, breaking Tad out of his thoughts. "Red," they called him, though Tad had no idea why and really didn't care. "The Renegades have brought in a good dozen reinforcements."

Tad grimaced. "It won't take them long to figure out we've planted a GPS in her arm," he said. "Scout out every Renegade's position around the perimeter and flank each with two of our men. Alert me when we're ready, and be ready to move on command."

They couldn't wait to act, or they would risk Sterling removing that device and escaping their radar. If Adam wouldn't have killed him for doing it, Tad would have taken that bitch himself and made sure she could never escape. Now there were no options, because once that tracking device was gone, it was gone.

Rebecca Burns was going to have to die before she left that motel.

Chapter 13

STERLING KNEW THE INSTANT BECCA DECIDED TO bolt; he saw the desperation to escape rooted deep in her eyes. So much so she didn't seem to mind she was only half dressed, without a shirt or shoes. And he hated she was that scared of him.

With a few effortless strides, Sterling placed himself in front of the door a split second before a petite package of soft curves and fiery determination barreled into him. Becca gasped at the contact, new to her ICE-induced physical prowess; she could crank up her speed, but apparently didn't know how to apply the brakes. He wrapped his arms around her, effortlessly derailing her attempt, and that only served to piss her off. With a burst of renewed energy, she squirmed and shoved at his chest. The chairs behind her began to shake, and more and more it became apparent that her emotions triggered her abilities.

Sterling gave her a minute of eruption, letting her work out some of that energy and anger before he gave her some space. Shackling her wrists with two hands, he had the displeasure of a firm knee to the groin. He grunted and ground his teeth. "Now that was unnecessary," he mumbled.

Her chin lifted defiantly, and she tried to repeat her offense. "Oh no, you don't," he said, wrapping a leg around hers, molding their hips intimately together.

There was no hiding how hot and hard he was right now. Her eyes went wide with instant awareness at the feel of him pressed against her stomach.

Behind them the chairs clamored from side to side. "I'm assuming the chairs rattling around like that means you're not so happy with me right now."

"How are you even back in my life?"

"I've asked myself that same question. I don't believe in coincidences."

She looked appalled. "You think I arranged all of this?"

He arched a brow. "Did you?"

"Did you?"

"No."

Her expression clouded in obvious rejection of his answer. "You lied to me."

"Never," he said. "I don't lie. I'm a 'what you see is what you get kind of guy.'"

"You're one of them."

"I'd die before I'd join the Zodius."

"The pictures—"

"I explained." He softened his tone. "If you want to be mad at me, be mad that I let you get captured, because I deserve that. You went through hell in Zodius City. But don't accuse me of being with Adam, because he is everything I stand against."

She searched his face, an earnest expression on hers. "If you aren't one of them, then how are you here? How did you escape?"

"Same way you are," he said. "Everyone around me took a nap, and I took advantage." He eased his hold on her wrists and let her hands settle on his chest, the ICE still wrapped in one of them, but she didn't pull away. "It killed me to let you go to that lab by yourself. When those alarms went off, and I saw all the bodies lying everywhere, I was certain you were dead. I hacked the security cameras and found you entering the ventilation system. I followed you, but I was too late. You were gone."

She studied him long seconds before her face dropped to his chest. "I'm so confused."

His hand slid to her hair. The feel of her in his arms pressed intimately to his body was right in ways he couldn't examine right now. "That makes two of us."

Turbulent guilty eyes lifted to his. "I was going to find you, Sterling. *I wanted to find you*, but I had to warn people about Adam, and Tad showed me those pictures of you. Then I heard voices, and—"

"You did the right thing." She'd thought of him. She'd wanted to come to him. It was enough. "I'm just glad you got out. You would never have found me anyway." He hesitated then gently prodded. "Can you tell me what happened back in the lab, Becca? Who is the Milton you mentioned?"

Her fingers curled on his chest, and Sterling could almost feel the simmering anger in her. "Another scientist they kidnapped," she explained, her voice tight. "They killed him." Everything that wasn't bolted down in the room was suddenly in the air, floating, rather than crashing against walls and floors. "I *begged* Adam to spare him, but he has no mercy."

"So Adam was there when all of this happened?"

"He left me with Tad," she said. "That was when Tad flung Milton's dead body to the floor, like he was a piece of trash, and said we were going to have some quality time together."

Sterling tensed. "Did he touch you?"

She shook her head. "No. I don't know what happened. I just lost it. Every emotion inside me just seemed to explode. The next thing I knew, glass vials were shattering, and the Zodius soldiers, Tad included, were on the ground." She was shaking and not from withdrawal.

He pressed his hand to her cheek. "I'm sorry."

"I can't control what's happening." She motioned to the room. "I can't control any of this. I'm so tired of not being able to control anything that's happening to me."

The absolute angst in her voice told him she was telling the truth. He believed her completely. "Maybe we can control things together." He laced his fingers in her hair and covered her soft lips with his. Redirecting her emotions, testing the effect, because he wanted to—damn it, he wanted to in a bad way. He didn't bother with coaxing and prodding. He was looking for fast and hard, lust that consumed, that left no room for anything else—intense, passionate, hungry. And so he tasted her deeply, with sensual strokes of his tongue, drawing her to the place they'd been in that bed, a place where everything outside the moment disappeared.

Stiff and unyielding for only a moment, her balled fist slowly opened, splaying along his biceps, as if she meant to push him away... to resist. But she didn't resist, nor did she push him away. A soft sound escaped her lips, pouring into his mouth, a sound part weak protest, part moan.

Sterling eased back slightly from the kiss, tenderly brushed his lips over hers, before delving deeper... this time with a possessive slant of his mouth that drew her further into the kiss. This time the man in him demanded her response. And she gave it to him, body melting into his, melting until they were one. Until she *became* the kiss, as he did. The moment this complete abandon overcame her, she moaned again, soft, sensual, willing. Desire coiled in his stomach, tightened his body, but Sterling willed himself to check it, willed himself to remember the purpose of this kiss. Another long stroke of his tongue, a deep taste of sweetness, and he forced himself to tear his mouth from hers and turn her in his arms to see the room.

───〜〜〜───

Becca stared at the aftermath of her emotions, the room in shambles, as if a small tornado had swept through, leaving only remnants of its destruction behind. Chairs rested on their backs, the Las Vegas picture speared on one steel leg; the table was turned over. Pillows were on the floor. The single lamp broken. But Sterling's kiss had calmed that storm. How could a kiss that stirred such intense passion actually calm the erratic telekinetic ability she'd developed? But it had. Everything in the room was as it should be—on the floor. Well, not where it should be exactly. The place was a mess.

"It's about focus," Sterling said from behind her. "Learning to tap into a particular part of your psyche that creates the telekinesis."

She whirled around to face him. "That's why you kissed me? To prove a point?" she asked, not sure why that upset her so much, but almost choking on her words as she realized he was standing right behind her, close—so close—she was practically back in his arms. She could see the light dust of a new beard that had brushed her cheeks moments before, see the teal of his eyes, the light brown lashes framing them like a beautiful fan. They stared at one another. They seemed to be getting good at that.

"I kissed you because I wanted to," he said, his voice low, gravelly. Sexy. "And for the record, I was asleep when what happened in the bed started. By the time I realized it wasn't a dream, you were seconds behind me, realizing the same thing. I want you *willing* or not at all."

He wanted her. His bold confirmation whispered through her body and made certain intimate parts tingle. "I don't know what to say to that."

He pulled her to him and kissed her, a brush of lips over hers. "You don't have to say anything, and I won't do that again unless you ask me to." He patted her backside and set her away from him, walking to the bed and grabbing his shirt from the floor. "Why don't you write down the personal items you want from your place, and I'll send someone to pick them up." He snatched a pillow from the floor and tossed it to the bed. "If we can find a pen and paper in this mess." He pulled open the nightstand to look inside and nonchalantly asked over his shoulder, "Did I mention the GTECHs can windwalk? It makes for speedy service. We can probably have your things here by the time you finish showering."

She blinked, surprised, and excited. "Oh please, yes. I would kill for some of my own things right now. And a shower? A little piece of heaven." She paused. "Wait. Did you say *wind-walk*? What does that mean?"

"No pen and paper in sight," he said, closing the distance between them again and offering her his T-shirt. "I can't find yours," he said. "And though I have nothing against you running around the room in only your bra, it's distracting."

Her heart fluttered with his words. She couldn't even remember what she'd asked him. She reached for the shirt, the idea of wearing it felt incredibly, wonderfully intimate.

He held onto it and her hand. "What you said about me having a GTECH power that allowed me to mess with your dreams, or your mind, or even your body—I don't have any of those abilities, and I wouldn't use them on you if I did." There was a warm promise in those words. That warmth washed over her and spoke more than his words. There wasn't a GTECH inside Zodius City who'd possessed such gentleness as she felt in this man. Right or wrong, foolish as it might be, she was going with her instincts. She trusted Sterling.

His gaze lingered on her swollen mouth, as if he were thinking of the kiss they'd just shared, and it was all she could do not to touch her lips. "I believe you," she said, summoning the courage to ask the question she so needed answered. "Why don't you pass out when the others do?"

He went stone still, his hand still covering hers, his expression indiscernible. "Maybe you have more skill than you realize, and you choose to protect me." He smiled, the tension fading, almost as if she imagined it. "And you like kissing me." He let go of the shirt.

Hiding her smile, Becca turned away from him, not about to admit that she did indeed like kissing him and that his logic actually made a bit of sense. With a quick tug, Becca slid the shirt over her head.

It smelled spicy and masculine like him. Hugging the shirt to her, she stuck the vials of ICE under her arm. She didn't want to let her lifeline go. "Wind-walking? What does that mean?"

He righted the wobbly table, muscles flexing deliciously. Now she was the one distracted. "Pretty much what it implies. We fade into the wind and hitch a ride. It's fast and efficient."

"Wow," she said, not questioning it being true. She was already living in a bizarre world. Still... "I mean... just wow."

He reached into the fridge to pull out a bottle of water. "It comes in handy."

He walked to her side and offered her the water. "Drink. You have to be dehydrated and hungry. I'll get you food while you shower."

"Thank you," she said, accepting the water only to have him hold it as he had the shirt.

"And keep the ICE," he said softly. "I won't take it from you. In fact, I want you to have a dose on your person at all times in case you start going into withdrawal."

The protectiveness in his voice washed over her and made her stomach flutter. "Thank you," she said again, far too comforted by his presence. Being alone was frightening. She didn't want to be alone.

He moved away from her, picking up around the room, but she stayed where she was. She'd never been afraid of being alone, never felt such a thing in her life. It scared her, made her worry her judgment was impaired, that she was trusting too easily. She hadn't even asked for evidence that those pictures didn't prove Sterling was a Zodius. She hadn't even asked where the safer place he was taking her was located. He kissed her, and she melted. She trusted… "I need proof you're not Zodius," she blurted.

He stilled in motion, the broken picture in his hand, then glanced at her and set it against the wall. And damn it, why was she staring at his pecs? She jerked her gaze upward to find herself captured in his steady one, his expression unchanged, indiscernible.

Long tense seconds passed before he said, "You'll get your proof."

It was thirty minutes after leaving her to shower, and Sterling sat in the back of a surveillance van outside the motel on a portable stool. He showered and changed into black fatigue pants and a black T-shirt in the adjoining room he shared with Becca. He'd spent that time telling himself to get a grip. Becca was turning him inside out, and he knew it—probably impairing his judgment. Not probably—she was. Why did it bite him in the backside that she wanted proof of who he was? Of course she wanted proof. She was smart. She'd been through hell and back. But it bit him already, like a big ol' grizzly bear chasing dinner.

"Explain exactly what happened in the warehouse," Caleb said from where he sat beside Sterling. Two flat-screen monitors hung on the wall directly in front of them—one displaying the motel door, the other, a live feed of Doc Kelly. Between her and Caleb, the two of them spat out questions about Becca like it was a contest—who could ask the most questions the fastest.

"She panicked when the other scientist was murdered.

She said glass started shattering, and the soldiers passed out. And now that I think about it, when the Zodius came to take her to the lab, her orange juice glass shattered. I just thought it was caused by some sonar signal from military testing Adam might be doing."

"And you're immune to passing out around her. Why?" Kelly asked, shoving a long lock of blonde hair back into the clip at her nape. "I don't like unknowns."

"I watched her freak out around a couple of humans, and they were fine, which I'm guessing to mean I have just enough of a deficiency in the GTECH area to make me desensitized to whatever she is doing."

Kelly pursed her lips. "That's interesting. I'm not sold on the idea, but it's a good hypothesis."

"Hmmm, okay," Caleb said, his light brown eyes thoughtful. He sat up straight and ran his hands down his jean-clad legs. "If Becca's emotions trigger these episodes she's having, then my ability to probe and influence human emotions might allow me to help her control it."

"Oh no," Kelly said quickly. "It's too dangerous, Caleb. So far we've seen GTECHs pass out from whatever mental compulsion she gives them. What if she has the ability to kill them as well? What if you're the first? What if the others weren't passed out at all? What if they were dead?"

"Jeezus, Kelly," Sterling said. "Enough with the what-ifs."

"She's right," said a stern voice from behind.

Sterling and Caleb swiveled around to face Michael, a remark on Sterling's tongue quickly swallowed as he found a cute, petite blonde package of sweetness next to Michael. Cassandra was Michael's mate, but she appeared to be his polar opposite—light and understanding where Michael was dark and unsympathetic. "It's too dangerous," Michael continued. "You can't go near that woman. I don't care what kind of story she's offered in explanation. I don't trust her. For all we know she has the ability to somehow influence your mind, Caleb. Maybe that's her goal. To get close to you, to convince you she needs to be inside your head—or you inside her. Adam wants you to join him in a bad way. You know this."

"Again—with the paranoia," Sterling said irritably. "I was with her. I saw how scared she was."

"Good acting," Michael said. "Do we even know she really has cancer? The medical records could be a cover. She was missing for months. She could have been with Adam."

Sterling wanted to punch Michael, and not because he was wrong, because he was voicing concerns Sterling had as well, but didn't want to face. "If Becca were working for Adam, he wouldn't have tried to kill her last night."

"Maybe it was a setup to make you think she could be trusted," Michael said. "He had to have seen how protective you are of her. You pretty much write it on a wall in fluorescent color. And amazingly, the Zodius knew exactly where she was at that club, despite the fact that she has no psychic imprint from sex with a GTECH."

"It was an ICE club that had security cameras," Sterling bit out. "Of course, they found her."

Michael's expression hardened. "It was a setup if I ever saw one. A way to make us feel the need to bring her into our inner circle and protect her." He shoved a bag of food at Sterling. "I don't know how I became your delivery man, but don't get used to it."

"Service with a smile," Sterling jibed because he enjoyed irritating Michael, especially considering his opinion of Becca. "Or no tip."

Michael ignored his comments as he did most jokes, eyeing Caleb. "You can't go near that woman."

"Becca," Sterling ground out between clenched teeth. "Her name is Becca."

Michael narrowed a suspicious gaze at Sterling that said, "Something you want to tell me? Like she's your Lifebond?"

A muscle in Sterling's jaw clenched at the silent prod, uncertain what he thought about his relationship with Becca at this point. The woman made him insanely hot and out of his mind.

Caleb, still focused on Michael's concerns, waved off his warning. "Rebecca Burns can't control my mind. She can't control her own. We need her in a lab, helping us find a way to deal with ICE. That means we have to help her, so she can help us."

Kelly tried to respond. "Yes, but—"

Michael cut her off.

"Assumed lack of control," Michael said. "It could be an act."

"If I touch her mind, I'll know if it's an act," Caleb said. "And that has to happen before we allow her near one of our facilities."

"Quarantine her at Neonopolis," Michael said. "Don't allow her inside Sunrise City. Our main headquarters needs to stay off limits."

"I agree," Kelly argued, never one to hold back her

thoughts. She'd been with the Renegades since the day of the Area 51 takeover, and she was as devoted as any of the men to protecting her country. "She can work in a lab there and communicate with me via webcam while I evaluate her myself. And for the record, I double-checked our initial information, and not only did Becca have cancer, her treatments were highly experimental. Frankly, I don't know how she got into the program. It's so exclusive. We're working on her detailed records. I'm curious to see how ICE reacts to her specific medication. It's the most logical cause of these abilities, since she's the only one who's developed them. And I have to say... as bad as all this is, there could be some amazing cancer cure discovered. So in other words, get me that blood sample, Sterling. I'm dying to see what's going on with Becca."

"I will," he said.

"She's going to need more ICE," Kelly added. "I have about three weeks worth for her, and that's it. And that's being really sparing in the lab to ration it."

"I'll get it," Sterling said. He had to. He would.

"Back to the prior topic, Caleb," Michael inserted, ignoring the rest of the conversation. "Don't underestimate how much he wants you by his side. He could use this woman to manipulate your mind. He believes together you will be unstoppable—that you could rule the world."

Caleb rubbed the back of his neck. "We'll extract at 1400 hours." Which gave them three hours until departure. He eyed Sterling. "I've already cleared nonessential personnel before her arrival."

Sterling inhaled a rough breath and let it out. "She wants proof we aren't working for Adam before she helps us." It bit hard that she didn't trust him, even if he was forced to question her. He knew better, but it still didn't sit well.

Caleb nodded. "I'll arrange documentation and a call to the White House."

"And we want proof she isn't working for Adam as well," Michael stated flatly.

Cassandra elbowed him. "Stop, Michael. You've made it clear you don't trust her." She removed the canvas bag from her shoulder. "I brought Becca some clothes and girl stuff to carry her over until we get to her place. I felt like this would be faster."

Sterling accepted the bag. "Thanks, Cass."

"I'm happy to help," she said. "I only wish it were safe for me to go into the room and talk to her. The poor thing has cancer, a forced ICE addiction, Adam chasing her, and now you guys to deal with. I can't imagine what she must be going through."

Sterling shook his head, amazed that this caring woman, a psychologist who'd worked with soldiers and their families, a friend to everyone who knew her, was the daughter of the mastermind behind the GTECH "immunizations." But indeed, her father was General Powell, now MIA and most likely up to some government plot to control the GTECHs. And she'd been brave enough to stand against him.

Michael grimaced at his Lifebond, now GTECH through their connection. "I told you not to go getting sappy over this woman, Cassandra. I don't want you to become attached and get hurt. For all we know, Adam has promised to cure her cancer by making her a full GTECH in exchange for her service to him."

"He'd never give the GTECH serum to a woman," she scoffed. "He believes women are beneath men, meant to be converted only through Lifebonding."

"Adam often makes promises he does not intend to keep," Michael reminded her. "*Especially* to women." He cut a glare at Sterling. "I will continue to believe he has sent her here to infiltrate our operation and tear us down from the inside out until I have proof otherwise." He glared at Sterling. "You'd be smart to do the same."

Sterling stared bullets at Michael, ready to launch himself at him, ready to throttle him once again for being right. Michael stared right back at him, welcoming a confrontation.

Caleb looked between Michael and Sterling, and then arched a brow. "Something I should know?"

"Nothing," Sterling said and meant it. Michael, in all his asshole delivery of the facts, was still right. He wasn't objective with Becca. Just thinking of the way she'd tasted on his lips, tightening his groin, and he knew it was more than that. He wanted her in a bad way, and fuck, fuck, fuck, he was emotionally involved with a woman who really could be the enemy. A soldier knew better than to be emotionally involved. No more. From now on, it would be all business.

It was a resolution he set solidly inside himself, just as a text message buzzed his cell phone. Thankful for the distraction, he yanked his cell from his belt and glanced at the screen. It was Marcus. "It's one of my street contacts," he told Caleb as he motioned to the door. He'd reply to Marcus once he was inside. "I'll be ready at 1400."

"We'll have a car and driver at the front door," Caleb

said. "You and Becca take the backseat. Make sure she's tranq'd, Sterling. For everyone's safety."

Damn. "Copy that, boss," Sterling said, heading toward the motel, a new attitude toward Becca firmly installed, or so he thought.

The instant he walked into the room and shut the door, the scent of Becca permeated his nostrils, seeped into his soul, and he had to remind himself that touching her would paint a bull's-eye on her for the Trackers. Becca was off limits.

He set the food on the table, walked to the bathroom, and knocked. "I have clothes and some other items one of the Renegade's Lifebond put together for you. They haven't had time to get your things as I'd hoped."

The door cracked open, and Lord have mercy... when he saw that tiny, white splotch of towel through the crack, he knew it was all she had on. A wild, hot image of shoving open that door and ripping the towel away tore through his mind right before the cruelly vivid fantasy of bending her naked body over the cabinet and burying himself inside her.

Off limits, he told himself, but he didn't move, didn't walk away. He stood right there, all but talking himself into pushing that door open and pulling every naked inch of her next to him.

Chapter 14

STERLING WAS STILL TRYING TO CONVINCE HIMSELF not to go inside the bathroom and strip away Becca's towel when she delicately cleared her throat.

"Thank you," she said hoarsely, as if she were as affected by the intimacy of the moment as he was. She backed behind the door and reached for the bag.

Sterling handed it to her quickly and turned away, adjusting his cock where it rested painfully against his zipper in a long, hard throb of pain. Sexual tension prickled him like tiny needles poking his skin. With a grumble, Sterling yanked the damn torn picture off the leg of an overturned chair and set it against the wall, and then finished. Still he couldn't get rid of the tension charging through his body; he dropped and did a hundred push-ups. Cock still throbbed. Shit. Damn thing was as stubborn as a woman. He did another hundred. His cell buzzed again, and Sterling cursed. He'd forgotten Marcus.

Sterling jumped to his feet and claimed a chair behind the table and opened the text message to read: *Where is my money?*

The blow-dryer sounded in the bathroom as Sterling sent a text message in return: *Where is my ICE?*

Marcus: *Don't tell me you screwed up a sure thing?*

Sterling: *Your idea of a sure thing is about as sure as getting lucky with a nun.*

A several-seconds pause, then: *If I get you another shot don't F it up*.

Sterling snorted: *Talk is cheap*.

Marcus replied: *My portion of this deal is not*.

Sterling would have typed more, but the door to the bathroom opened, and he all but swallowed his tongue. Becca stood there with her hair sleek and shiny, her lips glossed pink, her skin pale and fresh, looking like an angel come to save his tarnished, bedeviled soul. Of its own free will, his gaze traveled over the slim blue jeans she wore and flat, silver-strapped sandals that showcased delicate little feet. Then back up those long legs to her pale blue blouse that dipped deliciously at her neckline.

Her hands smoothed the silky strands of her hair as she walked toward the table. "I can't believe the clothes fit."

"We'll get your things later," he said. The earlier extraction had forced priorities to shift, but he didn't tell her that.

"I'm completely satisfied," she said. "You have no idea how wonderful it felt to have clean clothes and a private shower that didn't make me feel like I was the star of some porn flick."

Sterling's gaze riveted to her face, a hard punch of anger vibrating through his gut. "I'm sorry about Tad opening the bathroom door like he did. I would never have let him go inside."

Pink flushed her cheeks, and she sat down at the table trying to be nonchalant about her comment, but the visible shiver that shook her delicate frame gave her away. "I hate talking about that man. He might have been forced to keep his hands off me, but Tad raped me with his mind so many times, it makes my skin crawl just thinking about it."

Blistering anger bubbled inside Sterling and mixed with an acidy dose of guilt over ever letting Becca near him in the first place.

Becca inhaled. "Food smells so good."

He reached for the bag and offered her a burger and fries. "It's probably cold by now."

"I don't care," she said popping a fry and sighing. "I feel like it's been a lifetime since I had a good fry." She unwrapped her burger and spread the fries on the paper. "I'm actually hungry too. It's the first time in well… a really long time. Got any ketchup?"

He snatched up the packets in the bag and piled them on the table before reaching inside the fridge. "I've got water and Dr. Pepper."

"No Coke?" she asked, mockingly appalled.

"I have a pretty serious Dr. Pepper addiction," he admitted, passing her the can. "Doc Kelly—she heads up our scientific team—she gives me hell about it. Says all the sugar is bad for the body."

She accepted the soda. "But you don't care, I take it?" She gave him a smile, light and full of humor. The tension from her demand for proof he wasn't working for Adam had faded, if only for a short while. It was the first time he'd seen her at ease, and he liked her this way. He also felt like a complete asshole, because he was about to tranquilize her and betray what little trust he'd earned.

"If a GTECH can't survive a few too many DPs," he said, "he's in real trouble when the Zodius start shooting. I think Kelly thinks it makes us feel human if she acts like were human."

She dabbed her mouth. "I guess there is the plus side. You can now justify your vices." He leaned back on the chair and studied her, watching her slim, ivory neck as she swallowed. Delicate. Kissable. "Am I to believe you have no vices?"

She smiled, and it was as if the sun had shined right there at that table. Sterling had seen a lot of female smiles—demure, seductive. He'd not seen a lot of sunshine smiles. "Still like my Snickers bars."

He grinned, reaching inside the fridge again, before dropping a package of peanut M&Ms on the table. She laughed. "Your version of my Snickers bar?"

"You betcha, sweet plum," he said, winking.

She snorted. Feminine. Cute. "Sweet plum? That's a new one."

"What can I say?" he queried. "You inspire my creativity."

She waved that off jokingly and picked up the candy. "You keep M&Ms in the fridge?"

"A man has to do what a man has to do to protect his candy. This place is a dump. The air doesn't work half the time, and they melt, which turns a bag of peanut M&Ms into a bag of messy peanuts, and that's just not right."

She shook her head and laughed. Soft and musical. His cock jerked again. Damn. "Yet judging from the DP stock," she said curiously, "you come here often."

He thrummed his fingers on the table. "Places like this have ears to the pavement you won't find anywhere else."

"Not even the high-rise, high-security resorts?"

"They each have their value," he agreed, "but the

resort crowd requires a lot of time and even more of the green stuff. And why give away the green if you don't have to? Places like this one—you can get a guy to sell out his best friend and his wife for a cigarette." He draped an arm over the back of the chair. "This is life in the fast lane. The down and dirty of the city."

"God. The fast lane. My brother used that exact term so many times."

"It's a soldier's mentality," Sterling told her. "We like action. We like fast."

"My father wouldn't have agreed. He'd have taken strategic over the fast lane any day. He was always trying to slow my brother down and make him think."

"Because you act fast doesn't mean you aren't thinking," Sterling argued, defending himself through her brother. "It simply means you size up the situation and act before fear rears its ugly head, and you talk yourself out of it. Fear can get you killed."

A distant look touched her expression. "The last time my brother was home on leave, we went to the movies. On the way home, we witnessed a bad car wreck. A drunk driver swerved into the lane and hit another car head-on with his pickup truck." Her gaze fixed on Sterling. "Kevin didn't think about the danger. The car was on fire, and there was a kid inside, and he went after him as if there were no consequences. He pulled that kid out of the car and saved his life. I've never been so scared in my life, not even inside Zodius City. I was afraid he was going to burn to death. Afraid the car would explode. Afraid of losing my brother."

"I'm sorry," he said. "I know you loved them both very much."

She nodded shortly. "It was amazing Kevin came out of it all unscathed. He was a hero. He saved those people's lives."

"That's what soldiers do, Becca," he said. "We save lives."

"I know," she said solemnly. "But that doesn't make losing someone you love any easier. Being the wife or child of a soldier is far more terrifying than even Adam is. I don't ever again want to feel what I felt when I lost my father and brother."

She was telling him they had no future, whether she realized it or not. He already knew. He couldn't even make love to her without putting her in danger, marking her for the Trackers. He was bad for her in all kinds of ways. "Is that why you haven't told your mother about your cancer?"

"I didn't want to scare her," she said. "I thought I'd deal with it and make it go away."

"So you went through all that fear and treatment alone." It wasn't a question. It was more awe at such an unselfish and brave thing to do.

"Yeah," she said. "I just couldn't bear to see her hurt again. I guess at some point I'm going to have to talk to her."

"Not if we can find an antidote or a way to keep you on ICE long-term."

"Don't," she said, shaking her head. "Don't paint rainbows for me. I don't need them. I don't want them. I'm way beyond that now." She gave him a look that said that part of the conversation was over and swiftly changed the subject. "Why are the eyes of the Zodius black, yet yours are their natural color?"

Sterling froze with his drink tipped back, glad for the diversion to regain his composure before he set the can back down. "All GTECHs have black eyes, but they have the ability to camouflage them to their natural color with everyone but their Lifebond." Except him, but he wasn't about to say that.

"So your eyes aren't really teal anymore?"

"No," he said softly, too softly, and he knew it. "They're black."

Her expression softened. "I always loved your eyes, you know."

"No," he said. "I didn't know." But he was darn glad right then for the special nonprescription lenses Dr. Chin had made during his time at Area 51, even if Chin was a traitor. "I always loved your eyes too. I still do."

"Thank you." Her cheeks flushed, and she picked up a fry. "So why do all the Zodius choose not to camouflage their eye color?"

"The color is human," he said. "And humans to the Zodius are weak and part of the past. GTECHs represent evolution."

Her expression paled. "I really want to get to a lab and start working so we can stop Adam." She hesitated and shifted in her seat. "Where exactly are you taking me when we leave here?"

"Our inner-city hub," he said. "We'll have a live webcam set up so you can work with our scientific team."

She shifted in her chair again, looking increasingly uncomfortable. "And my proof that you are who you say you are, along with everyone else I'm working with?"

"Caleb's arranging documentation and a call to the White House."

"White House?" she asked with an arched brow.

"The Renegades have an alliance with the government, though half the time they still treat us as barely contained enemies. But we make it work, and so do they. No one wants Adam to get any more powerful than he already is."

She nodded, cutting her gaze from his, picking up a french fry and taking a tiny bite that seemed more about avoiding eye contact than hunger.

"Becca," he said gently, willing her to look at him. He knew she felt like she was alone, and being quarantined wasn't going to help.

Her lashes fluttered and lifted. "Yes?"

He opened his mouth and shut it. How did he tell her everything was going to be okay when it wasn't? Cassandra was right. Becca had the world on her shoulders. So he hedged. "Eat. It will make you feel better."

She stared at him, her eyes filled with trepidation that suddenly shifted to determination as she straightened and said, "Putting an end to the nightmare named Adam will make me feel better, but I'll settle for food now."

He grinned. "I like that plan." He snatched a fry and then reached into the bag and pulled out the four burgers remaining inside.

Becca laughed. "You do have that big GTECH appetite." She picked up a fry. "It seems I'm getting one myself. I sure hope ICE burns calories since I'm missing my five-mile daily run. And if it does, I don't want to think about how easily that could lure women into trying it. And I'm not joking."

"Thankfully Adam isn't good at thinking from a female perspective." He dumped fries on top of the bag.

"Let's hope we get it off the streets before anyone gets that creative idea for recruiting new users."

"You know," Becca commented, "the only thing keeping Adam from mass distributing ICE is the body count. He wants people alive and worshipping him from what I can tell. But I think he'll become impatient and risk the body count to get followers sooner than later. And the problem with that is we have no idea of the long-term effects ICE has on people. They could die. They could develop strange alien diseases. Go blind. Become cripples. The list of possibilities is daunting."

"Turn violent," he said softly, thinking of the conversation by the van. "Yes. We've thought of the possibilities, and they aren't good."

"Exactly," she said, pausing with her burger near her mouth and then setting it down. "I can't believe I'm saying this, but we have to cut off the supply source."

We. At least she was talking like she'd decided to join the Renegades, and he hadn't even gotten her that proof yet. "We're trying," he assured her. "I was hoping we'd figure out the ingredients in ICE to try and cut him off at the source before we left, but you don't get two chances to get out of that place. We were lucky to get out at all."

"But I did find out," she said. "I know how he's making it. It's—"

Sterling's cell rang at the same moment the room phone jangled to life. Adrenaline surged through Sterling's body at the warning. It was a signal. They were being attacked.

Becca's brows dipped. "Somebody really wants your attention."

Sterling pushed back his chair and stood up, walking

casually toward the bed, when he was feeling anything but relaxed. He found the bag Kelly had sent him, removing the sedative. He'd planned to warn Becca before he gave her the drug, but there wasn't time. The Renegades couldn't protect her if she laid them flat on their asses.

Before Sterling could turn around, the bag was in the air, as were the pillows on the bed. Sterling cursed. Becca's emotions. She sensed danger, maybe even sensed he was up to something. Sterling turned to find Becca standing a foot away.

"What's going on?" Her body was stiff with tension, her voice quavered with anxiety.

He reached for her, pulling her close. "Easy, sweetheart," he cooed softly, burying his fingers in the silky strands of her hair, his lips by her ear. She tried to pull back from him, but he held her easily. "I'm sorry, Becca," he whispered. "There's no way around this." He injected her arm.

She yelped and then went limp against him. So much for trust, he thought grimly. Sterling lifted her into his arms and headed for the door.

Chapter 15

SECONDS TICKED BY LIKE HOURS AS STERLING HELD Becca's limp body against his, waiting for the second coded call from Caleb with emergency extraction instructions, knowing he was once again about to carry Becca into who knew what hell.

Those seconds gave him time to think, and damn if an unfathomable emotion didn't surface—fear. WTF? Why was he thinking in the first place? Thinking got you in trouble. And fear was simply not an option. A good soldier saved lives and stayed emotionally detached. He acted. He *did not* think. He did not allow fear to come into play.

But he wasn't emotionally detached—not where Becca was concerned. These damnable, repeated circumstances kept thrusting her unconscious body into his arms, completely reliant on him to keep her safe. And though he wouldn't trust her with anyone else—hell no, not by a long shot—one of the two prior occasions hadn't turned out so hot. In fact, it had turned out pretty damn crappy. Not this time.

Sterling's cell rang. It was already in his hand, and he quickly answered.

"Car," Caleb said. "Front door. Now!"

Sterling didn't ask questions, and thank the good Lord above he didn't do any of that damn thinking from seconds before. He charged toward the door, and kicked it open. Wood splintered against hinges as Sterling exited the room to find a nondescript black sedan—the same kind used as high-end taxis all over Vegas—sitting there, the back door flung open.

He took a step forward, when bullets suddenly splattered the vehicle. With a curse, Sterling charged toward the car door. At the same moment, the wind lifted. Two Zodius soldiers boldly materialized on either side of him. Suddenly, Damion leaned out of the car, Glock in hand, and unloaded two rounds into the foreheads of the attackers.

"Give her to me!" Damion yelled, reaching for Becca.

"Hell no," Sterling said and then reconsidered when a Z materialized on top of the damn car. *Don't think—just do*, he told himself, and rode on instinct.

Sterling handed off Becca and snagged Damion's guns at the same time. Not a second too soon as bullets sprayed near his feet, one slicing along the side of his calf and way too close to Becca.

No way that this was a kidnapping attempt. It rang more like an assassination mission. Sterling pointed his gun at the Z guy on top of the car, but Caleb appeared on the roof and did the dirty work for him.

"Go!" Caleb yelled, as Michael and a squadron of Renegades appeared all around the car.

Sterling didn't have to be told twice. He was in the car in seconds flat, yanking the door shut behind him.

"Drive!" he yelled, damn glad to see Casar Alegra, the best damn driver they had in the Renegades, before turning his attention back to Damion. "What the hell are you doing here?"

Damion had Becca sprawled out over the seat,

running a handheld scanner that resembled a retail price checker over her body. He glanced up at Sterling. "What's it look like I'm doing? I'm trying to find out how they found her." The scanner buzzed over Becca's right shoulder. "Bingo. Tracking implant." He dropped the scanner and snatched a knife from his pants.

Sterling grabbed Damion's wrist, the eight-inch blade hovering in the air. "Don't even think about it," Sterling warned between clenched teeth. Damion, knife, and Becca did not go together.

Abruptly, Becca jerked, her lashes fluttering. Oh shit! She was waking up. The sedative wasn't working.

"Stop the car!" Sterling yelled.

"Are you nuts?" Damion asked. "We can't stop or—"

"Stop now!" Sterling ordered. "Put it in park."

Casar slammed on the brakes and shifted into park. Almost instantly, a Z soldier appeared at the front bumper. Casar looked at the Z and then over his shoulder at Sterling. "We're stopping, why?"

Becca started screaming. Marcus, Damion, and the Z in front of the car—all passed out.

"That would be why we stopped," Sterling mumbled, reaching for Becca. He had to get her out of here before the Zs sent in a human convoy to finish the job they'd started. Or, he thought grimly, just unloaded a couple machine guns into the car.

The man with the knife fell on top of Becca. She screamed again and scrambled backward in the seat just as strong arms circled her, the familiar, oddly safe scent of Sterling insinuating into her nostrils, the feel of him close, his voice near her ear from behind as he whispered, "Easy, sweetheart."

He reached around her and shoved aside the man's body, so that he leaned against the door away from her. Becca fought the sense of comfort that Sterling's voice and touch offered, unsure if she could trust him, wanting desperately not to be alone in whatever was happening to her, but not to be tricked or taken advantage of. Every time Sterling was near she woke up in a strange place, and she didn't remember how she'd gotten there.

That thought sent Becca whirling around, her hand on his chest as she shoved him away. Confused. Uncertain. Stating the obvious and wanting a reaction. "I'm in a car, and I have no idea how I got here. There's a man holding a giant knife that he intends to use on me. Explain that to me, Sterling."

"I'll explain," he said, as his cell phone rang. He snatched it from his belt and held up a finger to Becca as he snapped it to his ear and spoke.

"The sedative wore off," he said to his caller. "Everyone is down but me." His gaze went to Becca. "In her arm. Yes. I'll deal with it and contact you upon completion."

Becca was gaping at him when he hung up. "You sedated me?" she demanded. "You sedated me and then—" She stopped, thinking of his conversation, and urgently patted down her arms. A bad feeling twisted in her stomach. "What's in my arm?" Panic started to form, and she repeated the question before he could answer. "What is in my arm?"

His hands went to her shoulders. "A laser-inserted tracking device. That's how the Zodius found you in that warehouse last night, and that's how they found us in the motel. And yes, I sedated you when they attacked. The Renegades can't protect you if they are lying flat on their backs like they are now. Adam has human followers. They'll come for you, which means we have to move, and we have to move now."

He reached for the door. She grabbed his arm. "Out there? Where they can shoot at us?"

"Not us," he corrected. "Me. You stay where you are. Somebody has to drive us out of here before we start getting shot at."

He exited the car and she barely contained her need to pull him back, her fingers digging into her palms. She held her breath, waiting for gunfire, waiting for him to drop dead. Instead, in a flash, he was by the driver's door, shoving aside the man behind the wheel. He'd wind-walked; he must have to have gotten there so fast.

"Hold on," he said, putting the car in drive and peeling out.

With the acceleration, the man in the backseat tumbled on Becca, and she yelped.

"What's wrong?" Sterling demanded, eyeing her through the rearview mirror.

Becca heaved the man off of her, thankful for the ICE-induced strength, only to have another wild turn flop the man's body right back on top of her. "What's wrong is, the guy who wanted to use that knife on me doesn't like your driving any more than I do," she said, trying to position the man so he wouldn't fall on her again.

She felt like she was living in an alternative universe. That her other self was still having her happy, 6:00 a.m. coffee and reading the paper, then going to work, and later eating her lunch on the same bench as always. She couldn't have cancer. There was no way she could have been on that motel bed straddling Sterling, a virtual stranger, and all but having sex with him. Nor could she have spent days held in captivity by a madman who wanted to rule the world and who had turned her into a drug addict. None of this felt real.

Becca snapped out of her fretful ponderings as Sterling turned into the parking garage of a major casino, driving several floors before parking on a busy level.

Nervously, Becca glanced around the lot, feeling as if they had just cornered themselves with nowhere to go. And she would have said so, but Sterling was back on his phone.

"Red Dragon Hotel," he said. "Fourth level. I'm leaving the car with Damion and Casar inside." He hung up and reached for his door. "Get down and stay here while I get us a car."

In what couldn't have been more than two minutes later, she was sitting inside a Toyota with the engine running. "I never thought I'd see the day I'd be willing to steal a car," she said.

"Borrowing it," he said, cutting her a sideways look as he accelerated. "Buckle up."

After the way he'd been driving, she didn't argue. She was buckled in seconds. "Can't they use that tracking device to follow us?" she asked, studying his profile and finding comfort in the ease at which he handled the wheel, the road. *The danger*.

"Until we get it out of your arm," he said. "Yes."

Becca assumed there would be a doctor waiting for her at their destination. She didn't want to know more than that now. The stolen—correction—borrowed car, the running from the Zodius, the man beside her who made her want to trust him when she wasn't sure what to make of him—that was all plenty.

Or so she thought. They exited the hotel and took a couple sharp turns. Sterling pulled behind a closed nightclub and parked behind the Dumpster before turning to face her.

"We have to get the tracking device out of your arm."

"Right," she said. "I assumed it—"

"Now, Becca."

She swallowed against the sudden dryness in her throat. "Now? As in right here, in the car? Behind this Dumpster?"

He nodded, and she asked, "Is there a laser to remove it?"

Grimly, his lips thinned, and he reached to his hip pocket and pulled out a slender blade folded inside a casing. "Not here. And there is nowhere safe I can take you until it's out."

Becca's heart thundered in her chest and vibrated in her ears. "Which arm?" she said, managing to keep a steady voice, trying not to think about how much this was going to hurt.

"Your right," he said.

"Do it," she said, turning to offer her shoulder. "Get it out of me."

She grabbed the door handle, her eyes prickling with tears she refused to shed. She'd made it through cancer and Zodius City. She'd make it through this. She'd barely finished the thought when a piercing pain shot through her shoulder, and she saw stars.

Sterling had been a soldier long enough to know there was only one way to dish out pain. Hard and fast. He'd sliced his shirt for a bandage and sliced her shoulder before she ever knew what had happened. His stomach clenched at the sound of her whimpers as he worked. Within seconds he'd tossed the tiny device from her shoulder into the Dumpster and tied off her arm. The instant he was done, he pulled her close and held her.

He buried his face in her hair. "I'm so sorry, Becca," he whispered. "I didn't want to hurt you."

"I… know," she said, her voice hoarse, the pain she felt rasping through every syllable.

He leaned back to look at her and stroked her hair. Her eyes were red, tears streaming down her face. He used his knuckles to wipe them away. Damn it, he was always hurting her. "Hang in there. We'll get you some pain medicine pronto, sweetheart. Lie down, and I'll get us where we're going fast, so you get some relief."

She barely nodded, and he eased her down on the cushion. He wasted no time putting the car into gear. That tracking device put them in this location—exactly why they needed to be out of here and out of here now.

Chapter 16

LESS THAN FIVE MINUTES AFTER REMOVING THE tracking device from Becca's shoulder, Sterling pulled the vehicle he'd "borrowed" into the parking garage of the Renegades' inner-city headquarters and hit the security remote he carried with him. Steel, high-tech, electronic doors opened to the basement level, where the Renegades leased nearly ten thousand square feet beneath the Neonopolis. An unlikely place for their operation, the nearly one-hundred-thousand-square-foot entertainment facility—complete with games, gambling, and a movie theater—offered concealment they were careful to maintain.

With his wind-walking skills not as developed for long-distance travel as most GTECHs, Sterling stayed close to home base. "Neon," as he called it, was his baby, and the two dozen men who reported there, under his command, his responsibility. Together, he and his men made it a point to know every move the Zs made within the city before they made it—to protect unknowing humans from their predators—Adam's Z followers.

Beside him, lying on the seat, her head near his legs, Becca moaned as if she were biting back a sob. Before he could stop himself, Sterling ran his hand over her hair. He wasn't what most would call the warm, fuzzy type, but something about this woman made him want to comfort her.

"We're pulling into the facility now," he said softly. "Hang in there."

"I'm okay," she whispered, pushing herself upright to check her surroundings. And then as if trying to convince herself it was true, she repeated it louder. "I'm okay. My arm is getting better. I guess that's a perk of the ICE. But my head is killing me." She glanced over her shoulder as the silver doors slid shut. "I feel like I'm back in NASA." She grimaced. "Or Zodius City."

"Other than technology," Sterling assured, "there are very few similarities between us and Zodius." He pulled the car into a parking spot by the elevator and snatched his cell phone from his belt. "I need to find out where Caleb wants us."

Her chin lifted with a hint of pride. "You mean where I'm to be confined? That is what's going to happen, right?"

Sterling heard the uncertainty in her voice, and remarkably he would have delved into more of that unfamiliar comfort stuff, if Caleb hadn't answered the line. "Protected," he said softly. "I'm protecting you, Becca."

"I see you on the security camera," Caleb said into the phone without a hello.

Feeling Becca's stare, Sterling recognized this conversation might not be one best heard by her. "Hold on, Caleb," he said and reached for the door, speaking to Becca. "Stay here a minute."

She gave him a short nod, her body tense, her expression apprehensive. He actually had to force himself to get out of the car and leave her feeling like crap—worried, unsure what came next. Not that he really knew either. This was all unfamiliar territory.

The minute he'd shut the door, he asked, "Any word on Damion and Casar?"

"They're awake and fine," he said. "No aftereffects from whatever Becca did to them other than their attitudes. They're both pretty shaken up by how easily they could have been killed when they were out. This ability Becca has—it could destroy us—bring us to our knees and allow Adam to control us or kill us."

"I know she seems dangerous," Sterling conceded. "But she wants to stop Adam as much as we do."

"We don't know what the long-term effects of ICE really are," Caleb argued. "Look at what the GTECH serum has turned Adam into. What if the ICE users take on those violent tendencies? What if she does and turns on us?"

He didn't even want to go there. "All the studies show that the GTECHs are basically what we were before we were converted," Sterling argued. "Those who were violent simply become more violent. If that's true with ICE, then Becca isn't going to become a weapon."

"What about when Adam threatens to kill innocent people unless she does what he wants her to do?"

He had a point—one Sterling didn't like. "When the Zs attacked us in the warehouse, they didn't start shooting. They were trying to capture Becca. But not this time. This time they were trying to kill her."

Caleb clearly hesitated, then said, "Which I guess shouldn't be a surprise. I know my brother. Adam knew once the tracking device in her arm was gone, he'd lose her. He wasn't willing to risk her falling into our hands and being used against him. And like it or not, both her knowledge and her abilities are weapons."

"I know," Sterling said, eyeing the car that was be-hind him. Becca had turned around and was staring at him. His eyes met hers. The uncertainty in hers twisted him in knots. "Adam tried to kill her. Once she knows that, it should ensure her loyalty."

"She has terminal cancer," Caleb reminded him. "She needs ICE to survive. The only place to get ICE is Adam. She personifies what Adam is trying to create—a person forced into loyalty by the human will to survive. No matter how she fights it that need to survive will be there, driving her decisions and her actions."

Sterling inhaled those words like an acid burn and cut his gaze from Becca's before he became any less objective than he already was. "Right. Her cancer. Now the ICE addiction Adam forced on her. It's like one big poison. Damning in all kinds of ways."

"It's not a definition of guilt," Caleb said. "It's a warning to be cautious." His voice sharpened to an order. "Be careful, Sterling. You care about this woman. I don't want to see you or anyone else get hurt."

Sterling opened his mouth to say he was always care-ful, but that would be a damn lie. He was rarely careful. And nothing about Becca made him want to be careful. She made him want to throw her down on a bed and be all kinds of *not careful*. And Caleb knew him too well not to see that.

Tilting his head back, Sterling tried to ease the tension settling there. Staring up at the flat confines of concrete ceiling and feeling trapped by circumstances, by that damn diagnosis of cancer. This is why you don't get to know the people you are assigned to protect. Knowing the people made losing them so much harder. And he didn't want to lose Becca. In fact, he was pretty sure he wanted to save her more than anyone he'd ever tried to save.

"So where does this leave us?" he finally asked.

"I've cleared the west wing of the facility of all personnel," he said. "The lab included. You can stitch her up there and get a blood sample to Kelly. Cassandra and Michael are headed to her house to get some of her things. They'll be in her room. We'll evaluate what to do with her when I have Kelly's assessment."

"Copy that," Sterling said and snapped his phone back onto his belt. He walked to Becca's side of the car and pulled the door open.

"Let's get inside and get you some pain medicine," he said.

She stood, tilted her chin up, and studied him intently. "How are the two men that passed out?"

"Recovered fully," he said.

Her shoulders relaxed, and she stepped away from the door. "Oh good."

"Did you recognize the man with the knife, Becca?"

Her brow crinkled in this cute, pensive way as she considered. "No." She thought a bit more and shook her head. "Definitely not. But then I was pretty focused on the knife in his hand. Should I?"

"No," he said, not willing to scare her into thinking there were enemies inside the Renegade camp when he still had to convince her he was a friend.

"You were talking about me on the phone."

"Yes," he said, seeing no point in lying, but neither did he plan to tell her any more than he had to.

He reached for her arm. "How's my magnificent T-shirt bandage holding up?"

She ignored the joke. "It seems fine," she said. "I'm barely bleeding, and the pain is going away. What did… whoever that was on the phone… Caleb, I assume… say about me?"

He considered his response. ICE was healing her cut, just as it was healing her cancer. Who wouldn't desire a cure? A promise of another day, another minute. Another breath.

Yet, everything inside him screamed with trust. Desire, lust, want, need. He was screaming a lot of things where Becca was concerned, but trust was in there. And damn it, he didn't want to be a fool. He didn't want to risk the lives of many because this woman had gotten under his skin somehow.

"You're dangerous," he said, intentionally giving her an emotional push to put distance between them, shutting her out before he lost his ability to do so. Before this woman did more than get under his skin. Before she crawled right into his soul and turned all that black sludge living there into a mushy, pink pushover.

Her chin lifted defiantly. "Says the wolf to Little Red Riding Hood. If anyone is dangerous, it's you."

He almost laughed at how true that was. "That's right, little girl," he said, and before he could stop himself, his hands slipped around her slender waist, and he pulled her close, his lips near her ear. "And we both know how easy it would be for me to gobble you up."

Sexual tension radiated through his body to hers, hers to his. Her breath, warm and seductive, fanned his neck. His groin tightened, his body heated with demand. Memories of her on top of him, her breasts high, her nipples pink and pebbled, flashed in his mind. The thought of having her naked, all that creamy white skin pressed close, taunted him. Her body, hot and wet, wrapped around him, riding him.

With a low growl, Sterling set her back, put distance between them before he really did gobble her up and enjoyed every minute of doing it. Before he left her with that psychic imprint they had to avoid.

"I want you, Becca," he said. "But there are reasons I can't have you, a lot of reasons. The least of which being that if we were intimate, you'd carry the tracking residue."

She drew a shaky breath and let it out, that full bottom lip of hers that he so flipping adored, quivering. "Yeah, well, I can't trust you either," she said, clearly assuming that was what he meant.

"But you want to."

Reluctantly, she admitted, "Yes, I want to."

He arched a brow. "And?"

Confusion touched her. "And what?"

"And you want *me*."

Her eyes went wide. "You want me to say I want you?"

He nodded. "That's right. I admitted I want you. We might not have trust, but we might as well be honest with each other."

She shook her head as if clearing cobwebs. "You do realize that statement made absolutely no sense. Trust and honesty are the same. And based on that reality, I could say I want you and be lying."

"Fair enough," he said. "So humor me. Say it." He didn't know why he wanted to hear it so badly. He saw it in her eyes, and he'd tasted it in her kisses.

"Okay then," she said. "Yes. I want you."

His lips lifted in a smile at her confession. He had no idea why making her admit that out loud meant so much to him, why he'd burned for it so badly, but he had, and he did, and he liked it a lot. One hell of a lot.

She shook her head. "I could be lying."

His smile widened. "But we both know you aren't."

Adam and Dorian materialized in two silent strands of wind inside the parking garage where Tad awaited their arrival.

"Well?" Adam demanded of Tad. "Where is she?"

"Her tracking device was removed," he said. "But she couldn't have gotten too far. We have men all over the garage looking for her."

Adam leveled Tad in a stare. "This happened how?"

"We had her at the motel," Tad assured him. "But your brother showed up. He put himself in the line of fire to protect the woman, knowing we would not kill him."

Dorian tilted his head to the side. "My uncle is very strategic, isn't he, Father?"

"He is," Adam agree. "A talent we will appreciate more when he has joined our cause."

"I wish to meet him," Dorian said.

"You will," Adam assured him. "Just as the world will soon meet you."

Dorian tilted his head, staring into space a moment. "The woman is no longer in the garage," he said, clearly using his ability to read the recent events that had occurred within an energy source.

"Can you find her, Dorian?" Adam asked, never underestimating his son. Though the woman had not been marked with a psychic imprint that a Tracker would need to follow a target, his son was far more advanced.

Dorian stared blankly into space as he often did when accessing new skills. "No," he finally said. "But they removed the tracking device here in this garage. It left a certain energy residue." He tilted his head again. "Interesting. I can reach the part of her mind that feels pain, Father. Would you like me to make her feel pain for betraying you?"

"You can make her feel pain from a distance?"

"Yes," he said. "But it must be from this location, where that energy is strongest."

Adam was pleased. "Could you cause her enough pain to kill her?"

A slow smile slid onto Dorian's lips. "I do believe I would enjoy trying."

Chapter 17

BECCA FOLLOWED STERLING INTO WHAT LOOKED TO be a typical sterile, well-equipped lab. She scanned the room—several tables, microscopes, and the appropriate high-tech machinery.

She cut Sterling a sideways look, intent on asking him a question that she'd completely forgotten. He was leaning lazily on the doorjamb, his T-shirt torn from where he'd made her bandage, rippling abdominals exposed. Her mouth watered as she thought of touching all that taut hard muscle, and she dragged her gaze from the deliciously tempting sight to find him watching her, heat in his eyes. As if he knew what she was thinking.

She watched him too, unwilling to shy away. She'd had a few lessons lately on embracing life while she had it, and she wasn't going to waste it being embarrassed. And Sterling was just plain hot—indeed, she thought once again—a man her fantasies were made of. Tall and blond, hard in all the right places, he was a stud muffin like she'd never seen the likes of. She did want him. What woman in her right mind would not?

That he wanted her only made her hotter. That he didn't take her when he knew darn well she couldn't resist him… that only made her want him more. His concern about creating a psychic imprint built trust, no matter how much she hated the restriction—if a girl had to die, let her die in pleasure.

Becca delicately cleared her throat. "I assume you evacuated any staff for fear I might cause them injury?"

"We don't keep a scientific staff here anyway," he said, neither denying nor confirming her accusation.

"Point for you for being good at avoiding questions," she said, making sure he knew she wasn't accepting that answer.

Becca moved to stand beside a cabinet of supplies and removed two items she needed to draw her own blood. "I assume your people want my blood." She sat down on a stool. "So do I. How about drawing it for me? I can do it, but I've never been fond of sticking myself."

"What makes you think I know how?"

She laughed. "Aside from the exceptional T-shirt tourniquet you made? I know the GTECHs are all ex-Special Forces. That means trained medics. Not to mention you sliced my arm up like a pro."

He pushed off the door and sauntered to stand in front of her. Her gaze slid over those long legs hugged by snug denim, but not before she grabbed one more inspection of those abs.

"What I did to your arm had nothing to do with medic training and everything to do with necessity," Sterling said, reaching for the needle and syringe. "I had to get that device out of your arm before the Zs found us."

"Zs?" she asked. "Right. Got it. Zs are the Zodius." She wrapped a rubber band around her upper arm. The good one. "As for my arm, as painful as slicing it open was, I'm glad you did it. You were protecting me. So far, if I have to be a prisoner—I'd rather be one here."

He stilled, the syringe midway to her arm, his gaze snagging hers. "We don't want to keep you a prisoner,

Becca," he said, standing close. So close. Too close. Not close enough. "It's about keeping everyone safe, you included."

"I know." She studied him—the square jaw, high cheekbones, full lips. He was a beautiful man. Before she could stop herself, she reached up and touched his cheek. He didn't move, but she could feel the instant awareness in him, see the darkening of his pupils, feel the heat radiate off his body. But he didn't move, didn't reach for her, or stop her.

She allowed her fingers to glide over the stubble forming on his jaw, her gaze following the movement, amazed at how sensual the contrast between her softness and the roughness of those whiskers aroused her. Someone had once told her that when you tasted death, life found new texture. Perhaps it was true.

She swallowed hard. Death. It always had a way of shaking her right back into reality. Becca pulled her hand back and forced herself to remember what they'd been talking about. She was a prisoner. And he was her captor but claimed he didn't want to be. He had no choice. She got that. Really she even understood it.

"You don't have a choice but to keep me prisoner," she said. "I put everyone to sleep, and even if I didn't, Adam is coming for me. So either way, I'm confined. I get that." She held out her arm for the blood draw. "Let's get this over with. I'm ready to have at least an hour or two without needles and knives. Draw five vials," she told him. "But I get three. Your people can have two. And before you argue, it's my blood. I decide."

He hesitated an instant, as if he wanted to say more, but then didn't. He did what she'd said and drew her blood. Becca rather liked ordering Sterling around and having him actually comply. That he did—well—that was another point for trust. No one inside Zodius would have let her order them around. "My people can be your people too," he said, finishing the task, and then pressed a piece of cotton on her arm. He folded it at the elbow and held it there.

"I need to know the Renegades are really who you say they are before that can happen," she said. "I need proof." He stared at her, his eyes piercing hers, delving so deeply she felt they were touching her soul. All the while his thumb stroked a lazy pattern over her wrist. Warmth spread across her skin, up her arm, over her neck.

"You'll get your proof," he said finally, as if whatever he was looking for in that inspection he'd found. "Let me check out my handiwork." He shifted his attention to her shoulder. "See if I need to throw a couple stitches in that arm for you."

"You don't," she assured him, but let him unwrap her arm and study the wound. "It's almost healed, and the pain is all but gone. It must not have been as deep as it felt."

He tossed the T-shirt in the trash, and she glanced at her arm, confirming the wound had already begun to close.

"If ICE heals you this quickly," he said thoughtfully, "then surely Adam was right when he said ICE would cure your cancer."

Adam had told her the same thing, but she'd not dared to really believe it. She wet her suddenly dry lips and cursed the hope that flared inside her. She didn't want another crushing blow, like the failure in Germany. "It doesn't really matter unless we find an antidote for withdrawal. Until then, I'm dead when we run out of ICE."

He reached for her, and she held up a hand. "Don't. Don't feel sorry for me. God, please don't feel sorry for me." She laughed without humor. "That's *exactly everything* I don't want from you or anyone else."

He stared at her, his gaze probing, seeing too much. "You don't have to go through this alone anymore. You have me. And you have the Renegades, who are my family, who can be yours."

Not family. The people obligated to care for her, like the families at the cancer treatment center. The idea of that just destroyed her. "I don't want to talk about this."

"Becca," he said softly, trying to reach for her again.

She scooted off the lab stool and backed away from him, thankful he didn't pursue, yet upset that he didn't. "We need to find a common denominator in the ICE deaths. A variation in the ICE formula. A blood type. Sickle cell. Arthritis. It could be anything. It could be they are all smokers. Or they're diabetic. I need to run tests, and I need the records you have so I can get to work. Bodies would be better."

"We have the records and—" He motioned to the sink in the corner when she surveyed the blood staining her skin, remnants of the earlier incident with the tracking device. "You can clean up your arm there and bandage it."

"Thanks," she said and headed in that direction.

He kept talking behind her as she washed up. "We've

tried to get the bodies, but the government won't give them to us."

Becca dried her arm and then grabbed a lab coat hanging on a coatrack, eager to get to work. "I don't understand. Why give you the records and not the bodies?"

"They have their scientists working on the issue. We have ours. We get what they deem relevant." He walked to a desk and powered up a laptop. "As I said, we have a tenuous relationship with them at best. We all want Adam to be brought to justice and humanity to be safe. Unfortunately, the government believes safety means all GTECHs, us included, have to be controlled or eradicated. And since they've tried control and it didn't work, they're leaning toward eradication."

She shook her head. "Powell really created a mess with the GTECH program, didn't he?"

"Welcome to a little slice of my life." He motioned to the computer. "Let's get you online with our scientific team."

Becca closed the distance between them as he dialed the phone and set up the teleconference. Not long after, he offered her the chair in front of the desk and pulled another up to sit beside her. His finger hovered over a computer key.

"Ready to meet your new co-workers?"

She nodded, surprised at how ready she really was. For the first time since she'd found out about Adam and his evil plans, she might just have a chance to do something about it. To stop him.

Sterling punched a key. A pretty blonde woman appeared on the screen wearing a lab coat, her hair pulled back in a conservative knot.

"Becca," Sterling said, a hand motioning to the screen. "Meet Kelly Patterson, director of science and medicine for the Renegades, and a royal pain in my ass. Nevertheless, damn good at what she does."

"The only *ass* is Sterling," Kelly retorted, but there was no mistaking the tease in her voice. "But I'm sure you're figuring that out by now."

Becca barely contained a smile as she noted Sterling's grimace followed by a low grumble.

"Am I late?" came another female voice a second before yet another pretty blonde appeared on the screen. Her hair floated in silky strands around her shoulders as she murmured something to Kelly.

Sterling leaned closer to Becca. "That's Cassandra," he said, his voice low, for her ears only. "She's the Lifebond of Michael. The king of dark and cranky."

"I heard that, Sterling," Cassandra said, pursing her lips at the camera. "Don't be an asshole. Michael isn't cranky. He's protective and cautious. He's also *your friend*. And he's waiting for you in the east wing of Neon with some of Becca's personal items."

Amazingly, Becca found herself laughing at Sterling's exchanges with Cassandra, and it felt good. These people were friends who knew and loved each other, nothing like the stiff, cold existences inside Zodius. And the lead scientific director was a woman. Another something Adam would never have allowed.

Cassandra eyed Becca. "I wanted to let you to know that I went inside your house to pick up your things. I felt a bit like an intruder, but I tried to make up for it by picking out the things that seemed the most important to you."

Even though Sterling had told her he was having some of her things picked up, she'd never written out her list. "Thank you," Becca said quickly. "I don't mind at all. I can't wait to have some of my own things."

"Anything I can do for you," Cassandra said. "I'm here. I'll leave you to Kelly for now."

Sterling grabbed the tubes of blood and touched the small of her back. A gesture that spoke of a growing intimacy between them, that felt, well, right. It felt good. Confusing, but good. "I'll do the same," he said, before holding up the vials to the camera. "Michael will have Becca's blood samples to bring back with him." He eyed Becca. "Back in a bit."

He waited for her acknowledgement, protective, as if he didn't want to leave unless she said she'd be okay. It felt as nice as that hand on her back. Wonderful, in fact, and she dared to indulge in enjoying the feeling, if only this once. She didn't remember the last time anyone had protected her, not since she'd lost her father and brother over a decade before. She nodded. "I'll be here." And for the first time in a long time, Becca realized she felt safe.

———

Some time later Becca found herself in deep conversation with Kelly, during which Kelly not only shared the history of the Renegades, she set up a secure email and sent Becca proof the Renegades were working for the government. Finally satisfied she was playing on the right team and liking Kelly quite a lot, it was time for Becca to vocalize her theories and how she thought she could help in the lab.

"I'm going to email you some data on the GTECHs,"

Kelly said. "You can compare them to the ICE users. Some of the Zodius soldiers have what we call the X2 gene. It developed around fifteen months after conversion, and to put this in perspective, the lab rats that developed X2 all killed each other." She held up a hand. "And let me assure you Sterling doesn't have the X2 gene. None of the Renegades do... well... except Michael, but he's different in all kinds of ways. I'll send you his file as well. But please don't tell him. He won't like it."

This was not good news to Becca. "My biggest fear has been what happens with long term use, rather than the few who have died in the midst of thousands. Not that I'm dismissing that problem, but we're dealing with an alien component, and we have no idea how it will react or evolve in our environment."

"Believe me, I know," Kelly said. "Which brings us to the question I've been beating my head against the wall about. How do we keep that from happening? The ticking clock on that question is killing me." She visibly cringed. "Oh God, Becca. I'm sorry. That was insensitive of me. You know, I'm pretty excited about what I see in your blood work. I don't know if Sterling told you my thoughts on this, but if you really are cured then think what this could mean for cancer research when all of this is over."

Becca absorbed that and found herself smiling inside, thinking of all the times she'd dared to ask, "Why me?" She realized it might just come back to here and now. She might be able to help people beyond just the immediate trouble with Adam. Even Adam, in an unintentional way, might be helping cancer patients. She opened her mouth to say as much, when a loud screeching sound ripped through her ears.

Becca grabbed her head. "Oh God! What is that? Make it stop!"

"Becca," Kelly said. "I don't hear anything. Tell me what's going on."

"How can you not hear it?" Becca screamed. The sound ripped through her, seemed to carve out her insides, and rip a path along her nerve endings.

"Caleb!" Kelly shouted. "Caleb, help! Get Sterling back into that room!" Then, "Hang in there, Becca. Sterling is coming. He'll be right there."

Becca fell to the ground. "It's too late," she whispered. Death had her attention again. It kept calling her name. And death, she realized, as she felt *him* in her mind, was named Dorian.

Chapter 18

STERLING COULD HEAR BECCA'S HIGH-PITCHED SCREAM even before he burst through the lab door, leaving Caleb and Michael in the hallway, adrenaline pumping through his body like white lightning. He felt that scream right to his soul, the terror in it, the pain, and the desperation to survive. Becca thought she was dying. That someone was trying to kill her. How he knew that, he didn't know. But he knew.

The lab came into view in a whirlwind of flying debris that Sterling fought his way through as he spotted the computer and the overturned chair. Relief washed over him as he found Becca huddled beneath the desk, knees pulled to her chest, but no intruder.

He rushed to her, glass crunching beneath his boots as he squatted down in front of her. "Becca," he said, his hands going to her knees. "Becca, sweetheart."

She screamed again, clutching onto his arms, and then kicking and screaming. Hysterical… fighting for her life… scratching at him… wild. He backed away long enough to see her eyes. Wide… blank… as if she were blind.

"Get her out from under the desk," Caleb said from behind.

Sterling looked over his shoulder. "Are you nuts? We have no idea what she might do to you."

Caleb appeared above him. "I have mental shields

other GTECHs do not. So does Becca. I can feel her
energy, and if she doesn't start using them and using
them now, she's going to die. She's being attacked. So
get her out now."

Sterling didn't need to hear another word. He reached
for Becca, curling his fingers around her arm, and pulled
her kicking and screaming from under that desk.

"Hold her still," Caleb ordered.

"Right," Sterling muttered, sitting down on the floor
and positioning Becca in front of him, pinning her arms
to her sides from behind, her back against his chest.
Still, she kicked wildly. "That's as good as it gets."

Caleb kneeled at their side, out of the range of her
kicks, and pressed his hand to her forehead.

She let out one sharp final scream and then gasped.
Her head fell forward. "What just happened?" she panted.

Sterling had no idea what Caleb had just done, but he
was thankful. Quickly he turned Becca in his arms, his
hand sliding over her hair. "You're okay."

"Sterling," she whispered a moment before her eyes
went wide on Caleb.

"She won't be," Caleb said. "Not if we don't act now."

"Adam!" Becca yelled, trying to pull back, shifting
to her knees.

"Caleb," Sterling and Caleb said at the same moment.

"Becca, listen to me," Caleb insisted. "Someone attacked your mind. They're going to attack you again.
You have the ability to shield yourself. I need you to
focus with me, and let me teach you how."

"I can't," she said. "I don't have any idea how to
do that."

"You do," Caleb insisted. "Relax, and let it happen."

He eyed Sterling with a keen glance, before returning his attention to Becca. "Do you trust Sterling?"

"I…" She cut a look at Sterling. "I…"

"Good," Caleb said, as if she'd admitted trust. "Let him help you. Let him be your anchor. Find him in your mind first, and when you start to lose focus, you go back to him."

Sterling had never been anyone's anchor and never thought he wanted to be. Nor was he sure he was made of the right stuff for such a task. But he'd do just about anything for Becca. He took her hand. "I'm all yours, sweetheart," he teased. "Take me when you're ready."

She laughed. It didn't matter that there were tears welling in her eyes. That sound was like honey on a hot sunny day. Sticky sweet in all the right ways.

"You'd like that, wouldn't you?" she challenged, her voice hoarse, but not without a playful twang.

"I would," he said, shifting his weight to one knee. "So do it."

Caleb reached out and pressed his palms to both their forearms. "Close your eyes."

To Sterling's shock, warmth spread up his arm, energy almost like electricity, moving through him into Becca… or maybe through her into him. "Find his mind, Becca," Caleb ordered.

Seconds ticked by. That warm energy flowed through him, getting hotter, more pronounced, until Becca's mind was there. Sterling could feel Becca in his head.

He wouldn't be able to explain that feeling to anyone if he had to; he didn't understand it himself. But it rocked his world, the intimacy of her inside his head. For just a moment, the idea that she might read his past, know his weaknesses, almost made him jerk away. Caleb's hand tightened on Sterling's arm, as if he knew what Sterling was feeling, what he was about to do.

Then, suddenly, someone else was there, in his head—no, in Becca's head. She gasped at the malevolent touch. In his mind's eyes, Sterling saw a boy—young, strong, evil. Then a flash of himself cutting open Becca's arm. Pain wrenched through him as he felt what Becca had felt when he'd cut her shoulder.

"Find Sterling in your mind, Becca," Caleb said. "Find that anchor, and center yourself in that place. Then fight back. Seal out the pain. Block the intruder. This is your mind. Not his. Get angry. Fight!"

"Fight," Sterling whispered, out loud, or maybe it was in his mind, in hers. He didn't know exactly, but he felt Becca shaking. Sterling was shaking with her. That energy that had drawn him closer to her was pushing him away. He could almost feel the pressure on his chest like a hand.

"Don't let him win, Sterling," Caleb said softly. "Be her anchor. Reach for her mind."

Anchor. He was supposed to be her anchor. Sterling tightened his grip on Becca's hands as Caleb had on his arm. "Becca," he said. "I'm here."

Her fingers curled around his, and he could hear her breathing rasping out faster… more shallow. Long moments passed. She pressed hard against his mind, pulled him toward her, and wrapped him inside out with her presence. The pain faded in a sudden rush of awareness.

"He's gone," Becca said, her shoulders slumping. "He's gone! I did it!"

The energy he'd felt spiking along her nerve endings

faded instantly. Sterling let out a sigh of relief, and it was all he could do not to pull her into his arms. Had he ever felt such protectiveness for a woman? For anyone? Her grip on his hand tightened, her eyes meeting his, awareness between them.

There was something as intimate as sex in that connection they'd shared. Something beyond physical contact, a sense of knowing each other on a level no other person could. It was remarkable. On some level he knew her fears, her joys, her needs. And, he thought, with a hard swallow, she knew his. She knew things he'd never shared with anyone.

"Can you feel your shield in place, Becca?" Caleb asked. "Protecting your mind?"

"Yes," she said, and obviously struggled to pull her gaze from Sterling to Caleb. "I feel it."

"Keep it in place," he said. "Practice releasing that shield and then pulling it back into place. Use Sterling as that anchor if you need to, especially when you go to sleep. You have to feel that shield before you allow yourself to rest."

Sleep. Bed. Him with Becca. Sterling mentally shook away that image. "If she lets down the shield, then can't her attacker come back after her again?"

"I can't be certain, but I don't think so," Caleb said, releasing their arms and leaning back on one foot, settling his arm on his knee. "Emotions create a type of energy wired to the brain. That energy leaves a residue that lasts for a short period of time. Once it's gone, it's gone. He'd need another strand of her energy to attach to. And the good news here is that Becca, in essence, has the same ability to shield herself as a full GTECH, minus the help of a Lifebond." His gaze touched Sterling's. "Not even a Tracker could find her should she ever be marked." Sterling inhaled. Caleb was telling him that he could be intimate with Becca without consequence.

"Is this because I'm using ICE?" Becca asked.

"I don't think so," Caleb replied. "After the connection we shared, my feeling is that this has to do with a natural ability you possessed without awareness before using the ICE. Or maybe before combining the cancer treatments and the ICE. I don't think your abilities can be recreated in other people without the same dormant skills." He shrugged. "The whys, whens, hows, and mights—those are questions for you scientists."

"This is all so… surreal," she murmured, tilting her head to study Caleb. "You look so much like Adam, but yet, you are nothing like him."

"I consider that a compliment," he said in what was meant to be a nonchalant tone, but failed. Sterling knew Caleb's secret fear of becoming like Adam one day.

"You don't communicate with wolves?"

Caleb shook his head. "No. That is my brother's ability." His tone darkened. "Who was he, Becca? That boy who attacked your mind?"

"Dorian," she whispered, then firmed her voice. "It was Dorian. I hate even saying his name. He's Adam's son."

Sterling's brows shot up. "Come again? Adam's son is six months old. How would he attack your mind?"

Grimly Becca explained, "Dorian is only six months old, but he's aging at the rate of two years per month. He's the DNA source for ICE. And let me tell you, he is the epitome of evil, beyond Adam, and he's getting stronger and more dangerous every day."

"Holy mother of Jesus," Sterling murmured, his eyes meeting Caleb's troubled stare.

"You can say that again," Caleb agreed. "I felt that boy's energy. If he's this powerful at six months old, what will he be at a year? Or five?"

"He's pure evil," Becca repeated. "I can't stress that enough. He'll kill just to watch someone die, because it entertains him. I saw him in action. And that's the kind of evil these Clanners are ingesting daily." Her lips thinned as her face paled. "That I'm ingesting every day."

The parking garage was a scurry of activity as police tried to get to the car that had been reported as stolen. Zodius soldiers held them at bay.

Meanwhile, in the exact spot that stolen vehicle had once been, the spot where Rebecca Burns had experienced the pain Dorian was now using to connect and hopefully kill her, Adam watched as Dorian's eyes rolled from the back of his head and came into focus. "I have met my uncle, Father," Dorian said. "You were right. He is very powerful. He has defeated me. He has saved the woman's life."

Adam inhaled a bittersweet breath. Caleb's abilities, his strengths, however cumbersome at present, would be immensely useful when Caleb assumed his role as a leader by his side.

"He does not wish to join us, Father," Dorian said. "But I know that you wish him to. He is concerned for the humans. Why not kill some of them? He will join us to save them."

"Because killing humans scares the other humans,"

Adam said. "Until we control enough of them, we must cater to their many sensitivities. We do not want to scare people away from using ICE before its use becomes a national epidemic of sorts. Which will be soon." He was already hard at work planning expanded distribution.

Adam redirected to matters most urgent. "Do you know where the woman is, Dorian?"

"I know only what I saw in her mind," Dorian said. "She is still in the city—not far, I think. In a lab with the one they call Sterling. He was in her mind, too. Sterling is fond of the woman. She could be used against him if need be."

Adam smiled at the way Dorian instinctively found weakness and turned it into a strategy. He snapped his fingers at Tad who stood nearby. "Find Sterling. Follow him. He will lead you to Rebecca Burns."

She'd introduced Caleb to Dorian, the source of ICE. That screwed up his plans to use Dorian as a secret weapon when he'd reached his prime. Adam balled his fists at his side. He should have killed that bitch himself when he had the chance.

Adam cut Dorian a look. "Give the humans something to think about besides us."

Dorian's eyes filled with a mixture of menace and excitement. "Thank you, Father," he said. "I so enjoy playing with the humans."

A moment later, flames shot from a nearby car, then another. And another. Adam laughed as voices lifted in the air, people scrambling to safety.

Adam and his entourage faded into the strands of wind whistling through the screams.

Chapter 19

BECCA'S BLOOD WORK WAS ALMOST NORMAL, AS IN barely a trace of anything pointing to cancer. It was a miracle, but Becca didn't celebrate. Kelly and Sterling seemed to understand she needed to set herself aside, including the threat Dorian represented, and focus on the big picture.

Six hours later, Becca punched a computer button to end a session with Kelly and turned away from the lab table to run smack into Sterling.

His hands settled quickly to her arms, steadying her. Heat curled in her stomach, and she had the most exasperating desire to push to her toes and run her fingers through his spiky blond hair.

"You're hovering again," she reprimanded.

"I was bringing your dose of ICE," he said and then grinned. "But yeah, hovering too."

"My mental shield is up," she said. "I can feel it. I'm okay. I swear. You don't have to stand over me and wait for Dorian to attack."

"I'd rather be safe than sorry," he said. "I'm staying close by your side. So just deal with it." His hands slid away from her arms, leaving her cold and eager to have him touch her again. He held out the vial of ICE. "I don't want you going into withdrawal."

Reluctantly, she reached for it, but closed her hand around his instead, as she suddenly remembered something she'd learned while in his head. "This isn't about me surviving this addiction," she said, needing him to know that for some reason. "I know you're worried about that, maybe even worried that I will have second thoughts about destroying ICE. But I wouldn't have told you about Dorian if that were the case. I know you might think I'll make decisions simply to keep myself alive, or maybe others around you will, but I won't. This is bigger than me."

He reached up and brushed hair from her eyes, gently, protectively. "Then I guess *I'll* have to keep you alive."

She wanted to melt into him at that moment, wanted to believe he could protect her, save her. But he couldn't. Why pretend otherwise? She slipped the vial of ICE from his hand and turned away from him. Ashamed by such an addiction, she didn't want him to see her take it.

Becca downed the ICE and set the vial on the lab table, the freezing sensation sending her hand to her throat. Suddenly, Sterling's hands were on her shoulders, and he was turning her toward him. Before she knew his intention, his fingers laced through her hair, and he was kissing her, his mouth hot, demanding. His body—strong, warm—pressed close to her.

With only a moment of hesitation, Becca leaned into him, wrapped her arms around his back, moaned as his tongue slid along hers, caressed and teased, hungry. He tasted like apple pie, and if she hadn't been so hot, she might have laughed at the fact that he'd been eating apple pie.

But she was hot, and for the first time since meeting Sterling, maybe for the first time ever, she kissed him— kissed a man—with complete, utter abandon. Kissed him like there might not be a tomorrow, like a woman who knew what she wanted, and what she wanted was him.

Long seconds later, Sterling tore his mouth from hers, staring down at her with heavy-lidded bedroom eyes that made her want to kiss him all over again. "I thought you had reasons not to touch me," she challenged, hardly recognizing the gravelly, desire-laden words as her own.

"I've never done real well at doing what I'm supposed to do," he said, his thumb caressing her cheek, the sensation somehow making her breasts heavy, her nipples tight and achy. Becca had never felt so ready to lose herself in a man. But then, she'd never been in a position where she had nothing to lose but herself. It was liberating in ways she was ready to embrace.

She drew a breath and willed away the flutters in her stomach, nerves that came from years of suppressing her desires. "I've always done exactly what's expected of me," she confessed. "I don't want to this time. I don't want you to either."

He lowered his head, his breath warm as it caressed her skin. The promise of his kiss brought her to her toes when suddenly he drew back. "Once we do this," he said, a deep, whiskey-rich quality to his voice, "we can't undo it."

He'd said something similar at her house, when he was about to tell her about the GTECHs. She didn't shy away then, and she wasn't going to now. And apparently neither was he, because despite his warning, he didn't move away, didn't put distance between them, and she could feel the thick ridge of his erection. Courage formed with those realizations. Becca flattened her hand on his chest, splayed her fingers, absorbed the feel of muscle flexing beneath her palm. She wanted to touch him, to feel him close, to forget everything else for just a little while.

"I don't want to die never having known you, Sterling."

Torment sliced through his expression. "Becca—"

She pressed her fingertips to his lips. "Don't," she said, easing her fingers away, letting them slide over his jaw. "Every day of our lives could be the last for every one of us. I'm simply living with that in mind. I regret not doing so my entire life." She'd regretted a lot since finding out she had cancer, and regret was something she could do without. "I want you, Sterling."

He stared down at her, and she'd never been looked at quite like that, with so much simmering heat. He really did look like he wanted to gobble her up as he'd once suggested, and thankfully, he apparently decided he would. He kissed her, more than kissed her. It was a claiming, a taking. A possessing. His lips pressed to hers, first soft then firm, his tongue pressing past her teeth, warm with demand, hungry… devouring her. And she wanted to be devoured, wanted to devour him right back. Wanted to do every wanton, sensual deed she'd ever dared to consider, ever dared to wonder about, and always allowed inhibitions to destroy.

Becca went to her toes, reaching for him, silently begging for more as she molded her body to his. Tugging his T-shirt free of his pants, she pressed her hands beneath. Warm skin greeted her, and she moaned into his mouth. She craved more of that skin next to her.

She shoved the shirt upward. "Take it off," she panted into his mouth.

Instead, she found herself lifted onto the lab table, her legs spread wide, Sterling between them. And still he kissed her, softly, deeply, then wildly, trailing his lips over her jaw, near her ear, down her neck. He shoved aside her lab coat, strong hands skimming her rib cage and then caressing the curves of her breasts.

Feeling bold in her need, Becca's hands were touching him anywhere she could, everywhere she could reach. When she finally managed to press her palm over the front of his crotch and trace the ridge of his erection, he moaned and pulled back.

"Are you sure about this?" he asked, his voice husky with desire. And that desire only served to make Becca hotter.

She caressed the hard length of him and found herself smiling. "Are you sure about this?"

He half-growled, half-moaned and kissed her again, long strokes of his tongue promising this was going to be the best sex of her life, and she was ready.

"Not here," he whispered against her lips. "In bed." He pulled back to look at her. "*My bed*. I want you in my bed."

Something about the possessive caveman way he made that declaration had her darn near trembling with need. "Take me there," she said, and almost laughed at the pun. He lifted her from the table and took her hand, leading her to the door when his cell phone rang. A soft curse slid past his lips as he fished it out of his pocket—a different phone than she'd seen him use in the past.

"I have to take this," he said, leaning against the door and pulling her close as he answered, as if he couldn't stand the idea of letting her go. She loved that feeling, and she curled into him, her hand on his chest... her lips on his neck.

Becca heard the muffled sound of a male voice before Sterling tensed. She leaned back, noting the instant strain etched in his face.

"What's the address?" he asked, then a few seconds later, "I'll be there in five minutes."

He snapped the phone shut and surprised her by pulling her close and kissing her. "That's in case you decide you don't want me to kiss you anymore when I get back." He set her away from him and charged toward the cabinet, removing supplies.

Like that could happen. "Back from where? What's happening?"

"That was the Vegas PD, or rather, my informant," he said, grabbing an army backpack from the coatrack and filling it with the supplies.

"You have an informant in the Vegas PD?"

"Young guy with a sick mom to take care of," he said. "I pay him. He helps me save the world. It works for us." He shoved the bag over his shoulder. "We have another potential ICE fatality. We're struggling with the government's incomplete medical records. I'm going to do my best to bring back the body. At the very least get blood samples. But I have to move now. The military has alerts set up with emergency networks for anything that resembles an ICE reaction. It won't take long for them to seize control of the patient." He started toward the door.

Becca followed. "I'm going with you."

He shook his head. "Oh no," he said, his tone uncompromising. "You aren't going. It's too dangerous. Adam's after you. You know this."

"There are things I might notice about the patient that

you won't," she argued. "We don't have much time to figure out this puzzle, Sterling. I have to be there. I have to use this opportunity to figure out what we're missing."

"Even if I would consider it and I won't, I have to wind-walk to get there before the military."

Desperation rose in her. This could be important. Critical. Their only hope. "Can't you transport me?"

"Transporting humans comes with the risk of death."

Urgently, she made her case. "I'm not like all humans. I'm not even like all ICE users. We've proven that. We can't risk missing something. You have to take me. I'll be okay."

"You don't know that."

"You don't know I won't. One life, my life, versus the country. You know there's no choice here. I need to go with you. We're wasting time debating." She grabbed his arm. "Let's go." He hesitated and she added, "I'm going to die anyway. I get to choose how. And I choose to do it saving lives."

He held his footing, cursed, and ran a hand through his hair. "I must be insane for considering this."

That was as close to a yes as she was going to get, and Becca acted on it. She rushed to the cabinet and grabbed some extra supplies before hurrying back to Sterling and handing them to him. "Put those in your bag."

He gave her a brooding stare. "I swear," he grumbled, "I've never known a woman who pulled my strings the way you do."

Thinking about what Caleb had said about his brother, she tilted her chin upward and repeated his words. "I take that as a compliment."

Sterling took her hand and pulled her with him. A

smile touched her lips at his resignation. She was about to wind-walk, and she was excited about it, not one bit scared. Seemed these days she was dying to live. Or maybe living to die. Either way—she was ready to get that sample.

Less than a minute later, invisible strands of wind slipped inside Neon as the steel security doors opened. Sterling pulled Becca close, struggling for several seconds over his decision to take her with him. He might not often do the expected, but he wasn't one for doing the stupid either. Taking Becca with him was somewhere in the middle of those two things, probably leaning toward stupid. But he wasn't exactly big on time for debate right now. This opportunity would come and go while he tied his shoe and kicked the sand, if he let it.

"I'll be fine," Becca said, touching his cheek, as if reading his hesitation, or maybe his thoughts. "Let's just go before we lose this patient."

Incredible. Unfreaking believable, in fact. Becca didn't seem the least bit scared. Didn't seem to have the concept that wind-walking could be deadly to a human. Sometime between the cancer and this hell with Adam, she'd developed an unnatural tolerance to fear.

Before he could talk himself out of it, Sterling grabbed a hold of Becca and a little faith along with her—seemed he was reaching for that more and more lately. He hit the button to seal the doors, and then faded into the wind.

Chapter 20

STERLING AND BECCA MATERIALIZED IN A NARROW alley to the right of the Magnolia Resort.

Urgently, Sterling inspected Becca, his hands framing her face. "Are you okay?"

She blinked and refocused. "Yes. I'm fine." Her eyes lit, little wisps of raven hair fluttering over his fingers, scenting the air with fresh, sweet female. "That was so absolutely amazing." She glanced around. "Where are we?"

"We never materialize out in the open," he said, grabbing her hand, on the move toward the end of the alley now that he knew she was safe. Pausing at the corner, he said, "You're my new assistant. Everyone in this town knows me as a 'for hire' bounty hunter, whatever brings in cash. You're in the field to learn the ropes. End of story—say no more." He didn't wait for a response. They were on a ticking clock here.

Sterling led her into the open and immediately spotted the EMS truck parked at the service door of Magnolia Resort. Marcus's resort. Marcus was sure to have questions about Sterling showing up right when an ICE Clanner crashed inside his club. But hell, Sterling's life had been one long series of difficult questions. He could handle a couple dozen more. Confrontation was the name of the game. He played it well.

"Score one for Eddie again," Sterling whispered as they walked toward the truck.

"Eddie?" Becca queried.

Sterling motioned to the plainclothes cop striding in their direction, the one who looked like the type of guy women called a "Teddy Bear"—young, with a buzz cut, and a husky build. "Eddie's the informant I told you about."

"It took you long enough," Eddie said, meeting them just past the scurry of curious bystanders. "They're wheeling the dude this way now, and he doesn't look good." He glanced at Becca. "Hi." Then back at Sterling. "Attending a death-by-ICE ritual isn't exactly what I'd call good date strategy, Ster."

Sterling grimaced with hidden amusement. Eddie was a funny guy when he wanted to be. "She's my assistant." Getting to the point, he said. "What do you know about the user?"

"Twenty-seven," he said. "A dealer—as in cards, not ICE, though he could be both. Don't know much yet. He's worked for the casino for a year, and for your information man, those two guys you called me about— the Clanners you wanted me to track by their driver's licenses—they haven't been home since you called me, as in MIA. But interesting detail—they worked at one of Magnolia's sister properties. Could be a connection. I'll follow up. Right now, you don't have time for trivial pursuit. The EMS guys already radioed the hospital. I wouldn't be surprised if the army showed up any minute now. If you have any hope of asking this guy questions, you'd better find a way inside that ambulance, and do it now."

"Wait," Becca said. "He's alive? I thought he was dead."

"Barely hanging on," Eddie said and dug in his pocket

to remove a small brown bag. "Vials of ICE, and now you owe me big."

Sterling and Becca shared a relieved look.

"That look says you owe me even bigger," Eddie added. "And on that note, I'm getting lost. I don't want to be seen with you. Good luck. Sterling's a royal pain in the ass."

Becca glanced at Sterling, her amber eyes twinkling. "You have a way of bringing out the love in people."

"It's a gift," he said, as Eddie disappeared into the crowd.

The EMS workers wheeled the stretcher out of the building at a fast run. "Show's on, sweetheart. Here's the plan. Rush toward the EMS guys, and throw some frantic emotions out there when you do. Tell them the Clanner is your brother, and make sure you get in that ambulance with him." He shrugged off his backpack and gave it to her. "I'll go to the front seat and make sure they don't stop you from drawing blood and doing your examination. Once it's done, we wind-walk the hell out of here. Anything goes wrong, same plan. We wind-walk the hell out of here."

Becca nodded, her face flushed. The EMS people approached. She waited until just the right moment.

"That's my brother!" she yelled, and Sterling watched her do a number on the emergency crew. Sweet. She was good at the fake frantic stuff. He frowned. Okay. Not so sweet. A fizzle of unease rushed through him. He didn't want to consider Becca might be deceiving him, but she'd been a little too certain she could survive wind-walking... as if she knew. Every instinct he owned screamed he trust her. No, he realized. Becca was like him. She'd become immune to the possibility of death, a realization that tore at his gut. He didn't want that for her.

He shook off the thought as Becca jumped into the EMS truck. Sterling made his way to the passenger's side door. The minute the engine started, he yanked open the door and was inside.

"Hey!" barked the driver, a middle-aged man with dark hair sprinkled with gray.

Sterling pointed a Glock at him. "Hey, back at ya." He ripped the radio out of the dash, as he ordered, "Drive to the hospital so we can save this man's life."

The driver put the vehicle in gear and took them onto the road.

"What the hell is going on up there?" A male yelled from the back, a moment before a short, stocky man with a buzz cut appeared.

Sterling pointed a gun at him. "What's going on is you're going to allow the woman in the back to do whatever testing she needs to do. And you're going to help her. So go help." He raised his voice. "How you coming back there, Becca?"

"I need you back here!"

"Go help her," Sterling ordered, following the man to the back where he joined another paramedic directly across from Becca.

"He's dead," Becca said, her face pale, her hand on her stomach.

No sooner did she make that announcement than the truck came to a screeching halt. Everyone jerked forward and backward again. Curses flew—supplies along with them.

Sterling was in the front of the vehicle in a flash, and he spewed a few curses of his own when he saw what had caused them to stop. Army jeeps. Three of them. And what was in front would be in back.

He returned to the back and bent down next to Becca. "The minute the doors open, we're gone."

"I can't believe I'm saying this," she said, "but we need the body for our research team."

"The body!" one of the paramedics exclaimed. "You're going to steal the body?" He made a move for the back door.

Sterling aimed his Glock. "I like shooting guns," he said. "Give me an excuse to shoot this one." The man eased back to a sitting position about the time Sterling heard the front doors open.

"I can't take him and you," Sterling said, hating that he wasn't like the other wind-walkers in that moment, that he had limitations the others did not. "One at a time."

"Take him, and come back for me," she said. "We can't risk losing this body. We need it."

"Not a chance in hell," he said as the back doors flew open, and Sterling grabbed Becca.

They reappeared inside Neon, and he handed her the remote, saying, "I told you I'd make choices to keep you alive, and I meant it. Wait inside." He faded into the wind.

Sterling materialized inside that EMS vehicle to find himself staring at three machine guns—one held by a familiar face—Lieutenant Riker, the ICE task force leader he worked with often. They respected each other, but they were far from friends. Riker motioned to his soldiers to stand down the instant he saw Sterling and then stalked forward.

"What the fuck are you doing, Sterling?" He eyed the EMS techs. "Get out."

The men scrambled out of the vehicle as Sterling replied, "Same thing as you, jackass. Saving the world one dumb-ass at a time."

"News bulletin," Riker said. "This one died. You failed."

"He might still be alive if we had the medical data to let our team do their job," he said.

Riker leaned forward. "Your medical staff has an open invitation to join ours."

"To become yours, you mean," Sterling corrected. "And you know, as I do, that's not going to happen. You can't have it both ways. Use us for protection, and lurk around for the chance to stab us in the back."

"I'm a soldier just like you," Riker said. "Taking orders."

"Like I *was*," Sterling said. "The government doesn't own me anymore like they do you. What happens when they decide to inject the new and improved whatever-it-might-be into you, Riker? What happens when they turn *you* into the enemy?"

"I know what they did to you was messed up."

"Innocent lives are on the line, Riker. I need this body to try and protect them. And I'm taking it with, or without, your consent. In the long run, I'm a much better friend than I am an enemy."

Riker's steely gray eyes narrowed for several tension-filled seconds before he gave a sharp inclination of his head, then stepped backward and slammed the doors on the truck. Sterling and that dead body were gone before the doors ever closed.

———ᴧᴧᴧ———

Iceman sat in a corner booth of one of his favorite restaurants, several sets of stairs setting him on a pedestal, among only a few other seats. Nursing a glass of Lagavulin Scotch straight up—the only way to enjoy a premium malt—he savored the flavor as he did his growing success.

Sabrina sat next to him, curled by his side, smelling like tangerines. He didn't know why she smelled like that, but now that scent meant only one thing to him— lust. Translation: money, sex, satisfaction.

"The girls did good tonight," she said, and the wad of cash they'd collected proved it. She ran her hand over his chest, under his jacket. "See. Tad touching me hasn't impacted my performance. I know how to get my girls motivated. I'm going to make you lots of money, baby."

He cast her a sideways look and then scanned the restaurant. From where he sat, Iceman had a full visual of every corner and every seat inside the five-star, fine-dining facility.

There was no denying Sabrina got him hot and hard. Or maybe it was the way she performed, both in bed and with her girls that got him hard. Either way, he'd decided his next move.

He sipped his Scotch. "I've been considering your new bond with Tad," he said. "Perhaps it can be useful."

She lifted her Merlot to her mouth. "How so?" Her tongue slid over her bottom lip, intentionally seductive. She liked games.

Out of necessity, he had already shown her the

tapes of Rebecca Burns at the club. And they had to find this woman. That meant he needed his staff looking for her.

"Once we have the woman—this Rebecca Burns," he said, "the Zodius will not be able to touch us. We'll get rid of Tad, and anyone else who gives us trouble." He'd keep Rebecca Burns attached to his hip if need be, his own personal ICE-addicted bodyguard. And as much as he wanted to kill Tad, he had uses for him—like getting to the source to make ICE since his scientific team couldn't seem to recreate it.

A slow smile slid onto Sabrina's lips. "Tad fucked me," she said, "so now we fuck him."

He was going to fuck Tad all right and Adam with him. Iceman's gaze lifted to the doorway as JC sauntered toward the table, a façade of casual, betrayed by the hard set of his jaw, the stiffness of his neck, and the interruption of Iceman's private time.

JC took the stairs with a double-step and slid into the booth across from Iceman and Sabrina. "Another Clanner died," he said. "At the Magnolia Resort. He was a staff member."

Iceman ground his teeth. Now he knew why JC was so tense. They'd made the decision to infiltrate the resorts, to bring all staff on board for future distribution. They'd been cautious, starting one resort at a time. But the two Clanners from the warehouse were staff from Magnolia. Now the dealer.

"He used Eclipse last night," JC said. "It will be in his system." He lowered his voice. "Every Clanner who has died has used ICE Eclipse rather than a straight shooter of ICE."

Not a positive development, but it could be managed. "Continue with our plan."

"Sooner or later law enforcement will figure out the Eclipse boost is causing the fatalities that have nothing to do with withdrawal," JC said. "They'll go public. They'll tell people to stop using ICE or risk death."

"And we'll tell our Eclipsers they're safe," he said, "that it's the non-Eclipsers, the straight-up ICE users, who are dying."

"People are told drugs will kill them every day," Sabrina added. "They keep using."

"There you go," Iceman said. "Problem solved. Anything else?"

"Sterling showed up while the paramedics were at Magnolia," JC said. "With Rebecca Burns. They left in the EMS vehicle, and my sources tell me that body never made it to the hospital. She's helping the Renegades."

"Sterling has a stock of ICE," he said. "I'm sure of it. So she's helping her newest ICE supplier. I need that to become me."

"You mean Adam," came a male voice a second before Tad slid into the seat next to JC. "He wants Rebecca Burns, and what Adam wants he gets. You cross Adam—you die."

Iceman schooled his features to an unaffected mask, silently reeling. What the hell? Where had he come from? There was no wind here. They were half a mile deep inside a casino resort. He knew damn well he'd seen everyone who'd come and gone since he'd arrived. Not to mention that Tad had slipped past the front door in leather pants and a leather jacket in a mandatory suit-and-tie establishment.

Tad eyed Iceman, taunting amusement glinting in his eyes. "You think you're irreplaceable, but you're not." He motioned to the seat beside him. "JC here knows the ropes, doesn't he? Bet he'd like a few of those fancy sports cars you drive on Adam's dime. Maybe you should buy him a couple. A good second-in-charge deserves to be looked after."

He reached for Iceman's Scotch, saluted Sabrina with a hefty dose of lust in his black eyes, and then downed it. "That is good stuff." It wasn't clear if he meant the Scotch or the woman. He glanced at Iceman. "Hard to believe you came from a longneck-beer kind of family." A challenge glistened in his eyes. He crossed his arms in front of him. "Now. Let's start planning a way to lure Rebecca Burns out into the open, so we can capture her. If she showed up when an ICE junkie died, then we need to kill another one and make it look like the other deaths." He barked a bit of dry laughter, followed by a lame attempt at a sick joke. "If we kill one, she will come."

Iceman stared at Tad, hatred burning acid in his gut. No one made Iceman look a fool without paying the price. Tad would soon learn that price was painful.

Becca tossed her pencil down on the lab table and pressed her fingers to her eyes. It had been hours since the Clanner had died in the back of that EMS truck, and the body had since been taken to Sunrise City for full scientific review, which was fine by Becca. Dead bodies were not her thing. She was an astrobiologist, not a coroner—an astrobiologist who was tired, hungry, and frustrated, wishing Sterling would return.

He'd been in a meeting with Caleb and some of the other Renegades for a while now, trying to decide what to do about Dorian. Considering her lack of progress, she hoped he was coming up with answers.

Dropping her hand from her face, Becca ran her palms down her legs and glanced at the clock on the computer. Good Lord. She really had lost track of time. Was it really two in the morning? No wonder she was tired. Unfortunately, the need for sleep caught up with even an ICE user, just not as quickly.

The buzzer on the computer beeped, signaling Kelly was hailing her. Becca hit a computer key, and the teleprompter came to life. Kelly's image filled the screen, her light blonde hair piled on top of her head, dark circles hovering around her eyes. Becca didn't doubt she herself looked just as exhausted.

They were both swimming in a sea of a million possible answers with a ticking clock pressuring them to find the right one. And thus they had decided to divide and conquer, and then compare notes every few hours. Kelly and her team were working on how to save the current ICE users, while Becca had found herself sidetracked by the idea of an immunization against ICE to block its absorption. "Please tell me you've had better luck than I have," Kelly said with a heavy sigh.

"I wouldn't call it luck," Becca said. "But I've been thinking through some of my experiences at NASA. When dealing with extraterrestrial microorganisms, you expect the unexpected. We operate under the premise that there are microscopic life forms we don't even recognize, because we don't know how to measure their existence, which makes this problem seem complicated, but really, I'm not sure it is. What if it's actually as simple as why we can't live on an alien planet and why they don't live on ours? So something we use every day could be the thing that creates an immunization or an antidote—something like oxygen, but not oxygen. A mineral. A vitamin. Since ICE is alien, we should look for an element that repels the DNA, and then maybe we could convert it for use. I'm going to review the GTECH information now and see if it gives me any insight." They talked through that concept a few minutes, both encouraged by the possibilities, before Kelly said, "I've been thinking about how to deal with the current ICE users as well. I'm going to talk to Caleb about more aggressive measures. Bring a few of them in, and begin weaning them off ICE under medical supervision. It's not the way I'd prefer to approach this, but it's in the interest of saving lives. I'm going to talk to Caleb about it in the morning." She glanced at her watch. "Okay. It's already morning. We both need some sleep."

"You rest," Becca said. "I'm fine. I want to work on this idea I have on the immunization while it's fresh in my mind."

"There's no possible way anything is fresh in your mind right now, Becca."

"I really need to keep working, Kelly," she said. "I need to figure this out."

Kelly studied Becca a moment. "You mean, before it's too late and you're dead like that Clanner you watched die today. Isn't that what you wanted to say?"

"Yes," Becca said, her throat suddenly tight with emotion. "We don't know when that's going to be, Kelly."

"I've seen your blood work," Kelly said. "Several

samples now. As long as you keep taking the ICE, you'll be fine."

"Even if I had a never-ending supply of ICE, we can't be sure what side effects it will have on its users. We don't know how long I have until I'm no longer useful."

Kelly studied her a moment and then softly said, "Becca. It's okay to want to live. To care about your own future."

That tightness in her throat from moments before settled hard in Becca's chest. "It's easier to think about everyone else's future." A truth that slipped out without her meaning it to.

"Fair enough," Kelly said after a short pause, her voice firmer now, taking on a hint of stubbornness. "We'll worry about you, for you. I'm going to call Sterling and order him to feed you and put you to bed. End of story. Night, Becca." The screen went blank.

Almost instantly the door to the lab opened, and Sterling entered, looking as country-boy, hot-cowboy delicious as always, and with him a wave of spicy-smelling food that made her stomach rumble in demand.

"I have a late night connection," he said, holding up the bag as his cell phone rang. "I brought Chinese."

"It's Kelly," Becca said. "Telling you to feed me." She left off the "take me to bed" part, despite it being as appealing as the food.

He grinned. "Now who has psychic ability?" He snatched his phone and answered it. "I'm about to feed her and then," he hesitated, before adding, "take her to bed." Their eyes connected at that last statement, his rich with the promise that "to bed" meant *his bed*.

Chapter 21

BECCA SHRUGGED OUT OF HER LAB COAT AND ALLOWED Sterling to pull her toward the door.

"Time for food, a hot bath, and bed," he promised.

"Hot bath?" Becca asked hopefully. "You have a tub here? Really?" It had been weeks since she'd had such a luxury.

"I have a whole apartment here," he said. "Nothing fancy. Not the apartment or the tub. But it'll hold plenty of water and a pretty woman to boot."

Becca smiled at his not-so-subtle, country-boy charm. He was a gift in so many ways, just what she needed right now. He didn't demand. He didn't overwhelm. He didn't try to be suave and debonair. There were no airs or niceties. He was who he was, and she loved that about him.

"By the way," she said, as he led her down a hallway that looked like any one of thousands, basic carpet with doors on either side. "Where'd you get Chinese food at two in the morning?"

"I know the Chinese couple that owns the joint in the complex above. They hold a late-night kitchen poker game every Wednesday. If they're winning, I can always talk them into cooking for me."

"And if you're winning?" she asked as he stopped at the end of the hall and shoved open a door.

"I never gamble. But I do enjoy the ritual of watching

everyone else lose their backsides to Mr. Ling, who always wins. And no matter how many times the same people lose to him, they keep coming back for more. It's worse than basic-training soldiers begging to be punished."

She walked past him, their eyes briefly touching, her stomach fluttering with awareness as she entered the foyer. "I find it hard to believe you don't gamble." She brought the apartment into view and found it very basic—a place to live, not a home—brown leather couch and chair, leather-covered coffee table with built-in ottoman. Not much more.

"I'll never so much as toss a dime in a casino's direction," he said, stepping inside and shutting the door, so close their shoulders brushed. Becca bit her bottom lip at the feel of him next to her. Had she ever wanted a man so badly?

He motioned to a simple table to the right of the living area. "Like I said. Nothing fancy." He set the bags on the table and walked to the kitchen and opened the fridge. He continued talking over the bar that divided the two areas. "Sunrise City is really home. These are temporary quarters I use as needed."

"Funny," she said, sliding into a seat and removing the Styrofoam containers out of the bags. "I totally read you as a gambler."

Sauntering back to the table, he set a Coke on the table. "Got your favorite." He sat down at the end of the table next to her and popped the top off his Dr. Pepper. "And old faithful for me." He took a sip and responded to her comment. "I'm a risk taker, not a gambler. I can control when I take a risk. Gambling would control me. I want no part of that."

"I see," she said. "You're a control freak."

He grinned. "Nah. Control is an illusion. None of us really have it. We just trick ourselves into thinking we do."

Becca grabbed her Coke and popped the top, trying to hide her reaction. His words reached right inside her and twisted her in knots. No one knew better how true his statement was than a person who'd lived through a cancer diagnosis.

She tilted the drink back and swallowed as he continued. "So I just go for it when I have to. Live or die, I let it all hang out."

Becca was seized by a sudden, gut-wrenching emotion, only it wasn't hers.

Her gaze jerked to his, her heart in her stomach. "You don't have any family," she said, certain it was true. "You don't worry about living or dying because you think no one will care if you're gone."

He arched a brow and stared at her, expression unchanged for several seconds before he opened the lid on one of the containers. Instantly, an alluring scent of simmering food teased her nostrils and made her stomach growl. "Spicy beef," he said. "Extra soy sauce for the white rice."

"You're not going to comment on—" She stopped midsentence. Did a double take at the food. "How did you know what I like? Surely I don't have a file this detailed."

"So I was right then," he said. "Huh. Strangest thing. I was standing there talking to Mr. Ling about what I should order for you, and somehow I just knew. Just like I know you love chocolate, but hate caramel. How you take two creamers and one Sweet'N Low in your coffee. And you could live on macaroni and cheese if there weren't so many carbs." He shut the food lid and sat back. "I have to tell you, Becca, I've never been much into analyzing food based on carb content—can't think of one time in my life in fact. So I'm thinking this has to be me some-how getting inside your head and reading your thoughts." He studied her. "Am I right on any of this?"

Shocked, Becca nodded. "All of it."

He leaned back in his chair. "I'll be damned," he said, his brows dipping. "Are you somehow linking our minds together now?"

"Not that I know of," she said. "And I could feel when we were connected before." Intimately… almost erotically. "No. We aren't connected now. Maybe this is all information you picked up when we were, and you're remembering now… when certain triggers occur, like you ordering me food."

She studied him, dumbfounded by this new turn of events. No wonder it had felt so intimate when they'd merged minds. They'd somehow delved into each other's personal lives, dug deep into each other's core. She wasn't sure she wanted him to know what was there inside her. The battles she'd fought with herself recently—the insecurities, the fears. It was easier to think about what she'd learned about him, his thoughts. "You don't have any family."

He shrugged and then sipped his drink. "Like I said, the Renegades are my family."

She gave him a gentle glower. "You know what I mean. You never talked about your mother back in the library. I remember you lived with your grandmother and that your father was killed in combat. Do you have siblings?"

"My mother died during childbirth. My grandmother died a few years back of a heart attack."

A sudden memory flashed through her mind. *Sterling's memory*—of him jumping off a building onto a car. His last thought—he could die, but not before he freed the little boy being held hostage in that car and returned him to his parents. He wasn't afraid of dying. She felt not one tiny iota of fear in him.

She blinked away the image, thinking of the terror she'd felt over dying these past few months. "Don't you ever feel afraid?" Her voice cracked. She wasn't sure why, but there was emotion balled in her throat, tightening her windpipes.

Suddenly, he was on one knee in front of her, turning her to face him. His hands settled on her knees. Strong. Warm. His eyes searched hers. "You know when I feel afraid? Every time I think something is going to happen to you. I had nightmares about what Adam was doing to you at Zodius."

"Because you blamed yourself," she said. "It wasn't your fault. You tried to save me. I knew that."

"No," he said, rejecting that idea. "A soldier finds a place to put that stuff. We have to if we're going to keep going. That's not what this is with you, Becca, and it wasn't from the moment I met you. So in answer to your question… again, yes. I feel fear." His hand slid to her neck, callused fingers sending goose bumps down her spine. "You aren't alone anymore. We'll be afraid together."

Uncertainty rose inside her, along with one of the many fears her cancer had brought with it—the fear that had kept her from telling her mother about her diagnosis.

She didn't want to have someone taking care of her...
draining the life out of those around her while she died.

She tried to pull back. "No," she said. "I don't need
you to do this. I don't want you to make me feel better."

He kissed her, a light brush of his lips over hers,
followed by a seductive sweep of his tongue against
hers that seemed to touch her all over. "I don't want
to make you feel better," he said, his voice rough with
desire. "Better doesn't begin to describe what I want to
make you feel." Again he kissed her, featherlight. "I've
wanted you since the moment I laid eyes on you, most
definitely since I saw you walking up that sidewalk to
your house."

As she had him. She remembered him standing there
on her porch looking like sex and sin, recalling every
pleasurable moment of her life she'd missed. She wanted
to take what he was offering, to forget everything but
him, to escape if only for a little while. But damn it,
unlike in the lab earlier, she was now in her head, and in
his for that matter, thinking instead of just feeling. She
didn't want to be selfish, to act without thinking about
the aftermath.

Sterling leaned in and brushed his mouth over hers
again, his teeth nipping her bottom lip, tongue caressing. Becca moaned softly, unable to contain the sound
despite her best efforts. Control was not her friend
right now.

Her hands settled on Sterling's shoulders, the feeling of muscles flexing beneath her palms enticing her.
To touch... to feel... Okay. Maybe she did want to be
selfish. She wanted to rip his clothes off, wanted to
see him naked—*really* wanted to see him naked. She

barely stopped herself from arching into him, somehow reminding herself that when this was over she'd still be the girl with cancer that had become an ICE addiction, a load better carried alone.

His fingers trailed down one of her bare arms, and she felt that touch all over her body. Her stomach fluttered. Her thighs ached. Her breasts felt heavy and full; her nipples tight and sensitive.

"I'm trying to do what's right here," she whispered, her voice quavering as she struggled to find the will to resist him, even with words. There was something so enthralling about this man, so demanding about the desire he evoked in her. He was wild and thrilling, yet amazingly, what should feel dangerous felt safe.

His cheek brushed hers, whiskers erotically scraping against her skin, his breath warm against her ear as he whispered, "If I instinctively know something so simple as how to order your dinner, think what else I might know about you. What we might know about each other. How to tease each other... How to please each other."

There was an emptiness inside her that shuddered with hope, with a plea that he would drive it away, fill it with something that wasn't icy and cold.

He pulled back and looked at her, his eyes dark, passionate. Compelling. "No regrets, Becca," he vowed, and she knew he'd found those words in her head. Words she'd sworn to live by when she'd left that German hospital without a cure. Words she'd spoken in her head in the lab earlier with him there.

She rolled them around inside her and let them take root, rewarded herself with a deep inhalation of

Sterling's addictive, masculine scent. "No regrets," she said softly.

A slow smile formed on his lips. "I love it when you agree with me," he teased.

Becca laughed. "You're crazy."

"About you," he said huskily.

She felt a little schoolgirl rush from that. In the past, she would have felt like the geeky bookworm with the quarterback, uncomfortable and out of her league, but not with Sterling. Never before had a man taken her from such dark emotions to laughter. A place she might just find real escape.

She pressed her hands to his face, her lips to his. Absorbing him. Breathing him in like a little piece of life. They lingered that way, heat simmering between them. Expanding… drawing them in closer to one another without ever moving.

His tongue flickered against her lips, pressed past her teeth as he slid it against hers for a long, sensual taste. "Your kisses taste like honey," he murmured. "What does the rest of you taste like?"

She shivered at the erotic comment—the promise he was going to find out. He kissed her again. Crazy-wild, hot-kissed her, and she loved every second of it. Loved his tongue, his lips, and his hands sliding through her hair, over her face.

Becca ran her fingers through his thick, blond hair. She loved his hair—a little wild like him. Hot like him too. With each stroke of his tongue, each touch of his lips, she felt liberated.

Her palms traveled over his chest—warm, hard muscle, her reward. She was extremely, intensely interested in those muscles, like the best science project in the world that had to be studied. She explored his arms, his biceps, how they felt beneath her palms. Inching forward in her chair, she arched into him, for research purposes, of course. To explore how he would feel pressed close to her. Her breasts ached for his touch, her nipples tight and swollen, in need of his mouth. God. Had she really just had that brazen thought? She was a good girl; she always had been.

His hands slid over her breasts, fingers teased the stiff peaks of her nipples. Her hands covered his, silently telling him she wanted more, because she couldn't ask or demand. Because she was still that "good girl" at heart and couldn't seem to let it go.

But she didn't want to be a good girl. If anyone knew the meaning of "life is short," she did. Becca ran her lips over his jaw, hid her face in his neck, and nibbled as she said, "You know what I want?"

He slid his hands around her waist. "If you say Chinese food, I'm going to object."

"I'll give you a choice then," she said, feeling braver with his jest. "Feed me, or take off your clothes."

"I'm all for getting naked, if you are," he quickly agreed.

"You first," she bargained.

And while the idea of standing in front of him naked, him fully clothed, would make her feel vulnerable, exposed, it apparently had none of those effects on him.

"Okay," he said, unaffected by the idea as he pushed to his feet and started undressing. And only seconds later, he stood there in all his naked glory, and she sat there, fully clothed.

Becca wet her suddenly dry lips as her gaze traveled

over that hot body of his, with the lithe muscles that bulged and rippled in all the right places. Her eyes lingered on his abs—oh man. The man had abs. Really, really nice abs. Etched like a canyon of hard rock with delicious dips and mountain, all of which called for her tongue. They needed to be licked, every single one of them. She swallowed, her throat now as dry as her lips, her gaze traveling over his jutting erection. Big, hard, and ready. She was wet. She squeezed her thighs together against the ache there.

Part of her wanted to rip her clothes off and just feel all that perfection next to her. The other wanted to savor every second of looking, exploring, touching.

Slowly, her gaze lifted to the smoldering heat in his stare. "Can I touch it?" she asked.

"If you don't," he said, "I might have to beg."

Sterling, naked and begging. She was pretty sure she'd died and gone to heaven.

Chapter 22

Erotic images rushed through Sterling's mind as Becca walked toward him, anticipation for the moment this gorgeous, sweet, yet incredibly sexy woman would touch him. She stopped in front of him, her gaze lifting to his, simmering heat expanding between them. He swayed slightly, then silently reprimanded himself, despite the very male, very caveman-like desire to reach for her and say "mine." He knew that wasn't the right move. Just as he had known what to order for her at that restaurant, she didn't feel she had choices, like she was spinning out of control. Well, she was going to have them with him. Whatever she wanted, she needed—he wanted and needed.

Slowly, her lashes lowered as she pressed her palm to his chest. It was soft, cool—a contrast to the fire licking at his limbs, spiraling between them. She splayed her fingers, flexing them against his skin before trailing one finger downward to his lower abdomen, and then flattened her hand on his skin again with the promise she wasn't going to stop there. And man, oh man, did his cock know it. He was standing at attention, thrumming with anticipation, his heart pounding in his ears.

Her fingers walked a path downward to the base of his erection, and then she caressed straight to the tip. His cock jerked instantly with the pleasure.

Becca sucked in a breath and tried to pull her hand

away, her eyes seeking his. And before he could stop himself, he stole a little piece of that control he'd vowed to relinquish to her. His hand closed around hers, wrapping her fingers around his cock. "Don't stop," he ordered, barely recognizing the husky voice as his own.

Her teeth scraped her bottom lip, and he all but moaned. Lust licked at his limbs like a four-alarm fire. That soft, amber gaze of hers so often full of innocent uncertainty flickered to his face, innocence no longer there. Instead, her eyes shimmered with a combination of desire and hesitation. And then, blessed be, her hand tightened around him.

"Oh yeah, sweetheart," he said hoarsely, releasing her hand, allowing her that freedom of choice, as long as it involved her hand on his cock.

"You like that?" she asked, more teasing than confirming.

"Just to be clear," he said, his voice gravely and affected. "You pretty much can do anything you want to me… and I'll like it. Aside from the use of teeth, that is." Amending quickly, he added, "If used in limited capacity, of course, teeth can be kind of sexy and remain on the table for acceptable use. And being a scientist and all, I know you have an experimental instinct. Feel free to go with that. Just let it ride."

She laughed, loosening her grip on him, teasing him with her fingers. "I've never known anyone quite like you before, Sterling."

"Ditto to you, sugarplum," he managed, despite her voice strumming along his nerve endings like a musical aphrodisiac, helping her hand kill him with lust. Oh yeah. He was going to die if he didn't feel the wet heat of her body wrapped around him in the real near future.

Her smile widened, her hand working him mercilessly, pumping him. She had control all right. He had a love-hate thing about that too. He wanted to take control and rip off her clothes. *Her, naked, now*.

"I should probably tell you," she said softly, her lashes lowering, her gaze hot as she watched her hand exploring his cock. "My experimenting has been limited to a lab."

Hell yes. He loved that. "Baby, it turns me on just thinking about being the guy that changes that." He closed his hand around hers again, around the pulsing heat of his erection, moving their hands together, moving his hips in rhythm. "The idea of being the one to make you wetter and hotter than any other man ever has—you feel how turned on it makes me?"

Her chin jerked upward, her expression registering shock. "You're outrageously bold."

"You like it," he said. "And if you don't get naked soon, I'm going to do it for you."

"I'm not ready yet," she said, smiling. Soft. Sexy. Playful. And then she went to her knees. Holy crap and thank you Lord. She was going to put that sweet little mouth on him. "I'll need to do some research before undressing," she said, staring up at him, his cock jutted out mere inches from her lips. She closed her hand around the base of his shaft. "Tell me. How does this feel?" She touched the tip of it with her tongue. He moaned with the sensation. "I'll take that as a 'good.'" She drew the head into her mouth and then rolled her tongue around him. "And that?"

"Good," he said. She arched a brow. "Do it again, and I'll judge better."

She did, and silently, he commanded. *Suck me deeper*. His hand went to her head, the words lodged in his throat as he reminded himself he'd vowed to give her choice and control. Ah, but she seemed to know what he wanted. She drew him deeper and deeper, a sliding motion up and down his length that had his hips pumping again, which felt damn good, until a sudden thought slid into clarity.

She was hiding from her own pleasure, from the vulnerability of losing herself to that need. That's why she wasn't naked. That's why she was on her knees. And he was letting her. Selfishly taking what she offered by convincing himself he was giving her freedom of choice, when what she needed was freedom all right. Freedom from pain, fears... inhibitions.

With forced willpower he eased Becca away and went down on his knees in front of her. "What are you doing?" she asked, instant confusion clouding her lovely eyes, uncertainty flickering in her face.

"Kissing you," he said, pulling her close, one hand twining into her silky mass of raven hair, the other sliding up her back, molding her closer, pressing her soft curves and full breasts against him.

Sterling kissed her like he was making love to her, using his tongue to caress, coax, and yes—to heck with handing over control—demand. He took his time, seducing, making love to her with his mouth. And when he thought for certain he'd kissed away her insecurity, he vowed, "I'm going to make you come. And then come again. And then come some more." He pulled on her shirt hem and tugged it over her head, her bra quickly following. "Say and do all kinds of things to make you call me outrageous and make sure you love every one of them."

His gaze raked hungrily over her bare upper body. Her breasts weren't large, but they were high and full, the perfect size for his hand. "You're beautiful," he said. "I love your nipples." He played with one of them, tweaked it. "All rosy pink and plump. Perfect for my mouth."

"Sterling!" Becca said. "Do you say whatever comes to mind?"

"You have a problem with me telling you I love your nipples?" he asked, molding her breast to his palm and kneading.

"No," she said softly.

"Good," he said, dipping his head down and lapping one with his tongue, his arm still supporting her from behind. One lick, nip, and yes, bite, at a time. His teeth scraped her nipple, and she moaned with pleasure. "That's how you use teeth properly," he declared proudly before kissing her again. "Damn, I like how you taste." He kissed her again. "All hot and sticky sweet." He took her down on the carpeted floor. "I want to know how the rest of you tastes."

He pressed his mouth to her neck, her collarbone, those hot little nipples again, and continued to travel, until his tongue dipped into her navel. Her flat, sexy tummy quivered with the touch.

It didn't take him any time to strip away the rest of her clothes. He kissed his way from her ankle up to her knee, and then gently nudged her legs farther apart.

"That's it, sweetheart," he said. "Open for me."

She raised to her elbows. "Sterling," she whispered, nervous energy pouring off of her.

His hands slid up her thighs. "This is where you lie back down and enjoy this as much as I'm going to."

"I can't—"

"You can." He slid his fingers along her core, and she moaned. "See how good that feels." He caressed her some more, coaxing another moan, his gaze meeting hers as he continued to touch her, intentionally pushing her to let go of her inhibitions. "You're so hot and wet. Just the way I like you."

She fell backward, sighing in an admission of defeat, giving herself to him. A smile touched his lips, one born of satisfaction, of conquest. His fingers explored, playing with her like a kid would a new toy, discovering hidden secrets—triggers that made her moan, sigh again, arch her back.

When she looked at him with bedroom eyes that begged him to take her, he gave them both the ultimate reward, the pot of gold, almost as good as having that hot, wet heat wrapped around his cock. His tongue lapped at her swollen clit, and she arched into him, breasts high in the air, fingers digging into the carpet. He suckled and caressed with a tongue experienced in such devilish acts, but never so eager to perform. Expertly he used his fingers to stroke and caress, to drive her to the edge, then he took her to a shuddering climax that had her muscles milking his fingers, the sweet honey of her release pouring around them.

She gasped with the impact as the moment faded, her gaze bouncing off his in a red-faced flush of embarrassment as she turned her head away.

"Oh no," he said. "Don't even think about it."

He reached for her and in one easy move sat up against the wall and pulled her on top of him, his cock pressed to her backside, swollen and pulsing.

Shoving her loose hair away from her face, he told her, "We don't do embarrassment, you and I. We are just getting started, sweetheart, just cracking the door on a long night that'll never end."

"Sterling—"

He kissed her, silently telling her what words already had, then met her gaze and said, "That was fucking beautiful—just like you are. Understand?"

She kissed him. Slid that sweet little tongue right into his mouth and took him like he planned to do her.

His hands went to her hips as he shifted her weight. She obeyed the command, the one that said—let me the fuck in before I die—and her hands went to his shoulders, anchoring herself to take him.

He nudged open her feminine lips and eased his shaft inside her, intending to go slow, but she didn't seem to agree. Becca slid down him in one fast, hard move that sent the head of his cock driving into her core. A blast of pleasure rocketed through him with such force it about shot his heart out of his chest.

They connected, intimately joined like their minds had been. And when she pulled back, searching his face, he knew she felt it too, the undeniable bond between them. Intense. Consuming. Seconds passed, their bodies smoldering, unfamiliar emotion expanding in his chest. This woman was doing something to him, taking him over, reaching right inside him and touching his soul. And all he could think was how much he wanted her to keep doing it.

His hands settled on her waist, pressing her down, swiveling his hips, urging her to move with him. A slow, sultry dance of lusty need started. She braced herself on his shoulders, her breasts bouncing with each pump and thrust. He palmed them, kneading, molding. Then he pulled her nipples between his fingers so that each movement of her body applied just the right amount of erotic pressure on the sensitive peaks. She rewarded him with soft sounds of pleasure.

He watched her face, the way her lips parted, her brows dipped. Passion colored her ivory perfect skin. She was fucking beautiful, just as he'd told her she was, and in a way he'd never thought a woman could be. She did it for him. She was the beginning, the middle, and the end.

She gasped and buried her face in his shoulder. He pressed her close, pressed deep inside her as she moved in a frenzied rush that said she was on the edge... about to come. And he took her there, took them there, pumping hard and fast, molding her closer and tighter, until she stiffened in a moan a second before her body grabbed a hold of his cock and spasmed around him.

Somewhere in the near distance, a shattering sound splintered through the air. A glass, no two, maybe three, shattered with her orgasm. He didn't care, and she didn't seem to either. She clung to him, and he pulled her down hard on his shaft, thrusting into her one more long, hard time. With a low, guttural groan, he exploded, spilling his seed inside her, seeing nothing but the black place in his mind that exploded in the colors of pleasure.

Long seconds later, they collapsed against each other, and he could have held her like that forever. She ran her fingers through his chest hair and leaned back to stare at him, sudden awareness rushing over her features. "I think I broke something when I..."

He arched a brow. "Came? Had an orgasm? Rocked my world?"

She flattened her hands on his chest. "You love to make me blush, don't you?"

His lips curved, and he ran his knuckles along her cheek, right where the flush of red appeared. "You're very pretty when you blush."

"Thank you," she said shyly, like there was any reason to be shy with him at this point. Damn, she was adorable and sexy.

"I loved making you so hot you shattered glass," he confessed. "It's good for a guy's ego. But if it really bothers you, we can try that whole anchor thing. You need to practice controlling your reactions." He wiggled an eyebrow. "We can use orgasm as practice. But I do have to ask. Are you using me for sex? Because, you know, if you are, I can live with it. I just want to know." Oddly, what started as a joke left him hungry for an answer, his insides twisted in a knot, waiting.

"I'm dying, Sterling," she said, suddenly serious. "Of course, I'm using you for sex."

His heart splintered in a thousand pieces with those words, and he framed her face with his hands. God, how he'd hoped they were Lifebonds, that he would save her that easily. But he wasn't giving up, and he wouldn't let her give up. "You are not going to die," he said. "I won't let you."

"That," she whispered, "is just outrageous, and please just stop bringing this up." Anger filtered into her voice.

"Saying it… that you can save me… is mean." She pushed away from him, trying to get up.

He held onto her. "Becca—"

"Don't," she said. "Let me up."

He pulled her close and buried his face in her neck, inhaling her soft scent. "No. I won't." Instead, he pushed to his feet and carried her to that hot bath she wanted. After that, he'd feed her and take her to his bed. And if she wanted to argue, he had no problem showing her who was in control.

If he pretended it was him instead of her, maybe she would believe him.

Sabrina sighed with the sweet bliss of satisfaction as Iceman rolled off of her and sat up on the edge of the bed, disposing of the condom. He insisted on using one even though she'd told him she was on the pill and disease free.

He didn't want "babies" he said, disdain in his voice. Like she did? She'd seen how her mama had been tied to the house and babies, while Daddy ran around with women like… well, her.

Sabrina wasn't stupid like her mother. She knew the way to a man's heart was his dick, not a houseful of screaming kids. She knew how to keep a man like Iceman—a man who was all about power and pleasure.

She rolled onto her stomach and pressed her hand to her chin, watching as Iceman poured himself his standard, after-sex Scotch. She kept the bar stocked for him—an easy enough task when you worked for a casino and lived in one too. Satisfaction—all forms. Any way he liked it. That was what she gave him. That was what he gave her in his arrogant, bossy kind of way. But that was okay. Those things made her hot. She didn't want a pansy-ass bringing her flowers and kissing her feet.

"So what are we going to do about Tad?" she asked.

He glanced over his shoulder. "Get rid of him," he said. "Lure him where we want him and then take him out. And while Rebecca Burns would be a prize we will continue to pursue, we aren't waiting for her. We deal with Tad now. And as much as I'd like to hold him captive and pick his brain about Adam's operation, I'll shoot the bastard and throw him to the bottom of a river if necessary."

"Good," she said quickly. She liked a jealous man, though she liked Tad's rough, forceful approach. His talents were quite extensive. "It was like he came out of nowhere at the restaurant."

"Indeed, it was," he said, downing his drink and grabbing his pants from the floor. He glanced at his watch.

She eyed his ass while he did. It was nice and tight, a fine specimen. She didn't want him to cover it. "Don't leave, sugar," she said. "I've not had my fill of you yet."

He zipped his dress pants. "I'm going to look at the security feed. Try and figure out how Tad surprised us. I don't like surprises like you do."

Sabrina pushed to her feet and pulled on a sheer pink robe. "You liked it when I hid under your desk and blew you while you talked to your secretary."

He cut her a look. "And I warned you not to do it again."

To feel in control. Check. She got that. But she also knew he didn't mean it. "When can we get rid of Tad?" she asked as she walked him to the door.

He turned and leaned against the frame, crossing his arms in front of his broad chest. "What are you willing to do to get rid of him?"

An uneasy feeling fluttered in her stomach. "What did you have in mind?"

Iceman stared at her, his eyes steely cold, like ICE, and then pulled her roughly against him. "Play the same sex games you do with me," he said. "Seduce him in a location that will leave him distracted and exposed so that I can kill him before he escapes."

She could barely believe her ears. "You want me to let that man touch me again?"

"I want you to help me destroy him," he said, pulling her close, rough—his voice sharp. "Do you want to please me, Sabrina?"

"I'd rather please *you* in bed, not in someone else's," she said. That was how this worked. The woman who drove the man of power, who "made" him in ways no one else ever could.

"But you'll do it," he said. It wasn't a question.

It felt like a heavy weight was crushing her chest. "Yes."

A slow smile lifted his lips before he crushed her mouth with a kiss that ravished her and tasted of greed. But not for her, she realized, for power. She was nothing but a token in a game. He left her a few seconds later, set her away from himself without another word, nor a look behind.

He'd asked her to let Tad touch her again. Told her, ordered her, expected her to "do" Tad to please him.

Sabrina leaned on the door and slid down its surface. Her eyes prickled—tears! No. No. No. She balled her fists, half-growling, half-shouting into the room. She was not her mother. She would not cry over a man, especially not one who was using her, because no man who cared about her would ask her to do what Iceman had.

Iceman was no better than Tad, she realized. They were both using her to get to each other, to gain power and control. That was the greed she'd tasted on Iceman's lips.

Damn it, she wasn't her mother. She wasn't stupid and blind. If she was going to survive this, she had to look out for herself. She inhaled. Iceman had a plan. Well, so did she.

A simple bathroom of white tile and silver accessories surrounded Becca as she lounged in a tub of hot water, waiting for Sterling to return from the kitchen. Bubbles, manufactured from shampoo out of desperation and irrational shyness, covered the top of the shoulder-deep water, her legs stretched out in front of her, head against the wall.

It didn't matter that she'd just spent hours making love to Sterling in every gymnastic position she'd thought possible, and some she wouldn't have believed possible, until he'd proven otherwise. Bottom line, she still felt shy in the aftermath. Emotionally, more than physically, but somehow the bubbles provided a security blanket, an extra layer to protect her, while she tried to understand what she was feeling.

She'd never done the kinds of things with a man she'd done with Sterling. Sex had been stiff and uncomfortable—an awkward, hopeful attempt to find pleasure that had always come up short of expectations. Never the all-consuming physical bliss she'd shared with Sterling that had managed one minute to be darkly erotic, the next, playful and filled with laughter.

Becca sat up and pulled her knees to her chest, where emotion welled in a tight ball. She'd thought living a little was a smart move, a natural move, a way of facing death. The truth was living made you crave life. And Sterling made her realize how little she'd really lived.

All of a sudden, Becca felt an odd tingling at the back of her neck. "What the heck?" she murmured, running her hand over her neck, under the bottom of her hair where the water had dampened it.

"Something wrong?" Sterling asked, appearing in the doorway in nothing but jeans—unbuttoned and hanging low on lean hips—and holding a glass of wine.

"No," she said, realizing the tingling sensation had gone away. "Nothing."

He sauntered forward, lithe male, with his ever-present, casual façade that never quite hid the lethal soldier beneath the surface. Her mouth watered and not because of the wine. It was all about the man. His hair was rumpled, sexy. Thick, light blond, always a bit wild—it fit him. And his body, what a body! Every time she inspected it, she found another place she wanted to lick.

She'd never thought such a thing about another man. Well—not that she knew. What woman hadn't had that kind of thought about her preferred Hollywood hunk—a Brad Pitt or George Clooney. But that was a safe fantasy a girl knew would never come true. This was Sterling, a man she had licked in quite a few places, but apparently, not enough places to satisfy her urges.

He sat down on the toilet seat and offered her the wine. "I bought this when I got the Chinese food. Thought it might help you relax."

"Thank you," she said, accepting the glass, thinking how incredibly thoughtful that was. "Aren't you going to have some?"

"Nah," he said. "I don't drink. Never acquired a taste for it. Besides, GTECHs are immune to the effects anyway."

Surprised, she sipped her wine and studied him over the rim of her glass. Dry, but a bit sweet. Perfect. A treat—just like the bath. "Surely a Texas boy like yourself—in the army to boot—has a beer here or there?"

"I slug one down for appearance's sake when I need to," he said. "But that's about it." He motioned with his chin. "How's the bath?"

Something flickered in her mind, a shadowy image—an emotional response to drinking that was his, not hers. "Why don't you drink?" she asked, ignoring his question, fragments of his emotions, a piece of a memory, splintering in her head. Unidentifiable, but for one question that came to her. "Who close to you was an alcoholic?"

His expression darkened. "Exactly how much did you get out of my head while you were in there? Because so far I got Chinese food preferences on you. That's not much."

She was pretty sure he'd managed a few of her fantasies as well and put them to good use while they were making love, but she wasn't about to say that. Instead, she indicated her glass. "And apparently my preference for certain wines."

"A far cry from the huge bombshells you keep

pulling out of my head." A hint of tightness in his words. Tension etched his jaw line, a raw discomfort in him she'd never seen before.

"I only had a feeling," she said gently. "Nothing more. I didn't see this part of your past." She softened her voice. "I promise. And I didn't mean to be nosy. You don't have to tell me if you don't want to." She hesitated. "If you want to, though, now or later, you can."

He ran a hand through his hair then let out a harsh breath. "Oh well, hell. It was my grandmother, but you know, she did rehab, and she died ten years sober. I don't know how, out of all my memories, you picked one this ancient."

"It must be a building block of your life," she said. "Something that defines you and stays with you, consciously or unconsciously, always."

One of those splinters of memory glinting in her mind. "Wait. You don't think she got sober because you went away, do you? That you made her an alcoholic?"

"That was part of the deal when I joined the military," he said. "They cleaned up my grandmother, and I enlisted. So yeah, she got sober because I went away. Losing your kid and raising your kid's kid isn't easy. She did the best she could. I made sure I did my best by her. I went away and gave her a chance at a real life."

"What do you mean that was part of the deal when you joined?"

He kicked back against the toilet seat, one foot on his knee. "I was in knee-deep shit at the time. Hacked a top-secret government computer program for cash. Told myself it was to get money for her rehab, but it was really about, you know, proving I wasn't a loser." He grimaced. "Which, ironically, made me a loser because I got busted, and by the way, that's why I stood you up that day we met at the library. They showed up at my house, and that was that. I was gone. I don't even know how the army intervened. My dad was a Special Ops guy—covert on the highest level. I still don't know what he did, but whatever it was, it apparently made them want me too."

"Or maybe it was your ability to hack that program," she said. "How'd you learn to do that?"

"Self-taught. I have a mind for it. And you're right. The army wanted that skill, and they've put it to use many times over the years."

"What did your grandmother say about you enlisting?"

"She was in a drunken stupor," he said. "I told them to clean her up and tell her I was dead. Never saw her again after that day. Not until she was in a casket." He ran his hand over the back of his neck. "Which was harder than I thought it was going to be."

Becca knew why—knew it to her core. "Because she was all you had left." Facing death, she had been feeling very alone, but in life, she had always felt loved. There had always been lots of unconditional love. Sterling didn't have that in his life.

"Yeah," he said softly, his gaze settling on the floor a minute. "Hadn't seen her in years, but knowing she was gone, it rattled me. But it was the right decision going into the army. It was where I belonged. Now I belong with the Renegades, trying to make the army and this country what it once was. Safe and free. The best place on earth." He tilted his head, studying her. "I've told you my deep, dark secret. Your turn to talk."

She sipped her wine. "What do you want to know?"

"When did you plan to tell your mother about your cancer?"

Sideswiped by that question, her chest tightened. Why she hadn't seen that one coming, she didn't know. The answer weighed as heavy on her tongue as her worry about her mother. But he'd been honest with her; he'd opened up about a part of his life she was certain he didn't talk about. He was right. It was her turn.

"Never," she said, and laughed without humor.

His brow arched. "And now?"

She set the wine on the side of the tub. "What do I tell her now? I have no idea."

"You mean you have an excuse to avoid that conversation, and you're taking it."

She hugged her knees tighter and rested her chin on top of them. "Now who's digging around in whose head?"

"I don't have to dig around in your head to know that," he said. "I can see it in your eyes. You should call her."

"And say what?" she asked. "Hey Mom, I was dying of cancer, but good news, now that I'm drinking alien DNA, I might live to become an evil monster like the source of that DNA. Thought I might say hi before that happened."

"You're not—"

She raised a dripping wet hand stop sign fashion. "Instead of you telling me what I want to hear—Becca, you're not going to die, or Becca, you're not going to turn into a monster—why don't you stop teasing me with the prospect of food. Let me get out of here, and let's heat up that Chinese food."

He pushed off the seat and squatted down in front of

her. "Becca," he said roughly. "Turn around, and let me see your neck."

She sucked in a breath, knowing what he was looking for—the Lifebond mark that could save her life. A mixture of hope and dread filled her. She wanted life, but she didn't want pity or obligation from him.

"Don't do this," she said. "The odds are next to zero." Yet she remembered the tingling on her neck, and there was no denying the passion between them was nothing she'd felt with any other man.

"We have to know," he said, his jaw set in determination.

She'd learned a few details in Zodius City about Lifebonding. "The mark appears during sex, and the female feels pain. No pain. No mark."

He fixed her in a steely stare. "Turn around."

With a chill inside her as cold as that first drop of ICE hitting her throat every day, she did as he bid. Turned around and lifted her hair with her free hand. Seconds ticked by before he kissed her neck, intimate, a caress. Goose bumps slid down her back, warmth replacing the chill. Was it possible there really was a mark? Could it be? Hiding the anxiety darting through her, Becca slowly turned around, butterflies attacking her stomach.

Tenderness rushed over his face as he reached out and ran his knuckles down her cheek, tenderness etched with sadness. "I'm insanely, wildly crazy about you."

The butterflies turned to a hard knot. "There's no mark," she said, her throat constricting with the words. The tingling she'd felt had been nothing.

He shook his head. "No," he said. "Becca—"

"Don't," she said, knowing he was about to apologize

because he couldn't save her life. Exactly everything she didn't want to hear from him. Besides she wasn't thinking about some miracle cure. She was thinking about not being Sterling's Lifebond, about how some other woman was out there, some woman who belonged to him, and him to her.

Uncertainly swirled in his gaze, and he looked as if he might say more. Finally, he simply offered, "I'll go heat up the food while you get dressed."

He didn't give her time to respond, not that she was sure she could have found her voice for the emotion lodged in her throat anyway. He was on his feet and gone in an instant.

She sat there a few seconds, the water chilling, and part of her with it. She wasn't Sterling's Lifebond, but she was falling for him. She cared about him, exactly why it wasn't fair to get involved with him, to burden someone with the pain of loss. It was a cross one should bear on one's own. To do otherwise was selfish.

Becca stepped out of the tub and grabbed the fluffy, white towel hanging on the rack and wrapped it around herself. Suddenly, that tingling sensation on her neck started again.

An instant later, Sterling appeared in the doorway, and when he did the sensation faded, almost as if it were warning her of his presence. She shook herself mentally and tried to act unaffected. But hadn't she heard Lifebonds had some sort of sensory ability to know when the other was near?

Surprising her, Sterling held her Burberry travel bag, the one her father had given her as a college graduation gift. "This is the bag Cassandra picked up for you. I thought you might want it." He winked and headed off again, and she knew he was trying to keep things light.

Becca would have delighted at having her bag, if not for the funny feeling at the back of her neck. She bit her lip and shut the door, then bent down and looked inside the bag, finding her makeup pouch.

She pulled out a handheld compact, turned to the mirror, and held up her hair. She gaped at what she saw—two faint circles, one inside the other, a good three inches wide at any angle. A tattoo that wasn't a tattoo had appeared out of nowhere clearly after Sterling had checked.

Becca turned to the sink and pressed her hands to the counter, her heart pounding like a drum, echoing in her ears. It couldn't be. "Oh God," she whispered and squeezed her eyes shut. When the lamp had shattered during orgasm—she'd blacked out in that moment of both pain and pleasure that must have been the Lifebonding process.

A mixture of elation and guilt filled her. With a blood exchange, Sterling could save her life. Her stomach twisted in knots, and emotion balled in her chest. If she died, he died. God, please let that be only if they did the blood exchange. What if the ICE somehow did something to her, something that would hurt him? He wouldn't consider the possibility and let her run tests. He'd feel obligated to save her. He'd insist. And sure, Sterling wanted her. He desired her, but bound for life was a big deal. It was like marriage without a divorce court.

She pressed her hand to her stomach, willing it to calm, and made a decision. She wasn't going to tell him about the Lifebonding mark.

As long as she and Sterling avoided a blood exchange,

there was no reason he had to know about the mark on her neck. So long as he never knew, there would be no guilt or obligation. This was a secret she planned to take to her deathbed—alone.

Chapter 23

HOURS AFTER THEIR MANY LOVEMAKING SESSIONS, Becca lay curled by Sterling's side, sleeping peacefully. Sterling, on the other hand, was wide awake, computer in his lap, back against the headboard of his bed.

He focused his tech skills on how and where to find the ICE warehouse. He punched keys and tried to hack Club Nebula to track down some sort of database of ICE users, any information that might lead to the main distribution source.

He punched a few more keys and cursed. Nebula's computer system was down. Sterling ran his hand over his face and tried to think, his gaze landing again on Becca, her silky dark hair spread across the black comforter as if it were a part of the blanket, her body pressed to his side as if she were trying to melt into him.

Holy shit, he was dying here over this woman. Not only had he talked to her about his grandmother, he'd wanted her *in his bed*. Those two things were huge anomalies. He didn't talk about his past, and even if it weren't for security reasons, he wouldn't have another female in his bed. He went to them and left when he was ready, which was usually pretty damn fast. He could have set Becca up in her own room, but she was here in his bed and exactly where she belonged. He'd never felt so possessive and hungry for a woman in his life.

But she wasn't his Lifebond. She was *supposed* to be his Lifebond. He knew it clear to his soul. He should have saved her, made her his—*loved* her. He scrubbed a hand through his hair, tormented. He'd actually started to convince himself the coincidence of them coming back together was about fate, destiny, crazy shit like that, things he'd never believed in, but wanted to with Becca. Maybe he couldn't Lifebond. Maybe that was one of those GTECH abilities he didn't possess. That would make him her worst nightmare, a Lifebond who couldn't really Lifebond.

On that sour note, he forced his attention back to the computer screen and was considering hacking the Empire Resort's computer, since Nebula was attached to that facility, when his cell phone rang from where it rested on the nightstand. Becca stirred beside him as he snatched it and looked at caller ID. Kelly.

Sterling answered. "What's up, Doc?"

"I need to talk to Becca," she said. "And Caleb said for you to meet him in the Cityscape room in twenty minutes." Cityscape was the room in Neon where they'd covered the walls with maps of every street, tunnel, and sewer in Vegas and the outlying areas.

"Morning to you too," he said and held the phone out to Becca. "Kelly wants to talk to you."

Her eyes went wide. He laughed and covered the phone. Damn she was cute. "She can't tell you're in bed with me from the sound of your voice."

Her cheeks turned rosy, and she sat up straighter, shoving hair behind her delicate little earlobes. "Right."

Sterling put the phone back to his ear. "She'll call you in ten minutes."

His gaze traveled over Becca. She looked sexy as hell in a slinky white tank that cut narrowly down the sides of her breasts, exposing the lush curves. "Make that twenty minutes."

Kelly made a frustrated sound. "Tell her the dead guy's tox report came back with some weird readings I haven't seen before. I'm trying to get a hold of the army's scientific team to see if this is an anomaly or a match with the other ICE victims. Not that I think they'll be straight with me, but I plan to leverage the findings—to trade information."

Anomaly. He was all about one big, fucking anomaly today. But there was one consistency. He wanted Becca so bad it hurt.

"Good plan," he said. "I'll tell her." He snapped the phone shut.

"Tell me what?" Becca asked.

Sterling eased her down onto the mattress, his lips hovering above hers. "That you're beautiful when you wake up."

"She didn't say that," Becca said, arms sliding around his neck a moment before his lips brushed hers. She sighed. "But you can tell me later."

Sterling walked into the Cityscape meeting room inside Neon, a no-frills ops room unlike the high-tech monster of a setup the Renegades sported in Sunrise City. Paper maps covered one main wall with an electronic monitor nestled in the center.

A large round conference table capable of seating ten sat in the middle of the otherwise empty room, with three men sitting around it. Caleb, Michael, and Sterling grimaced at the third—Damion.

"You're like a mole that keeps growing back," Sterling said, claiming the seat next to Caleb. "Or just a mole—period."

"This mole," Damion said, indicating the notebook computer in front of him, "is trying to hack into Nebula's computer and find out how they're managing their distribution."

"Already tried," Sterling said. "Their system is down. Interesting you happen to be messing around in their site right when it went down. For all I know, you did it."

Damion slid the computer across the desk. "Backtrack me, asshole. Set your mind at ease."

"Let's focus on the two points that brought us here, why don't we?" Caleb said irritably. Sterling and Damion glared at one another, and Damion jerked his computer back in front of him.

Seemingly satisfied no further conflict would ensue, Caleb continued. "Point one. We can't even think about eliminating or isolating the source of ICE, meaning Adam's son, if we don't have a better understanding of what is killing people. That means we don't wait until they die. Kelly wants active ICE addicts to study, and we're going to give them to her and quickly. While trying to find an antidote or an immunization, the general consensus is that producing one *and* ensuring it's safe in a short timeline is nearly impossible, which brings me to point two. How Becca can help us. The best thing she's done up to this point is to tell us that the source for creating ICE is Dorian. Deal with Dorian, and we deal with this problem."

"And Becca can give us Dorian," Michael said, breaking his silence with words that cut like fire through ICE.

Sterling's gaze shot to Michael. "How would she do that?"

"Dorian left Zodius City and came after her," Michael said in that cold tone he did so well. "Adam knows Becca is powerful, so he brought out his most powerful weapon, no matter how risky that move, to hunt her down and kill her. She's the bait, and we need to get Dorian out of Zodius City again and into the open where we can capture him."

"Forget it," Sterling said, ready to come out his chair and put a choke hold on Michael. "He'll kill her."

"She's powerful," Caleb reiterated. "With a little practice and you and me by her side, she can face Dorian without risk."

"We can't even allow her around our men," Sterling said, red-hot rage rolling inside him. "I can't believe you're saying this, Caleb, that you want to risk an innocent woman's life. I never thought I'd see that day."

"I'm protecting this city and quite possibly our world," Caleb reminded him. "Leaders lead, and we make tough choices. We need her help. And if you weren't so personally involved, you'd see that. I wouldn't ask this of her, if I didn't feel there's no other answer. We're desperate here. And we'll protect her."

"And we've done such a good job of that so far," Sterling half-growled. "This isn't the answer. There will be another Dorian, another child of Lifebonds. And that child might well have the same DNA. We need that immunization, and she thinks she has an idea for creating it."

"Exactly why we're going to capture, not kill, Dorian," Caleb explained calmly. "Our scientific team will then have his DNA to study. We'll take Becca out in public. She'll let her shield down and lure Dorian into the city."

Sterling pushed to his feet, fingers pressed to the table. He wanted the hell out of here. "What part of *no* do you not understand?"

His cell phone rang, and he yanked it off his belt, his glare lingering on Caleb a moment before he glanced at the ID, which read "unknown." He flipped it open, in case it was Marcus, and said hello.

"Hello there, Sterling, sweetheart," came a feminine voice.

Sterling frowned. "Who is this?"

"Who I am is not as important as *what* I am."

"Which is what?" he asked, punching his speaker button, instinct telling him this call was important.

"You could call me the Madame of the ICE dealers," she purred.

Sterling reclaimed his seat, his gaze settling on Caleb. "Do I call you Madame?" he asked. "Or do you actually have a name?"

"It's Madame to you," she said. "At least for now. And I can tell I'm on speakerphone. How many of those hot Renegade friends of yours are in the room? And can I pick one to rescue me when Iceman tries to kill me for helping you? I'd say you, Sterling, but everyone knows you have your hand up the skirt of that chick, Rebecca Burns."

"You haven't helped us yet," Michael said. "So don't count on being saved. Who is Iceman?"

"Hmmm," she said, ignoring the question. "I like the rough types. I pick you, whoever you are, to save me." She laughed. "Then again, if you don't even know the name of the man in charge, you might be the one who needs saving. If you want to shut down ICE distribution, I'm the ticket to success."

"And why exactly," Sterling asked, "would you help us?

"Revenge," she said with no hesitation. "I was loyal to Iceman. He has not been loyal to me. Nor has he been loyal to Adam. He's been selling his own cocktail of enhanced ICE. It's not only giving him his own cash flow, he's creating what he calls Eclipsers, followers who he plans to use to stand against Adam when the time is right."

Sterling and the rest of the Renegades went stone-cold still, a collective flash of shared glances colliding around the table—war with their own government, war with Adam, and now war with the Eclipsers.

"Eerily quiet there, boys," Madame said. "Guess I got your attention."

"What is it you think you can do for us?" Caleb asked. "What are you offering?"

"Depends," she said. "Who are you?"

"Caleb," he said.

"As in Adam's brother?"

"The one and only."

"Good," she said softly. "I assumed when Sterling didn't deny he was a Renegade, it was true, but confirmation is always preferred. And I'm of the belief that it's going to take one brother to fight the other. So here's the deal, Renegade leader. I can give you the ICE distribution center, the dealers, and a list of users. In exchange I want protection from the Trackers *and* a safe shelter to include immunity. I don't go behind bars."

Caleb shook his head no.

"Fine," Sterling said, eyeing Caleb defiantly. "You can have what you want. So how does this go down?"

"Oh no," Madame said. "Everyone knows Caleb's word is gold. I want to hear a promise from him."

Sterling, Michael, and Damion all stared at Caleb expectantly. Sometimes their leader was a little too much the golden good guy. Almost as if he needed to defy a connection to his brother by being something so extremely opposite, even when it wasn't the best choice.

"I won't give you immunity," Caleb said, "but I will give you protection."

Sterling balled his fist and came an inch from pounding the table. Madame was offering them the chance to slow down Adam, a chance they needed.

"Not even if I tell you that ICE didn't kill those users who died?" she said. "It was the cocktail Iceman created. The one he just started pumping onto the streets in high volume a couple of days ago. And you can stop him with my help. I'll call back in a few days when the body count gets higher." She hung up.

Silence filled the room, expanding with tension, until Michael said, "Becca can help us end this."

"She'll die, and Dorian will get away," Sterling said. "That solves nothing."

"Which is why I won't allow her to risk her life unless I feel she has adequate control over her abilities, enough to protect herself," Caleb said. "But I have to work with her to evaluate that. You know me, Sterling.

You know I wouldn't throw her to the lions." He hesitated and added, "But she deserves the right to choose for herself."

Sterling narrowed his gaze on Caleb, those words ringing with the assurance that Caleb had seen them in Becca's head, and that pissed him off. It also forced him to take notice. Becca wouldn't likely forgive him for taking away her choice, but he wasn't sure he could stop himself when taking away that choice was about protecting her. "Work with her, but don't bring up Dorian. Not until we know if she can pull off defending herself."

There. He'd agreed. Somewhat. And he could tell from the look in Caleb's eyes that his friend knew that was all he was going to get right now—perhaps ever. Protecting Becca was becoming as necessary as breathing.

———

Standing in the lab a good hour after Sterling had left her in his bed to make herself "at home," Becca was hard at work on an ICE immunization, making a list of common earth organisms and substances she believed to be the most worthy of a reactive evaluation.

The timer on the desk went off telling her it was time to dose. Sterling had left her a large supply in his apartment, and she dug into the lab coat she wore over her favorite black slacks she'd been thrilled to find in the items Cassandra had brought her and removed a vial.

She popped the lid, and her hands shook, a bit of the drug spilling on the pink shirt peeking out from her lab coat. She brushed it off, grimacing. The shirt was a favorite that she'd gotten from one of the NASA school tours, with "science is moon juice" on the front—some sort of knowledge is brain food kind of theme. She loved the crazy looks on people's faces when they saw it and didn't have the courage to ask what it meant.

She could use some of that amusement right now as she started to tip back the vial and hesitated, wondering why she was shaking so badly. She did have that tattoo on the back of her neck. The minute Sterling had left she'd raced to the mirror to see if it had faded, but sure enough, it was still there.

Becca eased the vial away from her lips and popped the lid back in place. What if the combination of the three—a partial Lifebond, cancer, and the ICE—had somehow changed her dosing requirements? She needed to draw blood before and after she dosed, because she didn't feel right at all. In fact, she felt pretty darn nauseous. *You need to eat*, she told herself.

But deep down, the woman and the scientist knew it was more than that. What if what she was feeling had to do with her partial Lifebonding with Sterling? But she had no one to talk to... not if she wanted to keep this bond a secret. Becca walked to the cabinet and pulled out the supplies to draw blood. A few minutes later, she placed the blood under a microscope and analyzed it.

Her breath lodged in her throat at what she saw, and she leaned back. Everything was not as it had been before the Lifebond mark. She'd been right. She had to talk to someone. Kelly or maybe Cassandra. Kelly. She'd simply have to claim doctor-patient privilege and pray that in this world of Renegades that still meant something.

Chapter 24

AN HOUR AFTER HIS ABRUPT DEPARTURE FROM THE Cityscape meeting, Sterling had exchanged a phone call with Eddie over the still missing Clanners from the club; unsuccessfully tried to reach Marcus and finally given up; and then did what any good, respectable soldier did when he was going to see the woman driving him insane—he picked up doughnuts. He didn't bother going to his apartment. He knew where he'd find Becca—already at work in the lab—and he was right. He shoved open the door and brought her into view.

Even before she turned to face him, awareness ripened in his limbs. He wanted her with the kind of hunger that ravished him inside out. And not merely her body. He wanted *her*. To wake up next to her... to kiss her good morning... to know what she felt, what she liked and disliked—things he swore he'd never allow himself with a woman, things his duty, his responsibility, had made impossible. No, her cancer, and now the ICE made them impossible, not his career. His chest swelled with the heaviness of regret and anger.

The instant she heard the door, she pushed off the lab stool and turned to him, lazily stretching beneath the oversized lab coat hiding the curves his memory was plenty ready to conjure up. He wasn't sure he could ever get enough of her.

"Hi," she said, blinking away a glazed look that told him she'd been in deep concentration for quite some time.

"Morning again," he said, walking toward her and indicating the box of doughnuts and coffee in his hands. "Brought breakfast since I knew you weren't likely to eat before you came to work."

"I've trained you well in such a short time," she teased. "And you're right. I didn't eat. I was eager to start testing my theory for an immunization."

He sauntered to a halt in front of her, and before he could stop himself, leaned forward and gave her a quick kiss—the kind of "hello" kiss a couple shared, the kind of kiss he didn't give women. And he enjoyed it, even wanted to repeat it. Right now, he'd be good with tossing the doughnuts on the table, stripping Becca naked, and finding his way back inside her.

"You taste like chocolate," she said, licking her bottom lip and accepting the coffee he offered her.

"Chocolate-covered glazed doughnuts," he corrected and set the box on the desk.

Her eyes lit, little specks of yellow swirling with amber, like a sunset pressing against a dark sky. "I love chocolate-covered glazed," she said, sitting down in a leather chair. "You saw my doughnut preferences while you were in my head too, I guess."

He claimed the seat next to her. "Nope," he said, teasing her. "No probing head games this morning. I just happen to like them, and we seem to mesh well when it comes to pleasure." He took a bite. "Hmmm... if this isn't pleasure, I don't know what is."

She shook her head. "You can't make me blush

anymore. You used up your blush quota several hundred outrageous comments ago."

He wiggled a brow at her. "Want to bet on that?"

"No," she said quickly and took a bite of her own doughnut. "I'll go with your 'no gambling' rule."

He finished off the one in his hand and brushed the crumbs away. "Ever heard of ICE Eclipse?"

"Not until Kelly called me about an hour ago," she said. "Adam knows nothing about this, or I'd know since I was testing for the cause of ICE fatalities." She sipped her coffee. "Kelly's working on the tox screen now, trying to identify what's in the Eclipse boost." She shook her head. "How ironic though that it's ultimately a human concoction of drugs that's killing people. We humans love to destroy ourselves. Not that I think ICE is safe. I simply think the side effects are going to manifest later with far more menacing consequences than death."

A knock sounded on the door, and Sterling went completely, utterly still. The doughnut he'd eaten rolled in his stomach. After the conversation he'd had with his fellow Renegades about Becca, protectiveness surged inside him.

"Must be urgent for someone to risk coming near me," Becca said, attempting a light tone and failing.

She felt isolated, and she didn't like it, he realized. And who could blame her? If only teaching her to control her abilities meant freedom rather than the danger of being used as bait.

With a few long strides, Sterling yanked open the lab door and did a double take when he found Damion standing there. Sterling gave his buzz cut and desert fatigues a once-over—Mr. All-American soldier, his ass, always preaching about rules and honor. He didn't even know what honor was. "You have a lot of balls coming here. What do you want?"

"For you to stop saying shit like that to me," he said. "I want to talk to Becca."

"I already asked her if she remembers you, if that's your plan," Sterling said. "She doesn't. And you know that, or you wouldn't be here."

Damion ran a hand over his hair. "See. There you go again." He ground his teeth. "I *did not* hand Becca over to Tad. Let me talk to her. She was scared when she saw me, reacting to fear. Give her a chance to remember me, so I can put your damn accusations in the grave where they belong." He lowered his voice. "Unless you're afraid she'll remember something you don't want her to remember."

"Pissing me off isn't helping your case," Sterling growled. "And news alert, smart guy—you can't come near her without passing out."

"Caleb said she has more control now," he said. "And I'm willing to take the risk of passing out to end this."

"Does Caleb know you're here?"

"No," Damion said, "but I'm all for including him if you want to. This thing between us needs to end, Sterling."

"Sterling," Becca said from behind him.

Too close to Damion for comfort. Sterling glowered at Damion. "Go away." He went to shut the door.

Damion's foot blocked it from closing. "Not until I see Becca."

"Sterling?" Becca said again.

Damn it. "Wait outside while I talk to her." Damion didn't move, his jaw set in stubborn determination.

Sterling made a frustrated sound. "Surprising her is not the way to meet her and stay standing on two feet. I need to prepare her."

"I'm not leaving until I talk to her. Eventually she has to come out of that lab." Reluctantly, Damion released the door and stepped away from it.

Sterling shut the door and turned to face Becca.

"I heard part of what he said. He wants to talk to me. Who is he?"

"The guy with the knife from the backseat of the car," Sterling said. "Damion."

"Right," she said, her expression thoughtful. "You asked me if I remembered him from the day I was abducted."

"Yes," Sterling agreed, hesitating as he selected his words cautiously. He didn't want her to start breaking glass and floating things in the air again. "Something happened that day. He insists it didn't. I know it did."

"Something bad, I guess." He nodded, and she asked, "Can't Caleb just look in his head? Or feel out his emotions. Or whatever it is he does. Can't he figure it out?"

"He says Damion is innocent. I was there. He isn't."

"I see," Becca said, looking uneasy. "He seems determined and certain he'll prove his innocence. Otherwise why would he be here?"

"For exactly that reason," he said. "You were passed out. You aren't going to remember anything. But him showing up here, demanding to see you, aware he might pass out, makes him look innocent—or so he hopes. He doesn't fool me for a minute. I don't want you anywhere near the man."

"What exactly do you think he did?"

Backed into a corner, Sterling contemplated keeping the truth from her. But the way she saw into his head, who knew when she'd find the truth anyway. "He helped Tad capture you."

She gaped. "And yet he's still here with the Renegades?"

"He insists the half dozen or so bullets I'd taken made me delusional," he said. "I wasn't."

"And Caleb?"

"There were other Renegades there that day," he said. "No one saw what happened but me. Caleb won't convict him on my word, not when I was injured. Damion is one of our most trusted Renegades. We were…"

"Friends," she finished for him. "And his betrayal hurts."

Could he hide nothing from this woman? "It didn't make me happy, no."

"I'll do it," she said decisively. "I'll talk to him. I have to. We need to know the truth with so much on the line."

We. Why did her using that reference make him feel so damn good? He'd never been part of a "we" in his life. "I don't like it."

"I got that from the way you tried to slam the door on his foot," she said. "Let's do this and get it over with."

A knock sounded on the door. "I'm not going away, Sterling," Damion yelled.

"Hold your damn horses," Sterling shouted over his shoulder.

Becca laughed, the sound resonating with nervous energy. "If he's this eager to throw himself under the bus, let him do it. Open the door, Sterling."

Sterling stood there, willing himself to move, but damn, if he didn't feel a "me Tarzan, you Jane" rush that made him want to beat on his chest, scream "mine," and then go hide Becca someplace safe. Only he couldn't hide her—not from what she faced. There was no place safe. And as long as Damion remained inside the Renegade operation, they were all in danger. Still he didn't move.

"I really don't like this, Becca."

"I know," she said and walked to stand beside him.

"The anchor thing," he said. "Maybe you should use me now."

"I thought of that," she said. "But you are pretty upset with him. I don't want to risk what you're feeling somehow clouding my own memories or upsetting me so much that I make him pass out." She reached out and took his hand. "But thank you, and if I need you, I'd appreciate it if that offer stays open."

Sterling stared down at their hands, hers so delicate. At that moment, he felt small and weak compared to the bravery of this little female. He'd been alone so long—all his life. Alone was easier. Alone didn't come with good-bye or the emotion he had welling in his chest. Yet he was crazy about Becca, unable to turn away from her.

He brought her hand to his lips. "I am here if you need me." *Always*, he wanted to add, but that inferred that "always" was possible. So he didn't.

Sterling released her hand and turned to the door, prepared to lay out some rules to Damion before he walked into the lab.

—◆◆◆—

With a deep breath, Becca steeled herself for Damion's

entrance by mentally touching the shield Caleb had taught her to erect around her mind. She found security in its presence. And by doing so, she felt a sense of much-needed control.

The door opened, and a man walked into the room— tall, broad, and athletic, like Sterling, but the similarities ended there. Damion wore army fatigues rather than the faded jeans and light blue T-shirt Sterling wore. His sandy brown hair was razored short, where Sterling wore his light blond hair thick and spiky. And the man's eyes—the true GTECH black concealed under a façade of his natural human shade of forest green—contrasted with Sterling's teal green.

For a moment they all stood there in silence, the unspoken expectation in the air that Damion would pass out, but Becca felt not even an inkling of fear. In fact, the way Sterling was standing over Damion's shoulder, looking like the big, bad, boogeyman ready to beat his face in if he made the wrong move, almost made her want to laugh. Instead she smiled to herself. She found his protectiveness adorable and sexy. And it filled her with warmth.

"Thanks for seeing me, Becca," Damion said, when he'd apparently decided he was not going to end up a floor mat.

Becca glanced from Sterling back to Damion, studying the sharp lines of his face, trying to find a memory of that day at her house. His skin was sun-stroked, the slight lines around his eyes and mouth aging him to what she guessed was early thirties. He was handsome in a rugged kind of way, but not familiar.

"I'm sorry," she said, her lips thinning in disappointment. "I don't remember you. Not from that day at my house, only from the backseat of the car, when you were trying to cut out the tracking device."

"Damn it," Damion cursed, shaking his head. "Try again. Try harder."

Looking exceedingly irritated, Sterling barked, "She said she doesn't remember. And if you think showing up here to see her somehow makes you look more innocent, it doesn't. It makes you look desperate."

Damion whirled on him. "We were in the same army unit together," he said. "I've fought by your side for years. I've bled for you. How can you think I'd hand Becca over to Tad?"

"A lot of men we both served with are now Zodius," Sterling said. "So tell me what part of serving together proves a damn thing."

Damion made a frustrated sound and turned to Becca. "Caleb says you have abilities you haven't accessed yet, like getting in people's minds. Try and get into mine. Try and see what happened that day." He took a step toward Becca, and Sterling grabbed his arm.

Damion shoved off Sterling's grip and turned his attention on Becca again.

"I don't know," Becca said, taken off guard. Could she do this? She'd been able to get into Sterling's mind because he'd let her do it. Or, she thought, maybe it was because they were Lifebonds. She wasn't sure she could get into Damion's.

"She's not giving you a chance to somehow open her up to another one of Dorian's mind attacks," Sterling said, stepping in front of Becca. "You're gone, Damion. You got your chance. It didn't work."

"Oh come on now, Sterling," he said. "We both know

why you don't want her in my head. You're afraid she'll see what really happened and hate you, not me."

The next thing Becca knew, Sterling had a hold of Damion and was shoving him backward. They crashed against the door in a hard thud that rattled the supply shelf resting a few feet away.

A horrible feeling twisted in Becca's gut. What had happened that day at her house that Sterling wouldn't want her to know about? She had to know—needed to know. She inhaled and charged toward the two men, no idea what she was doing, but determined nonetheless. She stopped at the side of the two men and grabbed both their arms, focusing her mind at the same time. And the images started to flow.

Chapter 25

IMAGES RUSHED AT BECCA, SPIKING HER MIND LIKE needles in a pillow—thin, sharp, precise. She gasped and stumbled backwards, landing on something sharp.

"Becca—" She heard his distant voice, an echo in a tunnel that suffocated her with darkness.

Suddenly she was in her house again, in Sterling's arms as he ran down the stairs, in his head, and in his body. There was pain, so much pain, and fear for her. He wasn't going to make it. He wasn't going to save her. He ran harder, smoke rasping through his lungs—time stood still as pain shattered his side, his back, his arm. He burst through the back door onto the porch and found Damion waiting for him. He resisted handing her over— something told him not to hand her over—but he trusted Damion, and he was no longer capable of protecting her. She felt the relief for her safety swelling inside Sterling, even as the pain of his injuries splintered through him like a million pieces of broken glass, biting through his muscles with unbearable pain.

Explosive anger roared through him a moment later at what he saw in the distance—her in Tad's arms. Sterling shouted in utter disbelief, but he was weak, and the sound was a hoarse whisper. He launched himself toward the stairs, running for her, but another bullet pierced his leg, then he fell and blankness followed.

The images shifted in her mind, and Becca was

seeing through Damion's eyes. Sterling was handing her over to Tad a moment before he crumbled to the ground. Damion was running toward them, trying to stop Tad from taking her, but it was too late.

Becca's fingers dug into her hair, curling around the disarrayed strands, replaying both men's memories, trying to figure out what felt so wrong. "It doesn't make any sense."

"Becca, sweetheart." Sterling pleaded. His voice permeated the confusion, warm and gentle. She blinked away the images, fighting a battle in her mind, and found Sterling squatting beside her on the floor. "Are you okay?"

"Yes, I..."

Damion appeared over Sterling's shoulder, an anxious look on his face, the deep hazel of his eyes melding with hope. She opened her mouth to speak when Sterling said, "Your hand. You're bleeding."

Turning over her palm, Becca stared at the blood, blinked twice, and then felt the rise of panic, the fear of accidentally creating a blood bond. She scrambled to get up. "I'm fine." She defied that claim by ramming into the bar stool and smacking her head. She sat back down. "Ouch!"

Sterling wrapped his hand around her calf. "Hold still, and let me help you. You're hurt."

"No," she said, pushing away from him again. She managed to get to her feet, noting the red blotch down her lab coat. "I'm fine." She grabbed the hem of the coat and pulled the material around her hand. "How did I cut myself?"

"One of the vials busted, and you fell on it," Sterling

said, his voice husky, waves of emotion pouring off him. He thought her panic was directed at him, that she'd seen something about him she found upsetting.

"If you touch me," she said, grasping for an excuse for her behavior, "I'm afraid I'll get confused. I'll lose the images in my head. I'm... I'm trying to make sense of what I saw."

"Becca," he breathed in a tormented whisper, unconvinced by her excuse. "Whatever you saw—"

"I don't know what I saw," she assured him, wrapping the lab coat around her hand with an iron-clad grip; the adrenaline pumping through her veins was, no doubt, making the bleeding worse. "One minute I saw Damion handing me off to Tad." She swallowed the heartbeat that darted into her throat and hoarsely added, "The next it was you handing me to Tad. It was... confusing... jumbled." Emotion swam inside her, and not her own—Sterling's.

"You said you didn't recognize me," Damion pointed out and gave Sterling a stern look. "If I'd been the one to take Becca from you that night, she'd have to remember me."

"I know what I saw," Sterling ground out between his teeth.

Damion cast a pleading look. "You don't remember me."

She was at a loss at what to say. "I was leaning over Sterling's shoulder shooting at the door when I was handed off, and the gun was ripped from my hand. I fought wildly, blindly." Her gaze flickered between the two men. "I could have been handed off more than once, I guess. I was rattled. It all happened so fast."

She glanced at Damion and weighed what she was about to say for certainty. She trusted him. Right or wrong, she felt it to her core. Not the way she trusted Sterling, but she trusted him.

Slowly, she shifted her focus back to Sterling. "Whatever happened that night, Sterling, Damion wasn't working for Adam. I'm sure of it."

Damion let out an audible sigh of relief while palpable tension banded around Sterling.

"I know this sounds silly, but I have this sense of illusion. Like someone made one or both of you see something that wasn't there." She shook her head. "I have to think, to process, and see if I can make sense of it."

"I'll go," Damion said. "Thank you, Becca."

"Thank you for trying to save me," she returned with sincerity.

Surprise flickered across his chiseled features, quickly masked. He inclined his head and turned to leave. Neither he, nor Sterling, acknowledged one another, the strife between them still too raw. Somewhere in the midst of what she'd experienced between these two, she'd felt friendship and trust—sadly, now torn apart.

As Damion made tracks for the door, Becca's gaze collided with Sterling's, his face guarded, impossible to read, but she didn't need to read his expression. She felt the need in him, the sudden, possessive desire, the white-hot lust, and fear—fear he was losing her, like he somehow needed her before she was gone. It all rolled off of him, a part of the tidal wave she'd sensed in him before, crashed into her, and silently pulled her toward him, engulfing her with the force, demanding response.

Respond she did. Desire pooled low in her stomach

as heat slid along her skin. Shaken by his ability to provoke such instant lust and how easily she could forget the danger of the blood on her hand, she cut her gaze.

"I have to wash up," she said, rushed to the sink, and turned on the water, all the while trying to understand what was happening. How had she gone her entire life without ever finding this kind of passion? Sterling appeared by her side and offered her a bandage he'd unwrapped. He frowned as he looked at her hand. "You shouldn't be bleeding that badly."

"I'm fine," she said, taking the bandage, but of course, she wasn't fine. Her heart sputtered and threatened to stop. It was how she'd bled during cancer treatments, when her blood had stopped clotting properly. Right then she realized what she'd done, what she'd sworn she would not do. She'd found hope, and hope had once again stomped all over her.

She covered the cut without looking at Sterling, and then forced herself to turn to him. "I should get back to work."

"We need to talk about what just happened."

She desperately wanted to touch him, to tell him she'd seen nothing but a hero in those flashbacks, but if she did, they wouldn't stop there. And she could feel the blood oozing through her bandage. "I don't want to talk about it right now." She tried to sidestep him. She needed to run tests, figure out what was happening, and keep Sterling away from her blood.

Before Becca could escape, she was in his arms. Warmth slid through her limbs, and she wondered why she had wanted to. But the minute her hand settled on his chest, another splintery piece of information pierced her mind, a memory both he and Damion had shared. "Caleb wants to use me to get to Dorian."

Sterling's expression darkened. "You're not doing it." He picked her up, set her on the desk, and stepped between her legs as if he belonged there.

"I have to do it," she said, ignoring his order, shaking inside at the idea of contact with Dorian, but knowing this was the right thing. "I want to do it."

He stared down, dark shadows swirling in his eyes. "No." He pressed his hand to hers where it still rested on his chest.

Becca sucked in a breath, realizing her hand, her bandaged hand was on his chest, like she'd subconsciously put it there.

Sterling's fingers slid to her face. "He almost killed you last night."

A terrifying, familiar reality. "But he didn't, and I'm learning to use my abilities. I'll be okay." She would be okay. She let those words fill her, convinced herself she believed them. And she did, until he lifted his hand, now covered in the blood seeping from her wound.

Sabrina delivered a drink to a forty-something, bald guy at the blackjack table. He grabbed the glass and did another long inspection of her cleavage as he dropped a chip on her tray. A flipping dollar. Her gaze slanted over the ring around his finger.

She leaned forward, next to his ear. "Let's invite your wife for a little ménage, shall we? Should I go find her?"

He went completely still and then dropped a green chip on her tray. She caught a glimpse of his ruddy face a moment before he turned back to the cards, and she all but laughed. Wife threats worked every time.

Of course, the tips were just for fun. She kept this job as both a cover and a way to scout local marks that happened through the casino, flashing credit cards and addresses.

Not anymore though. Soon "Madame" was going to be on top with whoever could get her there. Iceman. Tad. Hell, she'd resort to the Renegades if she had to. She was, after all, about to get to know them up close and personal. Of course, if she worked herself into the Renegades' inner circle and killed Rebecca Burns as Tad wanted, they wouldn't like her much. She shrugged. There was only so much friendship to go around.

It was an hour later when she strutted through the kitchen to the back parking lot, ready to take on her Madame role. The hot Vegas night slammed into her with a force of a two-by-four, and she felt a bit weak in the knees. The way she felt when she needed a hit of ICE.

Chapter 26

BECCA JERKED HER HAND FROM STERLING'S CHEST with a gasp and grabbed her lab coat, wiping his hand clean. "Are you nuts?" he asked. "Stop worrying about me. I'm worried about you."

He pulled her to the sink and washed her hand. She squeezed her eyes shut and told herself he healed quickly. There would be no open wound for her blood to seep through. And with his macho protectiveness in high gear, it was clear she had no option but to cave and let him tend her hand.

A phone call to Kelly, and then they drew her blood and rushed it to Sunrise City via one of the windwalkers. Then the waiting began. She wanted Kelly to run these results, to see what was there, to assure her the Lifebond connection had not put Sterling at risk. Becca sank into the desk chair and tried to work while her testing was evaluated, but she was silently panicking. She hadn't had time to talk to Kelly about the changes in her blood since the mark appeared, and she couldn't bring it up in front of Sterling. An hour passed, and Becca read through the GTECH research Kelly had emailed.

Sterling hovered and paced, then hovered and paced some more.

With a frustrated grumble, she shoved the doughnut box shut and rotated in her chair to bring him into view, resting her arm on the back. "That's it," she said. "No more sugar for you. Don't you have an ICE dealer to go hunt down?"

"We should go to Sunrise City," he said. "Right now—wind-walk there and let Kelly run proper testing on you."

That he worried about her touched Becca deeply, but it also told a story. He'd insist on saving her if he knew he could, and that was even less an option now. Dorian could kill her and Sterling with her, if they were bonded. "Far too much time has been spent on me and my health issues," Becca insisted. "We need to focus on an immunization and a cure for ICE addictions." She left off the part about capturing Dorian, because she didn't want to argue about why she should or should not be involved. She was going to be involved whether he liked it or not.

"Once you're there, you can work more closely with the medical team," he argued.

So much for not delving into Dorian territory. "We both know why I can't go hide in Sunrise City. And anything medically wrong with me makes what I have to do here more urgent."

"You're not going to be bait for that freak son of Adam's," he said, his voice as hard as his stubborn head.

"Macho bossiness doesn't work on me," she assured him. "My father and my brother were both macho and bossy, and it got them nowhere. The entire reason you came in search of me in the first place was to stop Adam. And if I can help do that, I am going to do it."

"You're not," he ordered.

"Stop being unreasonable," she ordered right back. "You've taken on protecting me like it's your duty." She pointed at him, his mouth already open to argue. "And don't say it is. Protecting this country—at this point, all of humanity—is your duty. Not one woman." And damn it, she didn't want to be his or anyone's duty.

She drew a determined breath. He needed to leave before Kelly called with her test results in case something about their Lifebonding showed up. "If you can't remember that fact, then you and I... well, we can't... then I need to stay in another apartment."

His expression darkened, and he took a step toward her. "You don't mean that."

"I do," she said, choking on the words. "I... it's for the best. So we both remain objective about our decisions."

"I've been in *your* head too, sweetheart," he said, the distance gone between them. He towered over her, his fingers teasing a strand of her hair, his stare heavy as it rested on her face. "You're trying to protect me like you've been protecting your mother. I don't need protection." He paused, his eyes boring into her with dark emotion pouring from him into her. "*I* protect *you*. You don't protect me."

People who loved each other protected each other, but she didn't say that. She didn't say anything.

"You can't push me away," he said softly. "I won't let you.

Becca squeezed her eyes shut against an unexpected sensation—the heaviness in her chest. Damn it. She wasn't going to cry. She wasn't. She couldn't. She was past crying.

Sterling's hand cupped her face, and she leaned into the touch, unable to stop herself, all her good intentions at pushing him away lost.

The computer buzzed, and Becca's stomach twisted in a knot. Trying to hide her apprehension, Becca forced her eyes open. "I need to do this alone."

"No," he said, his hardheaded stubbornness roaring to life yet again.

"Please," she said desperately. "I want to talk to her by myself. I need to deal with whatever is wrong alone first."

"You aren't alone," he said, and leaned over her and punched the computer key.

Resigned to defeat, Becca turned to the monitor as Kelly's image came into focus. "Okay, Becca," Kelly said wearily, her blonde hair piled haphazardly on her head with what looked like a pencil. "Here's where we are. Your blood count is all over the place, but we have no conclusive cause for the bleeding. I'm working on more detail."

"I had clotting issues during cancer treatments," she said.

"This doesn't mean your cancer is back," Kelly said sternly. "Stop thinking like that. I don't see any proof of any such thing."

Becca filled in the unspoken blank. "Please don't coddle me, Kelly."

Kelly pursed her lips. "I'm not. Stop trying to make this something it isn't." Sterling's hands settled on Becca's shoulders. Strong. It would have been comforting if Becca didn't so desperately need to talk to Kelly alone.

"Bottom line is this, Doc," he said. "What does all of this mean for Becca?"

"We want her to dose again and draw her blood immediately after."

"Can she do that?" he asked. "Dose again safely? I mean, I know she takes two a day now. But three?"

"Leaving her blood panel readings as they are now isn't safe either."

"So that was a no," Sterling said. "It's not safe."

"Excess ICE is disposed of by the body," Kelly explained. "That's why she doesn't overdose when she takes two vials a day and why we don't see people dying from excessive use."

What Kelly didn't say and Becca silently supplied was that they had no idea if there were other effects from larger doses.

"I'll do it," Becca said. "Thank you, Kelly." Trying to focus on something other than herself for her sanity, she added, "I was thinking about the vitamin C deficiency the GTECHs suffer. The reports you sent me say their bodies repel the absorption like oil and water. So what would happen if we injected someone with high levels of vitamin C? Would it repel the ICE absorption?"

"Interesting," Kelly said, her brows pulled together in thought. "You might just be onto something." She refocused. "But you need to go dose now. We can discuss this later."

"I agree," Sterling chimed in a moment before his cell rang. He grabbed it from his belt and cursed. "I have to take this. It's Riker." He frowned. "And Eddie."

Something was going on, and it must be big, but

Becca stayed on point. "Later" was a word she'd once taken for granted—not anymore. "Can you have a team start working the vitamin C theory?" she asked Kelly.

"I already planned on it," Kelly assured her. "Now you go dose."

Becca hesitated, relieved as Sterling stepped outside the lab, still on the phone. "I read through the basic Lifebond process you included with the GTECH material, but can you send me the more detailed version?"

Kelly tilted her head and narrowed her eyes, intelligence glistening in their depths. "Are there certain tests I should be running on you, Becca? Tests you'd rather were kept confidential?"

"Yes," she said, relieved at Kelly's ability to be both candid and discreet in the same instant. "That would be a good idea."

"I suspected as much, and I've already ordered the testing. The results aren't fully in yet, which is why I didn't mention them. My concern here is that you've started the Lifebond process and that your body might be trying to complete it without blood by perhaps replacing it with ICE."

Becca went cold. "How is that even possible?"

"This is the world of unknowns, but Cassandra had a similar situation. She and Michael didn't immediately complete their bond, and her body took over. She had a variety of health issues until they finished the blood bond. I'm of the opinion that completing the blood exchange immediately is critical to your safety."

"That means if I die, Sterling dies."

"Yes, but—"

"No. That can't happen. It *can't happen*, Kelly. What

if ICE caused something to happen to Sterling? Like turn him Zodius or kill him. And then there is the Dorian thing. If he attacks me, he attacks Sterling."

"What does Sterling say?"

"He doesn't know, and he can't know."

"We're talking your life here."

"Even if I didn't have these fears for his safety, I wouldn't tell him. I won't be some obligation he's stuck with."

Kelly tapped her pencil on the desk she sat behind and then thoughtfully rested her chin on her hand. "You want this to be a choice, not a forced bond that translates to a medical treatment to save your life." It wasn't a question. "I get that."

"I'm not sure you do," she said. Becca did want Lifebonding to be about choice. But Sterling was right too, when he said she was trying to protect him.

"No," Kelly insisted. "I do. So you should know that we have every reason to believe the couples who Lifebond would have fallen in love anyway. We think that's why Adam can't recreate it by throwing people together to have sex. In fact, he almost ensures he won't. And I know 'think' is a bad word in science, but when you read my reports you'll see why I say this. I really believe Lifebonding is an evolution of falling in love. Whatever you feel for Sterling isn't some scientific creation, Becca. It has real emotional substance."

Becca warmed with those words, with the hope that what they felt was real, but it didn't change things. "I won't risk Sterling's life."

Kelly studied her a moment. "If what you just said doesn't prove the love equation of Lifebonding," she said softly, "I don't know what does. I have to consult Caleb, but for now you have my silence."

"Thank you," Becca said, relief washing over her.

Kelly considered Becca a long moment. "You're taking his choice from him," she said. "You know that, right?"

Becca inhaled sharply at that observation. The door to the lab opened, and Sterling walked in. Becca turned and looked at him and saw his eyes reaching for hers, the look on his face warm with worry.

Heart fluttering, Becca recognized that what was between her and Sterling had started before the marks on her neck. It had started in that library years ago, when she'd had a crush that was the beginning of falling in love. She was still falling now. Becca turned back to the computer. "I might be taking his choice," she said softly, for Kelly's ears only. "But I'm also protecting him."

Sterling didn't miss the fact that Becca ended her teleconference with Kelly the minute he entered the lab. She rolled the chair around to face him, the splotch of bright red blood on her bleached white lab coat taunting him with the certainty of her fate. She was dying, and no matter what risk he took, no matter what mountain he climbed, no matter what building he jumped off—he could do nothing to stop it from happening. He couldn't even Lifebond with her, and he didn't understand it. If there was any woman in this lifetime he'd been connected to, it was Becca.

"What did Riker and Eddie want?" she asked, walking to a shelf and removing supplies to draw blood.

He closed the distance between them. "They both

wanted to remind me I owe them. And considering I pay Eddie—that takes big *cojones*. I guess that's why I really like that guy." He stopped in front of her and reached for the syringe.

"I can do it," she said, resisting weakly.

"You hate drawing your own blood," he said. "I'll do it."

She hesitated and then nodded, shrugging out of the lab coat and then claiming a seat. "Kelly wants blood before and after I dose."

"I was there, remember?"

"Oh yeah. Right."

He kneeled down beside her, resting his hand on her leg. "Becca—"

"I told you. Don't be the person who coddles me and says it's going to be okay."

"Okay," he agreed. "But only if I can be the person who tells you I'm crazy about you. I am."

She tried to laugh. "Bad choice. Don't be *that* person either, because you were right. I don't want you to get hurt."

"Hmmm," he said dubiously. "I'll take my chances." He wrapped a band around her upper arm.

"This isn't the time to start gambling." Her finger settled on his hand where it rested on hers. "I'm serious, Sterling. I'll stay in another apartment. End whatever this is between us before it gets any more complicated."

"No," he said, feeling her arm tremble. She needed to dose. He eased his hand back and prepared the needle.

"You like that word way too much."

"Because," he said, using his hand to extend her arm, tap her vein, and insert the needle. "You can't *argue* with 'no,' but if I gave you my reasons behind that refusal—scientist that you are—you'd have to analyze them, tear them apart, try and disprove them. A lot of time better spent working on the immunization, or even better, naked, in bed with me. By the way, that requires we be in the same bedroom in the same apartment."

She shook her head and smiled. "You're impossible."

He withdrew the needle. Blood seeped from her arm far too quickly, and he applied cotton and pressure. "I think you like impossible." He winked and walked to the cabinet again, setting aside her blood, grabbing a dose of ICE and supplies to draw yet more blood.

Returning to her side, he handed her the vial of ICE. She downed the contents then grabbed his hand. "I need to talk to Caleb," she said.

He stilled, certain he wasn't going to like where this was going. "Why, Becca?"

"I want to learn to protect myself against Dorian."

His jaw set. "You're not going after Dorian."

"That isn't your decision to make."

He taped her arm up, the ICE already slowing the bleeding, his answer coming slowly. "And if I refuse to let you do this?"

Her expression softened, her fingers grazing his cheek. "Then I give you one of those simple answers you like, and say, yes, I am. Then you agree, so let's skip the arguing, and go straight to that bed you mentioned."

"That's blackmail," he accused, snagging her hand.

A shy smile touched her lips. "Is it working?"

"Sweetheart," he said. "I'm taking you to bed no matter what. A good argument makes for great makeup sex."

A solemn look settled across her delicate features. "I have to do this, Sterling."

Sterling stared at her pale ivory face, wishing he could wipe away the dark stains beneath her eyes and the pain in their depths. Tormented not by what she had said, but what went unspoken.

She had to face Dorian while she still could, while she was capable. Everything inside him screamed to reject that reality, screamed that she was wrong. She *didn't* have to do this.

He wanted to take her to bed and keep her there, while all this hell went away, but it wouldn't. And he couldn't.

He had no idea what happened to him at that moment with those realizations, but he snapped. He could think of only one thing. How much he wanted inside this woman, her body, her soul. How much he absolutely had to be a part of her. How much it felt as if that were the answer to saving her.

Consciousness faded into pure need. He was kissing her then, wild and hot, barely a memory of when he'd pulled her into his arms. Suddenly, she was just there. And all he knew was the fire and ICE, of wanting what would surely be taken away, of the certainty burying himself inside her would somehow make this all go away.

He set her on the lab table as he had once before, spread her legs wide, and stepped between. Only this time they weren't making it to a bed.

Chapter 27

BECCA IN HER LAB COAT WAS MORE EROTIC THAN anything he'd ever seen. It was crazy, nuts, but Sterling had never wanted a woman the way he wanted her, never burned inside out. Never felt as if he might stop breathing if he didn't kiss her. But right there, then, with her on a damn lab table of all places, he was ready to ravish Becca.

"I want you," Sterling growled. "Here. Now."

Her fingers curled in his shirt, the heavy-lidded, desire-laden look she leveled on him telling him she was feeling pretty damn hot and needy herself even before she panted, "Yes. Please. Now."

He kissed her before the final word was completed, touched her tongue with his, and then caressed it nice and deep. Her hands, soft and delicate but not gentle, threaded through his hair and caressed his shoulders, his neck. Her touch drove him crazy. His cock stretched against his zipper.

Sterling pressed his hands beneath her jacket and filled his hands with her perfect high breasts, her nipples pebbling, hard little rosebuds teasing his palms. It was all he could do to keep from ripping off her shirt.

Forcing himself in check, he kissed a path down her neck, pressing her backward so that her hands rested on the table. Silky, raven hair cascaded behind her. Damn, he loved her hair—couldn't wait to have it draped over his chest. His mind raced with that imagery, but he was living in this moment. He kissed one of Becca's nipples through the thick pink T-shirt, nipped it with his teeth. He shoved off her lab coat and let his hand settle on the soft curves of her stomach. Why was she still wearing her shirt? He shoved it upward.

"Take it off," he ordered, reaching around her, already working on the hook for her bra. Both were gone in an instant. He tugged his shirt over his head as well and tossed it aside, burning for her skin against his.

He paused in admiration of her damn fine breasts with nice, plump nipples. He touched them and let their weight fill his palms. Becca covered his hands with her own as she fixed him in a heavy-lidded stare brimming with a raw, earthy quality that he could drown in—a happy man.

He kissed her, drank her in like the fine nectar she was, even as he pinched her nipples and stroked her breasts, rewarded with her soft, hungry moans, with the arch of her back, the touch of her hands. And he kept kissing her—her mouth, her neck. Lingering by her delicate little lobe he whispered in her ear, "You aren't going after Dorian."

Steel behind those words. She pressed her hands to his face and forced him to look at her. "Yes. I am. And you know it."

He inhaled, slid up her body, and pulled her hard against him, his hand raking her spine, molding her nipples to his chest. Lips lingered above hers. "No. You aren't."

"Another bet you shouldn't make," she told him.

Damn it to hell. Damn it to fucking hell. "No."

Her hand went to his face. "Yes."

He'd show her *yes*. He pressed her backward. "Lie down." He unzipped her pants and stripped them away, along with her shoes. "No panties," he said, upon that hot little discovery.

He spread her legs and stepped between them at the same moment that she sat up. "Panty lines," she explained, her hands going to his shoulders.

"I'm not complaining, sweetheart," he said, stepping back and easing her legs wider. "Open for me. Let me see my prize."

"Sterling," she whispered shyly.

"Your prize is coming too," he promised, mercilessly inching her knees wide. He was angry. At her insistence she put herself in harm's way. At Caleb's insistence there was no other answer. At the existence of a fucking disease called cancer. His gaze raked the pretty pink folds of her body. "Beautiful." His hands inched up her thighs. "How wet are you, Becca?"

"I can't believe I'm doing this," she said, her voice quavering. "We're in a lab on a table."

"And I'm about to do all kinds of naughty things to you on that table." His fingers stroked along her core. She gasped with the contact. "Oh yeah. Wet." He took her hand and guided it with his. She tried to pull away. He leaned forward and kissed her, a short, hungry tasting before he said, "Give yourself to the moment, Becca. Give yourself to me."

"Yes," she said, her mouth reaching for his. He gave it to her, that momentary escape she wanted. Then, lips lingering above hers, he guided her hand again, sliding their joined fingers along her slick, wet heat. She was breathing hard. Hell, so was he. He moved their hands together. Caressed, explored, and delved until she arched her hips against the touch. She was wet, so wet, but not wet enough. Sterling pressed her backward onto the table.

He reached for her legs and lifted them over his shoulders. "Sterling, what—"

His mouth closed down on her nub, ending any questions, any objections. He licked and tasted, caressing her with tongue and fingers, her soft little moans driving him crazy until she stiffened, and then shattered into orgasm. He took her all the way to the top and pulled her back down, unzipping his pants as he did, anticipating the moment he would finally be inside her.

He kissed a hungry path up her body and pulled her to a sitting position. "I have never needed to be inside a woman as much as I need in you right now."

"Yes," she whispered, sliding to the edge of the table and welcoming him.

He guided his cock inside her, intending to go slowly, but the wet heat of her was too much. She practically climbed on top of him, wrapping her legs and arms around him as he drove inside her, lifting her slightly off the table, pumping into her even as she rose to meet him, deeper and harder. Their bodies pressed tightly together. Their lips, hungry, molded in intimate, hot kisses.

She crashed into a sudden orgasm, her muscles grabbing his cock and pulling his release from him. Ripped it right from the core of his cock, and shot pleasure through his entire body. He buried his head in her neck, moaning with the intensity, spilling his seed inside her.

For eternal moments, they clung to one another.

Emotion replaced the pleasure, expanding in his chest as he rested his forehead against hers.

Her fingers curled on his cheek. "I have to try and capture Dorian."

"Not exactly the after-sex praise a guy likes to get from a woman," he teased lightly, leaning back to look at her only to find stark determination in her face. And he saw more, something he didn't want to see, but couldn't ignore. She needed a purpose, a reason to keep fighting, and she needed him to understand. "Then we'll do it together," he said. "But don't expect me to let you do the kind of crazy stuff I do out there."

She smiled. "I promise to only do crazy stuff while I'm with you."

"Add 'in bed' to that promise, and we have a deal."

"And here I thought that rule only applied to fortune cookies."

"Now you know better," he said and kissed her.

Early evening ten days later, Becca sat in the Cityscape conference room surrounded by Caleb, Michael, Damion, and Sterling. It was a miracle to her that, thanks to Sterling and Caleb's training, she was able to be here with them, able to control her abilities. And fortunately, increased doses of ICE had her feeling herself again, aside from a little nausea, which Kelly said was from her partial bonding with Sterling. And it was a good thing she was, because the four of them together was a lot of testosterone to swallow in a small room. Especially considering every last one of them was on edge and opinionated after three more Clanners had died. All of whom were packed up and toted away by the army before the Renegades could get to them.

And Sterling, well, he had done his best to keep her focused on science in the lab, or focused on him in his bed, and he wasn't pleased that it wasn't working—trying to convince her to stay out of the physical battle with the Zodius. But she'd continued training and felt more capable of using her skills in a confrontation each day. She knew her purpose in all of this, and it was about stopping Dorian, which was exactly why she'd been invited to this meeting.

"We have to shut down distribution," Michael said, a steely, determined set to his jaw. "Screw finding Iceman. Screw discretion. We'll send out a couple dozen Renegades today. Infiltrate the clubs and resorts. Let Adam know we mean business."

Caleb waved off that idea. "You'll force him out of the city and right into another one. Or two. Or three. Where we won't have the resources or manpower. It's too big a risk."

"I'll work Marcus harder," Sterling offered. "He's a greedy bastard. I'll up the pot of gold. Tell him my client is desperate for a large stock of ICE and willing to fork over the cash."

"He's probably having the same problem as us," Caleb said grimly. "Iceman is screening his users so well we can't find his dealers."

"We still have Madame," Sterling reminded him.

Damion tapped the table irritably. "She'll call back after a few more people die? Well, a few more have died. Where the flip is she?"

"She was taunting us," Michael said. "I doubt she

ever intended to help us. Iceman was playing with us, or setting us up, trying to get close to our operation, and Caleb shut him down before he got out of the gate."

Becca cleared her throat, shoving a wayward strand of dark hair from her eyes. "There's really only one answer," she said. "The one you're talking about because I'm here, even though we all know it's the reason I'm here in the first place. We have to deal with Dorian."

"Becca—" Sterling said.

Discreetly she removed her hand from the table and rested it on his leg. "I'm ready, Sterling," she said, finding his eyes with hers, willing him to accept what he couldn't change. She was touched by his concern, but mad at herself for being too selfish to leave his bedroom, too selfish to put distance between them when she knew it would be better for him in the end. "I've been working with Caleb. He's taught me a lot about control."

"That fluctuates in between the three ICE doses a day you're taking to fight off the cancer."

"Which could become four or five. Or kill me." She straightened her spine, determined, not willing to give in. "We need to do this. We need to deal with Dorian." Her gaze went to Caleb, telling Sterling this was happening with or without him. "What's the plan?"

She saw Caleb eye Sterling—the two men sharing a silent conversation only they understood, before a nod. "We get you outside Neon, making your presence known. We'll keep you under surveillance. Dorian will come for you, and we'll be waiting."

"We don't know what he's capable of," Sterling argued. "We have no idea if bullets, even Green Hornets, will slow him down. We know tranqs won't work."

"A nicotine dart," Becca said. "Kelly's been working on it after we tested it in the lab."

"Nicotine?" came the surprised rumble around the table. Damion asked, "As in cigarettes?"

"Right," she said. "Same substance, different composition. Nicotine depletes vitamin C, and as we all know, the GTECHs are vitamin C deficient. Boost them with nicotine, and the effect is weakened muscles and slowed organs, which is corrected only with the replacement of the missing C."

A stunned silence blanketed the table. "I want to be happy about this," Michael said. "But frankly, a weakness isn't something I enjoy. And his weakness is ours."

"Yes, well," she said cautiously. "We don't know if Dorian shares this weakness. He's not like the rest of you, or we wouldn't be dealing with ICE in the first place. It's a risk. We can't promise it will work."

"It's brilliant," Caleb said approvingly.

"And Kelly's idea," Becca said. "I simply introduce concepts related to different life forms. She made the magic happen. She's working with one of the engineers at Sunrise to create the dart and weapon to administer the nicotine, which apparently isn't a difficult task. It should be ready soon." She laced her fingers together on the desk. "Unfortunately, an immunization isn't as quick. It'll happen, but not fast enough to solve our problem. Not when we're accumulating a body count. But we now know that it's the combination of the ICE's effect on the body's organs at the same time the boost is used that causes the fatalities. Get rid of the ICE, and you stop the fatalities, assuming the one tox report we have is accurate. We still don't have the army's data."

"Riker still won't return my calls," Sterling confirmed, speaking to the room in general.

"Yeah, well," Caleb said, with a frustrated grunt. "I'm right there with you. No one is returning my calls either. Evidently, the government doesn't want to hand over those reports."

Completely baffled, Becca shook her head. "I don't understand. How do they expect us to operate like this?"

"They work with us when they're afraid Adam will kick them in the teeth," Michael explained. "Ultimately, they want us dead or controlled, just as they do Zodius. Truth be told, they're likely researching ways to use ICE to recreate the Super Soldier program they lost when the GTECH revolt occurred."

"We trade information for information," Caleb said. "Which is what we'll do now, if we can get a return phone call. We know about Dorian. They don't."

Sterling's cell phone beeped with a text message, and Michael grumbled, "Why do you always get these calls in the middle of meetings?"

"It's a text, oh dark and grumpy one," Sterling said, reading it. "Marcus wants to meet. Says he has a contact to get me that stash of ICE for a fabricated buyer." He pushed to his feet. "Gotta run. He wants to meet in fifteen minutes."

Becca stood as well. "I'm going with you. And don't say no, or I'll just…" What would she do? She glanced at Michael—big, intimidating Michael. "I'll have Michael take me."

Michael lifted his hands stop sign fashion, surprising Becca by laughing—something she doubted, until hearing it, he ever did. "I'm not touching that one with a ten-foot pole," he said. "Never get between a GTECH and his woman, but speaking from experience, Sterling, take her. It will be far less painless than fighting about it."

Becca's eyes narrowed on Michael. He arched a brow. He knew. He knew she and Sterling were Lifebonds. Her heart all but exploded in her chest. Sterling grabbed her hand. "Come on, woman. Before you make me have to kick Michael's ass."

Michael actually laughed again. "Like you have a chance in hell."

"Don't bet on that," Sterling called back over his shoulder. And despite the fact that she was about to become bait for quite possibly the most dangerous living being on their planet, Becca laughed too. She just hoped it wouldn't be her last.

Chapter 28

"OH MY GOD," BECCA SAID. "TELL ME WE DIDN'T TAKE Michael's car."

Sterling maneuvered the Mustang into the McDonald's parking lot where he was meeting Marcus. "Not just his car," he said. "His baby."

"He's going to be furious," she said.

"Good," he said. "He deserves to be furious."

"Don't pick a fight with him because you're mad at me," she scolded.

His cell phone rang. "I'm not mad at you," he said, yanking it from his belt. He was mad at the world, because it was going to take Becca from him, and it was going to do it soon. He could feel it in his bones.

He pulled into an inconspicuous parking spot near the back of the restaurant, scanned for Marcus and didn't see him, and eyed caller ID. With a low growl, he hit "send" and answered. To say he was in a foul mood would be an understatement.

"Ten fucking days you've been avoiding my phone calls, Riker," Sterling said acidly.

Unaffected by Sterling's mood, Riker replied, "Distance makes the heart fonder."

"Avoidance makes you a chicken shit," Sterling snapped. "We found out they had a drug cocktail in their systems. No thanks to you."

"I pick up the bodies," Riker replied, his words as dry

as the Vegas desert in mid-July. "I don't examine them. And I don't decide who needs to know what."

Sterling made a sound of disgust. "Bullcrap. You're running the army's ICE defense systems. You knew about Eclipse, and you knew I needed to know. You people want our help, yet you keep us in the dark."

"You people?" Riker asked in disbelief. "You mean the *U.S. Army*?"

"I mean the corrupt bastards above you, masquerading as the U.S. Army," Sterling corrected him, considered killing the engine, and decided to leave it running—in case Becca needed a fast escape. "While the army is busy plotting whatever they are plotting—no doubt something the Renegades won't like—Adam is gaining momentum, and innocent lives are being put in jeopardy."

A silver Porsche turned into the restaurant entrance. Fancy car spelled Marcus. Time to end the call. "ICE isn't made from Adam's DNA," Sterling quickly informed Riker. "You want to know more, you get someone to return Kelly's phone calls and make sure she gets what she wants. I don't care if it's the sticky note on your damn refrigerator." He hung up and eyed Becca. "Stay here."

She reached for her door. He shackled her arm. "I said, stay here."

"If I go unseen, then the purpose of me coming here was defeated," she argued, her eyes throwing defiant darts at him.

He grabbed her and kissed her, drank a long taste of what was fast becoming his own addiction. He didn't want her here, risking her life, when he hadn't even figured out how to save it in the first place.

"This isn't a bungee jump, Becca," he told her huskily. "We don't have those new nicotine weapons yet. We don't even have backup. Marcus misses nothing. He'll know you're here. That's all we're after." He let her go. "Lock the doors, and get the hell out of here at the first sign of trouble."

She nodded. "Okay. Stop acting so... angry."

"I freaking hate that you're doing this, Becca, and I hate that I can't come up with a reason that isn't selfish to stop you. So I'll be angry if I want to." He didn't wait for a reply. He shoved open the door and sauntered to the opposite side of the Mustang, masking the unease balled in his gut with a casual façade.

Marcus rested against the driver's side of the sleek silver Porsche, legs and arms crossed, a pair of Oakleys settled over his eyes. His fancy Italian, French, whatever-the-hell-it-was suit contrasted with Sterling's jeans and T-shirt.

"Great way to be discreet there, Marcus," Sterling drawled, giving the car a once-over. "Or maybe I misunderstood you on the phone, and you said 'don't be discreet.'" He snorted. "Would have gambled on you being a Lamborghini man though... *if* I was a gambling man, and I'm not."

"If you were a gambler, Sterling," Marcus drawled slowly, "we wouldn't be talking right now. We wouldn't be talking period. I don't gamble. I strategize to win, and then I win. And for the record, I have a number of cars. And yes, one of them is a Lamborghini."

Sterling wished he could see beyond those damn sunglasses, wondering what Marcus hid behind them. "For the record, your ego made you say that which makes it too big." Then, allowing impatience into his voice, "Why are we here, Marcus?"

"I know where you can get that ICE you want."

Sterling arched a brow. "I'm listening."

"Seems my casinos have been infiltrated by one of Adam's dealers," he said. "I've identified the woman in question. So here's how I want this to play out. You do your deal that you've been looking to make with her, keep my cut of our agreed upon deal, and I'll add another fifty Gs to your paycheck."

Sterling leaned against the Mustang, mostly because it would piss Michael off—and he was really in the mood to piss off the world today. "If this is the way you say I'm sorry for being a dick all the time," Sterling drawled. "I like the way you say I'm sorry."

Marcus tossed Sterling a data stick. "Pictures and relevant detail. Her name's Sabrina, a cocktail waitress at our Belladonna property, who several of my employees insist is high up in the ranks of the ICE operation, as in more than a dealer. Do your thing with her. Hell, *do* her for all I care. Then make her go away. I don't need her kind of trouble screwing with my business. She'll be back on duty Friday night—three nights too far away, as far as I'm concerned. She lives in the hotel. She'll be around."

Suspicion raked down Sterling's spine. This rang with bad vibes. A female close to the top of the food chain—sounded like his Madame caller. Coincidence? Few things were. Like Becca and him, he thought, shoving away the thought. "Why not use one of your security men?"

"The further this is from me and my staff, the better

for my business." His gaze shifted to the Mustang and to Becca in the passenger's seat. "That your new assistant?"

Sterling narrowed his eyes in a barely perceptible way. "Who told you I had a new assistant?"

"Just doing my part to pay off Eddie's medical bills for his poor, sick mother." He laughed. "You ain't got nothin' I don't got." He opened his car door and slipped inside, arrogant enough to assume Sterling would simply agree to his demands.

Sterling pocketed the data stick, watching as Marcus drove away. But there was something else bothering him. *You ain't got nothin' I don't got.* That statement bothered him. And not because of Eddie. Eddie was desperate to save his mother, though he'd be having a few, choice words with the man. It was about Marcus. Marcus was precise, exact in everything, even his speech. Maybe he was letting his guard down, but not likely. Marcus had a guard as steely as the defenses around Sunrise City.

Sterling shook his head. The way the man spoke wasn't the issue. There was something more. Why did the chance to get up close and personal with one of Iceman's top dealers have him so uneasy? Duh, asshole. Something wasn't right. He'd established that.

Sterling grimaced. Right. Brilliant observation. Of course, something wasn't right. He saw trouble everywhere he looked. Adam was trying to take over the world, and he himself was about to have his world ripped from beneath him because he'd gone and fallen in love with a woman destined to rip his heart out.

Sabrina lounged on her stomach across the foot of her bed, feet in the air, staring at Iceman where he sat tied to a chair, glaring at her with contempt in his eyes and a promise he would make her pay for this.

"You shouldn't have taken me for granted," she said. "Taking me for granted is what got you tied to that chair." She made a sound of disgust. "And good grief it was easy. I can't believe I thought you were powerful and sexy." She gave him a nasty inspection. "Now look at you. You're weak and pathetic. Easily outsmarted. You were all talk."

She didn't expect an answer. Not with that gag tied around his mouth. She liked him silent anyway. She'd listened to enough of his promises to last a lifetime.

The door handle rattled, and she sat up expectantly. The sheer red silk gown she wore she picked out especially for Tad. She'd hated him at first. But like her desire for Iceman, that had changed. She wanted him. Wanted what he could give her—a chance to be his Lifebond and live in the new kingdom of the world—Zodius City. A place her efforts would be appreciated rather than punished, as they would be with the Renegades.

The instant the door opened, her heart skipped a beat at the sight of Iceman appearing when he was tied to the chair. He slammed the door shut and in a single flash of a moment became Tad. She thrilled inside. The perfect fantasy man. He could be anyone she wanted him to be. That was pretty damn hot.

"How did it go?" she asked expectantly. "Did Sterling buy the story? Did he believe you were Marcus?"

"He not only believed it," he said. "He has Rebecca Burns with him right now."

Tad walked to the nightstand and opened a drawer, removing a dose of ICE and downing it. "So close and I couldn't touch her without the fear of passing out. No wonder Adam wants her dead. She's a menace."

"Do all the GTECHs take ICE?"

"They don't know the special skills it can give them," he said. "So why would they?"

She tilted her head. "And you don't want them to, do you? You like being something they aren't."

He sat down, offering her no response, but rather her own vial of ICE, along with a dose of Eclipse. Which she wanted, but... she cast him a dubious look. "I thought you said the Eclipse would kill me."

"Not taking it might as well," he said. "Lifebonding will eradicate your need for the drugs. You must stay strong until then."

She didn't know how to Lifebond, but she was all for being one of the royalty of Adam's world, which is what Tad said she would be. Excitement rose inside her. "When will that be again?"

"The same time I tell him about Eclipse," he said, guiding the vial to her mouth. "When the time is right." He turned the vial back on her lips and pressed the Eclipse star to her palm.

Pleasure rushed over her in a rainbow of color damn near as sweet as orgasm. She climbed on his lap, needing release, sliding her hands around his neck and glancing over at Iceman. She wanted to make Iceman watch.

But still, she hadn't forgotten her questions. "When is the time right?"

Tad ran his hands over her breasts, rough, measuring. "Adam is ruthless with his punishment if he does not get everything he wants when he wants it—generous with his rewards when he does. We will tell him of your Lifebond readiness when we share the news that the ICE deaths have come to an end. And so has Rebecca Burn's life."

She bit her bottom lip and smiled, arching against his crotch. "I can reward you now."

The room phone rang and so did her cell. She rolled her eyes. "It's JC. He's been calling over and over again. He says he needs Iceman."

Tad set her off him. "Tell him to come to the room," he said. "We may not need Madame. Sterling is here in the city with Rebecca Burns. We'll use those two Clanners from the warehouse he grabbed from the alley the other night to lure Sterling to us."

Damn. She really liked playing Madame. She grabbed the phone. "He's here," she said to JC, not giving him time to talk. "Come to my room. He wants to speak to you." She hung up.

Tad smiled. He walked over to his prisoner, watching as Iceman's eyes grew contemptuous. "I wouldn't look at me like that unless you want your balls in your throat." He kicked the chair over and ground his foot into Iceman's chest. "Then again, what's the point? I've decided I know what my reward should be for pleasing Adam. Your life. Fancy cars. Your woman in my bed. Lots of cash and power. I want to be you. I'm the new Iceman." Tad smiled. "Which means the old one has to die. Lights out, Marcus." Tad crushed his chest with his foot.

Chapter 29

NOT MORE THAN FIFTEEN MINUTES AFTER LEAVING the McDonald's parking lot, Becca slid into the wooden booth of the dimly lit, Texas-themed tavern not far off the strip, where they'd be meeting Eddie. Sterling followed her into the seat, his leg warming her bare one, her navy blue chiffon dress riding up her leg. A twenty-something bosomy blonde, who fit the showgirl persona of gorgeous with curves in all the right places, sidled over in short shorts and a halter. "What can I get ya?"

Becca realized right then this was the kind of woman she expected Sterling to be with, and she expected him to drool like the guy in the booth over her shoulder, who was gaping at the woman's backside.

Instead his hand slid to her leg, and he turned to her. "Coke?"

"Yes," she said, smiling at the tiny gesture of familiarity that felt really big. "Coke would be great."

He eyed the showgirl. "Coke. Chips and salsa. And tequila. A whole bottle of the best you have."

The waitress arched a brow. "Coming right up."

Becca turned her back to the wall to study him. "Alcohol doesn't affect you, and even if it did, you don't like it."

"I have the urge to try and overcome both obstacles."

"And that'll solve what?"

"Not a damn thing," he said. "But why not do it just to do it?"

"Why do I feel like I am in the middle of a *Seinfeld* episode?" she asked.

"Better *Seinfeld* than *Dexter*," he said. "Though I think our reality is a little more *Dexter* or *Twilight Zone* than *Seinfeld*." He rested his elbow on the back of the booth. "Friends in Low Places" by Garth Brooks replaced the sad melody of moments before. "When Eddie gets here, we have two choices. I drag him into the restroom and threaten to beat his brains in until he admits he sold information to Marcus. Or option two. You do your magical mojo thing and get in his head."

"I'll do the magical mojo thing," she said, knowing he didn't want to beat Eddie's brains in. He liked the guy. But she added quickly, "No promises."

The waitress set the tequila bottle on the table and two glasses. Sterling opened it and filled one. Becca grabbed the bottle to fill her own.

Sterling snatched it out of the way. "What are you doing?"

"If you're drinking," she said defiantly, her chin tilted upward, "so am I."

He glared at her and set the glass down. "We're Lifebonds," he blurted.

"What?" she gasped.

"It's been eating me alive," he said. "No Lifebond means I can't save your life."

"Sterling—"

"I need you to hear this, Becca," he said, his gaze one big thunderstorm of torment. "Please."

She nodded, unable to find her voice to reply. He

drew a breath and continued. "I've been going insane trying to understand how I could be so sure we would bond, and we didn't. I mean us... us... I would have gambled on. But then, driving over here a few minutes ago, I faced facts. I didn't take to the serum the way the other GTECHs did. I can't change my eye color."

Surprise washed over her. "You can't—"

"That's right. I wear special lenses to hide the black. And I can't wind-walk as far as the others either. Shit." He scrubbed a hand through his blond hair. "We're Lifebonds. I know we are. I just can't complete the process." Now his hand ran down his neck. "So I thought... I'll drink a couple bottles of tequila and try and get drunk. But it's not tequila I need. It's more serum. And the only person who has more serum is Adam."

Becca's heart was breaking. Her hand went to his arm. She had no idea about any of this. How had she missed something so important during their mental exchanges?

"You think we can't Lifebond because you are somehow not GTECH enough?" Like he'd thought he caused his grandmother's alcoholism.

"Yes," he breathed out in one word. "It has to be." And then he said the unexpected, the thing she realized she'd longed to hear more than anything, when she heard the words: "I love you, Becca."

"What I... you...?"

"I love you," he said hoarsely. "I tried not to, because I was afraid of losing you, but you know I do. And this isn't how I planned to tell you—in a bar with a bottle of tequila. Hell. I didn't know I was going to tell you at all, but it's done. Now you know."

She couldn't breathe. He loved her. Sterling loved her.

This changed everything. It made Lifebonding a choice, not an obligation. She opened her mouth to tell him, but a cold reality slid into place. If she told him, if they completed their bond and Dorian killed her, he'd kill Sterling too. She had to push him away, had to protect him.

Her throat constricted, but somehow she forced the words. "We haven't known each other that long."

His expression darkened, turned stormy, hurt burning deep in their depths. He let her go, started to turn.

She couldn't bear his pain. She grabbed his arm. "Wait. I... it's just... I don't want sympathy-love. That's guilt. It's not real."

His hands slid to her face. "I've known a dump truck load of guilt in my day, and this isn't it. *I love you*."

She felt those words straight to her soul. Saw the truth in his eyes. He loved her. "I love you too," she whispered.

A slow smile touched his lips. "Yeah?"

She nodded, his smile easing the sting in her eyes. "Yeah."

"We'll get the serum," he said. "You watch and see. This isn't over."

She remembered him talking about his grandmother, knowing he blamed himself for her drinking. Now he blamed himself for not being able to save her when he could. How could she not tell him the truth? "Sterling, there's something—"

"You rang, Master Sterling." Eddie slid into the booth. "Oh man. Guess I know what you two do on your off hours. Or all the time, I guess." He grabbed a chip and bit down. "Hi, Becca."

"Hi," she said. She didn't even remember the waitress bringing the food.

Eddie eyed the bottle of tequila. "Thirsty much?" he asked Sterling.

"I have a toothache," he said. "Pretty sure it came from grinding my teeth when I found out you've been selling information to Marcus."

Eddie bit down on another chip and froze, his face going stark white before he dropped the half-eaten chip. "One time," he said. "And I figured if he was stupid enough to pay to find out you had a new assistant—something you didn't seem to be hiding—I'd take the money. I needed it, man."

Sterling leaned closer, hands flat on the desk. "How do I know that's all you told him?" His voice was low, lethal. "How do I know you haven't told him about every conversation I've had with you?"

"Because I haven't."

Sterling glanced at Becca. "Your move or mine?"

"I need a connection," she said.

Sterling cut a look at Eddie. "If you want another paycheck from me, you'll slide your hand across the table and let Becca touch you."

Eddie's jaw slacked. "What?"

Sterling grimaced and reached forward, pulling Eddie's hand toward Becca. "It's painless." Becca slid her hand over Eddie's and shut her eyes. Images rushed through her mind. His mother in bed, him by her side. Marcus. Money. Eddie's sincere liking for Sterling. She let go of his hand.

"He's telling the truth." She smiled. "And he likes you too."

"Sometimes, Sterling," Eddie said, "I think you really have a loose screw between your ears."

"Sometimes, Eddie, I do. So you better watch yourself before I let a little bit of my 'crazy' loose on your ass. Or stop paying you. Don't cross me again."

Eddie gave an uncomfortable nod.

Sterling inched back in the seat and draped his arm behind Becca. "What's up in Eddie-town these days? Talk to me." And instantly, the tension was gone.

For the next half hour, Eddie gave them the lowdown on anything buzzing on his police turf about ICE, including locations and addresses of the most recent victims.

"If you aren't going to drink that tequila, I might have to call it my own," Eddie said. "I don't do much for entertainment these days. A drink in front of a football game would do a man right." His phone buzzed, and he reached for it.

"Go for it," Sterling said.

Frowning, Eddie read his text and eyed Sterling. "Those two MIA Clanners you've been hunting for since Nebula were spotted just headed into their apartment. You want to roll that direction with me?"

Sterling sat still, his expression unreadable. "You go," he said, sliding out of the booth, tossing money on the table even as he pulled Becca to her feet. He glanced at Eddie. "I know the address. I'll meet you there in ten minutes."

Sterling was already moving, tugging Becca after him. It was clear something was wrong.

The instant they were out the door, she asked, "What the heck is going on?"

"I have a bad feeling about this," he said, stopping by the car. "We meet Marcus, and he sees you, and then I have this bad vibe thing when I was with him that I blew off to my insanely uncontrollable need to protect you. Then suddenly, the two Clanners I've been trying to locate show up while you're here with me. It smells like a trap. They're after you, which means Dorian might show himself."

Before she knew his intentions, he grabbed her. Suddenly, everything went dark, and then light pierced her eyes. They were outside the Neon. He'd wind-walked from a public parking lot.

Sterling hit the remote and opened the door. "Go inside, and get Caleb or Michael. Not Damion. Tell them I'm at Mohawk's apartment. They'll know the address. And tell him to bring backup. I can't wait and risk Eddie's safety." He faded into the wind. Gone. She never got a word out.

Panic rushed over her. Sterling facing Dorian was exactly what she'd been trying to avoid. "Caleb!" she yelled, taking off running. The elevator door opened, and she rushed forward, almost smacking into Damion.

"Easy now," he said. "What's the rush?"

"I need Caleb," she said urgently. "I need him now."

"He's in Sunrise City," he said. "Left an hour ago. What's wrong? Talk to me, Becca."

God. This couldn't be happening. "What about Michael?"

"With Caleb," he said. "I'm all you've got, Becca, so start talking. Where's Sterling?"

She trusted Damion even if Sterling did not, and she didn't hold back. Becca spilled the entire story in a rush of barely coherent words.

Before she'd finished talking, Damion had already punched a button on the garage wall and set off some silent, flashing alarm. Another punch of a button and a panel slid open on the wall, displaying weapons.

"Go inside and call Caleb," he instructed, strapping a holster on his shoulder. "Tell him I took a team in to back up Sterling."

"He still doesn't trust you, Damion," she said. "You need to know that."

"Yeah well—" he said. "He'll have to get over *that* stick in his ass considering I'm all he's got."

The elevator opened, and three soldiers Becca had never met appeared, all in street clothes decorated with weapons, guns, and knives strapped to their bodies.

Fully armed, Damion motioned the men forward. Becca didn't wait for their departure. She was in the elevator, punching the button and willing the damn door to shut faster. And willing Sterling to come back safely, telling herself this wasn't a trap, knowing deep inside it was.

Chapter 30

IT WAS SUNDOWN. EQUIPPED WITH WEAPONS HE'D RE-
trieved from the trunk of the Mustang, Sterling materialized in the alley behind Mohawk's apartment. Off
Maryland Street, behind the Tropicana, it was the kind of
place where grunge and window bars counted as decor.
A nondescript black vehicle sat a few feet away—a police surveillance car, if Sterling ever saw one. Empty.

"Damn," he mumbled. He didn't want Eddie and his
men inside until... he eyed the Dumpster, a few feet
away, held his breath, and inched closer. Then cursed
again. The only good thing about the man inside with a
bullet between his eyes was that he wasn't Eddie.

Sterling glanced down the alley, noting a few pedes-
trians wandering nearby, and reluctantly left his weapons harnessed beneath the fatigue jacket he'd grabbed
for discretion. His gut clenched with the idea that Eddie
might be in another dark corner with a matching bullet
in his brain. He shouldn't have let him come alone.

He faded into the wind and reappeared at the edge
of the alley, scanning the front of the building, trying to
find Eddie, flipping open his phone to dial even as he
inspected the rows of cars lining a poorly lit street under
a rapidly darkening sky. Eddie's equally nondescript
Buick sat near the corner. Empty. He dialed Eddie,
walking toward the back of the building again, prepared
to enter the building.

Eddie answered on the first ring. Relief washed over him in a gruff demand. "Where the hell are you?"

"It's been a long time, Sterling."

Sterling stopped dead in his tracks at the sound of Tad's voice. "Where's Eddie?"

"Eddie and I are waiting for you upstairs," he said. "Me, him, the two Clanners you already met, and a very nice lady from down the hall who tells me she has twin baby girls at home. We're sitting here waiting for you to bring Rebecca Burns to me. I know she's in the city. You have fifteen minutes to get her here before the first of my guests dies."

"What are you going to do when you get her, Tad?" he asked. "Besides hit the pavement like the dumb lump you are?"

"Kill her long before she gets close enough to affect me," he said dryly. "Now who's the dumb lump? Whatever the hell that is. *Go get her*." His voice softened to a taunt. "I'll be easy on you though. First I'll kill the one Eddie tells me you call 'Mohawk.' You like him the least. But after that, I'll have to kill the woman." He hung up.

Sterling had an instant of contemplation, no more. Tad expected him to negotiate. If he were Caleb, he would, but he wasn't Caleb. He was Sterling. And what he lacked in GTECH mojo, he made up for in actions. Discretion no longer on his mind, Sterling drew two Glocks and checked his ammo, counting fire escapes as he did, when suddenly Damion materialized in front of him.

"Becca told me what's going down," he said. "I've got men on all corners of the building."

Sterling grimaced at Damion's presence, though he

wasn't about to dismiss backup. "Tad and four hostages. A dead cop in the trash can."

"Any idea what the end game is?"

"Tad intends to shoot a hostage in roughly eight minutes if I don't hand over Becca."

Damion cursed. "Any idea if Tad's alone?"

"None," Sterling said. "He's a showboater, but he's also quick to let someone else take a bullet in his place."

Damion hit the mike in his ear. "Talk to me." He listened and then looked at Sterling. "Nothing. No sign of trouble."

"I'll go in the back and take out Tad," Sterling said. "You come in the front and grab the hostages. The woman first."

Damion drew his weapons and smiled. "Always the women first." A double meaning. "We good, man?"

"Surprisingly yes," Sterling said. Working with Damion, well… worked. "This is where you normally tell me to wait and think things through."

"And you tell me to kiss your ass, and we go for it anyway," Damion said. "In light of the ticking clock… I'm trusting you on this one."

Sterling didn't miss the meaning, nor did his confidence waver. This was his zone, the place where far more times than not, his instincts were right. This was what he did—he acted. Never questioned.

Sterling checked his watch. Damion did the same. "Three minutes to go." They exchanged a nod, and both faded into the wind.

Sterling reappeared in a damn precarious position on the concrete ledge next to the metal stairwell. But soundlessness came with a price.

He eased around and glanced in through the curtain. Mohawk and his pal cowered against the wall, hands tied in front of them. Check. Woman crying, also with hands tied, pressing herself into a corner as if she wanted to melt into the wall. Check.

Where the hell was Eddie? Damn it. For all he knew he was in a Dumpster, and Tad had his phone. He should have demanded to talk to him.

Sterling eased back against the wall and checked his watch. Thirty seconds, and he didn't have a visual on Tad.

That was when Green Hornets started flying, one splintering painfully into his arm, another too damn close to his head.

"So much for backup, covering my ass," he mumbled, jumping onto the fire escape and none too silently. If the shooter hadn't already told Tad he was there, he'd just done it himself. Bullets splattered the steel stairwell.

There were shouts from inside the complex then, immediately after, the yell of a man falling off a nearby building. Backup. Late, but check.

Inside the apartment, the door burst opened. Sterling rotated around to find Eddie, not Damion, in the doorway. Sterling pounded on the window, and Eddie rushed over, gun in hand, and let him in.

"Where's Tad?" he asked, as Eddie rushed to the woman to untie her and then yelled for her to leave. "Go!"

"You mean the brawny asshole who held us at gunpoint?" he said. "He's fighting with some guy on the stairwell." He eyed the woman. "Go to your apartment, and lock the door."

That was all Sterling had to hear. He was through

the door in a run, taking the narrow hallway to bring the stairs into focus. Damion was almost at the top, dragging himself up the railing, bleeding like a stuck pig from his side and right leg, still hanging onto his own weapons.

"Where's Tad?" Sterling asked, as Casar ran up the stairs to help Damion.

"Your way," he groaned. "He headed me off at the stairs and took off toward the apartment."

Sterling turned away, guns ready to fire as he rounded the apartment door. The window stood open. Eddie was nowhere to be found. The two Clanners were still tied up, bullets through their heads. The woman was gone.

Weapons ready, Sterling rushed to the window and saw nothing then turned back to the room and narrowed his gaze on the closet. He yanked it open. Stunned, he found Eddie crumpled on the floor in a pool of blood, hands tied in front of him, which meant that the Eddie who'd let him in that window…

"Sonofabitch."

Sterling kneeled beside Eddie and checked for a pulse. It was faint, but he found one. There was no way Eddie could be in this closet, hands tied, with that amount of blood loss when he'd been standing in the middle of that room only minutes before. The time equation didn't work. What the hell was going on?

―∿∿―

While Eddie was in surgery, Sterling sat in the hospital in the middle of the stench of blood and death, hating every minute. If this was what had surrounded Becca every second of every day in that German treatment center, he wondered how she'd survived as long as she had. He wondered how he was going to deal with the doctor coming out of those steel, double doors at the end of the hall, telling him Eddie was dead, knowing it was because he'd fucked up and let him go into that apartment alone. Or how he was going to deal with it when Becca crashed, and ICE would no longer bring her back.

For three hours he tormented himself, until Caleb arrived and claimed the chair next to him.

"Any news?"

"None," Sterling said, running his hand over what would soon be a full day's beard growth. "Damion?"

"Sleeping it off," Caleb said. "His wounds weren't serious. He'll be fine in a few hours. Becca's worried. She says she's been calling your cell, and you won't answer."

"I can't talk to her right now," he said, pushing to his feet and walking to the wall across from the seats to lean against it. "I knew it was a setup tonight, and I let Eddie go in there."

"He's a cop, Sterling," Caleb said. "He's trained to do a job and do it well. He made his own choices."

"He can't make the right choices when he doesn't know what he's dealing with," Sterling said. "I didn't warn him. I thought I could get Becca to safety and return to him in time. But the one thing in my mind was my need to save Becca."

"Becca is more than someone you care about," he said. "She's a weapon we can't allow to land in the wrong hands. I would have done the same thing."

"But not for the same reasons I did," he said. "The idea of something happening to Becca was unbearable to me. It skewed my judgment. And now Eddie is in that operating room clinging to life, a sick mother at home with no one to take care of her."

"Eddie might still be in that closet, lying there dead, if you hadn't acted when you did," Caleb argued. "I would have negotiated. I would have been wrong."

Sterling cut his gaze, staring down the narrow hallway before turning back to Caleb.

He laughed bitterly, a choked sound even to his own ears. "I wanted to be Becca's Lifebond. I wanted to save her. I realized tonight that I'm not Michael. I can't go into combat and worry that if I die my Lifebond dies. When I hesitate, when I stop and think rather than act, people die. She will die." He inhaled a heavy breath. "The GTECH serum—"

"Sterling," Caleb said, cutting him off. "We need to talk about Becca, but now isn't the time or place."

A doctor came through the doors wearing scrubs and a mask pulled away from his face, hanging at his neck. Sterling and Caleb rushed to meet him. So did several guys from the Vegas Police Department. There was no family.

"He's stable but in a coma," the doctor said. "We are in wait-and-see mode. The next twenty-four hours will be critical." A few questions were thrown out, and visitors were rejected.

Caleb settled his hand on Sterling's shoulder. "Go to Becca," he said. "The rest will wait until tomorrow."

Sterling turned to Caleb. "I've asked myself over and over as I sat here—how did Eddie get into that closet so quickly? I'm telling you Caleb, I was in the hallway all of sixty seconds. It wasn't possible."

"What are you saying?"

"I keep thinking about what Becca said about the memories Damion and I have from her abduction. She said everything wasn't as it seemed. I thought I saw Damion when I handed over Becca."

"Thought?" Caleb said, quirking a brow.

Sterling ran his hand over his jaw. "I don't know, Caleb. Back in that apartment, I saw and even talked to Eddie, yet he was in the closet. He couldn't have been in two places at once. I've been wondering if I was drugged back at Becca's house. Maybe there had been something in the smoke. But this time, this time I was clean as a whistle. There's something more going on here."

"Maybe Eddie will give us some insights."

"If he wakes up," Sterling said grimly. He reached into his pocket and dug out the data stick. "Marcus gave me pictures and personal information on an ICE dealer who sounds an awful lot like Madame." He grimaced. "This is tread-carefully territory. He likely sold us out to Tad today. I was with him. He saw Becca. Suddenly, Tad was all up my ass?"

"Or he was followed," Caleb suggested. "He was handing over information on Adam's dealers."

"I don't know," Sterling said, skeptical. "I got a weird vibe off Marcus today. Everything about today, including him, stinks."

Caleb took the data stick. "I'll run down this woman and set up extra surveillance on Marcus. It's been a hell of a night. Go see your woman, and get some rest."

But Sterling couldn't go to Becca. Not yet. Not until he made one gut-wrenching stop. He had to go see Eddie's mother.

———

Despite it being 3:00 a.m., Becca was sitting on the bed with her laptop in front of her, fully dressed in jeans and a T-shirt, trying to focus on the research she and Kelly were exchanging by email. Impossible—considering she was a total mess, waiting to hear from Sterling, torn up about him not returning her calls. And going nuts over the necessity of hiding from Dorian, locked away like a prisoner.

Nevertheless, Caleb had kept her up to date, though it didn't stop the knots in her stomach over the "why" of Sterling's silence.

She should have told him about the Lifebond mark. And she would have in that tavern earlier in the evening had Eddie not shown up when he did.

But Michael knew about the bond; Caleb and Kelly too. Someone may have told Sterling, may have taken her chance to explain it to him her way to make him understand why she'd concealed their bond.

She was ready to say, to heck with waiting, and sneak out to the hospital, when the front door creaked open. Becca quickly set aside her computer and started for the door, eager to see Sterling, to touch him and know he was okay.

Before she made it halfway across the room, he appeared in the bedroom entrance, looking battered and exhausted. His hands rested on the door frame. Blood streaked the faded blue of his right leg, his black T-shirt matted with a dark spot she assumed to be more blood. Eddie's blood, she thought.

"Eddie is…" His voice trailed off.

"In intensive care," she said, rushing forward. "I

know." She wrapped her arms around him, never wanting to let go. Pressing her cheek to his heart, she reveled at the steady beat beneath her ear.

For a moment, he didn't touch her, didn't move as fear spiked inside her. He hadn't taken her calls. He wasn't touching her.

Then suddenly, he relaxed into her, his arms closing around her a moment before he buried his face in her hair. She still had the chance to tell him everything, to explain, before her silence created a barrier she wouldn't be able to permeate.

"I went to see his mother," he said, his voice hoarse.

She tilted her chin up, resting her hand on his chest. "How bad was it?"

"Had her nurse not sedated her, she'd probably be at the hospital as a patient, like her son."

"You did a good thing going there tonight. When Eddie wakes up—and he will, Sterling—he's going to appreciate what you did."

"Almost getting him killed?" he asked, a self-condemning bite to his words.

"You saved his life," she said, pushing to her toes and kissing him. "And don't tell me you didn't. Caleb already told me what happened." She took his hand. "You need a hot shower and rest."

He followed, his eyes heavy with an exhaustion she could tell reached beyond the physical. She turned on the water to heat and helped him undress. She would have stepped away, but he tugged her close.

"I need you, Becca. Join me." He trailed his fingers tenderly over her face and slid through a strand of her hair. "Please."

He needed her. Those words filled her in ways she fully intended to ensure he knew. "I need you too," she whispered, but a hint of discomfiture slid through her at the truth behind the words. She needed him to live on a literal level. How did she make sure he knew their connection was more to her?

Becca undressed quickly, eager to remove the barriers between them, starting with their clothes. They stepped under the hot stream of water, melting into it, and each other.

"Becca," he whispered, her name on his tongue, speaking a thousand unspoken words. *Pain. Longing. Need. Blame.*

She had to tell him about the mark. "Sterling—"

He kissed her, a long, drugging kiss that stole her breath and reached into her soul. A kiss that *became* her breath... became his. He devoured her with that kiss and the next... and the next, until he was devouring more than her mouth. He was devouring her body, touching her, licking her, nipping at her neck, her shoulder. Pressing her against the shower wall, he lifted her, one hand around her backside, the other braced on the wall beside her head.

All the turbulence she'd seen in his eyes, she felt in him now. His eyes met hers and held as he pressed inside her, filled her, stretched her.

Something wild snapped between them. Wild in a way Becca had never experienced in her life. She arched her hips and reached for more, bucked her hips as he pumped into her. Still it wasn't enough. There was no inhibition, no thinking. There was only need. Need she was willing to beg to have fulfilled.

"Sterling, I need…"

His mouth covered hers, his tongue sucking hers, licking and tasting. "I know," he murmured. "I need too." He maneuvered her around, away from the wall. "Grab hold."

Becca reached for the shower railing and tightened her legs around his hips, squeezed his cock tighter, deeper. He leaned in, licking the water from her nipples and suckling, and then pumping with his hips. Becca cried out with the pure pleasure of it, the pressure of his mouth on her nipple, darts of pleasure spreading through her. She called out his name, lost everything but him inside her, suckling her nipple and thrusting against her until she could take no more. In the same instant, she could not get enough. Becca exploded in a fierce rush of multicolored bliss, exploded with spasms that grabbed his cock and pulled him deeper. He moaned, low and guttural, and then tugged her hard against his hips.

They collapsed together, him holding her, her arms leaving the bar to wrap around his neck. "Is it me?" he asked. "Or is the water freaking freezing?"

"It's cold," she said, a shiver chasing a path along her spine. "Okay. It's freaking freezing."

He carried her out of the shower and set her down, snatching a couple towels from the cabinet. Becca began drying off, facing the mirror, when suddenly Sterling was behind her, brushing her hair aside and staring at her neck. Becca's heart accelerated, and the towel fell to the floor as she grabbed the counter to steady her suddenly weak knees. This was not how this was supposed to happen.

"Sterling," she whispered. Her gaze lifted to the

mirror to meet his, and the minute they connected there, she knew it had been a mistake. He could see the guilt in her eyes.

"You knew," he accused. "You knew, and you didn't tell me."

She heard the sense of betrayal in his voice and whirled around to face him. "I can explain."

"*Everything isn't as it seems*," he said, repeating her words. A coincidence that wasn't fate at all—it was planned. "What kind of game are you playing, Becca?"

Chapter 31

THE TRUTH OF THE MATTER BURNED STRAIGHT TO HIS soul. Anger formed, and Sterling embraced it, easier to face than the pain spiraling inside him. Becca had deceived him, let him torment himself over her death. "What's your agenda, Becca?"

She took a step toward him, and he let her, grabbing her and pulling her hard against his body. And damn her if those soft sensual curves didn't make his cock thick with desire. But then, if she was fucking him, why shouldn't he fuck her?

"Are you working for Adam?" he demanded, his mouth close to hers, hungry to taste the bitterness of lies on her lips, to embrace them and try to get over her. "He found out we were Lifebonds? Or you found out. It all makes sense now. That's why you weren't afraid to wind-walk. Why not just do the blood exchange, Becca? Why not trick me? Or was the opportunity just not there, so you had to continue to manipulate me?"

"What?" she gasped. "Sterling, no. Why would you think that?"

"Why else would a woman who is *dying* not tell the man who could save her life to do it? Why? It makes no sense."

"I had opportunity," she whispered hoarsely. "I was bleeding in the lab. I could have tricked you. But I did everything to avoid you."

"Don't lie," he said in a low growl, pressing his mouth to her ear. "We both know the blood exchange doesn't happen that easily. Stop playing me." He pulled back, fixed her with a steely, contemptuous look. "I don't like it."

"And I don't like you very much right now," she said, her chin tilting up defiantly, her lips quivering. "How would I know that?" Then suddenly her bravado melted into tears, the kind of tears someone dying sheds, the kind of tears, he realized, she'd never allowed herself since he'd known her.

"This isn't like giving me one of your kidneys and you keeping the other, and statistically, you're fine. This is forever, Sterling. How was I supposed to expect you to give me that when you barely even knew me? When you might have found out you didn't even like me? When it would have been pity and guilt, not love."

It was his turn to melt, into her, around her. "Becca," he whispered, thumbing away the dampness on her cheeks. "Baby, I'm sorry." He pressed his forehead to hers. "I'm so sorry. Tonight... Eddie... you—my inability to save either of you... it's been eating me alive."

"I was going to tell you," she said. "I just needed to know..." Her breath hitched. "I needed to know—"

"That I love you and can't live without you?"

Her hand rested on his chest. "Yes," she whispered.

"Well, I do," he said. "And I can't. And I'm not sure if that's a good or a bad thing for either one of us."

She swallowed, her delicate throat bobbing with the action. "So... I was right to worry. You don't want this."

He buried his face in her neck, breathed in her

flowery, feminine scent. "God yes, I want this. I just
don't know how, Becca."

"I don't understand. Sterling." Her hands were in his
hair, forcing him to look at her. She searched his face,
trepidation in her own. "You're confusing me."

He forced his gaze to hers, and he knew the stark
desperation that must be there. But he couldn't make it
go away. He couldn't tear through the torment. "I take
risks, Becca. I don't stop. I don't think. I just act. And
I save lives doing it. But that has been *my life* I was
gambling with, no one else's."

"You mean mine," she said, her hand curling on his
chest. "We don't have to do this."

"Of course we're doing this," he said roughly and
kissed her. She tried to object, and he kissed her again.
"We're doing this."

He scooped her up and carried her to the bed, spreading her legs as he did to settle intimately between them.
Her dark hair spread on the ivory pillow. God… she was
beautiful. She was his.

Resting his weight on his elbows, he declared, "We
live together, and we die together. And we'll save lives
together." He reached over and yanked open the bedside
table and snatched up a pocketknife. "Starting now."

"No!" she said, closing her hand over it. "Not now."

"Becca, baby," he pleaded. "Forget what I said. I
was just scared." Sterling inhaled against the impact
of the admission, his gaze traveling to the ceiling as he
regained composure. He leveled her in a stare and let her
see the truth in his eyes. "I've not been scared in years.
But I haven't been this alive either. I want this, Becca.
I'll deal with the rest."

"You have time to think about it," she said. "We can't do anything until after we catch Dorian."

"What does Dorian have to do with this?"

"One of us has to survive to keep fighting."

"Oh no," he insisted. "Live and die together. No negotiations on this. You'll be stronger and safer linked to me anyway."

"And if the Lifebonding somehow changes me? If Dorian can tell I'm different, and he doesn't see me as bait anymore? Or my ability is gone. Or my mind reads different somehow. We can't risk the lives that will be lost if we don't capture him. We can't."

A vice closed around Sterling's chest because he didn't want her to be right. But she was. Millions of lives were in jeopardy as long as ICE manufacturing existed. The free world was hanging by a string, ready to be snapped by Adam. His world crumbled around him as he realized... he might still lose Becca. He'd never felt so confused, so emotional, in his life.

He whispered her name and parted her legs, pressing deep inside her, becoming a part of her in the only way he could. Bond or no bond, she was his. She was in his soul, his heart. If she died, he'd be destroyed. He *would* die with her.

———

Becca woke in a warm, dark tunnel of sleep. Real sleep. The first she'd truly allowed herself in days—on her stomach and naked. A slow smile slid onto her lips as she thought of the many things she had done with Sterling. There were all kinds of reasons to be worried, concerned, and upset. But in that few seconds, she allowed herself to be something she had not been in months. Happy and in love. If she was going to die, she was going to do it as one satisfied, pleasured woman.

She pushed herself up on her hands, realizing the master of that pleasure was missing. Frowning at the muffled, but distinct sound of male voices from the living room, she quickly found a pair of soft, faded jeans and a T-shirt, passing on shoes out of urgent curiosity about what was going on. After a brief glimpse at her feet and her pale toenails, she wondered how a hot bath and bottle of red toenail polish had ever felt anything but adolescent and self-indulgent.

She opened the door as Sterling was saying, "I handed Becca to you."

"You handed Becca to Tad," Damion countered.

"We've been through this," Michael said. "What are we proving by beating this dead horse? You both saw something different."

"Tad wasn't Tad," Sterling said. "Eddie wasn't Eddie."

"Who the hell else could Eddie be, but flipping Eddie?" Michael asked roughly.

Becca had a sudden recall of Sterling's memory, of him handing Becca to Damion. She understood now. He'd handed her to Damion, and then... Damion had simply become Tad. She launched into action, bringing the room into full view, stopping behind the couch. Michael leaned against the wall across from her. Caleb sat on the black leather chair to her right. Damion, in the one to her left, looked fully healed from his injuries. Sterling stood in the center of it all.

Curling her fingers into the couch cushion, she steeled herself for the reaction she knew the insanity of her words were sure to bring and said them, "What if Eddie *was* Tad? What if he can become whoever he wants to become?"

"I'm sorry," Damion said. "But this isn't the answer. It can't be. I saw Sterling hand you to Tad. We couldn't have seen two different people at once. Sterling was delirious, shot up with Green Hornets or drugged. Maybe the Zs have some sort of hallucinogenic they are using."

Sterling whirled on him. "What if he shifted as I handed Becca over?"

Damion's lips thinned. "The timing had to have been perfect, right as I rounded the corner, but I guess in the world we live in, anything is possible." His brows dipped, his gaze locked on Sterling. "So you finally believe me? You don't think I handed Becca over to Tad?"

"I believe you," Sterling said.

Damion gave him a stunned look and nodded.

"You're back to trusting each other," Caleb said. "Good. And whether it was a shifter or a hallucinogenic, we need to operate as if nothing is as it seems and watch our backsides. Stack that on the pile with our other problems, the biggest being, how do we get to Dorian?"

Sterling's eyes met Becca's with stark despair. "Becca," he said solemnly, his voice sounding forced. "Becca is still the answer. They want her. We have to find a way to give her to them, but not to Tad. We have to make sure Adam believes he has to come for her himself. Seek out Adam's soldiers, and have Becca present when they go down. We kill them. Adam hates losing manpower because it forces him to use the limited serum he has to maintain his army."

"One step further," Michael said. "We target Tad.

Take him out of the picture." His words firmed. "I say Tad has to die. If Becca can be the one to pull the trigger—even better."

———

Feeling quite the Madame in a slinky turquoise dress that contrasted her red hair and hugged her curves in all the right places, Sabrina exited the elevator of Magnolia and headed to the executive office where Tad— masquerading as Marcus—waited for her.

Their plan was back on—she would be pivotal in delivering Rebecca Burns to her death. She would play the role of the Madame, afraid for her life because she was double-crossing Iceman. She'd find her way into the Renegades' operation close to Rebecca Burns and kill her. It was perfect. Sabrina couldn't be happier that Tad's plan the night before had failed. Now she would shine, show how valuable she could be, ensure she became Tad's Lifebond, and mark her territory inside Zodius City. There she'd be treated like royalty, as he'd promised. She was tired of bending over for the world, chasing money and men, struggling to pay bills. She'd thought Iceman was her trip out of hell. He talked all kinds of world domination crap and then fell flat on his face. She wanted to be where the real power existed.

Plush carpet beneath her heels, Sabrina knocked on the door. When it opened, she strutted into the office of fine mahogany with expensive art in carefully placed positions, a sultry smile painted on her red lips, which faded with a shocking discovery. Marcus was sitting in his office chair, gagged and bound. Alive.

She whirled to face Tad, and despite her shock about

Marcus, she didn't miss the hotness of him all decked
out in leather, looking like a mean fighting machine. He
wasn't handsome, not even close. But he was lethal—
rough in all the right ways.

"I thought you'd killed him," she said.

"Tossed some ICE down his throat and saved him,"
Tad said. "He's a present for Adam. Adam's enemies
are fed to his wolves in front of the city—eaten alive.
Makes for an interesting night of entertainment."

Even Sabrina, as cold a bitch as she knew she could
be, felt a wave of nausea with that image. Marcus—
formerly her powerful, vital Iceman—made wild
animal-like sounds behind her. He was desperate. She
didn't blame him. Dead was better than being puppy
chow any day.

Tad moved to the desk and leaned on the edge, his back
to Marcus, who fought uselessly against his bindings.

She sashayed toward him. "So what's the plan?"

"We're going to give Adam what he wants, his traitor, gagged and bound. The answer to why people have
been dying. Mass distribution of ICE. Control of this
casino and those connected."

She sidled up next to him, and he pulled her hard
between his legs. "I did exactly what the Renegades
believed I wouldn't do." He grabbed a handful of her
hair and pulled her mouth to his, slicing his tongue along
hers, his lust branding her, as it soon would his enemy.
And she was going to be there for the show.

Chapter 32

"SHUFFLE!" YELLED THE DEALER.

Sterling relaxed. "Thank you Lord, the pain is over, if only for a few minutes," he grumbled, eyeing the casino for any signs of Sabrina Walker, the redheaded cocktail waitress who Marcus had claimed was an ICE dealer.

"Any sign of her yet?" Becca asked from beside him, her leg pressed to his.

He was aware of her every move, her every touch, even the exact moment she needed to dose with that damn ICE that was keeping her alive. It was killing him to feed her those drugs, and then parade her around a casino as an invitation to Tad to try and kill her. It was like taunting the Grim Reaper—you didn't do that shit unless you really wanted the kind of stink that meant you were ten feet under.

Sterling wanted this over. He wanted her safe. And he'd made it clear she wasn't even going to the restroom without him. He didn't give a damn if she had to wet herself and mess up those nice black jeans that hugged her ass in all the right ways.

"Not yet," he said. "But her schedule says Friday at five. It's Friday at five."

"Marcus also said she lived in the hotel, but you've had men watching for her, and she's yet to be seen," Becca reminded him.

"She'll be here," Sterling said. "Because whether

Marcus is working for Tad, being followed by Tad, or whether Tad is masquerading as Marcus, this woman is the connection to Tad. We find her. He finds us."

"We're at a blackjack table," she said. "The only one who can't find us here is the waitress with the free drinks. There are cameras everywhere."

"You in?" the dealer asked.

"We're in," Becca said, scooting a chip forward for both herself and Sterling.

"Bingo," Sterling murmured. "Four o'clock, coming our way."

"The term would be blackjack," Becca teased, discreetly glancing in the woman's direction and watching her take a man's order. "Oh yeah. You're right. She's your Madame caller. She has that queen attitude that other women hate."

"Card?" the dealer asked.

Becca eyed the table and nudged Sterling. "You have thirteen. The dealer has twelve. He's supposed to bust. That's what the rule book says. You should stay."

He cut her a disbelieving look. "How do you know?"

"Bunch of guys at NASA used to play all the time." She smiled. "Okay. I played too." She motioned to the table. "You should stay."

"Fine," he said, glancing at the dealer. "Stay."

The dealer looked irritated, and Becca ran her tongue over her bottom lip, her eyes twinkling with amusement. "Use your hand."

Sterling kissed her because her lips were all shiny and tempting, inhaled the sweet scent of her that he wanted to breathe for a lifetime, and then cut a hand through the air.

The dealer flipped his cards and piled more money on Sterling's area of the table.

"You keep winning," she said.

Sterling shoved the money back at the dealer. "Tip." He eyed Becca. "This is why I don't gamble."

"Because you like to win?"

"Because I don't want to use up my luck at a damn poker table, instead of where I really need it," he said and motioned to their mark.

"Sabrina" or "Madame" narrowed her gaze on him and looked a little frantic. Fake frantic. Sterling wasn't an idiot, and she wasn't a good actress. She sashayed in their direction, her breasts barely concealed by her low-cut cocktail dress. She was pretty in a slutty, never-see-you-after-this, morning-after kind of way. The kind of woman he would have favored before Becca. The kind of woman who represented how shallow and empty his life had been.

"Here we go," Becca whispered.

"You in?" the dealer asked again.

Sterling cast him a hard look. "No, I'm not in, and I'll flipping tip you to stop asking me that."

Sabrina appeared by their table and made a not-so-discreet beeline for Sterling, ignoring Becca, who cast him an irritated look. "I have no idea how you figured out who I am, but you better make this look good, or you're going to get me killed. The deal is the same. So unless your boss is willing to meet my terms, this is over with your drink order."

So she *was* Madame, and she had no idea Marcus had sent him to her as part of a deal. Or so she wanted him to believe. "He is," Sterling confirmed.

She tilted her head, studying him as if weighing the

honesty of his words. "All right then. I break at nine."
She eyed Becca and then glanced at Sterling. "Crystal's
Dress Shop in the Forum. There won't be cameras there.
Dressing room two. Your woman comes in. Not you.
And if she can't negotiate what I want, I walk away."

And then she moved along to the next table and left
Sterling to wallow in the absolute certainty that this was
yet another trap with Becca as the target.

His eyes met Becca's, and for all the lighthearted
banter she'd managed today, he saw the trepidation.
He felt the waves of nervous energy balled around fear,
blasting off her and into him.

It didn't matter that trouble was what they'd come here
looking for, and trouble was what they had found. He
didn't want trouble, not when Becca was present. How
did Michael manage to focus in battle and not be scared
shitless for Cassandra? Sterling wasn't good at this. He'd
never cared about living or dying before. He'd lived in
the moment, used his instincts, and taken one risk after
another. He told himself to think of the bigger cause he
served, rather than the woman he'd come to cherish. Yet
here he was, faced with a bigger cause and her safety, and
the only thing he could focus on was the door, and his
need to throw her over his shoulder and take off running.

—⁂—

Becca's calm façade, the façade she'd played for Sterling's
benefit all day, was quickly fading into oblivion.

"I couldn't see into her head at all," Becca said, trying
not to panic. They were almost at the forum, after sitting
at the blackjack table another few hands to appear discreet.

Sterling pulled her behind a group of vacant slot

machines, his hands on her shoulders. "You're nervous. You're okay."

"What if *she* is Tad?"

He visibly shook himself. "Oh that is just a bad, bad image you put in my head. She isn't Tad. I promise you. He might shift, but I doubt he struts."

She frowned. "You thought she strutted?"

He smiled and ran his hand down her hair. "Like a call girl, baby."

"Oh. Yes. I can see that." Another horrible thought came over her. "What if my shield isn't working?"

"Try it."

"Caleb said no. He said I'll alert Dorian I know how to use it and give him time to probe it and find a way around it. I wanted to touch her and try to read her that way, but I didn't want to be obvious."

"First," Sterling said. "I don't have any reason to believe Dorian is going to appear here today. Not before Adam tries to have you taken out the more conventional way—good ol' human murder. But if he does, we have the weapons you and Kelly designed."

"That we don't know will work," she reminded him. "And Dorian came after me once before. You can't know he's not going to show up here today or even how close he has to be to attack my mind again."

"You have a shield," he said. "Caleb is in the hotel in case you need extra protection. And Adam isn't going to risk his greatest weapon and the source of ICE without damn good cause."

"Yeah, well that weapon is powerful," she said. "I'm not sure there is a risk for him to consider. He's that powerful."

"Baby," he said softly. "Please. You're making yourself crazy. Try your shield quickly, and pull it back down—long enough to give yourself the confidence of knowing it's there."

Becca forced a calming breath and did as he said. She slid her shield in place, felt the comfort of knowing it was there, and then cringed as she let go of the security it gave her.

"Well?" Sterling asked.

She nodded.

His lips lifted slightly. "Good."

"I should have touched her," she said. "Then I'd know if she was telling the truth. Maybe she really does need our help."

"And I think I really like blackjack," he said. "Potential temptation turned to addiction all too easily. In other words, potential danger equals danger."

"She gave us a warning. She gave us time to prepare. If she was planning to attack, why would she do that?"

"It's not because she's waiting for her break," he said. "Don't convince yourself that's an option, and let your guard down."

Becca hugged herself. "I won't. I know." But he was right. That was what she was trying to do.

"More likely, she had to call whoever she is working with—Marcus, Iceman, Tad—whoever it is, and make preparations for whatever is going to go down in that dressing room," Sterling said.

Chapter 33

THIRTY SECONDS. THAT'S HOW LONG STERLING WAITED after Becca walked into that store before he went after her—planned, counted-out seconds that were the longest of his life. It took him all of ten more to clear the entrance and a few rows of dresses, to draw a hidden weapon, and yank open the curtain to room number two.

Sabrina sat, legs crossed, lounging in a red velvet chair. Becca, stiff and prim, sat in a matching chair beside her, thankfully safe.

Able to breathe again, his gaze swept to the ceiling, the walls, the large mirror mounted on the wall, before they latched onto Sabrina again.

"I've always enjoyed a good ménage with a big gun," Sabrina purred. She pointed a red-tipped nail. "But shut the curtain before we get started."

He kept the gun on Sabrina. "Becca," he said.

She pushed to her feet and pulled the curtain, then stood close to him, as if she wanted to hang on if he decided to leave.

Sabrina sighed. "You two are clearly suffering from some sort of paranoia, so I'll get right to it, and let you go melt down somewhere that's not here. I gave your girlfriend a card with five of my dealer's names. A show of good faith."

Sterling cast Becca a sideways look, and she held up an index card.

Sabrina continued. "I can give you Iceman, his warehouse, his dealers, and his users. You give me what I asked for—protection without consequences. Tell your boss he has twenty-four hours to decide."

She pushed to her feet, and Sterling stepped to the side, giving her space. She paused, too close, and added, "Don't come back here. I'll call you. If you get me killed, who's going to give you all those juicy secrets?"

She slipped behind the curtain and disappeared. Sterling's instincts were screaming. Whatever had gone down here, it was more of the "not what it seems" variety. He had a bad feeling—the kind of bad that made nightmares like fairy tales. He grabbed Becca's arm. They were going to the nearest exit and wind-walking out of here.

No one inside the Renegades camp except Becca had ever seen Dorian, so the kid had walked by the throngs of Renegades and casino workers unnoticed and came straight to the executive office of the hotel where Tad waited for him.

Tad watched as Dorian meditated, eyes rolled back in his head, and waited for the announcement that Rebecca Burns was dead. The far left wall displayed camera footage of the dressing room, and Tad was starting to get antsy.

Sabrina had left the room, and now, so were Sterling and the Burns woman. Tad would have preferred to shoot the bitch from a distance, but any further violence at the hotel after the ICE fatalities could bring unwanted attention from military operations.

Abruptly, Dorian's eyes rolled back into position. "I cannot reach her mind from this distance without an emotional imprint to track," he said, speaking to both Tad and Adam, who was on speakerphone.

"She's headed for the door," Tad told Adam. "Say the word, and I'll order my men to shoot her."

"I will go to her," Dorian said, already headed to the door.

Holy shit. If anything happened to that kid, not only would he lose his abilities, but Adam would kill him. "Dorian! No!" It was too late. Dorian was out the door, too powerful for Tad to stop.

—✧—

"Put your shield up," Sterling ordered, whisking Becca to the back of the casino near the door he'd established with Caleb as their safety zone—where backup would be waiting.

"I thought—"

"Don't argue," he ordered. Every second she was unprotected was a risk.

"You think Dorian is here," she said anxiously.

"I don't know what I think," he said. "Other than my instincts are screaming, and when they scream, I listen."

"No," she said. "I'm not putting up my shield."

He stopped dead in his tracks in the protection of a crowd and glared. "What do you mean you aren't putting it up?"

"I want this to end, Sterling," she said. "I want it over. We walk out that door, my shields down, and we don't wind-walk to safety either. End this. No one is safe while Dorian is free. We can only hope your instincts are screaming because we have a chance to catch him."

Sterling stood there, the sound of slot machines and screams melting into an abyss. No—he would grab her and wind-walk her to safety the minute they exited.

She reached up and pressed her hand to his chest, as if she sensed the decision he was going to make. "We are trying to stop a monster before he can get his grip on the world. This is the time for you to learn to deal with reaching beyond your protectiveness for me. If you can't be objective under these circumstances, then you were right to question yourself and us, because you never will be."

Clarity came to Sterling. She was wrong. He would do the same for anyone. Okay, with a little more conviction for Becca, there was no denying that. But he saved lives. He took risks so other people didn't get hurt. He grabbed her hand. They were getting out of here. She yelped as he tugged her forward, pushed through the crowd. The instant they were away from the entrance cameras, they were riding the wind.

"Wait!" Becca demanded as he shoved open the door only to find her crumbling to her knees.

"Becca," he yelled, bending down to pick her up, only to have a piercing pain rip through his head. "Ah. God." In some distant place, he could hear Becca whimpering, hear people screaming. Somehow, he pulled himself to a sitting position, and holy shit, Jesus help them, found bodies lying everywhere.

Becca had gone fetal, and suddenly, a young boy was standing above him. Instantly Sterling was captured in the boy's mesmerizingly lethal stare—pale silver, rather than black.

"Sterling!" came Damion's shout from behind. The boy lifted his hand, and glass shattered—a fierce blast that collided with the pain in his head and made him gag. But somehow, he threw himself over the top of Becca. Screams permeated the air then utter silence. A heavy blanketing force replaced the glass. Holy crap. Becca was right. This kid was a nightmare. The only people coming to help them were coming from inside the casino. He wasn't sure that was possible; there could be a barrier there too.

Sterling hunkered over and reached for the nicotine weapon in his belt, when bullets would have felt a whole lot more comforting. So would the strength to lift the weapon. The screech in his head was depleting him, zapping his energy.

"Enough, Dorian," came Caleb's voice.

"Uncle?"

Uncle, meaning Caleb. Even in his current state of near insane pain, Sterling heard the whimsical fascination in Dorian's voice about Caleb—the child beneath the evil—with an idol, of sorts.

"Have you decided to join us now?" Dorian asked. "Father will be pleased to see you."

"Stop hurting the woman," Caleb ordered. "And we will go see your father together."

Sterling could feel Becca shaking beneath him, sobbing. And he knew if Caleb could help her, he would. He must have used whatever mind juice he had to get here in the first place.

But Sterling saw opportunity and distraction when it presented itself, despite the screeching in his head. He told himself to fire now and willed his hand to life.

Shoot the gun while Dorian was occupied. *He had to fire the gun*.

"I don't like to disappoint Father," Dorian said.

"If you bring me to your father," Caleb said. "I promise you, Dorian, he will forgive all else."

Sterling aimed the gun and fired over and over, but at the same moment, Dorian said, "I don't think so." He lifted his hand, and that barrier that had replaced the glass came down on top of them, crushing Sterling and Becca with the force of an eighteen-wheeler.

And then, suddenly, it was gone—as if Dorian or maybe Caleb had somehow destroyed it. Sterling gasped for air and reached for Becca, turned her over, and found no pulse. He screamed in horror. Frantically, for the second time since meeting her, he began CPR.

In his peripheral vision, he was aware of Dorian on the ground, proof the nicotine bullets had not only worked they'd crumbled the wall Dorian had created. Damion grabbed Dorian and faded into the wind as Caleb and Adam came toe-to-toe. Michael stepped to Caleb's side. Then Marcus stepped to Adam's side before shifting into Tad.

Sterling turned away and focused on only one thing—Becca. "No!" The word roared from his lungs, the pain and the impossibility of losing her. He should never have let her come here without the complete bond that would have protected her, made her stronger, safer, able to heal on a level beyond what ICE could give her.

Desperation rose in him, and he grabbed a piece of glass, sliced his hand, and then hers—pressed them together and willed her to life through the completion of their bond. He straddled her, holding her to him, begging her to live. "Come on baby. Come on."

And then, finally, she coughed and blinked. He had no idea why, but she was crying when she sat up and flung her arms around him.

"Tell me you're okay," he whispered. "Please. Tell me you're okay."

"Yes," she said. "I'm okay. Did we get Dorian? Did it work?"

"Damion got him," he said, amazed time and time again at just how brave she was. "I hope that means it's over."

She wet her lips. "Did you—did we?"

"Complete our bond? You bet we did, and you're stuck with me now."

A small smile touched her lips. "And you're stuck with me too."

He kissed her, scooped her up, and turned to find Caleb and Michael returning. Sirens sounded—raw and grinding, dozens of them.

Around him people were sitting up, waking from their unconscious state, thankfully alive. Sterling could see the headlines tomorrow. "Terrorist bomb set off in casino." Or "Angry gambler goes ballistic." Either way, there was a mess to be dealt with.

"It's over," Caleb announced. "Adam's not foolish enough to bring down the wrath of the army, or the Renegades, while he's not in a position to win. It's the big picture, rule the world shit, to him."

"Mark my word though," Michael said. "He'll come for Dorian, and sooner, rather than later. But for now, their production of ICE is officially halted."

Caleb looked at Becca. "You were very brave."

"Yeah, you were," Sterling murmured, staring down at her with more than love—he felt pride and admiration.

She smiled up at him. "See what happens when you listen to what I have to say."

He laughed, knowing they had plenty of time to argue about who was in charge. Right now, he simply wanted to take her to Kelly and make sure she was safe. And then take her to bed and keep her there by his side for an eternity—or as long as she would have him.

———

Adam returned to Zodius Nation, very aware of his son's absence by his side, but he shared a mental link with Dorian, and through him he would influence Caleb to join him. The world had a way of shaping destiny, and today was no different. Destiny was definitely afoot.

He'd left Tad back at the casino, squirming like a pathetic ant, begging forgiveness, trying to figure out how to maintain his Marcus identity without ICE.

Adam wasn't shortsighted enough to prematurely kill Marcus, though he wasn't about to share the details with Tad. Torture Marcus? Of course. Kill him? Time would tell. First Adam would evaluate his usefulness. His influence with those Adam wished to control.

He found his wife Ava in the women's quarters, lounging on a velvet chair in the center of the room. Chocolates and fruits adorned long tables, roses in every corner. Human females, her followers, surrounded her, eager to be future mothers of their new "perfect" lineage. Ava's ability to seduce them with her mind so that they would seduce his men with their bodies was arousing. But then, everything about his voluptuous Lifebond aroused him.

He sauntered to the lounge chair, the women around him all but falling all over themselves. Their king had arrived. He sat down and pulled Ava close. "Dorian has penetrated the Renegades' camp."

Apprehension slid over her lovely, heart-shaped face. "You are sure that Caleb will try to rehabilitate him rather than kill him?"

"He is a child," Adam said. "Of course he will try rehabilitation. And he will believe he has succeeded." He kissed her. "All is well, my love. And with time, it will be even better."

~~~

Sabrina tossed the duffel bag over her shoulder and rushed down her apartment stairs. She couldn't find Tad, and she was pretty sure, based on the mess at the hotel, his plan had gone badly. Which meant Adam would kill him and anyone near him. She had to get away. Quickly.

She exited the back of the building, the lot dark, a fine mist of rain starting to fall. Nerves jittery in her stomach, her heels clicking on the pavement, she all but ran to her car and yanked open the door when headlights shined on her. She stilled, feeling the squeeze in her chest of certain death.

All of a sudden, a car was there, a shiny black sedan. The back window slid down. A distinguished man appeared, his hair laced with gray, his features shadowy in the inky darkness.

"Hello, Sabrina," he said.

"Who are you?" she asked, wetting her lips nervously.

"A friend who wants to help you," he said.

"Help me how?"

"Stop depending on men with big promises and no ability to deliver."

She snorted. "And I suppose *you* can?"

"I'm the one who brings the right people together with the right solutions, even if they think it's a coincidence. It never is. I've been watching you, Sabrina." Moonlight shimmered across the twitch of his lips. "I can make you the first woman to enter the GTECH program—the 'Madame' of many others who will become like you."

"How?" she asked. No more running, no more hiding, no more wanting and wishing.

"All you have to do is come with me," he said, popping the door open and disappearing inside.

She looked at her broken-down Toyota and thought of the slim wad of cash in her purse that would last maybe a year. She climbed into the car and pulled the door shut. He wore an army green dress uniform, and she knew enough to know he was high-ranking. She glanced at a medal on his jacket and read the name.

Then she smiled, soft and sexy. She was cool with military men. She was cool with anyone who gave her the power, once and for all. "I'm all yours, Captain."

"That's General, Sabrina. General Powell."

———

Near sundown, two days after their Lifebonding was complete, Becca and Sterling were in Houston on her front porch, watching as Damion trotted from the moving truck to the porch and grabbed a box. "That'll do it. We're off." He smiled at Becca. "See you in the city."

As in Sunrise City, the Renegades' headquarters, and her new home. Becca smiled and leaned into Sterling. "See you."

When the truck pulled away, Sterling turned her into his arms and kissed her. Becca ran her hand down his cheek. "I've been thinking about you being a little more human than the other GTECHs." He stiffened and frowned. She frowned right back. "Don't look like that. Don't you see? It's just like we thought. There are *no* coincidences. You had to be as you were, so you could be my anchor and help me learn to control my abilities." Her voice softened. She loved this man so much. "You really do complete me, Sterling. It's the most amazing feeling."

Black eyes stared back at her, though to everyone else they were teal. After their bond, he no longer needed his lenses to camouflage their color, and he no longer had wind-walking limitations.

"There's something I need to ask you," he said softly.

A smile froze on her lips as she recognized the sudden tension in him. "What is it? What's wrong?"

The wind lifted around them, and suddenly they were on a balcony of a high-rise hotel, and she was facing a rail with Sterling nestled close behind her, miles of Vegas city lights around them, twinkling in spectacular glory.

"It's gorgeous," she said, leaning into him. "Where are we? What building is this?"

"The View Hotel and Casino," he said, softly, too softly. "In the honeymoon suite."

"What?" she turned in his arms to face him, and he went down on his knee. Her heart thundered in her chest, and her eyes watered. "What are you doing?"

He produced a small velvet box. "You didn't exactly get to pick when we Lifebonded, but you *can* choose if you live your life by my side. So Becca, I would very much like to take you to the chapel and make you my wife. Or anywhere in the world you want to go, whenever you want. I'm impatient though. I want you to be mine—tonight. I want to know you choose me, just like I choose you." He flipped the box open, displaying a single, elegant white diamond that would rival all the lights around them.

Becca bent down in front of him. "I choose you. Yes, tonight. I love you so much, Sterling, it hurts sometimes." Relief and happiness washed across his features, and she realized he'd been nervous. How could he possibly have doubted she would say yes?

He slipped the ring on her finger. "You like it? Because if you don't—"

She kissed him. "I love it and you."

Long minutes later, they were inside the room, stripping off each other's clothes. They went down on the bed together, Sterling on top of her, big and strong, and perfect in every way. "I thought we were going to the chapel?" she teased.

He slid inside her, stretched her deliciously, filling her in ways she'd never known possible. "I booked us for midnight." He brought her finger to his mouth, kissing the diamond that said she was his. "I figured we'd need some time to celebrate our engagement." He brushed his lips over hers. "When we come back, we'll celebrate the wedding." And he proceeded to show her just how well he understood the meaning of sin in the city.

Epilogue

A MONTH AFTER DORIAN'S CAPTURE, BECCA STOOD IN the amazing underground world that was Sunrise City, complete with restaurants, entertainment, living quarters, military, and scientific facilities. But the room that kept drawing her was this one—the mini surveillance room outside the two-way mirror looking into Dorian's room.

Becca stood at the window, watching him now as he read a popular teen novel, looking so very normal and so very alone. Behind her a pot of coffee brewed in the miniature kitchen, and a newspaper rested on the table next to her laptop, with speculation about the "terrorist" attack inside a popular Vegas casino.

The door behind her opened, and she turned to smile as Sterling entered. "Hungry?" he asked, carrying a box of—yes—his favorite doughnuts.

In the weeks since they'd Lifebonded, she'd worked with Kelly to perfect an immunization against ICE that was going to be flushed through the water system. With Kelly and Becca at the helm of the project, the army was actually supporting a community center to help ICE users endure the painful, but not deadly, withdrawal from ICE. The really exciting part of this to Becca was the cancer research some of the doctors here in Sunrise were beginning to embark on based on her medical records.

Becca shook her head at Sterling as he set the doughnuts on the table. "You're addicted."

He closed the distance between them and pulled her close. "I'm a 'you' addict."

"Says the man who's been Lifebonded for all of a month," she teased.

He brushed hair from her eyes, his expression softening. "A month I plan to turn into a very long lifetime."

She raised on her toes and kissed him. "I love you," she said.

"I love you too," he said. "But if you could say that with a distinctly happy vibe, not a sad one, it would do wonders for my male ego."

She rested her hand on his chest, the warm strength of him washing over her, reminding her how lucky she was to find someone so special. Everyone wasn't so lucky. She turned to the window and watched the little boy inside. "He's a product of greed," she said. "A victim."

He stepped beside her. "This from a woman who practically changed his name to 'evil' when we were trying to capture him?"

She touched the glass. "I'd never seen him like this. Being a boy. Maybe Caleb can change him. Bring out good instead of evil."

Sterling turned her into his arms. "Definitely not a bet I would take. But…" His eyes twinkled mischievously. "A group of the guys have a Friday night card game."

She gaped. "You want to play cards?"

"No," he said. "But it would really amuse me to have you play and win. They won't be expecting it. Oh yeah. Good times. What do you say?"

"And if I don't win?"

A slow smile slid onto his oh-so-sexy mouth. "I'll bet on you every time."